THE
LAST LEGION

THE LAST LEGION: BOOK 1

THE LAST LEGION

THE LAST LEGION: BOOK 1

CHRIS BUNCH

www.orbitbooks.net

ORBIT

First published in the United States in 1999 by Roc,
Penguin Group (USA) Inc.
First published in Great Britain in 2007 by Orbit

A CIP catalogue record for this book
is available from the British Library.

ISBN 978-1-84149-626-9

Papers used by Orbit are natural, recyclable products made
from wood grown in sustainable forests and certified in accordance
with the rules of the Forest Stewardship Council.

Typest in Garamond by M Rules
Printed and bound in Great Britain by
Mackays of Chatham plc
Paper supplied by Hellefoss AS, Norway

Orbit
An imprint of
Lirrle, Brown Book Group
Brettenham House
Lancaster Place
London WC2E 7EN

A Member of the Hachette Livre Group of Companies

www.orbitbooks.net

For
Don and Carol McQuinn
Megan Zusne and Gary Lothian
and Jim Fiscus
Not to mention
The Real Ben Dilley
and
The Real Jordan Brooks

ONE

Ross 248/Waughtal's Planet/Primeport

The police sweeper drifted past the alleyway, white faces under helmets inside staring straight ahead, disinterested.

Baka, Njangu Yoshitaro thought. He peered after them, saw the red-banded gravsled lift over the dome where the street curved. *Fools*.

Njangu wore dark brown pants and tunic, and a roll-down mask on his head. He pulled it over his face, adjusted the eye-holes, and went out of the alley. The wide boulevard was deserted under the hissing lights. Some shop windows were dark, more were lit with posturing mannequins, furniture, tron gear that no one in Yoshitaro's district of Dockside would ever own unless they stole it.

Njangu darted across the street to the steel-barred, blank doorway. The lock was a Ryart Mod 06. Not the hardest, not the easiest. Four numeric buttons. He would have three chances before the lock either set off an alarm or froze, depending on the store owner's paranoia and budget.

Try easy. The factory setting was 4783. He tried it, nothing happened. *The owner thinks he's clever But his sales-men open for him sometimes. Perhaps . . . the shop's address was 213. Blank first, blank second? Most likely first.*

He spun the dials, and the door clicked open.

Not that clever.

There were a dozen clear-topped cases in the thick-carpeted room. The half-sentient gems inside caught the light from the street, reflected it back in moving, kaleidoscopic splendor as they moved like jeweled snakes.

Njangu took a com from his pouch, touched a transmit button, held it down for a count of three, then a count of one, then three once more. Half a dozen shadows ran silently toward the shop's yawning door.

Yoshitaro trotted out, not looking back. He'd see the others later, get his share.

He ran for three long blocks, then turned down a dark street. He stripped off his hood, gloves, stuffed them in his belt pouch. He was walking quickly now, nothing but a tall, slender young man, respectably dressed, out a bit late, eager to get home and to bed.

The first shot rang dully from behind him, from the boulevard, then another and a third. Someone screamed, someone shouted. A metallic hailer shouted orders, inaudible but official.

Shit!

Njangu unsnapped the belt pouch, and took out a leather-bound book. He resealed the pouch with his burglar's tools, pitched it under a parked gravsled, and went on, strolling now, his *Tao-te ching* held in prominent view. *The temple closed, what? An hour, no, an hour and a half ago. You missed the last trans, eh? Yes, and stopped at a vend for a snack. See, here's the wrapper in my pocket. Good.*

It had better be.

He made another ten blocks before the spotlight caught him halfway across the street, and the sweeper's guns spat coiling rope. One straint caught him around the waist, the second pinned his arms, and he went down. He rolled to his side, saw legs coming toward him, the outline of a blaster.

'Do not move,' the voice said, hard, metallic, robotic. 'You are being restrained by a member of the Commonweal police as being under suspicion and a possible threat to life and public safety. Any movement will be determined as life-threatening.'

He obeyed.

'Good. Don't even breathe.' The voice became almost human. 'Eh, Fran. We have him.'

Another set of black legs came out of the police sweeper.

A boot nudged Njangu onto his back, a beam swept his brown face.

One cop dragged the wiry young man to his feet by the straints. Yoshitaro was taller than either of the men.

'Guess you didn't have squat to do with a little B&E back on Giesebechstrasse, eh? 'Bout ten minutes gone?'

'I don't have any idea what you're talking about,' Njangu said.

'Yeh. Guess you don't know anybody named Lo Chen, Peredur, or Huda, either? Among some of your other friends we netted.'

Yoshitaro frowned, pretended thought, shook his head.

'Wonder if the eye we had floating got you?' one officer said gleefully. 'Not that it matters, since we found this on you.'

He took a pocket-blaster from his boot.

'What were you going to do with it?'

'Never seen it before,' Njangu blurted, cursed silently for letting them draw him.

'You have now,' the second of ficer said. 'It fell out of your waistband when we took you down. Bad charges,

Yoshitaro. Violation of curfew, being outside your district, possession of firearms, and I'm not sure but what you were trying to pull it on us.'

'He was, he was,' the other voice said. 'I saw it clear.'

'Attempted murder, then . Guess that'll be more than enough, eh?'

Njangu's face was calm, blank.

The cop drove a fist into Yoshitaro's stomach, pleasure-filled eyes never leaving his face. Njangu caved in, let himself fall forward, turning to take the fall on his shoulder. As he fell, his legs lashed out, sweeping across the cop's calves. The cop screeched in pain and surprise, fell, his flash rolling away, sending swirls of light across the blank dark buildings around him.

Yoshitaro struggled to his knees, had one foot under him as the other cop came in, and Njangu saw the gloved fist smashing toward him.

Then nothing.

'It would seem,' the severe-faced woman said, 'there's little point in my recommending this matter be brought to trial.' She stared again at three screens whose display was hidden from Yoshitaro.

'All evidence appears in order, and your appointed defender advised he had nothing to offer on your behalf.'

Njangu's bruised face was stone.

'You've had quite a career for someone just eighteen,' the woman went on. 'I think it's a blessing for the Commonweal you weren't able to reach that pistol in time.'

She paused.

'Do you have anything to say for yourself, Stef Yoshitaro?'

'I do not recognize that name any longer.'

'So I understand. Very well. Njangu Yoshitaro.'

'I don't guess there's any point in saying anything, is there?'

'Show proper respect for the court,' the heavyset bailiff rumbled.

The judge touched other sensors.

'A long and unattractive career,' she mused. 'Beginning when you were just thirteen. What happened to you, Njangu? The file on your family shows no reason for you to be what you are.'

It wouldn't. Mother never went out until the bruises went down, and Dad bought his synth all over the city or sometimes made his own. And Marita would never tell anyone about our father's little nighttime visits. No. There's no good reason for me to be anything but what I am.

'Very well. Do you have anything to say for yourself? Are there any mitigating factors? The charges are most serious, even setting aside the matter of the attempted robbery of Van Cleef's with your fellow gang members. What I understand you hooligans call a clique.'

None you'd recognize.

'In consideration of your age,' the woman said, her voice formal, 'I offer two options. The first, of course, is Conditioning.'

Condit? A voice inside your head until you died, telling you just what to do. No spitting on the sidewalk, Yoshitaro. No alk. No drugs. Work hard, Yoshitaro. Don't criticize the Commonweal. Tell any policeman whatever he asks. A guaranteed job, dull eyes handling other people's credits and never thinking for a minute of slipping a handful into your own pocket for fear of that hidden voice.

I don't think so.

'The second is Transport for Life.'

It couldn't be any harder on the prison planetoid than here in Primeport.

'You may have half an hour to reach a decision,' the

woman said. 'Bailiff, escort this man to the holding cell.'

The man came toward Njangu, but he was already on his feet.

'I know the way.'

'Wait!'

The judge was opening another screen.

'There is another alternative, Yoshitaro, which I'd momentarily forgotten,' she said. 'We received a mandate a few days ago. Although I doubt if you'll consider it for even a moment.'

TWO

Capella/Centrum

Alban Corfi, Chief of Procurement, Undeveloped Worlds, Elis Sector, was a careful man. He read the entitlement twice before looking up and nodding at his superior, Procurement Head Pandur Meghavarna.

'Very unusual, sir,' he agreed. 'This is the what . . . thirtieth request for reinforcement and logistics this Strike Force Swift Lance — pretentious name, that — out there on the thin edge of nowhere's sent in this E-year?'

'Thirty-fourth, actually,' Meghavarna corrected.

'Something you might know, sir. All the others were spiked for lack of proper priority, unavailability of equipment, improper preparation of forms, and such. Why was this one not only allowed, but given a Beta priority?'

'An excellent question, Corfi, one which I attempted to find an answer to. I received none. Perhaps the Lords of the Confederation are practicing their capriciousness.'

'Very well, sir,' Corfi said, opening the file again. 'So what exactly do these noble frontiersmen think the Confederation is oh-so-willing and unable to give them? As if we aren't stretched to the limit and beyond already.

'Hmm. Six *Nirvana*-class P-boats with supply train . . . well, they'll whistle through their ears before they get any of *those*. Every one on the assembly line is tabbed for the Riot Troops. Alpha priority.

'Thirty-five heavy lifters, capable of carrying ten K-tons or greater for one thousand kis or more . . . I seem to remember there's some reconditioned items we could allow them.

'Assorted assault lifters, gunships, and so forth. Impossible, but with that curious Beta priority I suppose we'll have to give them what they want.

'Various other small vehicles, weapons, not a problem, not a problem . . .

'Twenty of the *Nana*-class strike boats? How'd anyone that far in the outback even *hear* of those? They haven't even been formally accepted by the Fleet. Beta priority, schmeta priority. I *hardly* think we need to worry ourselves —'

'Look again,' his superior said. Corfi obeyed, and his eyebrows lifted a trifle. That item was marked, in tiny green script, *Approved, R.E.*

'*Well*,' Corfi said, ashamed at his momentary lapse. 'So I was wrong. If *He* has approved the matter, it's up to *Him* to justify that to his superiors.' He sniffed, clearly distancing himself from future blame.

'Seven hundred and fifty trained men. The men they can have, heavens knows we've got enough of *them*. Take a few thousand more out of the slums for all of me. But trained? Doesn't he know there's a peace on?'

Meghavarna let a smile come and go. 'What about transport?'

'I've got the *Malvern* about through with her refit,' Corfi said. 'Terrible waste of fuel and all, but with a skeleton crew . . .

'Yes, the *Malvern*. And we can transship in a cycle,

perhaps two. Or as soon as they release those precious *Nanas*.'

'Good,' Meghavarna approved. 'I assumed you could expedite the matter.' He rose. 'I was a bit worried when your assistant told me you weren't in yet, knowing you live out toward Bosham.'

'I didn't even try to go home last night,' Corfi said. 'Stayed at the club, so I wouldn't get caught in the troubles.'

'What're they wanting this time?' Meghavarna asked. 'I don't really keep up on civ doings.'

'Bread, no bread, too much bread, the wrong sort of bread, or something,' Corfi said indifferently. 'Does it matter?'

'Not really.'

Corfi saluted perfunctorily, left Meghavarna's office. He took the drop to the main floor where his bodyguards waited, then rode the slideway for half a mile to his offices.

He decided he'd handpick the *Malvern*'s crew using his man in BuPers. That couldn't rebound on him, no matter what happened, since no one with sense concerned themselves with who went where in Transportation Division.

A nice obedient crew ... then he'd bounce the *Malvern* once, maybe twice, in various 'directions' before he jumped it toward its final destination through Larix/Kura. That should keep his boots clean.

Corfi reached his office, told his bodyguards to take a break – he wouldn't be needing them for an hour or so. Corfi neatly hung his body-armored overtunic on an antique wall rack, unlocked his safe, and removed the cleaner. He swept the office, found nothing more than the two standard bugs feeding prerecorded pap to Security, and keyed the vid to his assistant's line. Corfi gave the man some meaningless orders, while he checked the line with the cleaner. Still clean. He touched sensors.

The screen cleared, and he was looking at a tiny garden. Curled on its synthetic moss was a young woman, barely more than a girl. She was naked, and her ash-blondness was natural.

'Hi, darl,' she said throatily.

Corfi grinned. 'Suppose I was the bloc monitor?'

'He doesn't have my code,' she said. 'I didn't expect to hear from you until tomorrow. I thought you were seeing the wife-o tonight.'

'I was,' Corfi said. 'But seeing you like you are . . . I guess those damned riots'll keep me at the office another night.'

'Pity,' the woman said. 'I'll be ready.'

'You can be more than ready,' Corfi said. 'Remember that bracelet you were looking at?'

'Ooo.'

'Suddenly we can afford it.'

The girl squealed in delight.

'I *thought* that'd make you happy,' Corfi said.

'Oh, I am, I am, darl. Hurry home, so I can show you just how happy I am.' She parted her thighs slightly, caressed herself.

'Got to go now,' Corfi said, realizing he was having a bit of trouble breathing. 'I've got some work to take care of.'

The girl smiled, and the screen blanked.

Corfi waited until he calmed, then touched sensors once more. The screen blurred, became blank green. Again he keyed numbers, and the same thing happened. At the third screen he input letters and numbers he'd memorized several years ago, touched the SEND sensor. The transmission would be bounced at least a dozen times before it reached Larix.

As soon as he'd finished the final group, he broke contact, and, once again, checked for a bug. Still nothing.

Alban Corfi, soon to be somewhat richer, was a *very* careful man.

THREE

Altair/Klesura/Happy Vale

Tweg Mik Kerle stared glumly out at perfection. Utterly blue sky. Sky, even if it was a little reddish, beautiful, with a scattering of clouds. A spring breeze filtered through the open door, and Kerle smelled flowers, fresh hay, and, from somewhere, a woman's perfume.

He heard the tinkle of her laughter and snarled.

Perfection all around, and he was supposed to recruit for the Confederation's Army. Why would anyone here want to enlist and go wallow through the mud on some armpit world where people were actively trying to kill her? Leave a place where everyone seemed to know his place and, worse yet, like it? A place where all the women were gorgeous and happy, and the men stalwart and good-tempered?

Like that oaf looking in the window at Kerle's carefully spread-out exhibits. Here a tiny uniformed *tweg* ordered her twenty soldiers through a fascinating confidence course, there a *cent* was receiving a medal from his *caud*, while his hundred stood in stiff ranks behind, and in the center three *strikers* busied themselves learning some sort of electron-trade. He'd gape at the tiny mannequins, then guffaw and go harvest his turnips or whatever he harvested.

Kerle moaned, still looking at the bumpkin. Tall, almost two meters. Well-built. Good muscles. Blond. Human to the *n*th classification. Handsome, the sort men would follow anywhere, given a few years seasoning. A recruiting poster sort of yokel. *Don't walk away, boy. Come on through those doors and help a poor tired* tweg *make his quota.*

Kerle goggled. The yokel was walking through the door.

The recruiter came to his feet, beaming, well-rehearsed camaraderie in gear, while the back of his brain told him the young man had no doubt just slipped away from the nearest home for the terminally confused.

'Good aft, friend.'

"Day,' the young man said. 'I'm interested in joining up.'

'Well, this is certainly the place,' Kerle said. 'And you'll never regret it if you do. The Confederation needs good men, and will make you proud you decided to serve your government.'

'What I'm really interested in is travel.'

'Then the Confederation is your ticket. I've seen twenty, thirty worlds, and I've only been in ten years, made *tweg* in the first four, and should be up for *senior tweg* when the next promotion list comes out,' Kerle said. 'Not that you have to enlist for that long. Standard term is only four Earth-years.'

'Reasonable,' Garvin Jaansma said. 'Gives everyone a chance to see if they get along.'

'Any particular trade or skill you'd be interested in?'

'I'm not much on working inside. Prefer to be out-doors if I can. What about that?' The young man was pointing at a small model of an assault lifter. Kerle picked it up.

'That's a Grierson. Used in Armored Infantry. The

Grierson's the standard assault vehicle, called an Aerial Combat Vehicle, an ACV. Carries two attack teams. Chainguns here and here. Rocket pod here. There's a whole lot of different configurations. Ultrareliable. Dual antigrav units under here, give it about a thousand meters overground lift. We use it for patrols, or attack. In the assault it'd be backed up with heavy lifters, gunships like that model of a Zhukov there, and of course there'd be other assault lifters with it. You can even modify it into an in-system spaceship. You could command one of these in a year, maybe less. Five million credits the Confederation'd trust you with. Plus twenty men's lives, which is the real price. Not many jobs give someone your age that kind of responsibility,' Kerle said, sounding truly impressed.

'Sounds interesting,' Jaansma said.

'A couple of things first,' Kerle said, toes curling inside his mirror-bright boots, anticipating the bad news. 'Have you talked to your family about this?'

'They don't mind,' Jaansma said. 'Whatever I think is best for me they'll go along with. Anyway, I'm eighteen, so it's my decision, isn't it?'

'The first big one you can make,' Kerle agreed. 'Another question. I don't suppose you've had any trouble with the authorities?'

'None at all.' The answer came quickly.

'You're sure? Not even a joyriding or maybe a fight or two, or getting caught with alk or a snort? If it's minor, we can generally get clearance.'

'Nothing whatsoever.'

The young man's smile was open, sincere.

FOUR

Capella/Centrum

The *Malvern* bulged far overhead, dwarfing the line of men trudging toward its gangway. Garvin Jaansma gaped upward.

'Move along, dungboot,' a cadreman snapped. 'The Confederation don't want you to break your neck before you even get trained.'

'Good advice, *Finf*,' a voice grated, 'you being the experienced star-rover and all. I'm surely admiring all your decorations and such.'

The junior noncom flushed. His uniform breast was as slick as his shaven head. 'Quiet, you.'

The man who'd spoken stared hard, and the *finf* flinched back as if he'd been struck.

'Keep on moving,' he muttered, and scurried away.

The man was big in any direction, not fat, but heavy, solid. His face was set in a perpetual scowl under his forward-combed, thinning black hair. A scar ran down one cheek and faded out in the middle of his thick neck. He appeared to be in his early thirties. He wore unshined half boots, heavy black canvas dungarees, a green tunic that would have been expensive new, sometime ago, and had a small, battered bag at his feet. There was a military-looking stencil on it: KIPCHAK, PETR.

He eyed Jaansma and the recruit beside him, snorted, and turned away.

'I want to learn how to do that,' the other recruit said in a low voice.

'Do what?'

'Melt 'em with a look like that guy did. Cheaper'n a blaster and not nearly as convictable.'

Garvin extended his hand, palm up, and the other man repeated the greeting.

'Garvin Jaansma.'

'Njangu Yoshitaro.'

Garvin considered the other young man, who was about his age and height, dark-skinned with close-cropped black hair and Asiatic features. He wore charcoal trousers and a pale green shirt. Both fit poorly and looked cheap. He had a collarless windbreaker over his shoulder. Yoshitaro reminded Jaansma of an alert fox or hoonsmeer.

'Did anybody say where we're going?' he asked.

'Of course not,' Njangu said. 'Recruit scum don't get told shit 'til they have to know it, which I guess'll be whenever we get where we're going.'

'What about training?' Jaansma said. 'I enlisted for Armor, and so far all I've done is polish toilets.'

The older man turned back.

'And that's all you'll do 'til you get to your parent unit. The Confederation's got a new policy. They ship your young ass to your home regiment, and let them whip you into shape.'

'That isn't the way it is in the holos,' Njangu said.

'Damn little is,' the man said. 'It's 'cause the Confederation's falling apart, and they don't have time or money to take care of the little things like they used to.'

'Falling apart?' Garvin said incredulously. 'Come on!'

Garvin had seen troubles in his wanderings, but the

Confederation itself in trouble? That was like saying the stars were burning out tomorrow, or night might not follow day. The Confederation had existed for more than a thousand years, and would no doubt exist for another ten thousand.

'I spoke clearly,' Kipchak said. 'Falling apart. The reason you don't see it is because you're right at the center of things. You think an ant knows somebody's about to dump boiling water on its nest? Or a *wygor* ever realizes what the skinner wants?'

Neither young man understood the references.

'What do you think all the riots are about?' he went on.

'What riots?'

'You didn't watch any 'casts while you were farting around in the 'cruit barracks?'

'Uh . . . no,' Yoshitaro said. 'I don't pay much attention to the news.'

'Better start. A good holo-flash'll generally clue you how deep the shit is you're about to get tossed into, and maybe even give you time to pack hip boots.

'People are rioting, tearing things up because they can't get things. Centrum being a high-class admin center, nobody bothers to grow anything. Which means everything from biscuits to buttwipe gets shipped in, not produced locally. Since the system's showing cracks, sometimes those shipments don't get here in time for dinner.

'It's real hard to accept you're on the greatest planet in the universe, like the holos say, if you can't afford beans and bacon.'

'How come you know so much, anyway?' Njangu said, just a bit belligerently.

This time the look came at him. But he didn't quail. Kipchak let his glower fade down.

"Cause *I* pay attention,' he said. 'Something you better learn. For instance, I could tell you where we're going, what unit we're headed for, and even what the pol/sci setup is there. If I wanted to. Which I don't, much.' Perhaps he was about to add more, but they'd reached the ship's gangway.

'Your name and homeworld,' a synthed voice intoned.

'Petr Kipchak,' he growled. 'Centrum, when it suits me.'

'Noted,' the robot said. 'Compartment sixteen. Take any bunk. Next.'

And the huge *Malvern* swallowed them.

The compartment stretched into dimness. It was filled with endless four-high rows of bunks, with small lockers under the bottom one, and, like the rest of the ship, was spotless and smelled of fresh paint. Fresh paint and an incongruous odor of dust, as if the *Malvern* was an antique.

The recruits were ordered by a harried-looking crewman to strap down in their bunks and stand by for lift.

The *Malvern* came alive, a deep hum reverberating through every deck. The deck speaker said, 'Stand by.' The hum grew deeper until it made your bones sing, and the *Malvern* shuddered.

'Are we in space?' Njangu asked.

'I think so, but—'

The speaker interrupted Garvin, and said, 'Stand by for jump,' and moments later the slight nausea, disorientation came, and they were in stardrive. They waited to see what would happen next, but, characteristic of space travel, nothing did.

'Let's go see what there's to see,' Garvin said, unstrapping.

'I thought we'd be in zero gravity,' Njangu complained.

'Be grateful we're not,' Garvin said. 'Lots of people's stomachs would be real unhappy, and I don't get my thrills swabbing up puke in midair.'

'Oh yeh?' Njangu said. 'You been out before?' The phrase, heard on holos, rang tastily on his tongue.

Garvin smiled, shrugged, and led the way out of the compartment.

There wasn't much to see. More crew bays, deserted assembly areas, long corridors looking like the one they'd just left. There weren't any viewports, even on the outer decks, and neither Njangu nor Garvin could figure out how to operate the occasional screen they came upon.

Njangu stopped at one compartment hatch labeled LIBRARY.

'Let's go educate ourselves, like that goon told us we were supposed to do.'

Low tables lined the walls, with screens and keypads at regular intervals. Njangu sat behind one, touched a key. The screen lit:

ENTER REQUEST

'What?'

'Try, uh, destination,' Jaansma suggested.

Yoshitaro touched keys.

THAT LS NOT A PERMITTED REQUEST. TRY AGAIN.

'What about where we've been? Do what Scarface suggested and see what the holos say about riots.'

''Kay.'

A line scrolled across the screen: BASHEES NG, SERMON CONFED PUNDITS.

'Huh?'

Anotherline: BOSHAM RADS 4 STUN; then a third: LOK BLOOIES TURN WUNKIES BAK, 32 BAGGED, 170 INJ.

'I'm getting the feeling I don't speak Confederation,' Njangu said.

'Guess the journohs have their own shorthand, maybe?'

A rather voluptuous young woman smiled out. She wore nothing at all. Another line scrolled: PROKKY SEZ WORRY NU, SPORTY ALWAYS.

'Well good for ol' Prokky,' Garvin said. 'I'd sure sporty with her.'

'Wonder if we'll find something like her where we're going,' Yoshitaro said.

'If we do, she'll be officers only,' Garvin said. 'The hell with it. Let's get eddicated later.'

A crewman hurrying past spotted them.

'You two.'

They stopped.

'What're you doing outside your compartment?'

'Nobody said we couldn't,' Jaansma said.

'Nobody said you could, either,' the sailor snapped. 'And I just happen to need two servers in the mess hall. Let's go.'

Without waiting for a response, he turned and went back down the corridor, obviously expecting them to follow. Njangu and Garvin glanced at each other, then obeyed.

'What is this?' Jaansma said. 'Everything not ordered is forbidden?'

'I think we're starting to understand things,' Njangu said wryly.

On the third ship-day, they were ordered to pack their civilian clothes and issued gray tunics and pants, and soft-soled boots that strapped at the ankles. There were no patches, no insignia, not even name tags.

'We look like damned prisoners,' Garvin said.

'No we don't,' Njangu disagreed. 'Prisoners wear red.'

'Thank you for the educational information, sir.'

'Quite welcome.'

'By the way,' Garvin said carefully, 'that outfit you were wearing?'

'Yeh?' Yoshitaro's voice was flat.

'You, uh, don't look like the sort who'd wear something like that.'

'What do you mean?'

'You look like you'd thread a little better style.'

'I would. I did. But I didn't have any choice. Somebody bought my outfit before I shipped out,' Njangu said. His expression didn't encourage Garvin to ask more.

The ship schedule was simple: Stand in line to eat, exercise, stand in line to eat again, eat, try to find somebody to talk to or game with, stand in line to eat, eat, sleep . . . and the days ground past.

Petr Kipchak had a bunk at the far end of the compartment, but he was uninterested in making friends. He was either in a rec area, working out on the weight machines for endless hours, or in his bunk, reading a disk, completely engrossed.

'Dunno if I agree with this monosexual 'freshing,' Njangu muttered.

'Why not?'

'Liable to give some of us ideas.'

'Naah,' Garvin said. 'They put something in the food to keep it from happening.'

'Hey,' Yoshitaro said. 'You're right. I haven't had a hard since we've been shipboard!'

'See? Just listen to Uncle Garvin, and you'll know everything in time.'

'Allah with a yo-yo,' the recruit named Maev gasped. 'You won't believe this.'

'What?' Garvin and Njangu rolled out of their bunks.

'C'mon. You've got to see it.' Maev beckoned them to

the refresher, which was nearly full of men and women getting ready for the third-meal.

She pointed to one shower cubicle, large enough for a dozen people. But there was only one in it – Petr Kipchak, who appeared oblivious to their attention.

Garvin was about to ask what was so special, when he saw.

Kipchak was busily washing his genitalia with one of the stiff nylon brushes they used to scrub the shower walls and singing loudly off key.

'Good flippin' gods!' Garvin blurted, and the three retreated as Kipchak raised his head.

'What the *hell* . . . th' bastard's mental!' Maev said.

Njangu was about to agree, then realized – as he'd ducked back around the corner, he'd seen something very much like a smile on the burly man's face. *One way to have a little privacy*, he thought, and hid his amusement.

Garvin was awakened by a series of double-dings he'd learned told the time to the *Malvern*'s crew. It was deep in the ship's sleep cycle, and there were snores, some light, some hearty, around the compartment.

It was dark except for the dull red ready lights on the bulkheads, and, at the end of the room, white light from the refresher.

He sleepily decided he was thirsty and padded into the refresher.

It was deserted but for four men, two women. One woman stood by the hatchway on lookout, the other five sat or squatted around two blankets spread on the plas-slotted deck. All were older recruits. One was Petr Kipchak.

There were money and cards on the blankets. Kipchak had only a few bills and some coins, while the dealer had a wad of currency from a dozen worlds.

The five eyed Garvin. But he showed no particular interest, and went to the urinal. His expression flickered suddenly as he watched the game out of the corner of his eye, then became calm, innocent once more.

He finished, drank water from a tap, walked back by the game. One man, the dealer, a heavyset, balding man, looked up.

'Go to bed, sonny. This is way over your head.'

'Children's money's not good, huh?' Garvin asked.

The dealer started to snap, then smiled, a rather nasty smirk. He evaluated Jaansma, absently twisting a large silver ring on his left hand back and forth. Finally, he said, 'You wanna get burned, it's your business. I got no objections. Anybody else?'

Kipchak seemed about to say something, then shook his head. The others shrugged or nodded as well.

'Table stakes, so you best be ready for some hard ridin', troop, and no snivelin' when we wipe you out,' the dealer said. 'Go get your stash.'

Garvin went to his bunk, spun the combination wheels on his small carryall, took out a pair of socks. Inside was a thick roll of bills. He dressed hurriedly, making sure his boots were carefully strapped.

Njangu's eyes were open. 'What's going on?'

'There's a game back in the refresher. Thought I'd get in it.'

'Didn't think you were a gambler.'

'I'm not.' Jaansma hesitated. 'And neither is the guy with the cards. He's a mechanic.'

Njangu sat up. 'What're you gonna do about it?'

'Make me some money.'

'Be careful.'

'I'm always . . .' Jaansma broke off, thought a minute. 'You want in on the action?'

'I don't play cards.'

'You don't have to. Look, I just got an idea that'll make for a lot of fun for everybody.'

Garvin spoke in low, quick tones. Njangu frowned, then started grinning.

'One question,' he said. 'Why're we doing this? It could mean trouble.'

'Didn't you just answer your own question?'

'Maybe I did,' Yoshitaro said. 'Sure. We can do it like that.'

Jaansma peeled some bills from the roll.

'Here. Give me, oh, fifteen minutes.'

Garvin curled the five cards in his hand, examined them. Not good, not bad. This was the fourth hand he'd played. He'd dropped out of two, bet on one and lost.

'Ten credits to play,' the woman said, and tossed a bill into the center of the blanket.

Garvin tossed two coins on top of the ante, and other notes followed. Three players, including Kipchak, stayed in.

'Go ahead, kid,' the dealer said. 'You're off.'

'I take one,' Jaansma said, discarding and taking a single card from the five-card widow, and the dealer replaced it from the deck in his hand.

'No help,' he sighed, and tossed his hand into the discards.

Betting went around twice, and Kipchak took the small pot.

The dealer was shuffling when Yoshitaro slipped in. 'Hey, Kipchak,' Njangu said. 'I've got the money I owe you. Found a dice game yesterday.'

Petr blinked, looked hard at Njangu, was about to say something. Yoshitaro moved his head slightly up, down.

'Oh. Yeah. Hold my place.' Kipchak got up.

'I got it in my bag,' Njangu said, and the two went out.

Another hand was dealt, and the dealer won.

Petr and Njangu came back in. Kipchak's face was dark, stormy, then calmed. He sat down, and Njangu leaned against a bulkhead, not far from the lookout, someone who couldn't sleep and was boredly kibitzing.

The game went on for another hour. Garvin noted that one man licked his lips when he was bluffing, the woman pulled absently at a lock of her hair when she had a strong hand, other traits. But mostly he watched the dealer. The luck went back and forth, but the credits slowly and steadily flowed toward the heavy man with the ring.

Finally Garvin stretched his legs, and happened to tap Petr with his toe.

"Scuse me,' he said. Kipchak didn't answer.

'Wisht we had some quill,' a man grumbled. 'Losin' like I'm doin' is easier if you're not too sober.'

The dealer swept up the cards, shuffled them hastily.

'Mind if I cut?' Jaansma said.

'No,' the dealer said shortly. 'You're right.' He set the deck down on the blanket.

'Deep and weep, thin and win,' somebody intoned.

Garvin picked up the deck in one hand, cut it smoothly. The dealer looked at him carefully, took the deck, and cards flicked out.

It was quiet in the refresher except for the soft whine of the conditioner fans, and the snap of the cards being dealt, the sound a bit louder than it might've been.

The dealer's lips quirked when he picked up his hand. 'This one's got to be expensive,' he announced. He picked up bills. 'One hundred even to see if I'm braggin'.'

'I'll play,' Kipchak said, and put most of his small reserve in the pot.

'Me too,' Garvin agreed.

Two others shyed, two tossed in their hands.

'I'm taking two cards,' Jaansma said, and his hand passed over the widow as he discarded. His expression didn't change when he picked up the new cards.

'Dealer takes one.'

'I'll fly these,' Kipchak said, and stood pat.

The woman took two, the remaining man three.

'Another hundred,' the dealer said.

The woman dropped out, the remaining man increased the bet.

'I think I'm lucky,' Jaansma said. 'Up two hundred.'

'And a hundred back at you,' Petr said.

'Like I said, expensive,' the dealer said. ''Sides, it's getting late. Don't want to spoil my complexion with late hours.' He counted. 'Up five . . . six hundred.'

'The kid's going to be foolish,' Garvin said, and peeled bills into the stack. 'And up two hundred on you.'

'I'm short,' Petr said.

'No problem,' Njangu said, coming away from the bulkhead and taking notes from his pocket. 'Your credit's good.'

'Thanks.'

The dealer laughed unpleasantly. 'I think I'm gonna sleep real, real good.' He flipped his hand onto the table. All five were of a single color.

'Guess that does it,' and he reached for the money. 'High to the Protector.'

'Not quite.' And Petr slowly tossed cards faceup on the blanket. 'Ruler . . . Ruler . . . Ruler . . . Ruler . . . and the Alien for a fifth.'

The dealer's eyes went wide. 'You weren't—' and his hand went for his back pocket.

'Rube!' Garvin snapped, coming to his feet.

Light glinted as a tiny steel dart flickered across the blanket, buried itself in the dealer's forearm. He yelped, and blood spurted.

The lookout came forward, a short length of pipe appearing in her hand. Njangu sidestepped into her, and snapped a backhand strike into her temple. She tumbled across a player, lay still.

Another man was getting up, and Garvin drove a punch into his solar plexus, then smashed the back of his hand into the man's skull, and he went down.

The dealer stared at his blood-runneling arm, the knife still buried near his elbow. Petr pulled the dart free, and again the man screeched.

The other players were motionless, arms raised to their shoulders, fingers splayed.

Yoshitaro glanced into the troop bay. 'Nobody heard anything,' he reported.

Petr wiped the tiny knife clean, made it vanish. 'Don't like cheaters,' he said. 'Maybe I oughta slice your tendons for you. Play hell with your card game.'

The dealer moaned, shook his head pleadingly.

'You people see anything tonight, or did you go to bed early?' Kipchak asked.

Heads were vigorously shaken.

The lookout got to her knees, coughed, and threw up. She staggered toward a toilet. The man Garvin had hit lay motionless.

'You kill him?' Petr asked, not sounding worried.

'No,' Jaansma said. 'He'll wake up in an hour, and be sick like she is, but nothing lasting.'

'Good. We don't need any courts-martial,' Petr said. 'Now, isn't it bedtime for you folks?'

The players hurried out.

Petr pulled the dealer to his feet. 'You go on sick call, and swear you slipped and fell against a hatch dog. Got it? Anything different, and there'll be two witnesses who'll call you liar when we get to D-Cumbre.

'And then you'd better grow eyes in the back of your

head, which I understand makes a feller nervous after a while.'

'Nothin' happened,' the dealer babbled. 'It's like you said. I swear, I swear.'

'Good. Here. Take this towel and go find a medic.'

'Not quite yet,' Garvin said. 'For there's still a lesson to be learned before we offer our final benedictions.' He spoke in measured, liturgical tones. 'My man here has not yet learned how we discovered his villainy, and perhaps he could benefit from that information.'

'Don't tell the bastard,' Kipchak said. 'Then he'll do better next time, and rook another set of fools.'

'Not to worry,' Jaansma said lightly. 'For knaves such as he, there's never a lesson to be learned until the final one.

'I first noted this man because of the sound. Sound, you say, looking puzzled. Yes, sound,' he went on pedantically, 'for when a man is dealing seconds, that is dealing the second card instead of the top card of the deck, there's a certain sinful sibilance to be sensed.' He picked up the scattered cards, reassembled them.

'Listen, and you, too, shall be enlightened. Note how I hold this deck of cards, and observe well, as I hold this top card in place with the thumb of my left hand, and flick out the second card with my index finger and thumb of my right, there's a certain noise to be apprehended. Yes?

'Now, my second clue was that obnoxious silver ring the wastrel wears.'

He grabbed the dealer's left hand, and pulled the ring from his finger.

'Notice, it doesn't even fit properly, which would suggest he acquired it from some equally devious sort before we lifted. I noted he was not only turning it about his finger, but incessantly polishing it. So when he held the deck in his right hand, waving it about, like so, he could push out the top card a bit, see by its reflection if it was of interest, and then retain it by dealing seconds until he wished to possess it.

'The lookout was in on the graft certainly, and the mark I dropped might've been. Or maybe not,' Jaansma said indifferently.

'Maybe we ought to break this guy's thumbs,' Njangu said.

'We *could* do that,' Jaansma said, and the dealer moaned again. 'He's truly a malicious miscreant motivated into mopery by moroseness. But it might be as devastating for me to show him something.

'Look, you. You think you're a shark, eh? Or some other equally predatory creature. But you should learn there are always bigger sharks in any ocean.

'Observe. I take the deck, and shuffle it once. You saw, heard, nothing untoward?

'But watch. I will deal the top five cards.'

Each card snapped as it came off the deck.

'Protector ... Protector ... Protector ... Protector ... kicker. Not at all a bad hand. But I shuffle it once more. Now the top five cards are Companion ... Companion ... Companion ... Companion and a ten. A better hand. You would be inclined to bet such a hand like that hard, wouldn't you?

'You don't have to answer. But here is the hand I happen to draw.' Five more cards snapped off the deck. 'Nova ... Nova ... Nova ... Nova ... and how did that Alien show up once again? I thought it was in the last hand.

'You see? But of course you don't.' Jaansma's tone went back to normal. 'He's yours, Kipchak.'

'Go on, get!' Petr snapped, and the dealer half ran out of the compartment, clutching the blood-soaked towel.

'Gamblin'll be the death of me,' Kipchak said. 'Thanks. I owe you.

'No problem,' Jaansma said.

'Why'd you get involved?'

'Because,' Garvin said, 'of my deep abiding love for Truth, Justice, and the Confederation Way.'

Njangu snorted.

'All right,' Kipchak said. 'Another question. There was a little blood got spilled tonight. Neither one of you seemed real bothered by it. That ain't like most 'cruits I've met.'

Both young men looked at Kipchak, and their expressions wore the same amount of utter innocence.

'Mary on a pong-stick,' Kipchak swore. 'You two could be brothers.'

'My turn,' Yoshitaro said. 'Where'd you learn to spot somebody cheating like that?'

'I read about it in a book somewhere.'

'The same place you learned to deal like you did?'

'That's right.'

'What about the fancy talking? You sound like a god-shouter, or some kind of circus hustler.'

'That's what I am,' Garvin said. 'I've secretly enlisted in the Confederation to bring sinners into the welcoming hand of the Lord Pigsny.'

'Never heard of him.'

'That's why I became a missionary. Our sect isn't doing very well.'

'Do you ever give a straight answer to anything?' Yoshitaro asked in disgust. 'Like who was this Rube you were shouting to when the fighting started?'

After a moment, a low, sincere snore answered him.

Petr stopped them the next 'morning.'

'Wanted to thank you two clowns,' he said. 'I

would've chased every last credit down that rathole if you hadn't gotten interested.'

'Forget about it,' Jaansma said. 'I was having trouble sleeping.'

'Yeh,' Kipchak said. 'Anyway, I owe you.'

He didn't wait for a response, but pushed away through the crowd.

'So now we've got a debt of honor with Scarface,' Garvin said. 'Whoopie.'

'Don't slam it,' Njangu said. 'We might need a throat slit someday.'

The *Malvern* came out of N-space, and its nav-computer checked its position. It was on course.

A few minutes later, it shimmered and vanished on its next-to-last jump before the Cumbre system.

''Kay,' Petr said. 'Our destination's D-Cumbre.* It's a Confederation World, has a Planetary Government — a governor general plus some kind of council to advise him. Probably all the crooks with old money.'

'What's our unit?'

'It's supposed to be about ten thousand men. Called Strike Force Swift Lance.' Petr shrugged. 'Officers like flash names.

'Our *caud's* somebody.named Williams. Couldn't find anything out about him.

'The unit's assigned mission is keeping the peace.'

'Against who?' Njangu asked.

'It seems to be a little complicated,' Kipchak said. 'D-Cumbre's geetus is in mining another world. C-Cumbre, as I recall. The pick-swingers mostly come from a whole group of immigrants called 'Raum.' He gargled the initial

* See Appendix.

consonant. 'Spelled with a single mark in front, so you can tell it ain't pronounced like real people talk.

'The 'Raum came to C-Cumbre a few hundred years ago, my man told me. Believed they oughta own the universe. Instead, they're doon th' mine, like they say, which is where most fanatics belong, working for the smarter crooks who got there first.

'Guess some of 'em don't like the swing of things, so they're running up and down in the hills playing bandit and snipin' anybody who doesn't agree with 'em.

'That'll be one of our targets, I s'pose.'

'How do we tell them apart from the people we're defending?' Garvin asked.

'Hopefully because they're shooting at our young asses,' Kipchak answered. 'But they're supposed to be shorter, stockier, darker and, according to those who call themselves their betters, with all the bad habits anybody who's unlucky enough to be dealt the bottom card has.

'Anyway, the big squeaker is the mines are worked both by men and by Musth.'

'What're they?' Njangu asked. 'I never paid much attention to aliens. Never saw one to steal something from, I guess.'

'Big tall creatures,' Garvin said. 'I saw a holo on them. They look like big, skinny cats walking on two legs. Got a long neck, as I recall, and moved real fast. They looked like they could be bad news in a fight.'

'That's them,' Petr agreed. 'They're supposed to be as touchy as a whore the night before the troops get paid. I've never been around 'em, but a mate of mine has, and he said they're real quick to get nasty.

'Anyway, that's about all I know.'

'Can I ask you something?' Njangu said.

'I said I owe you.'

'You've been in the service before?'

'Yeh. I join up, get pissed off, get out, can't stand the way civilians piddle around, join up again . . . guess I oughta go one or the other,' Kipchak sighed. 'Tried settlin' down once or twice, but it didn't stick.

'Maybe this time I'll just stay in.'

'What . . . I don't know what to call it exactly, what branch do you generally serve with?' Yoshitaro asked.

'There's only one to think about, far as I'm concerned. Intelligence an' Recon. Snoopin' and poopin', we call it. Prob'ly be some of my mates from other times there. I&R's a small world, because most soldiers think we're brain-dead and suicidal.

'You operate by yourself or with a small team, so any ambush you end up in's your own fault, instead of stumbling along with a turd of hurtles like a common footso'jer does, or zooming into a hot landing zone with every other squid in a Strike Force.

'Still not a bad way to get killed, though. If I had a brain, I'd prob'ly go for Supply or Cooking.

'Appears Ma Kipchak raised herself a rock-solid fool.'

'Say, Njangu?'

Yoshitaro looked up from the disk he was reading. It was Maev.

'Ye-up?'

'I've got a problem with my bunk chain,' she said. 'Damned thing's got a kink, and I keep hitting it with my head. Could you see if you could yank it out or something?'

'Sure.' Njangu slid out of his bunk and followed the small redhead.

Petr and Garvin sat cross-legged on Kipchak's bunk, a small magnetic chessboard between them. Njangu grinned as he went by.

'Hmm,' Garvin said. 'White Queen takes Black Rook, I suspect.'

'What're you talkin' about?' Kipchak demanded. 'Your queen's not even close to my castle.'

'Never mind, never mind.'

Something woke Njangu. It took a minute for him to realize where he was. Maev was lying on the inside of the bunk, half-smiling in her dream. Her hand was between Yoshitaro's thighs. Her hair was very dark in the ready lights.

Neither of them had bothered with the third-meal, and had eventually fallen asleep from pure exhaustion.

Njangu felt himself stir, ran a finger down her sleek side, and caressed her thighs. Without waking, she lifted her leg, half rolled onto her back.

The loudspeaker blared: '*All hands . . . all hands . . . report to your Emergency Positions.*'

Njangu was out of the bunk, grabbing for his clothes. Maev blinked sleepily. 'What's going on?'

'Hell if I know. But we better get back with the others.' She dressed hastily.

'*All hands . . . all hands. Stand by to be boarded. Warning. Do not make any attempt to resist. I say again, do not make any attempt to resist.*'

'You got any idea what's going on?' Yoshitaro asked. Garvin shook his head.

'We're still in stardrive, aren't we?'

'Yeh.'

'How could anybody . . . another ship . . . get this close to us?' Yoshitaro wondered. Jaansma shook his head again.

'They could if they had a tracker waiting for us in N-space,' Kipchak said grimly. 'Or if they had our plot.'

'What does that mean?' Njangu asked.

'It means it ain't gonna be good,' Kipchak said. 'Especially with that bit about not resisting.'

The *Malvern* shuddered. 'Somebody comin' alongside,' Kipchak said. 'Not a bad trick in N-space. Damned near impossible unless you've got somebody on the bridge cooperating.'

'What's this about no resistance?' Jaansma said. 'Pirates?'

'Shee-yit,' Petr said. 'There ain't no such thing as pirates.'

'Then why'd they tell us not to resist? We — the Confederation isn't at war with anybody, is it?'

'Not as far as I know.'

'Then what—'

'Shut up. If I knew something, I'd tell you.' Kipchak snapped.

They waited for almost an hour. Normal lighting came on, and the ready lights dimmed.

'*All military trainees,*' the speaker said. '*Stand by for assembly. Secure all possessions and obey the orders of the men who will enter your compartments. You have nothing to fear if you obey absolutely.*

'*Any resistance will be met with the most extreme measures.*'

The troop bay was loud with questions and no answers.

Sudden silence, as the hatches at the far end of the bay slammed open. Two men entered the compartment. They wore spacesuits with open faceplates and held heavy blasters at port arms. They moved to either side of the door, froze.

A third man entered. He was tall, clean-shaven and white-blond. Like the others, he wore a dark spacesuit with no emblems, and had removed his helmet. There was a blaster holstered at his side.

'All right.' The voice boomed, and Garvin jumped until he realized the man had a portable loudspeaker mounted on his suit. 'This ship has been seized by lawful authority. All of you men and women are to consider yourselves prisoners. At the proper time you will be given an opportunity to redeem yourselves.

'Do not make any attempt at resistance, or you will be shot. You will not be harmed if you cooperate, and in fact could be richly rewarded in the future.

'Just remember – do what you're told, when you're told to do it, and you'll be all right.

'Disobey and die. Now, stand by for further instructions.'

The blond disappeared.

'Oh shit-oh-reilly,' Kipchak murmured. 'We're in for it.'

'Why?' Yoshitaro asked. 'What in the hell's happening?'

'You remember how I said I&R's a real small world? I know that bastard. Name's Celidon, and he's a proper shit. Kill you in a Vegan instant if you screw up.'

'I don't get it,' Garvin said. 'Why the hell should the Confederation highjack one of its own ships?'

'He isn't Confederation,' Petr said. 'Not anymore. He's freelance. Has been since they booted him out. I heard he was working for some Protector on . . . Larnyx . . . no. Larix. Double name. Larix and Kura, that was it.'

'What's going to happen next?'

'I think,' Kipchak said, his voice gaining confidence, 'we *did* get pirated. Odds are this Protector's after the ship and whatever's in it. Although how the hell he'd find out about a Confederation troop movement . . . beyond me. Way beyond me.

'Fair cagey, though. Unmarked suits, nobody in uniform, probably their ship's sterile, not a bad chance of getting away with it.'

'So what happens to us?' Garvin asked.

'We're still gonna be in the army,' Kipchak said. 'But it won't be the Confederation's. And it might be a real long time before we get back to anything resembling home, if it matters to you.'

'Wonderful,' Njangu said. 'Just goddamned wonderful.'

Petr wasn't listening, but making fast clicking noises with his tongue as he thought. 'Nope,' he said. 'Not for me, brother.'

'What's not for me?' Garvin asked.

'I'm not serving any Protector,' he said firmly. ''Specially not a renegade. When the Confederation comes down on this bastard, it'll be the high jump for anybody and everybody wearing his colors.

'Nope, not for me,' he said once more.

'What can you do?' Njangu asked.

'Don't worry about me. You fellows just keep your heads low and don't take any promotions. They mostly don't hang *strikers* in the rear rank. Sooner or later things'll shake out, or you'll get a chance to slide out from under. You'll be all right.' Petr's eyes weren't on them, but on the two guards at the hatch.

'You're taking off.'

'Better honk.'

'Can we come?' Garvin asked. 'Damned if I want to become any sort of pirate.'

'Don't be a prime idjiit,' Kipchak snapped. 'You'd just . . .' He stopped, looked at Garvin and Njangu critically.

'You serious?'

'Yeh.'

Njangu thought for a moment, then nodded. 'I've already got one strike on me, don't need another. I'll go, if you'll have us.'

'Well . . . I owe you, like I said. And being solo on a lifeboat can create problems, especially on a long jump, which I suspect we'll be making if we get that far.

"Kay. You can't take anything with you. We're gonna move backward, real slow. When the guards look at you, freeze. Don't look back. And for gossakes don't smile. Pretty soon they'll come for the others, which is when we go down past the refresher in the confusion, undog the hatch at the far end of the bay, then follow me. Hopefully that passageway's got air in it. We're going for one of the E-craft — escape ships — which should be on the mid-deck. All these goddamned troopships are built pretty much the same. If we're in luck, it'll be supplied and fueled. Otherwise . . . so let's go.'

Step . . . step . . . statue, I'm a statue, one of those bastards with the gun just glanced down the line, but not at me, not at me . . . step . . .

Half an eternity later the blond officer, Celidon, came back.

'All right,' his amplified voice cracked. 'Pick up your gear, and come toward me in single file. We're going to search you, then move you all to a smaller compartment, to keep you from getting yourselves into trouble. If any of you have a weapon, drop it right now. Otherwise, you'll be shot where you stand.

'First man!'

The recruits shuffled forward slowly.

Petr Kipchak slid down a side aisle. Behind him were Garvin and Njangu. Crablike, they scuttled away from the main bay entrance.

They passed the rumpled bunk Maev had taken Njangu to, and he had a moment of pain for what might've been but would never be.

Kipchak stopped at a small hatch, double-dogged. He pulled on one dog, and paint cracked, fell away.

'Goddamned shipyard assholes. If it don't move, paint over it.' He put his full weight on it, and the dog swung clear. He pulled the other one almost free, moved the dog back and forth experimentally, nodded satisfaction. There was atmosphere on the other side.

He opened the hatch, and the three crept out, into the bowels of the starship.

FIVE

N-Space

Garvin heard their silent footsteps as smashing echoes through the empty passages. Kipchak took the lead, Njangu behind him. Both moved easily, Jaansma noted, used to stealth, while he sounded like a drunken mastodon.

Petr gestured . . . down this passage . . . through this hatch . . . and the two followed. Twice he waved them back, and they ducked into an open compartment and space-booted heels clashed past.

There was noise ahead, and Kipchak chanced creeping to the passage's turning.

Voices came:

'Awright . . . stay in line, goddammit . . . look, I don't have the friggin' registry . . . I said keep it quiet!'

The sound of a blow, and a shout of pain.

Then Celidon's voice:

'Silence! I'll say this once only,' his voice boomed. 'Stay in the lines we've put you in. When you come to the noncom at the head of the line, give him your name, last first, and wait for him to check you off.

'You're now members of the armed forces of Larix and Kura, and you will learn we mollycoddle no one, and require utter obedience.

'Now, follow my orders!'

Petr nodded wisely, as if he could've given the speech himself, and waved them toward a red-lettered hatch.

EMERGENCY ACCESS TO LIFECRAFT.
WARNING: OPENING THIS HATCH WILL
SET OFF AN ALARM.
DO NOT OPEN EXCEPT IN EXTREME
EMERGENCY AND UNDER THE DIREC-
TION OF A SHIP'S OFFICER OR A SENIOR
OFFICER OF YOUR OWN SERVICE

Petr examined the hatch. Njangu was already looking at the dogs, then the hinges. He pointed to something Garvin couldn't make out, then opened and closed his fingers like a mouth . . . or an alarm going on and off. He pulled the warning sign a bit away from the hatch, then bent a corner of the plas back and forth until it broke free

Yoshitaro forced the plas into the back of one hinge, holding a tiny spring-loaded switch in place, held up his thumb with a grin, then crossed his fingers. Petr undogged the hatch. No alarm sounded. They went into a curving passage with smaller hatches at regular intervals, next to the outer skin of the ship. Garvin fancied he could feel the cold of space when he touched the bulkhead.

Petr pointed to one hatch. They opened it without setting off an alarm and entered a small airlock. Kipchak opened the inner hatch, and the three went 'down' into a single large teardrop-shaped room, with two hatches to either side labeled REFRESHER. The room was padded from floor to ceiling, and bunks were strapped to the walls. At the 'bottom' was a short ladder leading to a command station with three screens, a handful of sensors, a single strapped chair, and – in the center of the panel – a square button with a cover.

'Close the lock,' Kipchak ordered, and Jaansma obeyed. After he'd dogged the hatch, Petr checked the dogs, then secured the inner hatch.

'We're not in the clear yet,' he said in a pointlessly low voice. 'Sometimes these little bastards have a second alarm when the power's activated or when you boot out into space.

'You two pull down a bunk apiece. I don't know if we'll be doing any grav-maneuvers, but there's no point in getting bruised up unless we have to.'

Njangu and Garvin obeyed. Petr went to the command deck, strapped himself in.

'This boat is shit-simple,' he said. 'See this big mother button? That's power. When it goes on we'll have our own grav, and the screens'll give us real-time projections forward and aft, plus radar in the middle one. In N-space, all three'll be standard nav-screens. I hope.

'I'm talking because I'm scared I'm going to set something off.' He clenched his teeth, lifted the cover off the large red switch, pushed it.

Gravity swung 'down' from the nose of the teardrop to the deck of the boat, and the screens lit. Njangu felt a slight hum through the padding.

'We're live,' Petr said. 'Let's see if we can just hit this thing . . . here . . . and . . . here we go.'

Garvin felt movement as a hatch slid open in the outer skin and the lifecraft's davits moved it into space, let it float. He stared at the com deck's screens, couldn't make sense of the center one, but the other two showed the bulk of the *Malvern*. Hanging next to it was the sleek needle of a warship.

'Now the alarms go off,' Petr said, his fingers tapping keys. But nothing happened. 'I don't believe this,' he said. 'I've not lived that clean a life . . . but here we go.'

He touched a button, then the main button, and the world jittered a little, and the screens showed the blur of N-space.

'One ... two ... three ... four ...' and Kipchak touched another sensor. This time the screens showed normal space, and again Petr hit the main button, and they jumped again.

'Two blind jumps,' he explained, 'just to make sure they didn't have sensors out. They ought to have a button here labeled PANICKED FLIGHT.

They came back to real space. There was nothing around them, no stars, no worlds, no *Malvern*, no raiders.

'With luck,' he said, 'which we're having a plethora of ... that's shitpot-full for anyone without my advanced training ... we jumped maybe half a light-minute each time. That'll be far enough to keep the goblins from finding us, but not so far we lose the computer's base coordinates.'

'What happens if we do?' Garvin asked.

'We're screwed, blued, and probably not tattooed,' Petr said. 'This boat should ... emphasis should ... have our final destination as one option, a return course to Centrum as a second, and a jump to the nearest inhabited worlds the program's got in it for a third.'

Again, his fingers ran across sensors. Njangu was watching intently. Petr looked up, grinned.

'Didn't think a crunchie'd know this stuff, eh? Gonna have to learn, the more you know, the longer you live. There's no such thing any longer as an infantryman who can't run at least basic exterior ballistics while he's zigging like hell and hollering for his momma.

'Plus learning how to operate anything and everything, from whatever the goblins're armed with to ... to the *Malvern*.'

'You could've piloted that?'

'Could' ve gotten it off the ground and into space,' Kipchak said, 'with a couple dot-and-carry types to punch the buttons I couldn't reach. As for setting up for a jump – that's what computers are for. Now, shuddup.

'We're getting our options.' He scanned the screens.

'Mmmmh,' he said after a time. 'First possibility, going back to Centrum, is a little chancy. Seven, maybe eight jumps, since this turd doesn't have near the range of a real ship, and the life support'll be a little iffy by then.

'Next possibility is the closest human-occupied system. Which just happens to be Larix. What a coincidence. I don't think we want to go there, do we?'

The other two shook their heads.

'So it's on to the original destination, D-Cumbre. Two, more likely three jumps. Say a ship-week. Gad, but we're dedicated Servants of the Confederation.

'I'll bet there'll be a real shitstorm when the three of us show up instead of that hogwallower *Malvern*.'

Jaansma and Yoshitaro looked at each other, didn't mention the obvious. When . . . or if.

'So lemme set things up for the jump, and we're off,' Petr said, sounding impossibly cheerful.

Again, N-space swirled. Garvin's and Njangu's eyes kept being trapped by the kaleidoscope patterns, but Kipchak was oblivious.

'Pay attention here,' he said. 'This is why I wasn't blowin' smoke up your butts when I said this'd be better with more'n one.

'Whoever designed these boats figured he'd have shocky people who didn't know which end of a starship goes squirt trying to run it. So they set things up to be real simple. Find your program, hit the start button, then just sit there eating your fingernails.

'The only instruments you've got to watch in hyper-space is this needle here . . . which you keep between these two black bars with this little slider, and this timer. Every two ship-hours you reset it. If you don't, it'll kick the ship back out into real space.

'That's to keep survivors from getting too damned lost, I guess. And nobody I know's ever found a way to short around that fail-safe.

'So we stand watches.'

'Nice to know we're needed,' Garvin said.

'You are, boy. You truly are. Not just here, but in the most important way. Anything you consume gets processed, and you'll breathe it, drink it, or get it for breakfast all over again.' Petr grinned evilly, waited for nausea on the other two's faces, was disappointed.

'The recycler doesn't run at anything near a hundred percent. When the cycler's only got a single-source feeder, one survivor, it starts getting . . . sloppy is maybe the most polite way to put it, pretty quick. The more it's got to play with, within reason of course, the better off we all are.'

'There's got to be other supplies,' Garvin said. 'Otherwise, if we eat no more than we crap, we'll be thinking about Yoshitaro over easy in a couple of days. Diminishing returns and things like that.'

'Right,' Petr said. 'Supplies should be over there. Basics, plus quite a few luxuries. They realized anybody using these piddlers'd appreciate a little spoiling while they're waiting to be rescued.'

Njangu went to the indicated cabinet, unclipped the fasteners, and opened it.

'*H'rang-dao!*' he muttered. 'Guess what, guys? Somebody did a little self-enrichment at our expense.'

Kipchak was across the compartment.

'Fine,' he said, voice hard. 'Real fine. Somebody,

maybe in the shipyard when the *Malvern* got refitted, maybe even somebody in the crew, decided to sort through the goodies. For off-watch snacktime or to sell.'

'What do we have left?' Garvin asked.

'We won't starve,' Petr said. 'But we're going to get very tired of soyaglop before we make it to Cumbre.'

Other cabinets had been looted as well, including the one labeled ENTERTAINMENT. Petr wasn t upset by this.

'Gives you a chance to learn something else,' he said. 'There's two ways to pass the time when you're off duty and trapped somewhere you can't get a load on and get your ashes hauled, which'll be most of your military career. Believe it or not, you *can* get too much sleep.

'One is lying, the other's learning. Lying is the most common – everybody sits around and tells his or her life story, the most interesting thing that ever happened, the least interesting thing, and so forth.'

'Like everybody was doing on the *Malvern*,' Garvin said.

'Not everybody,' Petr said. 'Mostly those were the newbies. They weren't thinking about what happens when the lies run out. What happens when you know everything there is about somebody else? Real quick, you start hating their guts.

'It's always better to go first to your own resources. Read a disk, if you've got one. Or, if you don't, find somebody that knows something, and make them teach it to you.

'It'll give you something to think about, plus you can get pissed off at them and they at you for something that's got nothing to do with anything important.'

'So what do we do now?' Garvin asked. 'Njangu's got another two ship-hours before I relieve him.'

'I noticed, back when you were dealing with that gambler, you seem to like words,' Kipchak said.

'I do.'

'That's a good liking to have. So sit down over there. And listen.'

Garvin obeyed.

'Enter CHORUS as Prologue,' Petr began.

'CHORUS: *"O for a muse of fire, that would ascend*
The brightest heaven of invention:
A kingdom for a stage, princes to act,
And monarchs to behold the swelling scene . . ."'

Garvin and Njangu exchanged utterly bewildered looks.

Ship-hours and shifts later, a slightly hoarse Petr finished, '*Which oft our stage hath shown; and for their sake, In your fair minds let this acceptance take.*'

He stood, bowed.

'And that,' he said, 'I'm damned proud of.'

'I guess,' Garvin said haltingly, 'you ought to be. That's called a play?'

'Yep.'

'How many more of them do you know?'

'Oh twelve, maybe thirteen.'

'All by this same guy?'

'Mostly. And some others. Molière. Robicheux. Van Maxdem. Anouilh.'

'You memorized all of them?'

'Keeps you busy in the dogwatches.'

'Everybody in the army does shit like that?' Yoshitaro wanted to know.

'Nope. Just some.' Petr went to the fresher, drank water.

'Now it's your turn to entertain me.'

*

Half a lifetime later, they came out into real space, in the midst of a planetary system.

Petr lifted the com mike from its slot and touched a sensor. Panel lights glowed. 'We're broadcasting on standard distress freqs,' he said, and keyed another sensor. 'D-Cumbre, D-Cumbre, this is a lifecraft from the Confederation Transport *Malvern*. Please respond to this frequency. D-Cumbre, this is a lifecraft from the *Malvern*. . .'

SIX

D-Cumbre

The tall, silver-haired man opened the door. He wore the emblems of a *caud*, and was the commander of Strike Force Swift Lance.

Petr came to his feet at rigid attention. Njangu and Garvin awkwardly followed suit. All three wore brand-new uniforms, Njangu and Kipchak the mottled green of the infantry, Garvin the black coveralls of Armor.

'Come inside,' *Caud* Williams said, voice cold.

The three followed him into the office of Governor General Wilth Haemer. The head of the Cumbre system's Planetary Government, direct representative of the Confederation, looked like anyone's grandfather. But now he wasn't offering sweets but scowling in righteous anger. The door closed with a loud click.

'These are the three men, Governor,' *Caud* Williams said.

Haemer walked behind his huge, highly polished wood desk, bare except for an expensive-looking old-fashioned writing pen and single com button, stared as if they were diseased cells.

'I see,' he said. 'All three rank recruits.'

'Two, sir,' Williams said. 'The man to the left is a reenlistee.'

'Hmph,' Haemer said. 'Couldn't make it on the outside, eh?'

The back of Kipchak's neck reddened, but he said nothing.

'I should congratulate the three of you,' Haemer said, 'for surviving an . . . extraordinary experience. But I'm unable to, since one or all of you fools had to blab your fantasy to the journohs the minute you got out of the rescue ship.'

'Wasn't—' Garvin started.

'Silence!' *Caud* Williams snapped.

'Go ahead,' Haemer said.

'It wasn't us, sir,' Jaansma said.

'Then who?'

'I don't know, sir.'

'Certainly no one in the team I dispatched to pick up your lifecraft would've leaked to the holos without permission,' Haemer said. '*That* is an absolute fact.'

Garvin finally had sense enough to clamp his lips together.

'Your hasty story . . . I won't call it a lie, for I assume you three believe this nonsense . . . might well have sparked problems with Larix and Kura, and especially with their protector, Alena Redruth,' Haemer said. 'It's lucky I was able to release a clarification immediately.

'There's no particular reason I should clarify matters for anyone in your position, but I shall, for I believe all my personnel should be of a common mind.

'We are on the uttermost fringes of the Confederation. Our link to the Confederation lies through Larix and is not far distant from the Kura system, for your information.

'The goodwill of its people, and their protector, is very important to the stability of Cumbre. Your wicked tale might destabilize what is an extraordinarily close relationship.

'I realize you can't know it, but Protector Redruth himself was gracious enough to visit Cumbre a short time ago. Isn't that about right, *Caud* Williams?'

'Yes, sir. Actually twenty-three E-months ago,' Williams said.

'It was quite a satisfactory tour,' Haemer continued. 'He visited our mines, our cities, even took time to inspect your Strike Force, correct?'

'Yes, sir,' Williams said.

'And now our friendship, a friendship of three great systems of Man, here on the frontiers, is threatened by three fast-mouths,' Haemer said. 'This situation shall not be permitted to worsen,' he went on. 'Let me tell you what actually happened. Some renegades seized two of the Protector's ships. Possibly these criminals were even deserters from his own forces and wore the Protector's uniforms as a cover for their vile crime, which is why you became confused.

'There was an error made, but I have corrected it. You three have already released corrective statements to the holos after I personally allowed you access to our intelligence files, and wish to apologize. You wish to say something, young man?'

Yoshitaro's eyes were wide. 'Nossir,' he said. 'Nothing, sir.'

'I didn't think so.

'*Caud* Williams,' Haemer went on, 'I do not know what to do with these three. If we were anywhere close to civilization, I'd order you to discharge them from the service at once. But I doubt if any of them have employable talents on D-Cumbre, and we hardly want them to become a drain on the civilian economy.

'However, I want them to be fully aware of my displeasure, and while they will be permitted to serve out their term of enlistment, I do not wish to hear of them or see their faces again. Needless to say, this means I do not wish them to be promoted or achieve any recognition until I decide otherwise. Is that clear?'

'Sir, I cannot permit—'

'*Caud*, that is an order!'

'Yes, sir.'

Njangu and Garvin followed Petr quite numbly, about two meters behind the *caud* as he strode down the marble steps of the governor general's headquarters. Williams' Cooke – an open gravsled used for everything from ambulances to Command & Control – had its drive compartment open, and the pilot was muttering in a low tone and pawing in his tool kit.

'What's the problem this time, Running Bear?'

'Just won't start, sir. But I think I can get it going.'

'Very well,' the *caud* said. 'You three, across the street and into that park.'

The recruits obeyed.

'On line, and at attention,' he ordered. 'You heard what the governor general would like to do to you. That won't happen . . . unless you happen to get in his line of fire before he forgets your name.

'As far as being on any blacklist of mine . . . no. I'll never discipline a soldier for making an honest mistake. Nor are you disqualified for future promotion or awards, if you deserve them. You reported what you saw or thought you saw, and refused to back off.

'I admire soldiers with sticktoitiveness. But don't take things too far. Learn to think about what you thought you saw, and maybe reevaluate it.

'Remember one thing. Strike Force Swift Lance is, as the governor general said, far from the heart of the Confederation. We desperately needed the equipment and men on that ship, because it's been far too long since we've been resupplied, and the unit is badly under-strength. Some people we must respect might have overreacted to the bad news about the highjacking.

'Is what I'm saying making sense?'

'Yessir,' Petr growled, and the other two bobbed their heads.

'Very well,' Williams said. 'We'll forget about the whole incident. Welcome to Strike Force Swift Lance. You two new recruits'll begin your basic instruction immediately, which unfortunately won't be as formal as it should've been.

'We'll have to put you, Jaansma, directly into a unit to be trained on the job. As for you, Yoshitaro, you'll do the same with whatever unit personnel assigns you to. You, Kipchak, you've already been requested by Senior *Tweg* Reb Gonzales of the Intelligence and Reconnaissance Company. He says he knows you from another post.'

'Yessir. *Tweg* Gonzales and I were on Deneb-Nekkar together. A good man, sir.'

'You'll report to him when we return to post.

'That's all, gentlemen, except let me reiterate my advice – keep a very low profile and don't make anyone, not your noncoms, not your officers, and certainly not me, have to consider your sins for a *very* long time.

'*Finf* Running Bear seems to have gotten the Cooke started, so let's load up and get back to camp.'

He marched away, toward the gravsled.

Garvin and Njangu looked at each other.

'He seems decent,' Jaansma said in a low voice.

'Yeah? He doesn't believe us any more than that other asshole did,' Yoshitaro said. 'He's just more polite about it.'

Kipchak nodded. 'You're learning, boy. But give him . . . maybe both of them . . . some grace. How'd you confront the small problem that there seems to be a shark between you and the surface and cruising around your lifeline?'

'Strong point,' Garvin said. 'You can never convince a mark the wheel's rigged even after you show him the weights.'

The Cooke slid quickly away from the PlanGov fortress, down a sweeping avenue through the city of Leggett toward the gulf Dharma Island curled around. In the middle of the huge bay, twenty kilometers distant and barely visible through the heat haze, was Chance Island, Strike Force Swift Lance's base.

Running Bear accelerated, lifting the Cooke to a thousand meters. Williams turned in his seat and raised his voice above the windrush, trying to make conversation.

'Did all three of you take your oathing on Centrum?'

The recruits exchanged glances.

'Nossir,' Kipchak said. 'I've never been sworn in this time. Guess they never got around to it.'

Njangu and Garvin also shook their heads.

Williams reacted in horror. 'You mean . . . you've served for how long . . .'

'Two and a half E-months for me,' Petr said. 'Six months for Yoshitaro and Jaansma, since they had to transit from their homeworlds to Centrum.'

'Six months, and you're not even . . . great gods, what's passing through the minds of men these days? Oathing . . . that's the most important part of . . . I cannot believe no one, absolutely no one . . .' Williams sputtered. His lips firmed into thin lines. 'My apologies to you gentlemen, in the name of the Confederation. This is intolerable. Utterly intolerable!'

'Uh-oh,' Njangu muttered.

*

'Never seen so many goddamned soldiers in my whole friggin' life,' Yoshitaro muttered. 'Wonder what they're all here for?'

'Zip the lip,' Petr said. 'This is a solemn occasion.'

The three wore dress uniform – dark, almost midnight blue trousers, waist-length belted tunic, service cap with yellow piping on the trouser legs, cap, and epaulettes. The trousers were bloused into black mid-thigh boots. Petr had three rows of decorations above his left breast, and two winged emblems on his right; the other two nothing. All wore wide black-leather belts, with an ernpty knife sheath on it.

They were in the center of Camp Mahan's enormous drill-field, almost three kilometers to a side. The field was packed with soldicrs in dress uniform – almost eight thousand men and women of Strike Force Swift Lance.

From the farside of the field marched *Caud* Williams. Behind him was a color guard – three flagbearers with the banners of the Confederation, Cumbre, and the Force; then Williams' command staff and the Force band at the rear, blasting for all its might. Williams' bootheels smashed to a halt about fifteen meters distant. The band played for another four measures, then silence swept the square.

Garvin smelled the flower-scented air in the soft wind from the sea, the newness of his uniform, and his own sweat.

'Men of Swift Lance,' Williams' voice boomed from his throat and eight thousand belt speakers. 'We have come to honor three who've chosen to join us.

'Garvin Jaansma, Petr Kipchak, Njangu Yoshitaro, five paces forward! Colors!'

Two flagbearers marched out, one with the Confederation's flag, the second with the Force's.

Without a command, the Force guidon-carrier lowered his banner until it was level with the ground.

'You men, put your hands on the flag!'

They obeyed.

'Repeat after me. I, *Caud* Jochim Williams, do swear by all that I hold sacred, whether God or gods or my own honor, I will obey the lawful commands given me by my superiors and swear to defend the Confederation, its life-forms and its way until death, or until I am released from this vow.'

As they finished the oath, the band crashed into the Confederation's 'Galactic Anthem.'

'I wonder if there's any pickpockets working the crowd and if we can get a cut on the action?' Njangu whispered.

'Shut up,' Garvin whispered fiercely. Yoshitaro glanced sideways and noted his friend's Adam's apple working convulsively and what he thought to be a tear running down one cheek.

Garvin noted Yoshitaro's surprise. 'It reminds me of the circus, and he's a great ringmaster,' he managed, sheepishly.

'Quiet!' Petr snarled.

The band finished, and minor cheers rolled across the parade ground. 'Flags . . . return!' someone shouted, and the two bearers about-faced and returned to the guard.

'*Mil* Rao!' Williams shouted. 'Arm these soldiers!'

Prakash Rao, the Force executive officer, came out of formation carrying three leather cases. He gave one case to each man, returned to his position.

'Be worthy of this honor,' Williams said. 'Train hard, serve well, be a credit to the Force.' He stepped back, saluted. The recruits returned the salute.

'Unit commanders . . . take charge of your men and dismiss the Force!'

Yoshitaro opened his case. There was a cap emblem and two collar insignia, each a lance with a shock wave spraying from the tip, and a knife. Surprisingly, instead of being a stylized parade-ground device, it was a lethal fighting blade about 18cm long, single edged with its curving top edge sharpened about 7cm back from the point. The handle was leather, and the butt cap and hilts were silver. It fit his empty belt sheath perfectly.

'Strange,' he said.

'What?' Petr asked, an edge in his voice.

'I'm not slanging anybody,' Yoshitaro said hastily. 'But we get these emblems, which are all flash and filigree, and then this knife, which is damned practical.'

'So?'

'Which is the real Force?'

Kipchak looked uncomprehending.

'Never mind,' Njangu said. 'Let's go learn how to sojer.'

SEVEN

C-Cumbre

Jord'n Brooks let the drill yammer against the rock, blinking sweat back from his eyes. Grit swirled in the dusty air, caked on his face, dusted his hair gray. The stope he lay in was barely a meter high, half that wide, room enough for himself, the endless-belt carrier for the ore, and his drill. The rock under him, wet, hot, shuddered as someone in another drift set off a charge.

Brooks was very much at home in the mine, had been for twenty years.

He pawed rock back onto the belt, pulled back the sleeve of his insul-suit, checked the time. He shut off and slung his drill, wriggled back from the stope until the tunnel widened enough for him to get to his feet, his back just brushing the rock above him.

He went down the rise to the substation, the overhead taller and reinforced with steel beams. The air was a little fresher there, a conditioner chugging away beside the bank of controls.

His shift boss stood beside the vertical shaft, and a lift was waiting.

'You're covered,' she said, and Brooks took off his breather, set the airpak and drill down, got in the lift, and it shot upward. The shaft ended half a mile above, and he went through an airlock and transferred to a slidecar that took him to the mine's main shaft. He crowded into a cargo lift with twenty other men and women, boisterous and dirty, coming off shift, and it took him to the surface.

Harsh floodlights made him blink as he came out of the top airlock. Somehow Brooks always expected day when he came out of the mine, in spite of what the clocks might say. He inhaled air that was only dusty, dry, and cold instead of hard, oily, compressed, shivered a little until the insul-suit adjusted.

The other miners started for the gate and security. Brooks ducked around an orecar and slipped through shadows past the half dome of the mine's entrance, then high piles of spoil. He used an automated oretrain for a ride once, then continued walking. Twice he stopped, waited until the predicted security patrols passed, then went on. The night was lit with flaring burnoffs from other shafts not many kilometers away.

Beyond a second mine entrance he followed lift rails past more spoil until he came to a half-underground semicircular concrete bunker. Signs were posted:

EXTREME DANGER! EXPLOSIVES! DO NOT APPROACH WITH-OUT PROPER AUTHORIZATION FROM MELLUSIN MINING! NO INCENDIARY APPARATUS PERMITTED! UNAUTHORIZED PER-SONNEL WILL HAVE THEIR CONTRACT TERMINATED AND WILL BE PROSECUTED TO THE FULLEST EXTENT OF THE LAW!

Brooks went to one of the bunker's entrances. He took a strangely shaped key with four differently shaped and fingered arms from a hidden pocket in the leg of his insul-suit, fit it carefully into a slot in the door. He didn't notice a small crescent mounted above the door, just in line with the lock, didn't hear it click.

Brooks turned the lock once right, half back to the left, then to the right once more. The door clicked open.

Brooks heard the whine of a lifter, slid into darkness, watched the unlit vehicle ground five meters away. Two figures got out, came toward him. Both had guns ready.

'The Task,' a woman's voice came.

'The Duty,' Brooks answered.

The woman put her pistol away, came closer. She was Jo Poynton, and had once been part of his Fold, the 'Raum congregation. She was slender, medium height, in her mid-twenties, small-breasted, with surprisingly full lips that looked like they wanted to smile if their owner would ever let them.

'Were there any problems getting onworld?'

'None,' Poynton said. 'How long before you're missed?'

'I'm covered through the end of the shift,' Brooks said.

'We aren't that clean,' the other man said. 'The security tech we bought can only keep his radar down for another hour.

Brooks recognized him by the livid scar down his cheek as Comstock Brien, who'd left the 'Raum almost five years ago, one of the first of The Movement to go into the hills, now regarded as its most dynamic war leader. He was not tall, above average for a 'Raum, once stocky, heavy-bodied, but the time in the jungle, the time running, had worn him down to gauntness.

'Is it open?'

Brooks slid the door open. Brien took a lantern from his belt turned it on, and they entered.

'A candy store,' Poynton said.

Brooks made a noise like laughter.

'Telex there, Blok over there, and the primary ignitors are in this room here.'

'Get the detonators first,' Brien said. 'With those we can make anything go up.'

Brooks and the woman carefully took padded boxes of various detonators, carried them to the gravlighter, came back for another load.

Poynton had just stepped out of the bunker when a light blazed, and a voice said:

'Move and die.'

Both stopped.

'Mellusin Security,' the voice said. 'Put the boxes down. Slow. There's two guns on you.'

They obeyed.

'Five steps forward,' the security woman said. 'Prone on the ground, arms and legs extended.'

Brooks knelt, went on his face. A second lightbeam came on, pinned the two against the muddy ground.

'You,' the woman said. 'You in the bunker. Come out. Slow. Guess you three didn't think we've got our own snitches out listening for when somebody asks about explosives. Or that we'd set some extra alarms on the demo supplies just to make sure.'

Brien came out, hands half-raised.

'All the way up.'

His hands moved . . . and he dived forward in a shoulder roll. The guard's blaster went off and the bolt crashed above Brien's head into the bunker. Flame flashed, and smoke boiled as an alarm seared the night.

The guard spun, aiming again at Brien as he came to his feet, and Brooks was on his hands and knees, bear-walking forward into the woman's legs, sending her sprawling. The other guard's light flickered toward Brooks, just as Poynton got her pistol out and shot him.

The woman was rolling onto her back, both hands on her blaster, trying to aim, but Brooks was on her, hands clawing at her face. The gun spun out of her hands, and he had her throat and squeezed, squeezed, and felt bone crack, her heels drum against the ground, and smelled shit as she died.

He was off the corpse and on his feet. Another alarm screamed from a distance, matching the bunker's fire warning.

'Let's go,' Poynton said.

'No,' Brooks said firmly. 'We've time for one more load. And we'll take the guards' sled with us.'

His voice was calm, emotionless. The other two stared in surprise, then obeyed. Brooks trotted back into the smoky bunker, ignored the growing flames, draped slings of explosive portapaks on his arms, staggered out, and dumped them into the back of the security lifter.

'*Now* let's go.'

'What about you?' Brien said. 'I can't see how you'll be able to get back to your shift with the hue and cry out.'

Brooks got into the pilot's seat of the sled, examined the controls. 'It seems the One has decided I'm now on the run, like you.' He shrugged slightly. 'What happens, happens. Let's lift!'

He started the sled, brought it clear of the ground. The others jumped into their lifter, started its engine.

The air shock-waved as something inside the bunker exploded.

The lifters came off the ground, swung, then went to full power, banked around a rusting conveyor way. Jord'n Brooks followed, and the two craft fled into the night.

The only thought in Brooks' mind was: *Wish I'd had time to say good-bye to my children.*

Three minutes later the bunker exploded, destroying a square kilometer of the mine's aboveground equipment and buildings, and killing forty-five 'Raum miners, a dozen supervisors, plus nearly fifty security and firemen just short of the bunker. It was a month before that division of Mellusin Mining was able to resume operations.

EIGHT

'Looking for a *dec* named Ben Dill?' Garvin inquired of the legs sticking out of the Grierson's drive compartment.

'Inside the tin can,' the muffled voice came. 'Tell him from me he's a dirty bastard.'

'Uhh,' Garvin responded, and went to the rear of the assault vehicle. As he did, an antenna swiveled, tracking him, then waggled back and forth like a hound who's just lost the scent.

The ramp was down into the troop compartment, and inside was a man wielding a broom with great vigor. He was possibly the largest humanoid Garvin had ever seen outside the circus.

'*Dec* Dill?'

'That's me,' the man said. 'Armed, dangerous, and attitudinal with your basic Mark 1 Bristle Boomer.' He put the broom down and came out of the AV. Dill was in his mid-twenties, already balding, and had an amiable grin on his face. Garvin decided he didn't want to be around when Dill lost the smile. He guessed he wasn't supposed to salute, but brought himself to attention.

'Recruit Garvin Jaansma. Reporting.'

'Oh yeh,' Dill said. 'You're gonna be my new gunner. Relax. I ain't an officer – I know both my parents. Welcome to Third Platoon, A Company, Second Infantry, and may the gods have mercy on whatever pieces you've promised them.' His voice easily changed to a bellow. 'Awright, everybody! Unass the can!'

The legs came out of the drive compartment, became a grease-covered stocky man about Garvin's age.

'Stanislaus Gorecki,' Dill introduced. 'He's the driver/wrench, mostly wrench.'

'So it's my fault this pig runs one time out of ten?'

'Got to be somebody's fault,' Dill said reasonably. 'Not mine, 'cause I outrank you, and sure can't be the assholes in the Confederation who decided to issue us Mod. 2 Griersons instead of something livable, now could it?'

'Don't complain,' Gorecki said. 'We all could be crunchies, couldn't we?'

'Strong point,' Dill said. Garvin was lost, and the vehicle commander took pity.

'Here's the drill,' he explained. 'Pigs though they be, there's eight Griersons in each company. Takes two assault teams – that's twenty muddy infantrymen – crunchies. One Grierson per platoon. The other four are Company headquarters, heavy weapons, maintenance/recovery, and signal vehicles.

'We're part of A Company, and this Grierson is Third Platoon's. But you don't see the rest of Third Platoon hanging about here, do you? And if you look down the hangar, you see no more'n five people, plus idiots like the maintenance sergeant and his pukes, lurkin' about, trying to appear busy. You know where the rest of the platoon is?

'Today they're out painting rocks in front of Regimental Headquarters. Definitely part of learning to be a combat soldier.'

'I got you,' Garvin said.

'Study hard with us,' Gorecki said, 'or you, too, could carry the mil-specialty of Shit Shoveler First Grade.'

Gorecki eyed Garvin. 'You're the guy we paraded for day before yesterday?'

'I am,' Garvin said hesitantly.

'I owe you one. I was supposed to orderly for *Mil* Fitzgerald's mess, but she went and et with the *caud* at headquarters, all 'cause of you.'

'Glad I could be of service.'

Garvin heard a clang from inside the Grierson, and a small woman with archaic glasses and straight shoulder-length hair that looked like it'd been styled with a butcher knife came out. She wore the three rank slashes of a *finf*.

'Uh . . . hi,' she managed, nodding rapidly.

'This is our countermeasures yoodle,' Dill said. 'Ho Kang. Garvin Jaansma. She's *a finf*, so I'm the only one with rank enough to call her a yoodle.'

'Uh . . . hi,' she said again, promptly dismissed Garvin, and turned to Dill.

'Ben, I'm still getting false echoes on the close-scope. I tried tracking him around the ACV and got six people. Dancing.'

'Ho,' Dill said patiently, 'if I put that in the logbook, they'll redline us, and do you have any idea how long it'll be before we get parts?' He nodded at Garvin. 'Our newbie here was on the ship that got 'jacked, which probably had all the goodies we've been whining for.'

'Oh.' Kang readmitted Garvin's existence. 'They got everything?'

'Ship and all.'

'Who was *they*?' she wanted to know.

'Uh – I'm supposed to say it was pirates.'

'But who was it for real?'

'I'm in enough trouble,' Jaansma said. 'I'll stick with pirates.'

'I wish pirates,' Ho said wistfully. 'A lot more colorful

than those stupid bandits who call themselves The Movement, or the Musth, who never do anything except posture. Dammit, I want . . . I need . . . a fight!'

'We'll feed him a couple of beers and find out the real story later,' Gorecki said. 'Meantime, how do we fix that close-range pickup? I really like knowing when somebody's creeping up on me with a grenade.'

Kang glanced around, making sure she wasn't overheard. 'I could do it myself,' she said, 'if it weren't illegal, probably figure out a patch and pick up some stuff next time I get into Leggett. But who pays?'

Dill dug into the pocket of his coveralls, took out bills. 'Here. If it's more, I'll come up with it.'

The money disappeared into Kang's pocket.

'See what some people'll do to make *tweg*?' Gorecki asked. 'Even spend their own coin to look good.'

'Look good hell,' Dill said. 'This rustbucket breaks one more time, and it'll be a hangar queen and we'll all be on permanent solvent-tub duty. I'm just looking out for your best interests.'

Garvin was lost yet again.

'See,' Dill explained, 'that's this strike force's problem. We look real good on the surface – hell, you could shave in the reflection on this piece of shit.' He slapped the side of the Grierson. 'But ask it . . . or anything else to run for longer'n about a klick . . . that's another thing.'

'The motor pool's got shit in the way of supplies,' Gorecki added, 'but gods help anybody who fixes something with a nonauthorized part. So around here if you break down, you stay broke down and the asshole first *tweg* finds other duties for you. Shoveling shit.'

'Which brings up another problem,' Dill said. 'How much training do you have?'

'None,' Garvin said honestly. 'I was told I'd be trained when I got to my unit.'

'Just swell,' Dill said. 'As long as we're on the list of what we ain't got, try a budget for training exercises, ammo for training, rockets for training, try everything but fuel.'

'We've got simulators,' Kang said.

'Kang thinks sitting in a nice warm place shooting at things that don't really shoot back is the way to learn how to be a hero,' Dill said. 'She's a few microns short of a circuit.'

'Better than nothing,' the woman said stubbornly.

'Not much,' Dill said. 'You see, Jaansma? It ain't nothin' like the livies. Welcome to Strike Force Limp Dick.'

Alt Jon Hedley was less seated than sprawled atop his desk. His office would've been quite large if it weren't for the map racks, the several viewers, computers, and the map table that devoured space.

'Welcome to Intelligence and Reconnaissance,' he said, holding out a hand. Njangu blinked at the informality, but tapped it.

'Since we have our own way of doing things, we figure we should have our own flipping way of training people. We just started a cycle with four eagerly baying locals two weeks gone. You'll be able to drop right in.'

He glanced at the bulking, slightly going-to-seed senior *tweg* standing behind Njangu. 'Reb, would you mind buzzing Monique and ask her to drop in if she's in the company area?'

'Right, boss.'

Njangu's eyebrows lifted. Hedley caught it.

'This is a good place for instant flipping orientation,' he said. 'We have a few rules. First is that we're all flipping volunteers. Mess up, and you're devolunteered back into one of the regiments to become part of the madding herd.

'Second is not to get a big flipping head. We're nothing more than crunchies who happen to work in small lots. What we do, we do faster, better, and dirtier'n anybody else. So don' t go bragging about how billyjo-bad you are and pushing civilians or the herd around when you're outside the company area. Starting a fight is another reason to get punted out. Especially if you don't win.

'I said we're dirty, but when we're not, we're the cleanest. We depil, we bathe, we keep the boots shined and the uniforms as clean as we can. Any idiot can be a pig. We're not idiots.

'Three is that we've got our own ways, which aren't anybody's business but ours. I saw you look a bit surprised when I called Senior *Tweg* Gonzales by his first name, and he called me boss. But if there'd been an outsider around, I would have used his full rank and last name, and he would've called me sir.

'You can call people whatever you want . . . or, more precisely, what they'll allow you to. Senior *Tweg* Gonzales, for instance, happens to have about seven campaigns and two major wars behind him, so if you called him Reb when he comes back, he'd probably hammer you into a thin paste suitable for wallpaper. Save that for when you're trained and on a team. Or better yet, after you've been shot at a time or two.

'As I said, our business is our business. Keep it that way, and you'll be a credit to I&R.

'Petr Kipchak . . . who I just punted up to *finf*, because nobody stays in the flipping ranks in I&R if they're good, unless they want to . . . recommended you, and Reb thinks he's a good man, which is why I asked personnel if you'd be interested in volunteering. Don't screw up and make Petr . . . and me . . . out to be a liar.'

'Nossir,' Yoshitaro said, relaxing in the warmth of Hedley's smile.

The door came open and Senior *Tweg* Gonzales came in, accompanied by one of the more beautiful women Njangu had ever seen. She had close-cropped blond hair and an athletic body. As for her face . . . Njangu remembered a song he'd always hated, with the stupid lyric of 'bee-kissed lips,' and wondered what the hell a bee was. He still didn't know, but thought it looked pretty good.

'You wanted me, boss?'

'I did,' Hedley said. 'This piece of meat is yours. Njangu Yoshitaro, this is *Dec* Monique Lir, our training NCO and First Troop Gamma Team Leader. You'll find out that most of us wear at least two hats.

'I'm unit CO, which is a *cent's* slot, and Second Troop Leader, Reb is Company First Sergeant, which is a first *tweg* position, and so forth. The TO&E says we should have four officers, we've got myself and *Aspirant* Vauxhall, who's XO and First Troop Leader. If you qualify for I&R, you'll find yourself doing a couple of jobs, too.

'That's about it. Monique, take this disgustingly soft former civilian from my sight and transform him into something acceptable.' Hedley's voice was just as friendly as it'd been a minute earlier.

''Kay, boss,' the woman said. 'You . . . out!'

Njangu saluted, Hedley unwound from the desk, returned the salute, and smiled gently.

'Try to have some flipping fun.'

Garvin woke up with a headache.

'That's that,' Dill said.

'What's what?'

'You've seen the holos, where newbies spend all their

time marching back and forth, getting hollered at by drill *twegs* and such?'

'Sure,' Jaansma said. 'Can I get up?'

'Do it.'

Garvin slid out of the contoured chair, rubbed his arm where Dill had given him the injection three hours earlier.

'Now, about all that square-bashing,' Dill said. 'Group . . . ten-hup!'

Garvin, without willing it, slammed to rigid erectness, his hands at his side, slightly curled, his feet together, and his head tucked firmly into his chin.

''Bout . . . hace!'

Garvin lifted his right foot, put his toe behind his left heel, and pivoted through 180 degrees.

'I could march you back and forth and up and down,' the *dec* said. 'Make you do squads right about, flanking movements, and all that swaddle.

'You'd do it like you'd spent ten years on a parade ground. No muss, no fuss, one hypno-conditioning and three hours in the chair, and you've got it, without even one lousy little bead of sweat or blister.'

Garvin felt his skin crawl. 'That conditioning could've trained me to do anything?'

'Yep,' Dill said. 'That's why the injection can only be given by an officer, and a responsible medical team must be present during the application.' He laughed. 'See how careful the army is about your rights?'

Dill's laugh cut off as he saw Garvin's expression.

'Sorry. Guess it isn't funny the first time. The real answer is no . . . this kind of conditioning, a one-shot program, only takes because you don't have any objection to it. If I'd wanted you to go murder your mother, say, it would take a whole bunch more time. A year, maybe. That's why conditioning takes so long.'

'What's that?'

'You must've come from a pretty decent world,' Dill said. 'A lot of Confederation planets use that as a last resort for crooks. Three times, and they put a little voice in your head telling you what you can and can't do. Nasty shit.'

'Where I was,' Garvin said, 'when I enlisted, they didn't do anything like that. Just shot you for any serious offense.'

'Humanitarians, every one,' Dill agreed. 'Now quit lazin' about and get your ass out on detail. We're gonna do some *real* soldiering and give the *caud's* lawn a haircut.'

'Recruit Yoshitaro,' Monique Lir shouted an inch from Njangu's ear, 'that log isn't heavy, is it?'

'NO, *DEC*.'

'It's your favorite toy, isn't it, Recruit Yoshitaro?'

'YES, *DEC*!'

'Thought so. Squad . . . on the count of three, switch shoulders . . . one, two, THREE!'

In unison the five trainees lifted the eight foot long chunk of wood from their left shoulder to the right.

'Sloppy, very sloppy,' Lir shouted. 'Prepare to ground log, on the count of three . . . one, two, THREE.'

The chunk of wood thudded to the ground.

'Squad, ten-hut! Three deep breaths, in unison—'

Yoshitaro sucked air, tried to blink sweat from his eyes. He'd never hurt so bad in his entire life, not from his father's beatings, not from anything from the police. Why he didn't tell Lir to shove it and go find a place in a rifle company was beyond him.

Possibly, he thought, *pure terror from what the drill instructor would do to me if I even thought of quitting.*

He might've considered Lir beautiful on meeting, but

now she was a slavering demon from the worst pits of a hell he hadn't believed in until recently. As for bee-kissed, he hoped the mythical bee was about the size of a Grierson, and would come back for a return bout soon.

'Are we happy, squad?' Lir bellowed.

'YES, *DEC.*'

Njangu wondered how the other four in the team had managed to survive two weeks of torment before he got there. D-Cumbre natives must be tougher than they looked. Three days into this degradation, he knew little more about them than their names and what they'd done before. By the time Lir allowed them to crawl into the tents they slept in, across the street from the barracks Njangu now thought more palatial than any luxury hotel he'd ever burgled, there wasn't much inclination for idle chitchat.

Hank Faull was a former 'Raum, one of the miner/cultists Petr had told him about, seventeen, eighteen hundred years ago on the *Malvern*, when he didn't hurt all the time everywhere. But so far Faull hadn't proselytized, hadn't said much outside duty requirements other than when he showed Yoshitaro how to pitch his shelter, and told him not to worry, that Lir would certainly kill them all in the next few days and they could relax while the last rites were being read. None of the body-wrenching workouts Lir put them through, from the calisthenics before the sun rose to the night cross-country runs seemed to bother him.

Erik Penwyth must've been heavy before Lir got her hands on him, for his skin was a little loose around his gut. Now he was as skinny as everyone else. He spoke in an affected drawl, and Njangu gathered he came from one of D-Cumbre's rich families. Njangu thought Penwyth must be the insane member of the family, for why else would he be eating mud here at Camp Mahan instead of lolling about with whatever and whoever richies on D-Cumbre lolled with.

Angie Rada was short, small-breasted, and instantly made Njangu think of black silk restraints, scented candles, and sex wilder than anything he could dream of. He actually wondered what Lir would do if a little tent-swapping happened, but realized he was being really foolish, since he was too tired to raise even a smile.

The last was Ton Milot. He was also small, but very solidly built, always laughing. Like Faull, he never seemed tired or sore, and had told Njangu that Lir was a foam-bubble. Nothing she could come up with was as much an ass-buster as fishing.

'Plus,' he said, 'she hasn't figured out a way to drown us.'

'Yet,' Penwyth added.

The five stood by their log about fifty meters from the company mess hall. The sun was straight overhead, and soldiers were filing into the building.

'Is everybody hungry?'

'YES, *DEC*.'

'No, you're not. Are you?'

'NO, *DEC*!'

'We don't want to eat, we want to run, don't we?'

'YES, *DEC*.' Njangu felt his stomach start gnawing on his lungs.

'That wasn't loud enough! Right . . . hace. Forward, harch! Double-time . . . HARCH! Straight down to the beach, people. Let's see if we can run all the way to the swamp before anybody falls out! Maybe then we'll have a nice, refreshing crawl for a few hundred meters.'

Garvin checked the torque setting once more, put a little extra muscle on the wrench, and the nut snapped cleanly in half.

'Son of a bitch,' he muttered, remembering what Dill had said about the fate of those who were redlined. Would this take the Aerial Combat Vehicle off READY status? He pushed gingerly on the Grierson's intake shield, and it wiggled visibly. No way around it . . . somebody'd notice the bare bolt sticking out of the Greierson's roof and they'd be for the solvent tubs, great barrels cut in half, filled with corrosive muck used to clean weapons and parts. Jaansma climbed off the ACV's roof and started out of the hangar toward the far-distant Supply.

Half an hour later, he trailed disconsolately back. No such animal, the clerk had said snippily. Back-ordered. Sounds like you're down, he'd said, malicious glee in his voice. Always need a good 'cruit to polish some of the mung off these drive rollers, and maybe the rest of your crew'll give you a hand. Tough titty.

Garvin suddenly stopped. Were all those bolts holding the hangar's door-slider in place really necessary? They certainly looked the right size. He got his wrench and buzzed one nut free. Perfect, he congratulated himself, tossing the nut in the air and catching it.

'What the hell're you doing?'

Garvin jumped a meter, spun, and saw First *Tweg* Malagash, red face sculpted into a scowl.

'Uh . . . nothing, top. Just took a break, and I' m going back to—'

'With what in your hand?'

'Uh – nothing. Just this nut.'

'Which you're doing what with?'

Garvin tried to look innocent.

'You ever hear the word mil-spec, young soldier?' Malagash grated. 'As in military specification? That nut you just pirated off the door isn't authorized on any Grierson I've ever ridden.'

'Nossir, but—'

'ARE YOU ARGUING WITH ME?'

'Nossir, First *Tweg*, sir.'

'Perhaps you'd like to finish your training with the motivational platoon?'

Garvin shuddered. Their duties were simple – dig a hole on the first day, fill it in on the second day, dig another hole on the third day, and so forth, their shovel-work interspersed with extreme physical training.

'Nossir, First *Tweg*, sir.'

Malagash glared at him for a moment, relented.

'Go get your vehicle commander, young soldier. We'll have a chat about what you did . . . and whether he's giving you proper leadership. Then report to the mess hall. Tell the mess sergeant his grease trap needs cleaning.'

'This is what, in the end, you're all about,' Lir said. Njangu examined the rounded, black-anodized box in his hand. It was about 18cm long, 8cm wide, and 13cm high, and was featureless except for two locking clips on top, a guarded trigger mechanism and a safety switch on the bottom, and a feed slot in front of the trigger guard. It was also surprisingly heavy – about a kilo and a half.

'Blaster Mark XXI Operating Mechanism,' Lir went on. 'This is the guts to almost everything you'll be carrying. Look.' She held up an identical box to the ones the recruits held. Behind her in the arms room were several weapons. One was short, about the length of Yoshitaro's arm from shoulder to wrist; another, nearly identical but a meter long with a heavier butt, longer barrel, and fitted with a more elaborate optical sight. A third, even larger, sat on bipod legs and a fourth was on a low tripod mount.

Lir picked up the stubby weapon, turned it over,

dropped the box into it, and snapped the locks closed. 'Now you've got your basic-issue carbine. Pull the guts back out' – and she did – 'put them in this, and you've got a sniping rifle. This one's a basic Squad Support Weapon, and this one on the tripod's a Medium Crew-Served Blaster. All of them take the same mechanism, and the ammo is fed in through the base. Sometimes it'll be in a magazine like this, or a belt, or even a drum, which is what we generally carry on patrol, since I&R's policy is to hit 'em hard, break contact and scoot.

'A magazine'll give you thirty chances to kill somebody, drum a hundred, and the belt holds two-fifty or five hundred. Here's what the ammunition looks like.' She picked up a rounded cylinder the diameter and length of her little finger.

'Neat, no muss, no fuss. All the energy goes out the barrel, burning up the case while it goes, so you don't have to worry about leaving a pile of empty ammo for the goblins to find.'

Goblins, Yoshitaro noted. Petr'd used the same word. Obviously a generic I&R term for bad guys.

'We're now going to spend the rest of the morning learning how to field-strip and clean these suckers. Then we get to run and lift weights all afternoon,' Lir went on.

'Tomorrow morning, we'll start dry-firing, which is about as much fun as screwing your hand. But we'll do that for about five days, then we go out to the range and see what we shall see.'

'Gunner!' Dill warned. 'Stand by! Target!'

An alarm clanged on Jaansma's control panel.

'Enemy scanning,' Kang's voice said. 'Reaching . . . I have their TA radar diverted. They're blind.'

'Take it on down,' Dill ordered. 'Half meter nap of the earth.'

'Doing it, Skipper,' Gorecki said.

'Gunner! Search to the front.'

Garvin obeyed clumsily, moving his helmet back and forth, searching the display inside the faceplate. All he saw at first was a rocky formation, with a cluster of huts to one side.

'Gunner!'

Garvin looked more closely, and one of the huts moved.

'Target acquired, *Dec* . . . I mean, Skipper,' he said hastily. 'Enemy track . . . no, there's two of them.'

'Fire when ready.'

'Launch one,' Jaansma said, squeezing the soft grip in his right hand. The Grierson lurched, and a wisp of smoke curled past Garvin's vision as the missile spat out of its tube. Jaansma squeezed the grip in his left and became the missile. He moved the grip in his left back, forth, and the large track grew closer, blast-cannon aiming, then nothing.

'Hit!' Dill said. 'No flames, but it's dead!'

'Launch two,' Garvin said, keeping back the urge to exult, and became the second missile. The track at the center of his vision spouted fire, and Garvin rolled, bucked, was upside down, and the missile slammed into the hut beside the tank.

'Miss . . . launch three,' he said, and another missile went out from the Grierson, through the shock wave of another cannon blast, and exploded against the track.

Garvin jerked back to main control in time to see the tank's center turret flip back, tearing armor like paper, and flames gout.

'Area clear,' Dill began. 'Lift—'

'Negative,' Jaansma shouted, seeing movement. 'They're still out—'

'Shuddup, Gunner,' Dill said. 'I have them. Enemy infantry in the open, range three hundred meters.'

'Get them quick,' Kang broke in. 'They've got missiles, and they're seeking us. I've got serious indicators.'

Jaansma hit the selector bar with his chin to choose the chaingun and crosshairs appeared across the landscape. He found the infantrymen, put his sights in their center.

He slid a crossbar on his right grip, pulled his index finger tight, and the chaingun outside the Grierson roared. A red blast swept the center of the formation, and Jaansma hosed it back and forth.

'Targets destroyed,' he reported, and the landscape faded. He took off the helmet.

'Not bad,' Dill grudged over the intercom. 'Now, let's try it aerial. Another scenario.'

Garvin wiped sweat, put the helmet back on.

He . . . and the Grierson . . . were in close orbit off some asteroid. Below him on the surface missile launchers opened fire at other Griersons trying to land, and heavy gunships – Zhukovs – slammed smart shells down.

'Target,' Dill said. 'Enemy starcraft taking off.'

Jaansma looked back and forth, didn't see anything, then saw the ship – he didn't know what kind it was – climbing from behind a bluff.

'Acquired, Skip—'

He heard a dull thud, glanced down, below his faceplate, saw a cylindrical grenade land on the deck beside his chair in the simulator. An instant later, it exploded, and white, strangling smoke boiled out, enveloped Jaansma and tears poured from his eyes. He choked, gasped, tried to breathe.

'Come on, Gunner,' Dill's amused voice came. 'Where's the friggin' starship? Come on, man. Like I warned you, *anybody* can do it when it's easy.'

Njangu Yoshitaro lay in perfect position in the dirt, looking across a brushy field with dirt splotches here and there. His legs were splayed, toes pointing, feet flat on the ground at a forty-five-degree angle to his body. He was on his elbows, blaster tucked securely into the pit of his right shoulder.

Lir dropped down beside him, on his right, very close. She held a small transmitter in her left hand.

'Ready?'

'Ready, *Dec*.'

'Load and lock one round.' She handed him one shell. He slid it into the feed slot, worked the blaster's operating rod.

'First time you've ever shot for real?'

'Yeh,' Njangu lied.

'Safety off.'

He clicked the lever.

'Look downrange. Stand by.'

He obeyed, both eyes open, looking through the small optical sight. Lir's thumb twitched on the transmitter.

Movement! A man's torso and head came up from nowhere. Njangu put the dot in the sight's center on it, touched the stud.

There was a whiplash crack, the blaster's butt tapped his shoulder gently, and flame gouted in the center of the target.

'Hit. Center.' Lir said, handing him another round. He loaded.

'Downrange. Stand by.'

Ten rounds later, ten targets had gone down.

'You sure you've never shot at anything before?'

'Would I lie?'

Lir suddenly grinned, tapped him on the shoulder.

'Not bad, troop. You may make it.'

She came lithely to her feet, and moved to where Rada lay.

Yoshitaro sniffed, smelt ionized air, something else. It

was gentle, flowering, a bit like violets, a bit like frangipani.

Njangu decided his drill instructor, while certainly not human, had good taste in perfume.

NINE

'It's easy to dream about what will happen when Cumbre is ours, and we've finally got a chance to change things so all practice the Way of the 'Raum,' Comstock Brien said to the seven men and women in the jungle clearing, 'all knowing the Truth, all obeying the Truth, all empowered by the Truth.

'But to sit and dream is ultimately against the Cause, for the Planetary Government has real spies, their soldiers have real bullets, and death is a serious rebuttal to rhetoric. First we fight, then we debate.' He allowed himself a smile, and six of the seven laughed obediently.

Brien noted Jord'n Brooks' immobile face.

'You don't agree?'

'Of course I agree,' Brooks said. 'But there's nothing funny about our Duty. And we must always be sure we're following the right track, or we run the risk of falling into the same traps as the *soh*, our elders who taught that time and understanding would bring the Way to everyone, and were ground under by the pigs on the Heights.'

'Of course, brother. But we must never forget the human values of love, laughter, kindness, even in the midst of our struggle.'

'Humanity,' Brooks said flatly, 'is for after we hold the Heights, and eliminate PlanGov.'

Brien's face grew grim, then calm.

'Very well, brother. We can debate this matter this evening. But now is the time for action and learning.' He unstrapped a canvas roll, took out seven small weapons.

'Perhaps you recognize these, if you have children. They aren't quite toys,' Brien continued, 'but a young hunter's learning device. They're fairly accurate for about twenty meters, which is the real distance most fighting is done in these hills. The gun is air-powered, hand-pumped, and shoots small balls of copper. They strike hard enough to kill a bird or *felmet* . . . or blind a man.

'We cannot afford firing ranges like the Confederation has, nor do we have sufficient ammunition for training. But these will do well to teach you how to shoot . . . and hit.'

He passed six out, plus a palmful of the copper shot. Brooks was the only one he didn't give a weapon to.

'The first exercise we shall attempt is tracking. One of us will be a fleeing fugitive, the rest will be a patrol trying to find him.

'When you find him, please try to remember not to aim at his face. We cannot afford to lose a gun, but we can afford less to lose a man. Brother Ybarre, you will command the patrol.

'Brother Brooks,' Brien said, an unpleasant smile on his face, 'I'm sure, since you breathe and eat the theory of revolution, you'll happily be willing to play the part of the properly revolutionary fugitive.'

Brooks stood.

'You have a count of twenty,' Brien went on. 'Then we shall come after—'

Jord'n Brooks sprinted into the brush. Brien looked after him in surprise, then shrugged, and began counting. At fifteen he broke off. 'There is no fairness in battle,' he said. 'Go after him.'

The six obeyed, some moving with some familiarity of the wild, others more slowly and clumsily. Brien listened to them move away noisily, shook his head, remembered he, too, had once been that unpromising.

He went to the edge of the clearing, looked down the sweep of jungle toward the distant ocean. To the east, he could barely see the outskirts of Leggett. *One day*, Brien thought, *one day*. He heard a slight noise, turned, about to reprimand whoever'd given up on the exercise, saw Brooks crouched. He held the last air gun aimed at the center of Brien's chest.

'Brother, this isn't—'

There was a pop, and a pellet thwacked into Brien's stomach. It hurt. Brien jumped.

'I said—'

'Be so good as to lie down as if you were dead,' Brooks said. 'Or I'll be forced to shoot you again.'

Brien stared, then obeyed.

'You were right,' Brooks said. 'There is no fairness in battle.'

He crouched behind a tree, waiting in ambush for the others to return.

TEN

'You had no trouble before this?' Wilth Haemer, Governor General, asked, his voice worried.

'None, sir,' the communications tech said. 'I was making the normal commo check with my opposite number on Capella Nine, and discovered the channel was down. The autolog said it had been down for seventy-three E-minutes, to be precise.'

'You attempted to reestablish communication with the Confederation?'

'Immediately, sir. I've been trying constantly for the last three hours, without any result.'

'Nothing at all?' Haemer said. 'No static or whatever you call it?'

'I've never heard of any problem with a subspace com, sir,' the technician said. 'Especially a constantly open channel like this one is . . . was.'

Haemer fumed. 'You're the senior technician? Or is there someone at the station with more experience?'

'I'm the ranking operator, sir,' the man said. 'Trained on Centrum, seven years' field experience, all ratings AA-Plus.'

'Don't get huffy,' Haemer said. 'I just wanted to make sure.'

The technician didn't reply. Haemer gnawed his upper lip. 'Very well. Stand by to record. Message in Q-code, personal, to Alena Redruth, Protector of Larix and Kura.

Message follows: I have been unable to contact Capella. Are your channels still intact?'

'There'll be a problem with your message,' the tech said. 'I tried to send a query to Larix/Kura myself, to their Com Division, about an hour ago, and got a negative response. Nothing at all, sir.'

'Try again. Redruth won't fail to answer me.'

'Yessir.'

Haemer turned to his aide. 'Contact all Council members and *Caud* Williams. I want them at PlanGov headquarters within an hour!'

'Very well, Governor,' the woman said.

Haemer started for the door, stopped. 'Technician you're aware of the gravity, correction, potential gravity of this situation, I assume?'

'Yes, sir.'

'Do not inform anyone, and that means anyone, of this incident.'

'My superior's already been notified.'

'I'll take care of him myself,' Haemer said.

'She's a her,' the tech said.

'Regardless, dammit! Don't tell anyone anything, and that's a direct order!'

'Yes—' The governor general was gone before the technician could add 'sir.'

He whistled soundlessly, touched a sensor, and a microphone dropped from the ceiling. 'Scramble IX-N-8.' A speaker blatted, then cleared. 'Ybar, Qual, 23. Balar, Balar, this is PlanGov Central, over.'

'PlanGov Central, this is Balar, over,' a voice answered from C-Cumbre's single moon.

'Keren?'

'Me,' the voice said.

'The fewmets're in the centrifuge,' the technician said, 'and this time it's a *real* jewel.'

ELEVEN

Njangu was company runner. The duty wasn't much — sit in the company outer office, field the com, get whatever the Charge of Quarters, one or another of the company noncoms, wanted. It gave the recruits a chance to clean their gear and relax a bit.

This night was different. The CQ, *Dec* Alyce Quant, told Yoshitaro *Alt* Hedley was still in his office, and had been making calls on the secure com for the last three hours. He'd had a plate brought in from the mess hall instead of going to dinner. Something was up, and Njangu decided this perhaps wasn't the best time to be shining boots, and stayed in the background.

Aspirant Vauxhall and Senior *Tweg* Gonzales went into Hedley's office, followed by three officers wearing regimental staff tabs. All of them looked worried. Njangu wondered what was going wrong. He hadn't seen this many officers since his swearing-in.

Hedley opened the door. '*Dec* Quant, find *Finf* Kipchak and have him report to me.' Njangu noted the use of titles. This was serious .

'Yessir.'

The door closed. 'Recruit, you heard the man,' Quant said. 'Kipchak's in' — she glanced at the company TO&E board — 'Gamma Team, First Troop. Hipe!'

Njangu found Petr in Gamma Team's squad bay. He had a combat vest hung on pegs and was examining it carefully. He unclipped a holster, moved it from high under the right shoulder to a canted position on the right side, frowned, shook his head, and put it back where it'd been.

'The old man wants you,' Yoshitaro said.

'Uh-oh. What about?'

'Dunno. He just said get you.'

'Uh-oh twice,' Petr said, found his cap, checked his uniform, and went out the door. Njangu hurried to keep up. 'How've you been?' Kipchak asked. 'Haven't seen you since the giant group grope on the parade ground.'

'Keeping busy,' Yoshitaro said.

'I've heard Lir's good at that. You staying above water?'

'I dunno,' Njangu said. 'Don't think so. I'd settle for drowning a little.'

'Who wouldn't?' They dropped down the lift to the first level, hurried into the company office.

'Go on in,' Quant said, and Kipchak obeyed.

'I'm going for caff,' Quant said. 'They'll1 be wanting something to drink, the way officers jawjacknjive.'

She left. Njangu considered, went to the first *tweg's* desk, and turned on the intercom into the company commander's office.

'. . . nossir,' Kipchak's voice came. 'I hadn't heard. We were out on the range all day.'

'You're the only one who's been in-Confederation in the last year we know of, let alone on Centrum,' a voice came. '*Tweg* Gonzales thought you might be able to give us some skinny.'

'I can't really say, sir,' Petr said reluctantly. 'I'm not an analyst. And it'd probably be best for me to keep my tongue.'

'Why?' That was Hedley.

'Because . . . because what I think probably isn't going to sit well.'

'Try us,' another voice came.

'Go ahead, Petr,' Hedley said. 'My compatriots are more interested in facts than what fits.'

''Kay, sir,' Kipchak said, and said, coldly, 'I think the Confederation's falling apart. Maybe that's what's happened now.

'Sir, I spent a year on civ-street after I got out the last time, and things were really screwed. I know sorta-careerists like me're supposed to think the world's going to hell in a helmet, but this time it was different.

'I never got my proper mustering-out bonus, kept going back for it, and the paperwork was there, there and never here. Every time I went near GovRow, there were more people like me in lines, people needing things, and nobody helping them, or some lardass bureacrap just saying no.

'I started noticing things that were wrong, things that I remembered from before, and nobody seemed to care about, at least nobody in authority. The Met didn't run on schedule . . . sometimes didn't run at all. The lift-ways'd be busted, or cracked, and people just shrugged. Crime was way up, but weird crime. People killing each other just to be doing it, not robbing, not getting anything of advantage I could see. Pols got indicted it seemed like every day, and people shrugged and said that figured. Maybe I was just sensitive, but it felt like the rich were really rich this time, and the poor were jack-busted. You never saw the rich much — they stuck to their own districts, to their own enclaves. They came outside, they came with bodyguards or maybe got a brick through the windscreen. Everybody thought that was pretty funny.

'There were riots,' he went on. 'Like there's been for the last dozen years off and on, like *Tweg* Gonzales and I had helped put down, back when we served together.

'But these were different, at least on Centrum. They weren't just the slummies and poor folk burning for the sake of burning, or because the food shipment hadn't come in. Now it seemed like everybody had some kind of grievance they couldn't get taken care of.

'For a while the holos talked about the same things happening on other worlds, but then that kind of reporting stopped like the government'd pulled the plug on honesty. There were a lot of rumors, rumors about systems dropping out of contact, about some sectors talking about going independent and quitting the Confederation. I heard a couple of stories about shootings on the floor of the Confederation Parliament, but I didn't believe them. Maybe I should've.

'I don't know, sir. Maybe it's all in my head. I read a lot, and what I saw reminded me of what I've read about other empires when they started tottering. Rome, England, Second Mars, Capella. I'm not real surprised at this loss of contact.

'Anyway, sir. You asked me, and that's what I think.'

'Thank you, Petr,' Hedley said. 'You can carry on. Thank you.'

'Yessir. Thank you, sir.'

Njangu had barely time to shut the intercom off before Kipchak came out. He was a little pale. 'Damn, damn,' he muttered. 'I *don't* like talking to officers. 'Specially when there's more'n two of them.' He hurried out, and Yoshitaro went back to the intercom.

'. . . hardly inconceivable,' a voice said.

'But to collapse after all this time? I mean, how long has the Confederation been around?'

'A thousand years, more.'

'But when things fall apart,' Hedley said, 'they can fall apart really fast.'

'Especially,' Gonzales said, 'if the whole thing's been a façade for years, and everybody's been running around propping things up and slapping fresh paint on every crack. The whole thing can be dead, and never show any signs until . . .' his voice trailed off.

'The real question,' another voice said, 'is what about us? If there's some problem with the Confederation, if there's a break in the chain of supply, communication, whatever, where does that leave us?'

'Define *us*,' Hedley said. 'The Force? The Cumbre system? Mankind?'

'Screw mankind,' the other voice said. 'Start with the Force.'

'Well,' another officer said, 'we're unquestionably the big bang in Cumbre. I can't see the 'Raum in the hills getting any worse, can you?'

'I sure can,' Hedley said. 'The minute they hear PlanGov doesn't have the Confederation behind it, doesn't that make it a lot easier to listen to their dissidents and say screw the Rentiers and PlanGov, too. If you were a poor goddamned 'Raum miner, who'd you be taking seriously?'

'I don't think we need to discuss *that*, since it's obvious,' someone said. 'And does the loss of the *Malvern* fit somewhere into this?'

'*Pirates*,' someone said harshly. 'Does *Caud* Williams really believe that shit?'

'He's got to,' Hedley said. 'Otherwise, he'll have to start wondering what the hell Redruth is getting up to.'

'I don't like the way this conversation is going,' an officer said. 'We're getting a little close to dissension, so

I think we'd better end it. But I can't stop myself from adding this — could Redruth have known about the Confederation's troubles — I'm assuming your man Kipchak isn't an empty doomcrier — and started taking care of himself ?'

'That's another question we'd better not answer, and we don't have to, as far as I'm concerned,' Hedley said. 'And yes, let's change the subject. Angara, you're married to a local. When it sinks in there's no more flipping Big Momma, are people going to go apeshit? Like Petr said they're evidently doing on Centrum?'

'Don't think my love life makes me any kind of an expert,' another voice said dryly. 'But as a wild-ass guess, I'd think not. Cumbre's always been on the farside of nowhere, so there never was that much contact with the Confederation. The Rentiers have their own little empire carved out, so they could give a rat's nostril about the Homeworlds. The 'Raum carry their own Nirvana with them.

'Maybe there'll be trouble down the pike, when things we can't produce here start running dry. But even those are mostly luxuries, and nobody's going to tear down the state because they can't get Vegan champagne.'

'What about the Musth?' Hedley asked. 'What happens when they find out we humans ain't got no flipping Big Stick to call on if things get rowdy?'

Njangu heard footsteps, hastily turned the intercom off, and helped *Dec* Quant with the tray laden with drinks and snacks. When he'd finished, he asked if he could go outside for some air.

He stared up, at two of the three moons, one hanging in the sky, the other racing across the stars, then at the stars beyond, here on the fringes of empire, the coldly glittering stars.

What *would* happen if the Confederation was gone,

had torn itself apart? If he was stranded in nowhere for the rest of his life?

Njangu Yoshitaro felt real fear for the first time since childhood, fear of something he could not see, could not attack, could not run from.

TWELVE

Jord'n Brooks listened to the roar of the crowd inside the giant arena. *Good. The pigs are at the trough, watching their brothers hammer at each other.*

He nodded to the other two, and they got out of the lifter they'd stolen the day before and walked toward the auditorium's entrance. All three wore knee-length raincoats against the drizzle whipping in from the bay.

The two private guards at the entrance noticed them, stopped their chat.

'Sorry, boys,' one said. 'We're halfway through the match, and they've closed the gate.'

'Boys my ass,' the other said. 'They're friggin' 'Raum and—'

Brooks flipped his raincoat open, brought the blaster up, and shot the guard first in the gut, then in the head as he folded. The other guard had an instant to see death, then went down in the *spat* of another blaster.

None of the crowd inside the arena's rotunda noticed the shots.

The three 'Raum dragged the bodies to the side, behind some ferns, pulled the main door open, went unhurriedly inside, past the crowded wine stand, up stairs to a door labeled EMPLOYEES ONLY.

A 'Raum shot the lock open; Brooks kicked the door

open, and the three burst in, flattening against the wall on either side of the opening.

There were four people inside the office, two men, two women, and piles of credits being loaded into a counting machine, whispering out the other side neatly baled and marked.

A woman looked up, saw the guns, opened her mouth to scream.

'Don't!' Brooks said flatly, and her mouth banged shut.

'The credits,' he said. 'In those sacks. Now.'

A man looked worriedly at the men.

'We'll do it,' he said hastily. 'Just don't get upset. No money's worth dying for. Just let us go.'

Brooks nodded, and the four hastily dumped bills into the sacks. The other two 'Raum picked up the bags when they were full, shouldered them.

'There,' the man said. 'We promise we won't call anyone 'til you're well gone.'

'Yes,' a woman said. 'Just let us live. We never did anything to anybody, and we won't remember any faces.'

Brooks nodded the two 'Raum out the door, backed toward it as they went out.

'Thanks,' the other woman said. 'Thanks for not killing us.'

Brooks, face blank, lifted his blaster, touched the firing stud.

'Your Brooks is quite the hot wire,' Comstock Brien observed. 'Four appropriations this cycle, without any casualties. The last one netted close to a quarter million.'

'We should have had him go active years ago,' Jo Poynton agreed. 'For the first time, I don' t have to worry about finding credits for my agents, or for other tasks we have. But hasn't he about run his string in Leggett?

Shouldn't we be thinking about getting him out? Isn't it possible our brother Brooks has even greater talents than robbery?'

'Perhaps,' Brien said.

'We are short-handed in the Planning Group after T'arg and Miram's deaths,' she said.

'I know.'

Poynton looked intently at Brien.

'You don't like him.'

'No,' Brien agreed. 'I don't.'

'Why not?'

'He . . . he burns a little too brightly for my tastes.'

'Do any of us have the luxury of tastes?' Poynton asked.

Brien gnawed at a lower lip

'No,' he said reluctantly. 'No, we don't. And maybe we need a brighter fire, and maybe we can end this in our lifetimes.

'Maybe Brooks is someone we need.

'Bring him out of Leggett,' Brien said. 'We'll see what happens when he's thrown into deeper water.'

THIRTEEN

'Take it, Mister Jaansma.'

'Thank you, I shall, Mister Dill.' Garvin's smile got a little fixed as he slid into the Aerial Combat Vehicle commander's seat. 'Tell me when you're strapped in, Mister Dill.'

'I shall, Mister Jaansma.'

The intercom crackled. 'Driver to ECM . . . did those two get a mind-whop ray or something?'

'This is ECM. Definitely whopped.'

'Silence in the vehicle,' Garvin said, and there was. He took a deep breath. 'Driver, twenty-five percent power.'

'Twenty-five percent, Vehicle Commander.'

'Take it off, Mister Gorecki.'

The Grierson came gently off the deck and drifted out of the hangar, a delicate dinosaur in ballet slippers. Garvin felt panic as his mind said, *This is for real, this isn't the sim anymore*, and he buried the thought.

He pushed the select bar with his chin. 'Control, this is Two-Alpha-Three, clearing for lift.'

'This is Control,' a voice said. 'Reported traffic . . . two Zhukovs at east end of pad, three Cookes doing touch-and-go's on the grassy field . . . clear to lift at commander's discretion.'

'Two-Alpha-Three, lifting to one thousand, proceeding

west toward Tiger Maneuver area. Be advised vehicle commander is trainee.'

'Roger that, Two-Alpha-Three. We'll stand by with the whisk broom. Clear.'

'Take it up,' Garvin ordered. 'Fifty percent power.'

'Lifting, VC,' Gorecki said, and the ground on-screen grew distant.

Jaansma touched a sensor, and a map appeared on another screen. 'Do you need directions?'

'Negative,' Gorecki said. 'I could do it in my sleep.'

'Negative on faking it,' Dill ordered. 'Jaansma's still learning. Fly by his instructions.'

''Kay, VC . . . I mean, Gunner.'

'Don't skate on me, Garvin,' Dill ordered.

'Sorry.' Jaansma studied the map. 'Hold altitude, bring speed to ninety. Set course two-three-two degrees.'

'Altitude one thousand, speed accelerating to niner-zero. Now over water.'

The Grierson's course led south-southwest, across the gulf toward the finger of land enclosing it, and the restricted training area named Tiger.

'Set it on auto,' Dill ordered. 'Here's what I want you to do when you get to Tiger. Bring this pig down to about two-hundred meters . . . I'll have you on the deck next time, but I'll give you some slop now . . . bring it across the beach, jump over the foothills, and straight in across the target zone. Got it?'

'I think so.'

'Not think so, dammit,' Dill said. 'You have it or you don't.'

'I have it, Skipper.'

''Kay.' Dill switched channels. 'Tiger Maneuver Control, Tiger Maneuver Control, this is Grierson Two-Alpha-Three, inbound your area.'

'Two-Alpha-Three,' came the response. 'We have you onscreen. What's your flavor today?'

'Set program, uh, Seven-Three-White.'

'Seven-Three-White, roger.'

'We're making a low-level assault on a strong enemy-held base,' Dill said, switching back to the intercom, 'part of a regiment-sized assault force, backed with, uh, five Zhukovs I think I remember. Enemy has strong air-to-air capability. ECM, full standby.'

Kang turned the air-conditioning up in her tiny cubicle. 'ECM ready, Skipper.'

'Gunner ready,' Dill said from Garvin's normal station. 'Take it, boss.'

Again, Jaansma had a moment of fear, then a swell of confidence.

'Driver . . . accelerate to three-five-zero. Stand by for contact!'

Just ahead was the 'enemy' coast.

Njangu Yoshitaro decided he'd had enough. Enough of every muscle screaming as it tore, enough of his lungs trying to suck wind and not having the strength, enough of Lir's never-satisfied howls, enough of I&R, and especially enough of the frigging cliff he was only halfway up.

'I quit,' he muttered.

'No talking up there,' Lir shouted from below.

'I said I quit,' Njangu said more loudly.

'One more word, whoever's gossiping, and he or she's for the grease trap,' Lir shouted.

I can't even quit *this horseshit excuse for a life*, Yoshitaro thought, feeling very sorry for himself.

'Hey,' Angie Rada whispered. Yoshitaro crammed the side of his hand into the spider-crack, hoped his toehold was better than it felt, chanced looking across.

'Looka me,' she whispered. Angie sat on a ledge that looked to Njangu like a parade ground, almost 10cm wide. 'Don't I look cute.' She put one hand behind her head, jutted her breasts.

'Screw you,' he managed.

'You can if you ask nice,' she said. 'But love stories later. Guess what I'm on?'

'I can see.'

'No you can't,' she said smugly. 'This ledge widens beyond me. It's a frigging turnpike, and goes straight around the shoulder of this cliff to the road. C'mon up. This is the *real* way to do free-climbing.'

'What's that going to give me?'

'All Liverlips Lir said was get to the top, right?' Rada said. 'Not how, right? I&R encourages improvisation, right?'

Njangu wheezed agreement and found the strength to scrabble for a foothold to the side, and strength to lever himself up, up again, then across to Angie's ledge.

'Follow me, like the ossifers say,' she said, and Yoshitaro obeyed, sidling along the ledge, not looking a hundred meters down to jutting crags, until it indeed became a path, winding upward.

'Aren't you glad I think you're sexy?' she said.

Njangu managed a nod, while panting.

'Not like Faull, old strong-and-silent low-class 'Raum,' she said. 'I would've let him rot hanging there.' She gave him a sly look. 'Or made sure Lir heard him quit.'

'Doesn't matter,' Njangu said. 'Easy way, hard way, I'm still out of this shit.'

'Aw, c'mon,' Angie said. 'We've only got, what, another two lifetimes, then they'll put us into a fighting team. Doncha wanna be a *real* soldier boy?'

'Whoopie.' Njangu bent double, sucked air. 'I'm history,

I'm gonna be a nice happy grass-trimmer and garbage-can-emptier 'til my enlistment's up.'

'And then what?'

'I'll find a job somewhere.'

'Maybe working for my da,' she suggested.

'What's he do? Probably, with my luck, guide mountain climbers.'

'Nope,' the woman said. 'He's got six department stores, so you'd best be nice to me.'

'If he's so rich, what're you doing in the service?'

'I thought it'd be a hoot,' she said, defiance coming into her voice, then she looked away. 'And me and Da weren't . . . getting along.'

'Foolish girl,' Njangu said.

'Shut up,' Rada hissed. 'We've got to get up to the crest and look proper exhausted for Monkeytits Monique.'

'No you don't,' a voice came. 'You can stay just like you are.'

The two trainees froze, turned slowly. Just ahead of them on the path stood *Dec* Monique Lir.

'How' d you—' Angie managed.

'Beat you? Because I'm strong, clean-living and your friggin god,' Lir growled. 'Now, double-time right on up to the top.'

Before they reached the crest all the aches came back in waves to Njangu. The other three recruits were waiting, grateful for any respite from Lir's sadism.

'You were correct, Recruit Rada,' said Lir, who didn't appear to even be slightly out of breath. 'I *didn't* say how you were to get to the top of this, and I&R does encourage creative thought. I'm actually proud of you two.'

'Uh-oh,' Yoshitaro said under his breath.

'So proud, I'm going to let you be an example to the rest of us. I want you to go back down the cliff, while the rest of us stroll leisurely to the bottom and take a long break. Go back down – straight back down. Is it clear?'

'Yes, *Dec*,' the two chorused.

'Bad harmony,' Lir said. 'Drop down and do me some press-ups. Maybe twenty-five or so.'

She waited until they finished.

'Now, let's see some nice technique in descending,' she ordered. 'No slips, deaths, or even screams. You first, Rada.'

Angie gave Lir a hate-filled look, slid cautiously backward over the edge. Lir peered over.

'*Do* try not to fall,' she advised. 'Now you, Yoshitaro.'

Njangu obeyed.

'Oh, by the way,' the *dec* asked. 'Did I understand you have something you want to tell me?'

Njangu was about to bellow his resignation, and then suddenly everything was funny. He'd broken through some kind of inner barrier, and from now on, it might not be easy, but he'd do it. Hell, he felt good. He could duckwalk down the cliff if Lir wanted him to. Yoshitaro laughed.

Lir looked at him closely.

'That's all?'

Njangu nodded.

'Then get your ass down this cliff. It's a long run home, and I want to be back before retreat.'

The Grierson grounded at the same instant as the other Aerial Combat Vehicle and the two Zhukovs to make the points of a perfect square.

A moment later a courier boat settled in the middle of the formation. Its nose was the dark blue/white of the Confederation, with a ring of stars behind it. Below the pilot's cabin window on either side was the green/white/brown flag of Cumbre.

The Combat Vehicle's ramps dropped, and their crews formed up in front of their craft. All wore dress uniforms.

The lock of the courier ship opened, a gangway slid down, and Governor General Wilth Haemer strode out, flanked by *Caud* Williams and a polish of aides.

'Couldn't you have left a big booger on the pointy end, dammit?' Garvin whispered out of the side of his mouth. 'We didn't have to look *this* sharp.'

'Quiet, Gunner,' Dill said. 'You don't have anything to worry about.'

'Easy for you to say,' Jaansma said. 'You weren't the one who got told by His Holiness if he saw me ever ever again I was for the high jump.'

'Don't worry,' Kang said. 'He isn't interested in reviewing us. Too windy, too cold.'

It was that on Dharma's high plateau, wet mist blowing past the ghostly trees. Haemer and the others walked quickly, trying not to look like they were hurrying, to the formation of Musth waiting outside their headquarters, a series of high-ceilinged, polygonal buildings seemingly made of clear glass broken with onyx paneling.

The Musth were in a formation humans found strange. A dozen, probably underlings, formed a wide, shallow vee, and two others stood in the mouth of the vee, one behind the other. One Garvin guessed was the Musth's commander in the Cumbre system, Aesc.

Jaansma shut the governor general out of his mind and stared at the Musth. He'd only seen the aliens in holos, and found them mildly awesome. They were big, almost three meters, with long, sinuous necks. They were fur-covered, their only clothing a wide belt with crisscrossed straps to a neck-ring and a pouch in front like an oversize Scottish sporran. On either side were sheathed weapons. Garvin craned for a look, but all he could determine was that one was an incredibly long-barreled pistol-looking object, the other was an unprepossessing box with a strap on it.

Their fur was color-banded, coarse, light to reddish brown, going to black on their paws and tail; with a solid patch from throat to stomach that was anything from yellowish orange to rich orange.

Their lower legs were big, almost like a kangaroo's, but intended for upright walking; their front arms were smaller, ending in double-thumbed paws with retracted claws that would work well in a knife fight. They had short tails for balance.

The Musth ceremonials evidently didn't require rigidity like Man's, Garvin noted, seeing their heads dart about, peering here and there.

Dill's Grierson had been chosen with three other combat vehicles as honor guard for the governor general's monthly visit to the Musth base on Dharma's Highlands.

Haemer bowed to the forward Musth, half whistled, half hissed something in the alien's language.

'And I greet you, Governor General,' the alien replied. 'It isss well to face you once more.'

He turned.

'I would like to ssshare with you the knowing of my sssoldier-leader, Wlencing.'

The Musth behind Aesc bobbed his head. 'It isss interessssting to sssee your face,' he said.

'Ssshall we go into the building?' Aesc said. 'I sssee you mussst be chill.'

'If you have no objectionsss,' Wlencing said, 'perhapsss I might view your sssoldiery, for I have encountered Man but ssseldom, and am poor at diplomacccy.'

'Of course not,' *Caud* Williams said. 'I'll be happy to come with you.'

'There isss no need,' Wlencing said. 'You have busssi-
ness with Aesssc, I am sssure, and I am content to find
my own obssservations.'

Williams frowned, then nodded reluctantly. 'Very
well. I'm sure you'll be impressed.'

'I'm sssure,' Wlencing said, and came toward Dill's
Grierson.

'Do I salute him?' Dill whispered in panic.

'You better,' Gorecki said. 'We ain't fightin' them yet.'

Ben smashed his hand against his forehead, held it
there. Wlencing's neck extended sharply another 30cm
in surprise, darted back and forth like a snake's. 'That isss
a sssign of recognition?' he asked.

'No, sir,' Dill said. 'It's honor to a superior.'

'I sssee,' and Wlencing brought his forearm up, lowering his head, and stood motionless. 'I asssume it is to
be anssswered in same, like thisss.'

Both creatures dropped their arms.

'You have large beingsss in thisss crew,' Wlencing said.

Dill wasn't sure what to reply, so just said, 'Yes, sir.
Pure chance, sir.'

'Which one isss the gunner?'

'I am,' Jaansma said.

Wlencing walked to Garvin. 'Are you good?'

'I'm still learning,' Garvin said.

'But they choossse you, and your crew, to guard your
highessst? That is unusssual,' Wlencing said. 'Let me
asssk you, Gunner. When you practissse, do you ussse
machines?'

'Yes, sir,' Garvin said, suddenly at ease. 'We call them
simulators.'

'Sssimulators,' Wlencing said, tasting the unfamiliar
word. 'Who are your enemiesss on these sssimulators?'

'Other machines,' Jaansma said. 'Spacecraft. Armored
ground vehicles. Soldiers.'

'Are the sssoldiers Musssth?'

'Nossir,' Garvin said. 'Men. They wear different uniforms, depending on the problem.'

'I wasss told different,' Wlencing said.

Garvin started to argue, kept his mouth shut. The Musth eyed him. 'But of courssse you would be told to lie and not embarrasss yoursssselves,' he said, and went to Kang.

'Your dutiesss?'

'Electronic countermeasures, sir.'

Wlencing hissed, 'Are you good?'

'I am the *best*,' Kang said firmly.

The Musth snorted, a noise Garvin thought might be approval, might be amusement. 'That isss a warrior ssspeech,' he said. 'Each of usss is the besssst, are we not?'

'But I really am,' Kang said firmly.

'It isss a pity there isss no way of tesssting your boassst,' Wlencing said. 'We ssshould play gamesss of war between our two racesss. It would be good for usss, good for you.' He turned away, then his head swiveled. 'It will have to passssss another time,' he said. 'When the war comesss.'

Wlencing saluted again, walked toward one of the Zhukovs.

Garvin glanced sideways at Dill, found the big man looking at him.

'I hope he's still learning Common Speech,' Jaansma said, 'and didn't mean what he said.'

'Want to bet you're wrong?'

'Not a chance.'

'Can I ask something,' Njangu said, 'without pissing you off too bad?'

'You can try,' Hank Faull said amiably. The two sat on Faull's bedside locker, cleaning field gear.

'You're a 'Raum, right?'

'Ex-'Raum,' Faull said wryly. 'Or so my *soh* would tell you. He'd also call me a backslider, a traitor, an unbeliever . . . you know, the general sort of thing that makes up a good soldier.'

'*Soh?*'

'An Elder,' Faull said. 'A deacon. Someone who intercedes with the One, and interprets the Task for us.'

'One is like God, right?' Njangu said. 'But Task? I can hear capital letters.'

'Task is our mission . . . all of us and each of us . . . here on D-Cumbre.'

'What's the group goal?'

'All of Cumbre,' Faull said precisely, 'should belong to us. As should all of space.'

'Nice unambitious ideals,' Yoshitaro said. 'What about the rest of us?'

'You can either join us, or else . . .' Faull drew the back of his thumb across his throat.

'How *very* excellent,' Njangu said. 'By what right do you . . . sorry, the 'Raum who still believe . . . claim this?'

'Our *sohs* tell us that we are First Men, both in creation and here on Cumbre. We came here hundreds of years before the Rentiers and their cronies, even if archeology tends to suggest we showed up in steerage about a hundred years after the first non-'Raum.

'But the legend says when the men who became Rentiers arrived, they had the guns, and we were forced to do whatever they wanted. Into the mines, which is where most of us work today.'

'How'd you get here first? And from where?'

'That,' Faull said, 'is one of those things we're a little vague about. Our holy writ is called *The Crossing*, and it's very mystic about that. Our homeworld is never named, just described as a paradise, of course. Some say we came here pre-stardrive.'

'What, in one of those old-timey punt-it-out-with-a-rocket-and-pray?'

'*The Crossing* says the Sail brought us here, on a wind given by the One.'

'A solar sail?' Njangu said.

'I don't know,' Faull said. 'Our *sohs* aren't real great on us reading *The Crossing* for ourselves. Better we let him or her read it to us, and tell us what it means. Mostly the book is a bunch of lectures that somebody gave to a Fold, a congregation. The guy, or maybe it's a woman, who's preaching never gets named. That's really when I started getting in the shit, when I got a copy of *The Crossing* for myself, read it and had a whole bunch of questions the *soh* didn't do a real good job of answering.

'My father taught me to make up my own mind from whatever facts I could come up with. Maybe good, maybe bad, but that's the way I was taught, and that's why I started having trouble.'

''Kay,' Njangu said slowly, 'I understand the programming. But do the *sohs* tell the 'Raum they've got to live separately, like I gather they do?'

'If you're a 'Raum,' Faull said, some bitterness in his voice, 'everybody knows it. Knows it by your name, by your address, by where you went to school.'

'With no way out?'

'Except maybe the Force.'

'Which is what you're doing?'

'Which is what I'm *trying*,' Faull said. 'At least you off-worlders don't seem to give a rat's nose about shit like that.'

'If you'd stayed a 'Raum,' Njangu asked, 'you would've had to become a miner?'

'Actually, there's a ton of us who never pick the pick,' Faull said. 'We're merchants, traders . . . a lot of us are fishermen or live outside the cities, small-farming.

'I'm missing something,' Njangu said. 'If you've got all those options, why'd you go soldiering?'

'Those options are bullshit,' Faull said sharply. 'You can trade . . . to other 'Raum. Farm . . . but you better not get too big. Open a store . . . but it better not compete with the Anciens and their crew.'

'That,' Njangu said, 'sort of blows corpses.'

Faull nodded, turned back to his gear.'

'That's the system the Force is defending?'

Faull nodded again.

'One other question. Everybody calls the rich types Rentiers. What's that mean? Or was that the name of their ship, or something?'

'That was something I had to look up for myself,' Faull said. 'It's an old Earth word for rich people who get richer by making everybody dance around their money piles.'

'Shit. So much for Truth, Justice, and the Confederation Way,' Njangu said. 'It's the same here as anywhere else. We got the Golden Rule – whoever's got the gold, rules.'

Gorecki was teaching Jaansma how to pilot a Cooke. 'It's bone-simple,' he finished. 'Now let's take it out for a field test.'

'Good,' Jaansma said. 'Like where?'

'Off post, maybe around the island,' the driver said.

'Even better,' Garvin said, and climbed into the driver's seat.

The drive was already on. Jaansma fastened his safety straps as Stanislaus clambered in. He eyed the empty gunmount in front of him. 'If we had some ammo, I'd chance doing a little cross-country,' he said. 'But I guess—'

'Hoy,' someone shouted, and Garvin saw Ben Dill

trotting toward them. Over his shoulder was a belt, and holstered on it was the biggest handgun Jaansma'd ever seen. 'You two clowns thinking about going for a ride without me?'

'Never happen, *Dec*.'

'Good,' Dill said, vaulting into the passenger compartment. 'Let's get out of here before somebody finds work for us to do.'

'I was gonna have him do a circumnav,' Gorecki said.

'Sounds good to me,' Dill said. 'Let's go beachcombing. Take it away, Mister Jaansma.'

'Immediately, Mister Dill,' and Garvin pushed the drive pedal, and pulled the upside-down U of the control stick toward him. The Cooke hiccuped, then soared away.

'Didn't like that sound,' Dill said.

'If you don't like failure,' Gorecki said, 'don't hook with a Cooke.'

'Funny,' Dill said. 'I'm choking with hysterics. Take it low and fast, Garvin. I want to eat some spray.'

'Happy to oblige,' Garvin said, and dived toward the water.

'Come on children,' Lir shouted, 'or we'll be late for our morning prayers.'

Njangu wanted to curse, but was too out of breath. He thought he heard Gerd wheeze something obscene, but it was probably wishful thinking. Lir seemed determined to make sure none of them survived training, and had started taking the recruits for daily two-kilometer beach runs, with a five-klicker every third day.

'Most important muscle a good rifleman's got is his legs,' she observed cheerfully, easily running backward along the water's edge.

'Wrong,' Angie Rada managed. 'It's what's between them that's important.'

'You got enough breath for talking,' Lir called, 'sing something.'

'Aw shit,' Rada moaned, but obeyed:

> 'Oh once I was happy, but now I'm forlorn,
> Riding in Griersons all tattered and torn
> The drivers are daring, all caution they scorn,
> And the pay is exactly the same, the same,
> The pay is exactly the same.

> 'We glide through the air in our flying caboose,
> Its actions are graceful just like a fat goose,
> We hike on the pavement till our joints all come
> loose,
> And the pay is exactly—'

She broke off, hearing the whine of an approaching vehicle. 'Straighten up, you hounds,' Lir shouted. 'It's liable to be your mother!'

The five closed into tight formation, and a Cooke flashed around the point ahead. As it closed, the vehicle slowed. Njangu wondered who'd be this far from Camp Mahan. *Probably some officer with his popsy*, he thought wistfully, trying to remember the last time he'd made love to anything other than his hand, and wondered why he'd never tried to see if Angie was serious.

He squinted at the Cooke, saw three men in it. The man in the back stood, and Yoshitaro blinked at how goddamned *big* the bastard was. The man wore the four rank slashes of a *dec*. He threw an elaborate salute, and shouted, 'Hyp, heep, hoop, there, brave soldiers! Give us a cheer for the Force!'

Lir: 'Crash, you bastards!'

Yoshitaro: 'Eat it!'

Milot: 'Hope your dick falls off!'

Penwyth: 'I screwed your sister!'

Rada: 'Your mother gives it away!'

Only Faull stayed silent.

'That's the spirit I like to see,' the *dec* shouted, just as Njangu spotted Garvin at the controls of the combat car. He managed a feeble wave, thought Garvin recognized him, and the car swept past.

Bastard, bastard, bastard, he thought. *Knew I joined the wrong branch*, and the Cooke banked back. He was too out of breath for more than a crude gesture, but a couple of the others found lung space for an obscenity.

The Cooke was about a hundred meters past when Yoshitaro heard sudden silence. The combat car's antigrav went on automatically, and the Cooke bounced to a soft landing on the beach. The I&R runners were in hysterics, hearing the drive starter grind, grind, grind again, then they were even with the car.

'Going anywhere soon?' Lir taunted.

Dill grimaced.

'Hey, Garvin,' Njangu said. 'It's a real interesting walk back. You'll have time to admire the wildlife.'

Jaansma recognized Yoshitaro and grinned for an instant, then hit the starter again.

Njangu listened to the long grinding as the runners went around a bend, then heard nothing.

'God sort of does paybacks when you're being a wisebutt, doesn't he?' Dill observed.

'*I* wasn't saying anything, at least not much,' Gorecki protested.

'The innocent suffer with the guilty,' Garvin said. 'So we're gonna let *him* carry us back.'

'Awright,' Ben said. 'Gimme the com. I'll snivel for help.'

Garvin passed him the mike and heard the *crack*, saw a bright brass streak paint itself on the Cooke's hull about a finger length from his left arm, heard the *boom* of some sort of propellant weapon, then the burbling whine as the bullet ricocheted away.

He stared at the mark of the near miss for one instant, then dived over the Cooke's side. He landed on top of Ben Dill, who was scrabbling for that enormous handgun.

'Son of a bitch, son of a bitch,' Dill was muttering, then he was up on his knees, peering at the nearby brush, pistol sweeping back and forth. The gun went off, nearly rupturing Jaansma's eardrums, then Dill was running for the brush. Garvin didn't know what to do, decided he'd rather be a brave idiot than a cowardly logician, went after the *dec*. Stanislaus wasn't far behind.

They crashed through the brush, found Ben kneeling over some carefully piled branches. He held up a dull brass shell casing.

'Look at the antique that bastard tried to kill me with,' he said. 'He must've made himself a bed, then lurked for a target, and only had the one bullet. Or else he ran out of courage.'

'Wonder why he didn't shoot at the crunchies,' Gorecki said. 'More of 'em, and a slower, easier target.'

'Guess he thought we were more important,' Dill said.

Stanislaus and Garvin were staring at each other, realization having penetrated at the same moment.

'Somebody tried to frigging *kill* us,' Gorecki said in a hushed tone.

'No shiteedah,' Dill growled, from his vast experience. 'The big question is how in the hell did some goddamned bandit get all the way out here to Chance Island?'

The three glanced reflexively across the bay toward Dharma.

'We gonna go after him?' Stanislaus asked.

Dill thought. 'I'm not that sure he only had one bullet,' he said. 'And what would I do with you guys? He'd probably sneak around and pot you while I was thundering around in the tules.' He shook his head. 'I'm still not sure I believe this.'

'Somebody,' Garvin decided, 'is gonna shit five-credit pieces when they hear about this.'

But all they were told by their company commander, *Cent* Haughton, repeated by *Alt* Wu, their platoon leader, was to 'be more careful when you're outside the camp, and what the hell were you doing out there anyway?'

Nobody ever reported seeing the sniper again.

Lir looked the five up and down.

'You call this combat-ready? Your gear looks like you've crapped in it for a week. Fifteen minutes, full dress. Move!'

The five clattered back into the barracks, cursing steadily as they stacked their rifles, dumped combat vests and equipment, and started pulling on dress blues.

'I'm gonna kill her,' Angie managed. 'Kill her dirty and seal my goddamned tunic for me willya, Njangu, thanks.'

'Two minutes left and we're ready,' Faull managed. 'We're getting good.'

They pelted back out, and froze. Waiting in full dress uniform, were *Alt* Hedley and Senior *Tweg* Gonzales.

'Fall in,' Lir shouted. They obeyed, and the *dec* about-faced, saluted the *alt*.

'Sir, the troops are present.'

'Good,' Hedley said, taking a piece of paper from his pocket.

'General order such and such, effective this date, signed personally by *Caud* Jochim Williams, the following are promoted from RECRUIT TO STRIKER:

'Faull, Henry; Milot, Ton; Rada, Angela; Penwyth, Erik; and Yoshitaro, Njangu.

'Congratulations. The bullshit's over with. You made it. All of you.

'Welcome to Intelligence and Reconnaissance.'

They were waiting for Garvin Jaansma near the pond by Regimental Headquarters. Dill knocked his legs out from under him, held him pinned, while Gorecki and Kang grabbed his arms. He flailed, but they lugged him to the edge of the water.

'One . . . three, and yo-heave-ho,' and Jaansma splashed down.

'What the hell was that for?' he sputtered when he surfaced.

'You ain't a slimy recruit any longer,' Stanislaus said. 'You is one of us, you poor sad bastard. Plus you now get to get off this stinkin' base and go into Leggett and get into trouble without us.'

Jaansma stood knee-deep in the pond, oblivious to the lily pad dangling from one shoulder.

'Come on, Striker Jaansma,' Dill said. 'Stop crying and get your ass back to barracks. The old man wants to do it official-like in an hour.'

Garvin was sitting on his bunk, dress blue tunic beside him. Once more he reached out, ran his finger across the new red cloth of a striker's single slash.

'It ain't gonna go away,' a voice said. Jaansma looked up, saw Njangu leaning against the bunk behind him. He, too, wore a striker's insignia.

'Can't believe we made it.'

'I sure as hell can, you candy-assed armored idiot,' Yoshitaro said.

'But I didn't wander down here where you elite swine

swarm just to congratulate you. We got a week pass, y'know.'

'I vaguely remember the *cent* telling me that,' Garvin said. 'But I've been a little . . . excited.'

Njangu grinned.

'Me too. But I paid attention to the important shit. Especially because we got Force Maneuvers when we get back, and that'll be a pure whore on roller skates. You want to try to get in some serious trouble with some I&R rascals?'

'Why hell yes,' Garvin said. 'I thought you'd never ask . . . *Striker* Yoshitaro.'

FOURTEEN

The cave's entrance was tiny, barely a meter high and hidden by a thicket. Ten meters within, it opened into a great chamber in the heart of the mountain. It was cool, a relief from the tropic night outside.

Twenty men and women sat on blankets in a semicircle, three lanterns casting shadows on the high walls and ceiling. All had weapons, and kept them close at hand.

Comstock Brien stood in the center of the group.

'Are we sure, sister, this report is accurate?'

Jo Poynton shrugged, held out her hands. 'My agent has never been in error before. But I will admit he's never reported anything this important.'

'So if it's true, if the Rentiers have lost contact with their overlords in the Confederation,' Brien mused, 'it is now the task of the Planning Group to determine what advantage we shall take of this.'

Jord'n Brooks stood. 'Excuse me,' he said politely. 'My name is Jord'n Brooks. As you know, I'm the newest member of the Planning Group, so forgive me if I don't remember the names you've chosen to use, or if I'm violating protocol in not waiting until more senior members speak.

'It seems to me this opportunity must be seized

immediately! We must begin with a hard strike, an attack that clearly throws down the gauntlet.'

'Such as?' someone asked.

'I would suggest a direct assault on PlanGov head-quarters,' he said. 'Select a small squad, equip them with explosives, and attack. The men and women will die, naturally, but die as martyrs to the revolution.

'With proper planning and a bit of luck, they will die in the knowledge that they've taken a goodly percentage of the Confederation satraps with them, including that slug of a governor general, if we strike carefully and at the proper moment.'

'Pah!' Brien snarled. 'That's the purest of adventurism, very close to antirevolutionary wrecking! We must move slowly, in a considered manner.'

'Insults, labels, have no part in a reasoned discussion,' Brooks said coldly. 'Are your ideas so bereft of intrinsic merit you must instantly attack any contributions from others? Be careful, brother. Such behavior smacks of elit-ism. We have no intent of fighting against the harsh arbitrary hand of the Confederation and the Rentiers only to have another dictator emerge from within.'

'Brother Brooks, you also must be wary,' Poynton said. 'You are also coming close to antimovement behavior in your choice of words.'

'I am sorry,' Brooks said. 'And thank you for the admonishment. I acknowledge my error, apologize to Brother Brien and withdraw my statement. Of course we must move carefully, and be aware of the possibility of failure, and not sacrifice all on a single cast of the dice. But we must be careful not to be paralyzed with inertia that might be seen as cowardice, either.

'Since my first idea was received with such scorn by Brother Brien, let me offer an alternative:

'The Force will hold its annual maneuvers in a few

weeks. These maneuvers, here on the main island, have been a popular entertainment for some years, have they not? In fact, isn't it common knowledge that the final battle game is to be witnessed by most of the PlanGov and a goodly number of the Rentiers?'

'They are, and it is,' someone said.

'Why can't these swine be attacked while they're out in the open, away from their guards, sensors, and fortresses? How heavy will the security be in a time of festival?'

'Even if it is a play war, we still must worry about the Force, who'll be thronging the area.'

'And able to fight back with what? Blanks? And why do we worry so much about them? They're under-manned, their equipment is aging rapidly, and their morale must be low with this loss of contact with their overlords in the Confederation. Even the stupidest, most bestial soldier at Camp Mahan must be dimly aware of how repressive he is, and how his iron heel smashes the 'Raum.'

'You think more of the average helmet-head than I do,' someone called, and there was a ripple of laughter.

'That *is* an interesting idea,' Poynton said. 'I gather you have developed an overall strategy of your own from there?'

'I have,' Brooks said, voice excited. 'Hit now, hit hard, hit often. Hit not just PlanGov and the Rentiers, but hit those loathsome vermin the Musth wherever we find them, in Leggett or up on the plateaus where they plot our doom.'

'What could that give us? Their empire doesn't appear to be tottering,' a woman asked. 'Suppose they strike back? Not just with the soldiers they've got in the Cumbre system, but with a battle force from their homeworlds?'

'Good,' Brooks said. 'If they do, they'll hit all men, not just us. That'll mobilize everyone to join together. Since we are the only ones who'll have a plan, that'll give us Cumbre on a platter, then, together, we may destroy the Musth.'

'You think we can defeat the Musth?'

'Of course,' Brooks said scornfully. 'We are 'Raum. Is there anyone among you who think the One who created us to rule would allow the Musth any victory? Why would the One contradict his simple message and deny us their worlds, the worlds of the universe He promised us?'

A moment of silence, then shouts of 'no,' 'of course not,' and some smug, satisfied laughter came. Brooks put on a smile, let it linger for a moment, then went on.

'So we can set aside that impossibility. We hit the Musth, we drive them back into their enclaves, then off D-Cumbre. From there, as the situation develops, we will be in position to attack them on their base world of E-Cumbre, and drive them from the system. With the riches of C-Cumbre ours we can rebuild and continue our triumphant expansion.'

'Again I must remind you about your willingness not only to create empires in the clouds, but attempt to move into them,' Brien said. 'Return to this world, and what happens after we strike during these maneuvers. No matter how hard we hit them, there'll be enough left of the Force to come after us, into these hills. That will be a brutal campaign, although I, for one, would welcome it, for it fits directly into our *already-approved* strategy,' Brien said with emphasis.

'In my plan, the Force does come into the hills after our victory,' Brooks said. 'But we won't be there to be targets.

'This revolution should . . . must . . . bury itself in the

heart of the people. We can sit here in the jungle, and preach to the odd farmer, hunter, or peasant, and our numbers increase, but slowly, agonizingly slowly. And for each convert, we lose two to sickness and one to the Force? I do not like those figures.

'Other soldiers here in the wilderness are people like me, people who've given the most they can in the city and been forced to flee for their lives.

'I will be frank. I do not feel I am giving my full effort to the struggle, I do not think my talents are properly used, in these hinterlands. I was born and raised in Leggett, and worked in many jobs before I was forced to become a miner and joined The Movement.

'I know the cities, and they're jungles more impenetrable than these hills. That is where we should be fighting the oppressor, for the targets are close, and easy to study. When we strike, we strike from such close range he can't use his assault craft, his rockets, his missiles, his strike ships and his artillery.

'If that is the path we decide to follow, the pressure will be instantly increased. People hear of a patrol being shot at here on the Highland walls, and they yawn. But if an element of the Force is ambushed and wiped out in the heart of Leggett, and people see our power . . . victory is much closer.'

Brien started to say something, but Brooks overrode him.

'When we have a little power, PlanGov and their thugs will turn up the heat. Checkpoints, forbidden zones, brutality, all the criminal behavior of a tottering regime . . . the people will see at firsthand what we've been telling them about the reality of their world.

'They will hurry to join us, and the Force will panic and further intensify its persecution.

'It then becomes a feedback cycle, brothers and sisters.

Instead of a handful of feverish, wan, emaciated half-forgotten jungle fighters waging a bitter war, the entire population rises in frustrated frenzy, and as they do, become our brothers and sisters.

'That is the day of real, final victory !'

Brooks stopped abruptly. There was complete silence in the cavern, and he felt the power build, felt the will of the twenty people strong within him, and someone applauded.

Brien was on his feet. 'Brother Brooks is one of our most inspired agitators,' he said. 'I think we should admire the power of his rhetoric. However—'

'Forgive me for interrupting you, brother,' Poynton said. 'I'm not sure these matters should be fully debated now, for our blood is running hot.

'I would suggest we table this discussion of Grand Strategy for a time, while we all have a chance coldly to consider it, and discuss it with our cell members.

'With one exception,' she said.

Brien's lips pursed.

'I like what Brother Brooks suggested about using the Force's maneuvers against the system,' Poynton went on. 'We *have* been looking for a major action to show our strength.

'What is the matter with Brother Brooks' idea? We would not be risking that many fighters, we would be striking far from our homes and secret bases, and there would be an excellent chance of doing major damage to our persecutors.'

Silence for a moment, and the members of the group eyed each other, consideringly. A man stood.

'I agree. Let's hit them now, hit them hard, and then we'll see what happens from there!'

Another, and then a fourth spoke up.

'I see,' Brien said coldly. 'Brother Brooks has come up

with a very popular idea. I must admit to reservations, but it may, indeed, be time we took the war home to the enemy. How many favor his plan?'

Hands went up.

'There is more than a majority,' Brien said. 'I must bow to Brother Brooks' eloquence, and make it unanimous. We shall begin planning the details at once.

'Now, it is very late, and I would suggest we break up this meeting. Some of us have long kilometers to travel and places we must be seen at by dawn.'

As the twenty picked up their gear, Poynton came to Brooks.

'There are those who might think this small action might give you a base to build from,' she said in a low voice.

'I suppose so,' Brooks said, indifferently. 'I care little about that. What I care about is that there can be no real compromise for our struggle. Not now, not ever, not until total victory.'

FIFTEEN

'Balls,' drawled Erik Penwyth, staring at the Recreation Center. 'Just like the barracks, only painted more colors.'

'And a shittier location,' Njangu agreed. 'The only thing we look to be close to is the sewer works.'

The Force RC did look like former barracks, clinging to a hillside overlooking Leggett's biggest lubricant dump.

The five strikers wore undress khakis, short-sleeved shirts and shorts with matching knee socks and black-leather sandals.

'Balls said the queen,' Angie added, apropos of very little. 'If I had 'em, I'd be king?'

'Balls ain't no big thing said the duke,' Garvin finished. 'I got 'em and I ain't.'

'Ha. A *capital* jest, as I don't say,' Njangu said.

'You five have fun, fun, fun,' Faull said. 'I'll see you in a week.' He hurried down the hill, and through the rather perfunctory security check at the Rec Center's gate.

'Dump on us and run,' Ton Milot said. 'What's he got going?' He whistled, seeing a rather pretty, obviously pregnant woman embrace the ex-'Raum. Beside her was a boy, two or three years old. 'Question answered, the lucky dog.'

'And who's she?' Erik wondered. 'Is ouah Hank married? Or just cohabitin'?'

'Either way's against regs, isn't it?' Milot wondered.

'Sure is,' Angie said. 'Shall we drop the heat a wink?'

Njangu Yoshitaro's face went hard. 'You want to nark him off, Rada? Why?'

'Dunno,' Angie said, looking uncomfortable. 'He 's a 'Raum, isn't he?'

'He's one of us,' Yoshitaro said. 'And snitches aren't.'

'It was just a joke,' she said.

'Yeah, joke,' Njangu said.

'Hey, screw you and—' the woman broke off. 'Never mind, huh?'

Njangu was unmollified but had the sense to nod.

'If we're through bickering,' Garvin said cheerfully, 'is there anybody who really wants to stay in this fine joint, known for its heavily armed roaches since Buddha was a *finf*?'

'Big choice,' Milot said. 'Unless you armored wicks get better pay'n we do.'

'My folks gave me two hun for actually graduatin' from something,' Penwyth said. 'I'll toss that in the pot, but I don't think it'll make much difference spread five ways.'

'Ah, so it's nothing but a matter of money,' Jaansma said. 'Shall I see what I can do about that?'

'You need juicing?' Njangu asked.

'Don't think so.' Garvin held out his hands. 'Now heed me well, brethern and sistern, and may thy prayers be with me, for I go forth among the unwashed and heathen, with the hopes of gladdening our hearts and enriching our life experiences.

'Brother Penwyth, select a place where we shall reassemble, one suitable to my soon-to-be rich-bitch status.'

'A very classy joint is the Shelburne,' Erik said. 'Right down on the beach.'

'Then meet me there, perhaps by dusk, eh?' Without waiting for an answer, Garvin went toward the gate.

'I don't get it,' Erik said.

'Our friend is doing what I think he calls hitting the hustings, looking for a sucker with credits, which he'd probably call pecuniary emolument,' Njangu said.

'Your friend sure talks pretty for a striker.'

'Your friend is pretty, for a striker or anybody else,' Angie said dreamily.

'Yeah,' Yoshitaro said. 'He doesn't like narks either.'

She moved close. 'Hey, I'm sorry I said something wrong.'

'Forget it,' Njangu said. 'Let's go dump our ditty bags and check out Leggett.'

Leggett's center was a broad park, with winding paths and lush gardens.

'Nighttime,' Milot said. 'The hooks'll be out over there.'

'Oh yeh?' Yoshitaro said, interested. 'Any murphy men?'

'Huh?'

'Guy who hides in the bushes,' Njangu explained. 'The whore lures the mark in, her mac slaps him upside the head, jackrolls him.'

'Hell no,' Milot said, sounding shocked. 'What kind of an armpit do you think Leggett is, anyway?'

'Not nearly armpitty enough, evidently,' Njangu said. 'Good money to be made dry-gulching murphy men. But I guess us noble sojers shouldn't think like that. Lead on.'

The downtown streets were winding, close. The four soldiers pressed close to a small gravsled parked on the narrow pavement as a lift eased past.

'Expensive part of the world, eh?' Njangu asked Penwyth as he eyed a window full of jewelry.

''Tis that,' Erik said. 'And if you got it, flaunt it.'

'Look at that,' Angie said, voice hushed. She was pointing to a show window with a single shoulder bag in it. The bag was shimmering gold chain mail. 'Isn't that flauntable?'

'Yep,' Erik said. 'Only . . . six hundred seventy-eight credits. Two months' pay. It'd go well with your dress blues, Angie.'

'Maybe we'd better go back to the park if you're thinking like that,' Milot suggested. 'Njangu could pimp for you, since I get the idea he's used to crime. Or maybe I do, what did you call it, Murphy? Anyway, no soldier ever made enough money for something like that.'

'There's a way,' Rada said dreamily. 'There's *got* to be.'

'So much for my marriage proposal,' Njangu said. 'I'll never be able to keep you in that sort of style.'

Angie laughed, slid her arm around Yoshitaro. 'I'm forgiven?'

'For what?'

'Thanks,' she said.

'Hey, Erik,' someone shouted, and the four turned. Across the street a woman was waving.

'Jasith!' Erik shouted, and darted between two lifters. The others went after him through the heavy, slowly moving traffic.

Njangu decided the woman was worth risking death by antigrav for. She was model-slender, long black hair worn down either side of an oval face, about eighteen. Her lips were very full, and her sloe eyes promised infinite delights. Small breasts almost showed their nipples over her top, a multicolored silk kerchief casually tied around them with a bow on the side. She wore matching shorts and yellow high-heeled slingback sandals.

He watched enviously as she melted into Erik's arms, but noted hopefully that she kissed him close-mouthed before she pulled back. 'You make a *very* sexy soldier,' the girl said, her voice a throaty near whisper.

'I make a very sexy anything,' Erik said. 'I heard you were workin'. Mellusin Mining's on hard times?'

'Oh, you know, it's so dead, and there's nothing happening, and I thought I maybe would want to run some kind of store sometime, so Daddy wanted me to see what it's like. Veeeehry booooring,' she said. 'I thought it'd be interesting, selling lingerie, but it's just like working in a butcher shop or something like that, I guess. 'Though I don't think I'd care about a twenty-five percent discount on rib roasts. Maybe I'll get married instead.' She looked around. 'Who're your friends?'

Penwyth introduced them. 'And this is Jasith Mellusin. She's an old friend of the family.'

Jasith touched hands with the soldiers. She and Angie exchanged looks of instant hatred.

'So they let you out of your cage?' Jasith asked.

'Had to,' Erik explained. 'I was just simply too good for them to believe. Supersoldier, standin' right here.'

'Good is hard for *me* to believe,' Jasith said with a laugh. 'But since you've got a furlough, or an AWOL or whatever you soldiers call it, I assume you're going to Bampur's party tomorrow night?'

'Nope,' Erik said. 'Nobody invited me, now that I'm one of the uniformed unwashed.'

'Oooh, it'd be a *tragedy* if you didn't appear,' Jasith said. 'You *must* come. I've just invited you. You, and your friends. Allah knows we need new faces.'

Njangu bowed. 'And if there's faces like yours at the party, Allah knows we need you,' he said.

Angie glowered, and Njangu pretended not to notice. Jasith giggled.

'My friend here's from Centrum,' Erik said. 'He was on that ship that was taken by pirates.'

'You were,' Jasith said. 'How'd you ever escape?'

'It's a long and bloody tale,' Njangu said. 'Not suitable for the ears of virgins, the easily shocked, or the young.'

'Well that *certainly* doesn't include me,' Jasith said.

'No shit,' Angie muttered. Jasith pretended she didn't hear.

'Tomorrow night,' she told Erik. 'But don't be *deadly* and show up before midnight.'

'I don't even open m' eyes before then,' Penwyth said. 'We'll be there . . . with bells on.'

'What's in there?' Yoshitaro asked, eyeing a set of open gates.

'Where we don't go,' Angie said.

'Why not? Looks colorful. And there's four of us, all battle-trained and such,' Njangu wondered.

'It's the Eckmuhl, the 'Raum section,' Penwyth explained. 'We don't go on their ground, they stay on theirs.'

'Nice society you got here,' Yoshitaro said.

'It works,' Angie said defensively.

Milot snorted. Njangu waited for his comment, but none came.

There were seven men about Njangu's age just inside the gates. They were dressed flashily, and leaned bonelessly against the stone wall.

'There's seven good reasons not to go visitin' the 'Raum,' Erik said. 'Local fellers of ill repute, who'd like to see the exact dimensions of our purses.'

Yoshitaro buried a grin – the toughs looked and stood about the way he and his friends had, back on Waughtal's Planet. 'Thanks for the tip,' he said, sounding sincere. 'How deep does the 'Raum section go?'

'Three, p'raps four kilometers on a side,' Erik said. 'Ends right up against the base of the Heights.'

'How many people live inside there?'

Penwyth shrugged. 'A million? Maybe more? The census doesn't go inside, any more'n anybody else.'

'What happens when there's trouble?'

'The 'Raum take care of themselves,' Angie said. 'The coppers convoy half a dozen lifters through twice a day to pick up bodies. They don't slow down much.'

'The second mate on my boat went in there once,' Milot said. 'Nobody knows why. He always thought he was tougher'n anything. Maybe he spotted a girl. The heat found his head on the gate the next day,' Milot said. 'We never heard no more. Not ever.'

'Subtle bastards these 'Raum, aren't they?' Njangu said 'What about Hank? Won't he get in the shit, being 'Raum and in the army?'

'Who knows?' Angie said. 'The only people who think like 'Raum are 'Raum.'

'Guess that's why the Force is so successful against the bandits,' Yoshitaro muttered to himself.

'Hey,' Njangu said. 'Isn't that yours?'

The sign read: RADA'S FOR EVERYTHING. It occupied about half a block and looked, from its cluttered windows, like it indeed sold everything. And at a bargain, for there were signs everywhere: IF WE DON'T HAVE IT, YOU DON'T NEED IT. NO PRICE UNBEATEN. EASY PAYMENTS. NO FOLD UNWELCOME.

Angie nodded reluctantly. 'Yeh.'

'Whyn't we slide in there,' Milot suggested, 'and you get maybe six months' advance on your allowance? That'll grease us for the party.'

'No,' Angie said shortly. 'Can't do it.'

'Why not?' Erik asked innocently. 'Here's their own

lovin' child, just graduated from the hardest school the army's got and all. Why wouldn't they want to make some kind of love offerin'?'

'Love?' Angie laughed bitterly.

'What's the matter?' Milot asked. 'Don't you get along with your people?'

'Leave it, 'kay?' Angie's voice was sharp. 'Just leave it.'

'Sorry I even bothered to learn to read,' Milot said. 'Consider it left.'

Njangu let the others go on ahead, looked at Angie. 'Can I ask you a question?'

'Not if it's about my family,' she said. 'Right now, that's not something I can deal with.'

'It wasn't,' Yoshitaro said. 'Or, maybe, indirectly. What's that sign mean – No *Fold* Unwelcome?'

'My family's stores sell to anybody,' Angie said. 'But mainly to the 'Raum.'

'I'm lost,' Njangu said. 'If that's where you get your money from . . . why're you down on them?'

'They're dirty, they breed like rats, they'd like to wipe anybody out who isn't 'Raum, and they ought to be run off Cumbre,' Rada said bitterly. 'If people had any sense, they'd get rid of 'em, and work the damned mines with their own people. But they won't. People always let somebody else sling their shit. One of these days, it's gonna come back on them.'

Njangu eyed her, decided he'd gone close enough.

'Hey,' he said softly.

'What?' she snapped.

He cupped her chin in his hand, kissed her. Her eyes went wide in surprise, then her mouth opened, and her tongue curled against his, arms going around him.

'Hey,' Penwyth shouted, 'come on, you two. No frat-ernizin' in ranks!'

She looked up at Njangu. 'I hope you're not giving

out tickets you don't plan on punching,' she said a bit breathlessly. 'I thought you were going to go antsy over that rich bitch back there.'

Njangu wiggled his eyebrows. Angie laughed, and Yoshitaro thought it was a very pleasant sound.

'So much for wild, banzai soldiers on reckless leave,' Angie snorted. 'Turn us loose, and what do we do? Stroll the friggin' docks like friggin' tourists looking at friggin' boats. We've been on pass most of a day now, and had two beers each, one pretty crappy meal, and a nice frigging stroll is all.'

'What's the matter with that?' Milot asked. 'Being close to the sea is relaxing.'

'If I wanted relaxation, I could've taken a nap at the Rec Center,' the woman said. 'I'm looking for something resembling action. You know . . . dicks, drugs and doowah?'

'Pick a bar, any bar,' Erik said. 'They all look like we might find a disgustin' brawl.'

Njangu looked up and down the waterfront. 'No kid,' he said. 'But would just a plain simple brawl make our Angie happy? Doesn't there have to be a good body count and — and what the hell's going on over there?'

Six men were pushing a young, ragged-looking peddler around. Yoshitaro heard shouts of 'damn 'Raum,' 'toss him in th' bay,' and 'boot him, Sayid.' The boy's wares — brightly plated knickknacks — were scattered in the street.

Sayid was about to obey when a quiet voice stopped him. 'You don't even want to do that.'

He spun, saw Njangu. 'Butt out, sojer boy.'

'Sure,' Yoshitaro said agreeably. He spun sideways, and his foot snapped up, raked down Sayid's tibia, and smashed the arch of his foot. Sayid howled, bent, and Njangu snapped a punch into the man's jaw, recovered, dropped him with a hammer strike on the base of the neck.

Another man grabbed Njangu's collar, and Njangu turned into him, brought a knee up into the man's stomach, let him fall, vomiting, as he turned again.

A third man had a knife out of a belt sheath, and Milot had his arm in both hands, smashed it across his lifting knee, and the bone snapped.

Ton barely ducked a punch as Angie's knife hand struck into that fourth man's gut. The man gagged and collapsed.

Njangu kicked the first in the head twice, very hard, without lowering his foot. The man whimpered, staggered away, both hands over the bloody mess that had been his face.

The last man was holding up both hands, backing away, as Erik, grinning savagely, closed on him.

'Nuh-uh, nuh-uh, not my doing, not my concern,' he said quickly.

'Then get the hell out.'

The man obeyed, ran about ten meters, then started screaming, 'Police! Help! Police!'

Njangu helped the boy to his feet. 'You better scoot, little friend.'

The 'Raum glowered, spat, and ran into an alleyway and was gone.

'*Nice*,' Njangu muttered sarcastically, mopping his face with his sleeve. 'Virtue's sure as hell its own reward. Now let's beat feet before the law materializes.'

'Wup,' Njangu said, as they trotted past the entrance to a hotel fairly oozing class. Several luxury lifters were unloading ostentatiously wealthy passengers, and uniformed help hustled here and there. 'In here. Nobody'd look for four soldiers in a ritz dive like this.'

'And we *are* supposed to meet your friend here,' Penwyth said. 'At the very least, we can feed our darlin' Angie a drink.'

They slowed, tried to look suitably arrogant, failed, and entered the Shelburne. The lobby was all old-fashioned over-stuffed leather chairs, dark wood, and engravings of people in red coats jumping four-legged beasts over fences.

'Now, where would the bar be?' Njangu wondered.

'These are sure not my people,' Ton Milot said. 'Let's scoot. I'd rather face the cops.'

A clerk curled a lip as he saw them, then his expression changed.

'Mister Penwyth! I didn't know you'd gone into the services.'

'I felt it was my patriotic duty,' Erik drawled, in as snotty a tone as he could manage.

'But of course, and it's a delight to see you. Are you planning on dining here?'

'My plans,' Erik said, 'are nebulous at the moment. Actually, we were hoping to meet a friend. A Mister Jaansma.'

'Yessir,' the clerk said. 'He checked in about an hour ago. Oh, you must be the party he told me to expect. Your rooms are waiting. Six seaview rooms . . . I was able to put all of you on the ninth floor . . . I do wish Mister Jaansma had told me you'd be among his party, Mister Penwyth.

'Perhaps if you'd sign in . . . and how are your parents these days?'

'Spending most of their time on the out islands,' Erik said. 'They've closed down the main house on the Heights.'

'Ah,' the clerk said, pushing an archaic register toward them. 'That explains why I haven't seen them for a while. We're delighted to welcome you all to the Shelburne.'

'I had your stuff brought over from the Rec Center,' Garvin said, lounging on the bed. 'Save the wear and tear.'

'You must've found somebody real rich,' Angie said.

'And dumb,' Ton Milot added.

'That's a big affirm to both,' Garvin said. 'Now go brush your teeth, and we'll rendezvous in the bar in half an hour.'

Njangu lingered for a moment.

'You did a pretty good job of impressing those people.'

'Njangu, my friend, I did a pretty good job of impressing *me*, even if it was my deck. Those fools insisted on handing me money in bales, almost like they thought it was a straight game. So we should have a fairly adequate leave.

'I've found one thing in his life,' Garvin added. 'Whether you're rich or whether you're poor, it's nice to have credits.'

Njangu wandered around his room, face still, his mind on the past, touching the raw silk curtains, playing with the sensors on the com center, looking at the array of bottles in a wall cabinet, staring out the window at the calm twilight sea. *Not ever like this*, he thought. I *never ever thought I would—*

There was a light knock . . . no more than fingernails . . . at the door. Njangu opened it. Angie was there, holding her small ditty bag.

'You ready to go downstairs?' she asked.

'Mmmh,' Njangu said neutrally.

'I told Garvin we might be a little late.'

'Mmmmh?'

'I don't know about you,' she said, 'but I'm a lot hornier than I am thirsty.'

'Mmmmh.'

'Would you be interested in doing something about that?'

She stood next to the bed, hipshot, and slowly ran a thumb down her tunic seal, let it drop. She wore a black, lacy brassiere, not issue khaki. Her nipples were hard, erect.

Njangu undressed, watching her take off her shoes, socks, and pants. She lay back across the bed, lifted one heel up, let her leg fall to the side.

'Well?' she murmured.

Njangu walked across the room, bent over her.

'That was quick,' she said, a few minutes later.

'Sorry,' Yoshitaro apologized. 'It's been a while.'

'Don't apologize,' she whispered. 'You're still ready.'

'Trying to be,' Njangu said. 'So whyn't you put your legs around my back and we'll see what happens?'

Angie obeyed, and her wet mouth opened, moved for his. They never did make it to the bar that night.

'You appear a bit disheveled,' Erik said cheerily as he poured caff the next morning. Njangu yawned, made a rude gesture, and Angie curled a lip.

'He,' Penwyth went on, indicating Garvin, 'looks like rat-shit on rye.'

'If you think I look bad from there, you oughta see things from the inside,' Garvin moaned.

Ton Milot chortled.

'We sat at the bar waiting—'

'—and drinking,' Erik said.

'—and drinking,' Ton continued, 'and all of a sudden it got drunk out.'

'I was staying pretty clean-cut,' Garvin objected. 'For a while.'

'Actually, he was,' Erik agreed.

Njangu evaluated Jaansma. 'Then what happened? You step on a rhinoceros or something?'

'There was a band,' Garvin offered weakly. 'And they had a singer.'

'Who's partial to blonds,' Erik said. 'Marya's got a *savage* reputation for what she does to men. The rest of us lesser mortals had to make do with availables in the audience. Thank Heaven.'

'My available wasn't all that fine,' Milot complained.

Garvin moaned.

'Poor baby,' Angie offered, patting his hand.

'My peck . . . my something feels like it went through one of those old-timey clothes wringers,' Garvin said. 'That woman has more strange ideas of what's a good time . . . guys, we can't be drinking in that bar anymore. She said something about getting together again. One more night like that, and I'm undone.'

'Tsk,' Penwyth said. 'Don't forget the party tonight. Bound to be clusters and globules of beautiful young debutantes, just itchin' to make the acquaintance of a long-dicked stranger with money.'

'What party?' Garvin demanded.

'That's right, we forgot to tell the lad,' Erik said. 'A terribly big thing. At Bampur's – he's a bit richer'n the Creator – estate. It'll be interestin', because either the family's around, in which case it'll be old farts tryin' to get naked with young talent, or else the Bampurs're off on their island, which means it's the daughter's shinny, and everybody'll be tryin' to get naked with everybody else.' He slapped Garvin on the shoulder. 'So buckle up, old boy. The best is yet to come.'

'What am I gonna do?' Garvin moaned again.

'You need some nice water sports,' Njangu offered.

'That was what Marya said last night,' Jaansma said. 'And I didn't. Lord, Lord, how I didn't.'

'Off your dead ass and on your dying feet, troop,' Njangu said. 'A little clean-cut exercise is all you need.'

Garvin reluctantly admitted he might live after an hour being smashed by the long, rolling swells that swept onto the manicured sands of the hotel's beach.

He came out of the surf to where the others lay on the sand.

'Enough,' he announced. 'It's time for a beer . . . then shopping.'

'Who put you in charge of this glee club, anyway?' Angie demanded.

'I'm buyin',' he announced. 'So we're all flyin'.'

'For what?' Milot asked.

'For clothes what don't look like uniforms,' Garvin said.

'What's the matter with uniforms?' Milot asked.

'They make you look like a soldier,' Jaansma explained.

'And what's the matter with that?'

'Lordy, Lordy, Lordy,' Njangu said. 'I can see why he likes fishing. It's an intellectual match between him and ol' Scaley. Hipe!'

Ton Milot drank beer and eyed Njangu and Garvin.

'Got a question for you two.'

'Anything,' Garvin said.

'Yeh. We lie cheaper'n anybody,' Njangu said.

'Since you're offworlders, and it appears nobody's

gonna get back to the Confederation for a while, are you gonna go career and stay in the service?'

'Screw you.'

'I'm not being cute,' Milot persisted. 'It's pretty easy to guess what's gonna happen to the rest of us. Erik'll go back to being rich and working a couple hours a week at his da's trading company. Angie . . . well, up 'til she ripped my face off yesterday, I would've guessed she would've done her hitch, got out, and maybe taken over one of her family's stores.'

'Hey, Ton,' Angie said. 'I'm sorry. I didn't have any right—'

'Forget it,' Milot said. 'I never was good at sub-tile, anyway. Me, I get out, wonder why the hell I went in in the first place, get on a boat, and hopefully do good enough to get one of my own.

'But you two? What you just said, Njangu, makes me think you would've just done your time, and gone back to wherever you came from—'

'Wrong on that one,' Yoshitaro said. 'I go back, there'll be a judge wanting to talk to me. Exile's permanent where I came from.'

''Kay, then,' Milot persisted, 'what will you do?'

'Dunno,' Njangu said, staring into his beer. 'Get out, for sure. Whatever's cut us off from the Confederation can't last forever. Get my ass back to something resembling civilization, I guess. Maybe figure out some kind of hustle for Centrum.'

'Which brings up my question,' Penwyth said. 'Yesterday, when we got into it with those Neanderthals over the 'Raum offspring, I noted you behaved in quite an experienced manner.'

'I paid attention in hand-to-hand fumbling,' Njangu said.

'I name that pure bullshit,' Erik said. 'They never

taught *me* to kick head-high once, let alone twice without recovering. It would appear to me you've been some sort of professional at this bodily damage business?'

'Not me,' Njangu said. 'A little peaceful lambikins.' He ostentatiously changed the subject. 'Isn't it interesting that here we are, cut off from Big Momma Empire, and nobody seems to give a shit or go jumping around in a blind panic? That ain't the way it'd be played in the holos — everybody'd be running around skreekin' and skrawkin', "Catastrophe, Catastrophe."'

'Big things take a long time to trickle down,' Garvin said. 'Sooner or later, we'll feel it, when we can't get Earth pepper, or granny's little annuity doesn't come in. Thank gods the beer at least's made here on Cumbre.' He poured about half his glass down, signaled for more.

'Come to think about it, what the hell happens if we've got to handle problems offworld? Say about the mines on C-Cumbre, which I understand is part of our terrain. Speaking as a big-time gunner on a Grierson, it'll be a long and crowded goddamned trek with a couple assault teams in the back.'

'The Force has civilian cargo ships already under charter for pappery like that,' Erik said. 'My father makes just *pots* of money off the government keepin' a couple on standby.'

''Kay,' Garvin persisted. 'That's for simple things. But suppose we have to go interstellar? Suppose somebody like *Caud* Williams or Governor Dickhead T. Haemer decides we should go out and find those "space pirates" who just happen to hang their helmets on Larix and Kura? Where's the Confederation Navy that's gonna haul our asses over there, beat shit out of whoever the hell's king shit's navy, then give us fire support on a landing?'

He looked around the table. Only Njangu appeared interested in the topic.

Angie yawned ostentatiously. 'You're raving, Garvin. Drink more beer.'

'Somebody'll no doubt figure out something if that happens,' Erik said vaguely. 'Besides we're just line-slime. We're not *s'posed* to worry.'

'But . . . aw, screw it,' Garvin said, and followed Angie's suggestion.

'Let's go back to my first question,' Ton said. 'What about you, Garvin? What happens when they hand you the discharge?'

'My fate is easily determined,' Jaansma said, striking a noble pose. 'I shall return to my rightful place as the dauphin of the continent of France on Earth, and collect sluts by the score.'

'Yeh, Dauphin,' Milot said. 'I was being serious.'

'So was I,' Garvin said, 'but you won't believe me. So how about this: I'm gonna find me a circus on hard times, buy it and make the damned thing go, and show the folks in the outback the biggest hooraw you've ever seen.'

Njangu was about to laugh, then saw Garvin's expression. 'Circus?' he said, before anyone else could try a wisecrack. 'Sounds like a good way to go crazy.'

'It is,' Jaansma said, still serious.

'Enough of this nonsense,' Njangu said, standing and fishing in his pocket for money. 'Let's go make ourselves look pretty.'

Laughing, joking, none of the five noticed the unobtrusive man follow them down the beachfront walk.

'Well?' Angie said.

'Well,' Ton Milot said skeptically, 'I don't look like a fisherman . . . and I sure don't look like a soldier.'

'Exactly what we wanted,' Garvin said. 'You're supposed

to be one of the idle rich, assuming Erik gave us good advice on what's fashionable here in the capital.'

All of them wore civilian sandals. Angie wore a multicolored short dress of a silky material that iridesced light reds, oranges, pinks. The men wore loose-fitting drab-colored pants, and brightly colored shirts in various styles. Garvin had chanced a floppy-brimmed hat.

'So what now?'

Njangu checked a watch finger. 'Going on three . . . maybe back to the beach, then something to eat, then nap 'til this party, which we were told not to show up for until midnight.'

'I've been thinking about tonight,' Milot said. 'No offense, Erik, but I don't want to go there and step on my dick.'

'You won't, my man,' Penwyth said. 'It's just going to be a bunch of people relaxin', not some horrid sort of formal banquet.'

'People who're all rich,' Milot said.

'Not all. Some of 'em are just pretty an' available.'

'That's not my kind of thing,' Ton said. 'If it's okay with you, I'd just as soon slide on out.' He looked sheepish. 'I kind of want to go see what my family's doing.'

'I'm with you,' Angie said. 'I'd prob'ly do something stupid, some asshole'd say something, and I'd have to do him. You want company?'

Milot looked surprised, then nodded. 'It's just a little village, on the other side of the peninsula.'

'Issus?'

'Sure,' Milot said. 'You know it?'

'When I was a kid,' Angie said, sounding wistful, 'my ma took me there for . . . I guess it was three days. She and Da were having some kind of trouble. I remember we stayed in this little hut, and ate a lot of fish, and nobody bothered us. I liked it a lot. I thought things

were like they must've been in the old days, before —
well, before things got weird.'

'Hey,' Milot said. 'Nothing's changed much. Come on.
You'd be welcome.'

Angie looked at Njangu. 'I'm sorry, babe.'

'What sorry? Sorry you didn't invite me?'

'I thought—'

'There you go,' Yoshitaro said, 'thinking again. You're
only a striker, woman, and you're trying to do Mark II
thinking with a Mark I brain. I love the tules, and since
Milot has the manners of a toad, I'm inviting myself to
go fishing, 'kay?'

Garvin made a face at Penwyth.

'How about *that* shit? Forsook and forlorn by my best
comrade.'

'Doesn't bother me in the slightest,' Erik said. 'No one
ought to do what she or he hasn't the inclination.'

Garvin dug into his pocket. 'Here's two . . . three hundred each, children. Don't spend it all in one place.'

'Thanks, Father,' Njangu said.

'Don't thank me,' Garvin said piously. 'It's all to the
good — having too many people around who know me
cramps my style.'

The unobtrusive man followed them back to their hotel,
then found an alcove and took out a small com. He keyed
numbers. There was a click, and a woman's voice said
'Report.'

The man keyed a second set of numbers into the com's
built-in scrambler.

'They now wear civilian garb,' he said, and described
what the five were wearing. 'No attempt made to communicate with anyone. I tried to get close to them in the
bar, but all I could hear was they were talking about the
Force. I don't know if it's important, but they were talking

about military things I don't think an average soldier would know about.'

'Was there any indication on what they hoped to achieve with that carefully planned rescue of that child of ours?' the woman's voice asked.

'Negative,' the man said.

'Continue surveillance, but take no other action,' the listener ordered.

'Understood.'

Ton Milot had stubbornly insisted on changing back into uniform before they caught the 'rail over the mountains.

'Twenty percent discount for people in uniform,' he said. 'Plus my folks'll be pissed if I'm not looking purty.'

'If they expect purty,' Angie said, 'we better bring along a plastic surgeon,' but she and Njangu had done the same.

'We've got half an hour 'til the pod goes,' Milot said. 'I called my folks and told them we were incoming.'

'Yeh,' Njangu said absently, staring at the glass window of a shop.

'Entranced by his own reflection,' Angie said. 'That's okay, 'cause he is pretty.' She squeezed his arm.

'Pass on pretty,' Yoshitaro said. 'Don't look back, but check our reflection in this next window.'

'Definitely three good-lookin' sorts,' Milot said.

'With a tail,' Njangu said. 'See that little guy back there . . . no, goddammit, don't look!'

'Looks like not much of anybody,' Milot said.

'Good beaks don't,' Njangu said.

'You're being paranoid.'

'He was with us the last two turnings,' Yoshitaro said. 'I'm paranoid.'

'Who cares? We've got nothing to hide,' Milot said.

'I *always* do,' Njangu said.

'So what do we do? Dry-gulch him?' Angie asked. 'If he's copper, we'll get our butts in a tangle.'

'No. We'll turn right here, and go down this block,' and the two obeyed him. 'Cut in this store, then we'll go back out the other entrance. Come on now! Run!'

The three darted around a corner. A moment later, the unobtrusive man appeared, looked about, muttered under his breath, went into a doorway, and dialed numbers on his com. When the ringing stopped, he said, 'Three-one-one-five.'

'Listening,' the woman's voice said.

'I still don't know what they are,' the man reported. 'But they lost me, very neatly.'

'They're professional?'

'Looks like it.'

'Go back to the hotel,' the voice ordered. 'There's still two of them there. Team with Lompa, and this time *stay with them*!'

'There'll be no more surprises,' the man said grimly.

SIXTEEN

The silver monorails arced across the city, the center of the spiderweb a hangarlike stone building. The pod for Issus slid out of the station's roof and the track climbed. Njangu saw the broad lawns around PlanGov Headquarters, then the Eckmuhl, the walled 'Raum quarter with its high-rising, shabby apartments leaning together, about to tumble into the narrow, winding streets.

The rail climbed the bluffs on nickeled pylons, passing close to the wealthy enclave of the Heights. Angie chattered away about the great mansions and the beautiful gardens. Njangu wondered for an instant why, if she were so fascinated by this wealth, she hadn't wanted to go to the party tonight, somewhere down there.

Then he went back to worrying about that follower. *Who? Some friend of the idiots we gave lumps to? Not likely — if they'd been able to find out where Njangu and Company were staying, they might've gotten twenty other yutzes and lurked in an alley. But just trailing us? No. Who else? Coppers? But why? The police could give a shit if a few waterfront goons get their body structure readjusted.*

Military Intelligence? Njangu assumed, without any reason, the Force had spies. But he'd done nothing wrong, at least on this world. *What about the others? Ton*

Milot? Fishing without a license? Angie Rada? For being oversexed? Balls. Which leaves . . . leaves nobody. At least nobody I can think of.

Njangu let it swirl around his brain once more, then dismissed the matter and looked out and down lush jungles, wondering what was hidden under the canopy, realized he'd no doubt find out shortly, either in the war games or the real patrols I&R ran against the bandits.

Njangu leaned back, and Angie put her head on his shoulder. That sparked another curiosity. Why hadn't they just stayed in their hotel room if they hadn't wanted to go to Erik's friend's party? Angie certainly was an interesting enough pastime. That *had* been a third option. Why hadn't she suggested that? Did she think, maybe, Njangu wouldn't have been interested. Why hadn't *he* come up with the idea? Screwing was better than fishing from any perspective.

Oh well, he thought. *Nobody's dumber than a soldier. Of any sex.*

'Good gods,' Njangu shouted, leaning close to Ton Milot, 'did you tell them you'd been made commander of the fleet or something?'

'We're pretty patriotic,' Milot shouted, and the band broke into another ragged but enthusiastic march. A very pretty girl, about two years younger than Milot, with brown wavy hair, clung to the soldier's waist like a limpet. She'd been introduced as Lupul.

'Isn't that the national anthem again?' Angie asked.

'I think so, so maybe we better stand up,' Njangu said. They did, weaving just a little bit.

Issus sat around a nearly enclosed bay, on a low cliff twenty meters above the water and docks. The houses were hardly Angie's remembered 'huts,' but simple wood-framed shelters with sharp angled roofs. The

center of the town was a turf-paved square with businesses, the monorail station, and the town hall around
it. Njangu guessed it was some sort of D-Cumbre
custom to put a park in the town center, and thoroughly
approved.

It seemed every one of the village's two-thousand-odd
people were packed into the square, cheering their son
who'd made good.

'Yeh,' Njangu agreed. 'Patriotic. Pass the jug.'

'Better not,' Ton warned.

'Why not? Everybody's a *lot* drunker'n we are.'

'Yeh,' Ton said. 'But they ain't going fishing. We are.'

'What's this *we* shit?' Angie said, grabbing a passing
flask and inhaling the clear, slightly oily-tasting local
distillation with enthusiasm. 'You got a midget in your
pocket?'

'You don't have to,' Milot said, 'if you want to play the
old weak, feeble, helpless woman excuse.'

'Uh-uh,' Angie said. 'I'm no dummy. Water's fine for
a bathtub, but there's waaaaaaaaaay too much of it out
there for me. You big bwave men go into the vasty
deeps.' She fluttered her eyebrows. 'I'll stay here and
worry myself drunk.'

'Any possibility I could get away with the same line?'
Njangu tried.

'Not a chance,' Milot said. 'I've got to prove that I
haven't forgotten my roots, and you've got to prove your
worthiness to be honored by Issus. First we fish, then we
come back and there'll be a big celebration.'

'What do you call this?' Njangu asked, waving a hand
at the crowd.

'Just warming up,' Milot said.

'And what're we fishing for, anyway? It's getting
dark.'

'We're going after *barraco*,' Milot said. 'They're big,

nasty mothers, carnivorous, that'll go about, oh, eighty kilos or so. We harpoon 'em.'

'Are they good eating?'

'The best.'

'What do they think about us?'

'The best.'

'Whyn't we think about something a little smaller . . . and, maybe, safer,' Njangu suggested.

'Don't worry,' Milot said. 'I'll be the one with the harpoon.'

'What do I do? Hold your hat?'

'Nope. You'll be bait.'

Milot wasn't being funny. Njangu Yoshitaro clung precariously to the pulpit railing, gently moving a lantern back and forth, while the lifter floated slowly just above the calm, phosphorescent sea. Ton Milot was beside him, a long, barbed spear roped to floats in one hand. Alei, Milot's brother, was at the controls of the lifter.

Neither soldier wore his uniform, only a singlet and ragged shorts.

There were twelve other fishing craft out, lights gleaming, reflecting in flashing lines across the water. Behind them were the lights of Issus.

'Movement,' Ton warned. 'Move the lantern around some more, like you' re a worried bird with a flashlight up its butt.'

'Why?' Njangu said. 'I'm real happy with him staying down there.'

'Don't you want dinner?'

'Sure,' Yoshitaro said. 'A nice, yummy piece of fruit'll suit me just—'

He jumped as a slender silver arrow, teeth gleaming, came out of the water at him.

'Shit!' Njangu shouted, as Milot hurled the spear into

the monster's mouth. He staggered back, flailing for the railing, and toppled overboard. As he hit the water, something landed on top of him, something cold, smooth, and deadly. He kicked wildly, and the *barraco* hit him with his tail, and was gone. Njangu dived deep, kicking hard, then ran out of air and went for the surface. The lifter was about five meters away, and between him and it the *barraco* thrashed in its death agonies.

Milot and his brother clung to the lifter's safety cage, roaring with laughter.

'Would you two idiots get me out of this,' Njangu shouted. 'The son of a bitch might have a big brother.'

'Sure, sure,' Alei called. 'Maybe there is a big brother, and we leave you in there to bring him up, eh? You're the best bait we've ever had.'

'I'm going to kill someone,' Njangu promised, treading water, afraid to look into the dark depths below. 'And I'm not particular who.'

'Damn,' Garvin said, eyeing the long line of sleek lims. 'I didn't know there was this much money in the whole friggin' Cumbre system.'

'Best believe it,' Erik said. 'Mines are pure gold, even if they don't mine gold.'

'Now there's something we didn't talk about,' Garvin said, as they strolled toward the mansion's gates. 'If we're cut off from the Confederation, who's gonna buy the minerals? Isn't all this geetus on thin ice?'

'Cumbre uses a lot of what it digs out,' Erik said. 'And the Musth'll buy anything that comes out of the ground to take back to their own worlds. They don't give a rat's earlobe whether it's dug by their own people or by the 'Raum. This is secure wealth, m'friend. We'll get by.'

'Evening, Mister Penwyth,' a uniformed security

woman said. Erik nodded, and they went up the broad steps.

'The Bampurs do have real money,' Garvin agreed. 'No stinkin' security 'bots here. And it's nice to be with somebody they know.'

'What, automation?' Erik pretended horror. 'When there's always a lower-class flunky or a 'Raum to be hired? If we elite bassids started usin' robots, who'd steal from us and blackmail our fool asses when they caught us in bed with somebody we shouldn't be there with?'

'Careful, Striker,' Garvin said. 'You're startin' to sound like a revolutionary.'

They went through the portico of the Bampur estate. Garvin thought he was still in the open air, and the columns on either side of him stood alone, then realized they supported a long, curving roof exactly matching the sky above.

'Clever, that,' Erik said. 'In day, it looks just like daytime, at night, well, you can see for yourself.'

'Why'd the Bampurs go to the trouble?'

'Guess they don't like rain,' Erik guessed. 'Besides, the Rentiers – the very rich – aren't as you and I, remember?'

'Thought you were rich.'

'Not *this* rich.'

'So how are they different?' Garvin asked. 'Never had the opportunity to be around rich-rich much.'

Erik leaned close, and whispered: 'They find *really* dumb ways to spend their credits.'

The columned walk curved down a gentle slope to a lake, with a mansion in the middle, on an island.

A covered causeway led across the water. A man crawled along the causeway toward them. 'I'm a fish,' he explained. 'Crawlin' up . . . hic . . . stream t'spawn.'

'Did we maybe get here a little late?' Garvin asked.

'Nope. If we were late, good old Raenssler'd not even be movin'.'

'I see. Nice layout here,' Garvin said.

'When the Bampurs feel private,' Erik said, 'they roll up the carpet and you've got to hail a boat to go a-calling.'

'Clever, I suppose.'

'I suppose. Ah-hah,' Erik said. 'I knew Jasith wouldn't steer us wrong. Listen. The band sounds drunk, so the party must be starting to catch fire.'

Garvin listened, nodded. 'Nobody could be that bad sober.'

They went into the mansion's central room. It was huge, open on all sides with a twenty-meter-high domed ceiling. There were big now-raised storm curtains to let down in bad weather. Corridors spidered off here and there to other parts of the house.

The party was a swirl of people, some dancing, some drinking, some doing both, badly and well. Here a man sat staring at a holo of ballet dancers, sobbing bitterly, there a man leaned against a bronze life-size statue of an Earth mermaid, whispering his life's story into its sympathetic ear.

Garvin tried to look cosmopolitan, but it was hard. Not only were there three bars around the room, but each had four bartenders. Human bartenders. Even more exotic were the human servitors, more than twenty of them in white coats. The Bampurs had a *lot* of money.

He wondered wistfully if there was any way he could get his hands on some of it, then forgot that, seeing the dark-eyed small woman who darted up to Erik. Jasith Mellusin wore a quite incredible outfit – a black form-fitting floor-length asymmetric gown made even more immodest by missing side panels. The dress was held in place by large silver five-centimeter clips from mid-thigh to under her arm. She clearly wore nothing underneath it.

'You didn't forget me!'

Eric kissed her. 'How could I? And I'm right on time, Jasith, as you told me to be. Have I missed anything?'

'Two or three fights . . . a couple of people went swimming . . . one proposal of marriage . . . three engagements broken. Very, very slow so far.'

'What could we do to enliven things?' Erik asked. 'By the way, this is my fellow defender of freedom. Jasith Mellusin, Garvin Jaansma.'

Jasith evaluated the tall blond. 'Are you with someone?'

'Just him,' Garvin said, indicating Erik, 'and he's no fun. He leads.'

'Erik, I think you just enlivened my evening,' Jasith said in her throaty near whisper. She linked her arm through Garvin's. 'Do you dance?'

'Like an angel,' Garvin assured her.

'What's an angel?'

Garvin grinned sharkishly. 'You and I are going to get along very, very well.' He bowed to Erik. 'Thank you for the introduction, m'lad, and I believe we'll circulate.'

He moved Jasith toward the center of the floor, extended his arms just as the two bands, in exceptionally ragged nonsynchronization, broke into a new number.

'Oh,' Jasith said in disappointment. 'This is that new dance . . . well, I guess it wouldn't be new to you, 'cause it came out from Centrum a couple of years ago, so it's old journoh by now. Anyway, I don't know the steps.'

Garvin thought of telling Jasith the deep, thorough knowledge he'd gained of the Confederation capital's recreational tastes in three weeks in the recruit reception depot mainly spent cleaning 'freshers, decided there wasn't any point in spoiling the woman's fondest beliefs.

He was about to ask if he could get her a drink when he caught the tune's rhythm line.

'Hell,' he said, 'this one is easy. I'll show you.' He drew her out onto the dance floor. 'It's all flash,' he explained. 'Keep about, oh, five or six centimeters between us, hold your hand up like this, I put one hand around your waist, and it's step to the side, to the side, back, back, to the side, to the side, and so forth. Every tenth measure or so I put pressure on your waist, and you spin using your hand as a pivot . . . that's right. Then turn back . . . see, you've got it.'

Jasith, pink tongue clenched between her teeth, concentrated on her movements for a time, then looked up at Garvin. 'You're a very good dancer. Where'd you learn?'

Garvin smiled wryly, remembering a handsome man and a gorgeous woman, dressed in archaic formality, turning in a spotlighted ring, with hundreds of people cheering.

'In a circus,' he said.

Another memory came – an old-fashioned tarred tent. roaring in flames, screams, howls of fire lifters and a small boy, sitting in ashes, crying for the world that had just died around him. He pushed the thought away.

Jasith laughed.

'Sure. A circus. And you were the, what did they call it, master of the ring?'

'Ringmaster, actually. But that was a long time afterward.'

'Oh, come on,' she said. 'I'm not that foolish. You're not old enough to have done that.'

'If you say so,' Garvin said. 'But I look a lot older with my hair dyed black, a phony pencil-line moustache, and a top hat.'

'Oh, stop! You know I'm not going to believe you. So what's the new dance on Centrum?'

'It's very interesting,' Garvin said. 'First, you tie your

arms together at the wrists, both men and women. Then you loop your hands over the other person's neck.'

'That sounds romantic,' Jasith said.

'Oh, 'tis, it truly is,' Garvin agreed. 'When the music starts you prance backward and forward, four steps, while shouting "Ha! Hoo!" at the end of each sequence. Oh yeh. And everybody's naked.'

'You took it too far,' she said. 'I almost was believing you.'

'That's the story of my life,' Garvin agreed, as the music stopped for a minute, then became a syrupy ballad. 'Here's another new style,' Garvin said, and took her in his arms, holding her close.

'It's nice,' she breathed into his ear.

'So are you,' Garvin said, feeling a little drunk without having had anything at all to drink, her sleekness warm and giving against him. 'Your hair smells like a soft tropical night, with the wind whispering through it.'

'Maybe you *did* work for a circus,' Jasith said. 'You sure can use the words.'

'Ah, milady, when you're poor and in love with someone far above you, words are your only help,' Garvin said.

'Only?'

'Well,' Garvin said, 'the only ones you can use on a dance floor.'

'I'm not going to ask,' Jasith said. 'Because if I did, I'll bet you were going to say something dirty.'

'Not me,' Garvin protested, 'for I'm as pure as . . . as . . . as what?'

'Flower petals?' Jasith suggested.

'Flower petals,' Garvin agreed. 'And I'd like to take you in my arms, put you down on a carpet of them, and then lie down at your side.'

'Careful,' Jasith warned. 'I think I know what comes next.'

'I put nine meters of tongue in your ear and drill for uranium?' Garvin said.

Jasith giggled. 'That's enough, silly.'

'That's only a beginning,' Garvin said, and the music came to a halt. 'Now we both deserve a drink.'

They walked off the dance floor. Garvin stopped to admire a fountain, brass cups of various sizes and shapes, each cascading water down into the next with a soft tinkling sound like half-heard bells. A dozen people, mostly men, were gathered around it, listening to a darkly handsome man a few years older than Garvin, who sat on the banquette around the fountain.

'Of *course* there's a supreme being, Jermy.'

Jermy, a man very bald for his years, shook his head vigorously, a smile on his lips.

'Prove it, Loy.'

'Quite easily,' the other man said. 'If there is no god, put him or her in upper case if you choose, then all would be chaos.'

'Not necessarily,' Jermy said. 'Natural order. Evolution and that.'

'Fiddle,' Loy said. 'Nothing happens accidentally, or quote naturally end quote. Show me an example of natural order ... which you needn't bother trying, for there's none.'

'Better, since you're the one trying to make a point,' Jermy said. 'You give me an example of your god-dictated system that shows things are always as they ought to be.'

'Easily. Look about you. We freely concede the 'Raum are a distinctly lesser class and, I believe, race as well, correct?'

Garvin's skin crawled as he heard too many murmurs of agreement.

'Therefore, they must function in a lesser capacity. Do

you think it's chance that our servitors are 'Raum, fitting quite comfortably into their meniality? You'd hardly expect to see one of them on the dance floor or standing with us, would you? We are their superiors, of course, so therefore they are content with their god-ordered role as servants, whether it's working in the mines or' – Loy held his empty glass out to a nearby white-clad man – 'getting me another drink.'

The man, old enough to be Loy's father, bowed and took the glass, expression blank. As he turned away, his eyes met Garvin's, and the soldier noted the hard glitter.

'Yet another example—' The handsome young man yelped in surprise as water cascaded down his back. He whirled, to see Garvin, looking ostentatiously aghast, moving one of the brass cups, so the water fell into it once more.

'My apologies,' Garvin said. 'My hand must've conflicted with the natural order.'

The man came to his feet, flushing in anger. Garvin smiled, a tight, unpleasant smile. His hands curled, lifted, his left foot slid out and he centered himself, then semi-crouched.

Loy hesitated.

Jasith hissed, 'Men!' and flounced away.

Garvin waited, but Loy didn't move. Garvin ducked his head in dismissal, and went after Jasith.

He found her outside the great room, at the edge of the lake staring out at the night. 'Hey.'

She didn't move.

'Hey, beautiful,' he tried again.

She spun. 'Why do you men have to do things like that? You and your damned testosterone!'

'The crap that idiot was spouting needed interruption,' Garvin said. 'And I've learned you can never argue with a bigot. Nothing testerone about that.'

'What bigot? Loy Kuoro's well educated and a good friend of mine! His father's publisher of *Matin*, and he'll take over the holo in a few years. He's *very* clever.'

'Okay,' Garvin said equably. 'He's a very clever asshole. But do I have to like him to be permitted to think *you're* wonderful?'

Jasith hesitated, then shook her head. 'No. But . . . but you can't behave that way.'

'What do I know?' Garvin said. 'I'm just a simple soldier, with simple desires.'

Jasith looked skeptical.

'Sometimes they overwhelm me,' he said. 'For instance, with the moonlight behind you, I've got an overwhelming desire to kiss you.'

'You can't—' Her protest was muffled by his lips. The kiss lasted quite a long time. Eventually she drew back. 'Oh dear,' she said. 'I've never been kissed like that that I remember.'

'You sure?' Garvin asked.

'No. Maybe you should do it again,' she said. He did.

'My,' she said softly, melting closer. Garvin slid his hand through the gap in her dress, cupped, stroked her hips, then her naked buttocks. He slid a finger between them, caressed her. She murmured wordlessly, breath coming more quickly as her tongue curled around Garvin's.

'Should we think about finding a nice, soft pile of flowers?' he whispered.

'We can't,' she said sadly.

'Why not?'

'The Bampurs put alarms everywhere, and I don't want a scandal if people came running and found us . . . well, found us.'

''Kay, that's out,' Garvin said. 'How'd you come here?'

'I brought my lifter.'

'Well?'

'It's a little two-seater. We'd never be able to . . . to be comfortable.'

'So let's go somewhere. I just happen to have a nice, luxurious hotel,' Garvin whispered. 'With a big soft bed, and nobody pays any attention to people's comings and goings.'

'Comings?' she whispered.

'Anywhere you want to,' he promised, and they kissed again. He brought his hand up, fondled her breasts, felt her rigid nipples.

'Hey,' a voice came. 'You. Shithead!'

Jasith squeaked in surprise, jumped back. Garvin turned, very quickly. Loy Kuoro stood, face angry, fists balled. Jaansma forced his mind away from Jasith.

'That was a shitty thing you did to me,' Kouro said.

'Those were some shitty things you were saying,' Garvin said reasonably. 'Especially in front of some people.'

'People? *Raum* people?' Kouro sneered.

'*Publishers?* People?' Garvin echoed in an equally nasty voice. 'I hear the only way you can breed is with your own sisters? Any truth to that?'

Jasith gasped, and Kouro turned white. Garvin had a moment to realize he'd touched on something explosive, and the man tried to kick him. Garvin stepped back, and the kick barely touched Garvin's jacket.

'Don't do that,' he said in a calm voice. Kouro stumbled, recovered, and Garvin realized the man was somewhat drunker than he appeared. He swung, and Garvin grabbed his hand, pulled, and Kouro stumbled forward, falling to his hands and knees.

'Go back inside and get yourself a drink,' Garvin suggested. 'You're pushing the framework.'

Kouro came to his knees, and lurched forward, head

down. He butted Garvin in the chest. Garvin almost fell, recovered.

'That's enough,' he said, still in the same mild tone, and slammed two straight forefist strikes into Kouro, the first into his eye, the second into his midsection. Kouro *whuffed*, puked staggered back, and teetered on the edge of the lake. Garvin reached out, pushed, and the man shouted surprise, windmilled his arms, and fell backwards into the lake, landing with a thoroughly satisfying splash.

Garvin Jaansma didn't bother seeing whether Kouro surfaced, saw Jasith was gone. Garvin swore, went after her, through the great room, along the causeway, and through the estate's entrance. He went down the steps in time to see a small, bright red lifter streak down the driveway.

'I should've killed him,' Garvin said, and went back, looking for Erik.

He couldn't find him anywhere. He looked at the crowd of utter strangers. 'No friends, no taxis. I think,' he said to himself, 'it's gonna be a long walk home.'

'Curious,' Jo Poynton mused. 'Most curious.'

The voice came again: 'Your instructions?'

Poynton keyed her mike: 'Stand by.'

She returned to her analysis: *A group of soldiers stops one of our children from being beaten. Odd. They then somehow have enough money for rooms in one of Leggett's most expensive hotels and outfit themselves in luxury. Even odder. Three of them then elude one of my most experienced agents and disappear. The other two attend a very exclusive party in the Heights, at the home of one of the most anti-'Raum swine. One is identified by an agent of ours, working as a waiter, as Erik Penwyth, whose family, while not the worst of the giptel, isn't considered an especially fervent supporter of our cause. He mysteriously joined the*

Confederation oppressors a short time ago, for no known reason.
Now his companion, name unknown, starts a fight over a minor
insult made by the giptel Kouro about the 'Raum. He then leaves
and is walking toward Leggett. All this is very unusual, and
we do not need unusual occurrences this close to Dawning Fury.

'I don't understand,' she said softly, looking around
her room in the depths of the Eckmuhl. Bare except for
three transceivers, it gave no answers. She thought of
trying to reach Comstock Brien or, perhaps better for his
fresh thinking, Jord'n Brooks. But there was no time,
and certainly she might have a better understanding of
the problem than they would, far distant in the hills.

She opened her mike. 'Is there traffic in your area?'

'Almost none.'

'Do you and Lompa think you could take him alive?
There must be no misunderstanding – alive or do not
make the attempt.'

'Wait.' Silence, then: 'Affirm. Lompa has a pacifier.'

'Take him then, before he leaves the Heights,'
Poynton ordered. 'Move him to a secluded area, and I'll
have a pickup craft ready to home on your signal.'

'Understood,' the voice said. 'Stand by.'

Poynton picked up another com. 'This is Watch
Control,' she ordered. 'Wake the alert team for action.'

'I forgive this *barraco*,' Njangu said in a noble tone,
trying to sound like Garvin Jaansma being pompous, 'for
trying to eat me, for I find the mother pretty goddamned
delicious.' He realized he was a little drunk, just loopy
enough for almost any silliness to sound like an excellent
idea. Njangu took another piece of grilled *barraco* from
the fire-warmed stone, put it on a disk of flat, unleavened
bread. He poured a dipper of fiery green sauce over it,
folded the top over, and took a huge bite.

'How many of those are you planning to eat?' Angie

asked him, speaking with the careful pronunciation of
the quite drunk.

'What do you care? I won't let it spoil my girlish
figure,' Njangu said.

'I don't want you to founder and not be able to . . .
take care of other things.'

'The day that happens,' Njangu promised, 'is the day
the heavens crumble.'

'Yeesh,'Angie said. 'Ego!'

There were five of them lying on mats around the
small fire — Ton Milot; his girlfriend, Lupul; Njangu;
Angie, who lay curled with her head on Njangu's ankles;
and a slender, large-breasted girl about sixteen named
Deira, with tied-back dark red hair, a slow smile, and lips
Njangu didn't want to think about kissing. She wore
only a wrap, tucked in above her breasts, and insisted on
showing far too much of her upper thigh to Yoshitaro.

'Men're all like that, aren't they?' Lupul said.

''Cept for me,' Ton Milot said. 'I'm perfect.' He
belched loudly. 'Wanna see?'

'It is about that time,' Lupul said, getting up. She tot-
tered a little. 'Wups. Earthquake season, I guess.'

Ton Milot clambered to his feet and stood, grinning
foolishly. He looked down the beach, where two or three
dozen fires guttered down. There were shadows around
them, some sitting, talking; others dancing slowly to
their own music; others on the sand, moving, twined;
still others motionless, paired or alone. 'Looks like
things're trickling down to the last hardcases,' he said.
'Guess I'll see you sometime after the sun comes up.'

'Would you come on,' Lupul said. 'You see these guys
every damned day, not me.'

'Coming, dear.' He followed her into darkness.

'So now it's just us,' Njangu said. He bent over, and
kissed Angie.

'Well,' she said. 'Not quite. There's Deira. She's locked, loaded, and ready.'

The girl giggled.

'Ready for what?' Njangu asked.

'Show him,' Angie said.

Deira stood, unfastened the tie, shook her head and let her red hair cascade down almost to her waist. She walked slowly around the fire until she bestrode Njangu, pulled the tie on her wrapper, let it drop. Her body was shaved clean.

'Don't you like these colorful local practices?' Angie asked.

'Uhhh,' Njangu managed.

'She came over,' Angie said calmly, 'while you were fishing, and told Lupul she thought you were very handsome, and wanted to know what our customs were, since she guessed I was already with you. She told Lupul that she thought I was handsome, too, and wondered what I thought of her. I said I thought she was pretty, and that I wouldn't mind if she wanted to kiss me. So we did. She's a very good kisser. And she does . . . other things real nice, too. We borrowed one of the huts while we were waiting for you.'

Njangu realized his mouth was dry.

'Well,' Angie said reasonably, 'she's awfully pretty, isn't she?'

'Uhh . . . yes.'

'Can I kiss him?' Deira asked.

'Sure,' Angie said, and laughed.

Deira knelt, and pushed Njangu gently down onto his back. She lowered her body onto his, her mouth opening. Njangu felt her breasts hard against his bare chest. An eon or so later, Deira lifted her head. 'I do like him,' she said dreamily.

'So do I,' Angie said.

'Now I want to kiss you some more,' Deira said.

'That could happen,' Angie said. She unbuttoned her uniform blouse, took it off. Then she took off her shorts and briefs .

Njangu'd turned on his side, was watching. 'You don't act like this is a total shock,' Angie said.

Njangu smiled slightly, inclined his head, said nothing. The girls in his clique *had* done anything and everything they thought might shock the cits, with each other or the boys.

'You're wearing too much,' she said, and Njangu obediently slid out of his shorts.

Angie tube-rolled her shorts and tunic, put them down on the mat about a meter away from her.

'Come here, Deira,' she whispered. 'Next to me. Put your hips on my pants.'

The girl melted into Angie's arms. After a bit, Angie pushed on her head, and Deira kissed down Angie's neck, across her breasts and stomach. Angie lifted, parted her legs, gasped as Deira's fingers found her.

'Oh yes, oh good,' she sighed. 'Njangu, come here. I want you to bite me on my tits, my stomach. Then do it to Deira while she loves me. I promised her she could be first.'

Garvin guessed he was no more than fifteen minutes from the hotel, and making good time on the curving downhill road. He was singing quietly:

> *Oh don 't you remember*
> *Dumb Carvin from Altair*
> *Who'd screw up a sure thing*
> *No matter where.*
>
> *His mouth was a terror*
> *It never would mind*

He'd say something stupid
And then get kicked blind.

He went to a soiree
Just lookin' for fun
The women were friendly,
And hot as a gun.

The prettiest was Jasith—

He broke off, looking for a rhyme for Jasith, failed to find one. 'She sure was lovely,' he mourned. 'Nice and friendly and warm and—'

He heard the scrape, jumped sideways. The first man's sap came down, missed, and he tried to recover, staggering on a few footsteps. The second man had some kind of gun. He pointed it at Garvin, who ducked as the weapon hissed and something spat past, very close.

At the side of the road was a tall, straight-limbed bush. Garvin tore off a branch, held it across his chest like a fighting stave.

'Oh you poor bastards,' he said. 'You poor sorry bastards. Did you *ever* pick somebody in the wrong goddamned mood.'

The second man aimed his gun. Garvin darted to the side, raked the butt end of the branch across the sapman's face, who cried out and stumbled back. Without pausing, he snapped the branch's other end across the gunman's wrist, and the gun spun away, into the street. Garvin brought his knee up, smashed the branch across it. Now he held two clubs about 10cm in diameter and 50cm long.

'Let's play,' he said. The second man reached in a pocket for something. Garvin clubbed his forearm, then smashed the other club across the bridge of the man's nose. The man screamed, had both hands over his face. Garvin drove the club like a sword into his gut, kicked the man hard in the side of the head as he went down.

'Now for *your* young ass,' he said grimly. The first man was holding up his hand, whining, pleading. Garvin smashed him on the elbow with the club in his left hand. The man howled, clutched his wrist with his other hand. Jaansma snapped the club in his right into the man's face, heard teeth crack. He kicked the man in the stomach like he was driving a ball into the score zone, and the man whip-snapped, fell backward, lay motionless. Garvin stood over the two for a short time, breathing hard, waiting for movement. There wasn't any.

'Stupid goniffs,' he said. 'Rob a soldier, who's never got any goddamned money anyway.'

He looked up and down the road, saw no vehicles. He spotted the gun, picked it up, and examined it. *Some kind of knockout weapon*, he thought. *Nice and new-looking. Thieves don't normally carry trick shit like this I wouldn't think.*

He picked up one man by the hair, ignored his ruined face, sniffed his breath. *No alcohol.* The same was true of the other. *That's also a little unique.*

He went through their pockets, found two ID cards, pocketed them, continued searching. Both had some money and, interestingly, two identical expensive-looking coms fitted with scramblers.

'Hmm. Wish I were some kinda detective, so this shit'd make sense,' he muttered.

He considered calling the police, found himself grinning. *Njangu would beat my butt for even thinking that.* Besides, they'd keep him up the rest of the night with stupid questions he had no answers for. He pocketed the coms, the money, and the ID cards, and trotted away, toward Leggett.

*

Half an hour later, he saw the lights of the Shelburne ahead. A woman came out of the shadows.

'Morning, sister,' he greeted. 'Up late, aren't you?'

'Looking for a good time, I am,' she said. 'You interested? Half price, and you can stay 'til you wake up?'

'No thanks.'

'You one of those who like boys?' the whore asked, not insultingly.

'Nope,' Garvin Jaansma said, thinking of Jasith Mellusin, and her melting lips. 'Just stupid.'

SEVENTEEN

''Kay, troops,' *Alt* Hedley told the company. 'Break ranks and gather around this tippy-top-secret map and hear the good skinny.' The men and women of Intelligence and Reconnaissance Company obeyed. 'First,' Hedley said, 'let's welcome the new fools. Monique's shattered 'em so much they actually want to flipping join us. Tsk.'

Njangu caught Penwyth's eye, grinned. They'd managed to get into Petr Kipchak's Gamma Team, First Troop. Ton Milot was in Alpha of the First, Hank Faull went to Vic Team, Second Troop, and Angie was in Eta Team, Second. Njangu was not unhappy Rada wasn't in his team. The rest of their graduation leave had been mostly spent in Issus with Deira. Njangu'd taken Ton Milot aside, and told him what'd happened, and asked if he was about to get in trouble with anybody in the village.

Milot laughed. 'Not here, my friend. We figure what people do is what they do. Everybody knows Deira's a wild one.' He looked wistful. 'She and I got friendly a couple of times, back before I joined up, and I asked Lupul if she'd mind if Deira stayed with us. Lupul said she'd cut off my whacker, because if that happened, I'd never have any energy for fishing. So don't worry and have fun.'

The three had . . . or so Njangu thought. He was starting to wonder if, indeed, all great things happen in a city. But at the end of the leave, Angie confronted him. 'Look,' she said. 'When we get back . . . I sleep alone. There's nothing between us.'

'I know that,' Njangu said. 'Screwing and work don't mix.'

'Good,' Angie said. She acted like she was angry. 'And don't be talking about anything else.'

'Like what?'

'Like what happened with Deira.'

'But Ton Milot knows . . .' Njangu said, puzzled, then stopped, seeing Angie's lips compress. ''Kay. I'm not much into giving away family secrets.'

'Best not,' she said, and started packing. And that appeared to be that. Njangu tried to forget about it.

''Kay,' Hedley said. 'War games in four days, right? Everything's a flipping secret, right?' Somebody snickered. 'Don't step on my lines,' Hedley warned. 'You could end up humping a sackful of rocks up and down the company area.

'Anyway, first thing is that we're going to be the aggressors, as usual. Plus they've detailed off First and Second Company, Third Regiment to play bad guys with us. We'll also get a couple of Zhukovs and half a dozen Griersons. They're looking for volunteer armor crews right now.

'Needless to say, what I'm gonna give you now is flipping classified, and not to be talked about outside the company, 'cause we're not supposed to know any of this.'

He pulled the cover off the map. Njangu recognized it as the mountainous center of Dharma Island, with the outskirts of Leggett at the far left-hand side. There were arrows drawn here and there. A woman wearing the slashes of a *tweg* groaned.

'You recognize it, eh?' Hedley asked, amused.

'Yessir,' the woman said. 'Same turf as . . . three years ago, isn't it?'

'Sure is,' Hedley said, sounding delighted. 'Same flipping scenario, too.'

He touched the first arrow. 'The general scheme is that the Strike Force is going to make an in-atmosphere landing here, about thirty kilometers east of Leggett, against an entrenched enemy – us. They'll drive us north, flipping killers that they are, to here, right at the foot of Mount Najim, where we'll regroup.

'Strike Force Swift Lance will then make a final assault on our positions, and we, instead of retreating farther east into the Highlands like sensible flipping folks, will let ourselves be driven up to about here, close to the crest of Najim.

'There we make a suicidal last stand, and get wiped out and-slash-or captured, then the Task Force, meaning *Caud* Williams and the staff, will host a luncheon for PlanGov and the Rentiers, so all the fat cats'll have a chance to praise our lethal beauty.'

Monique Lir held up a hand.

'Go, Monique.'

'No offense, boss, but wouldn't it make more sense for the Strike Force to be the defenders against, say, attackers from offplanet? Like, maybe, Musth? Or against those pirates who ripped off the gear we were supposed to be getting.'

'You don't understand the big picture,' Hedley said gently. 'Attacking is a lot more romantic than sitting in a hole in the ground.'

'Shit,' Lir said.

Hedley shrugged. 'We weren't consulted any more'n usual. The way it'll work is the two companies of line animals'll take care of the digging and follow the scenario the staff wrote up. I&R's going to play the part of rotten behind-the-lines raiders, and stir about gently trying to create a commotion. One thing that'll help us a bit . . . the met folks are predicting the flipping rainy season'll dump on in early this year. Like tomorrow or the next day, so we'll have some nice nasty weather to hide in.'

There was laughter, and Njangu saw evil, anticipatory expressions.

'Study up on the map,' Hedley said, 'and start thinking of ways to screw with our noble brothers. The rules won't let us baddies win, of course. But I'd like for the white hats to know they've been meddled with.

'One other thing, and I'll personally flipping crucify anybody who ever says anything about it. It's a *real* jungle out there, and there's some folks who don't like soldier girls at all. Each man will carry one magazine of real rounds in his backpack, just in case. If by any chance those real poppers get confused with the blanks you'll be issued, all the gods had better have mercy on your ass, for I'll have none. And if anybody gets hit, I'll have you prosecuted for murder, and deny anybody in I&R ever saw a real round except on the range. That's all. Noncoms, take charge of your sections . . . dismissed.'

Hedley started toward the orderly room.

'Sir?' Kipchak called.

'What do you need, Petr?'

'A few minutes alone,' Kipchak said. 'Striker Yoshitaro's got something you might be interested in.'

'In with the both of you.'

'Njangu,' Petr said. 'Go get the stuff.'

The 'stuff' was the two coms, sap, knockout gun, and the ID cards Garvin had taken from his attackers. Garvin had told Njangu what'd happened, asked for suggestions. Should he call the police? Njangu, as expected, had sneered. Should he report it to his CO? Njangu asked Jaansma what he thought of the woman. Garvin hadn't much contact with *Cent* Haughton, but if the company first shirt, Malagash, was any indication, he wouldn't expect much. Njangu said *he* could turn it over to his CO, Hedley, who seemed to have intelligence both upper and lower case and see what happened.

''Kay,' Garvin said. 'But try to keep me out of it.'

'Why're you so touchy? You were just a handsome lad, attending an Utterly party in the Heights, and got skulked on.'

'*Caud* Williams said he didn't want to see my loverly face ever ever ever again,' Garvin said. 'I'm following orders.'

'You worry too much,' Njangu said. ''Kay. I'lll prob'ly have to tell Hedley who the poor sinned-against fool was, but I'll ask him to keep it QT.'

Hedley examined one of the coms. 'Nice, new . . . and it's a mate to the other one,' he said. 'Why would a common thief be carrying one of these, especially fitted with a scrambler? He'd dump it to a fence for his night's buzz. Plus a knockout-type shooter,' he went on, picking up the gun. 'Your friend's friends were nonviolent . . . or else they wanted a live body.'

'That's what I was wondering, sir,' Yoshitaro said.

'These two ID cards,' Hedley said. 'They're 'Raum.'

'How do you know, sir?' Kipchak asked.

'The Rentiers pushed a measure through their Council and then PlanGov about seven years ago that all 'Raum have a Y prefix on their ID numbers. Any notion that those gentle souls might be a leetle bigoted is a definite slander, ho-ho,' Hedley explained. 'But why would the 'Raum, even the baddies in the boonies, want some rear-rank striker for a prisoner? I think you'd better tell me about your friend.'

Njangu obeyed.

'Why didn't he call the cops? Most soldiers who get mugged holler in that general direction,' Hedley asked.

'He sort of thinks like I do, sir,' Njangu answered honestly. 'Police haven't been our friends for a whole lot of our lives.'

'Mmmh,' Hedley mused. 'And he wants to stay clean now. 'Kay, I'll do what I flipping can. I'm going to take this little story up to some people I trust in II Section, and also some folks in Policy and Analysis. That's the Planetary Police Intelligence, and they're almost half as good as they think they are. Ought to be, since they've had two hundred flipping years to get organized. You two can go back to work. Thanks for reporting this – it won't get pigeonholed, whatever the blazes a goddamned pigeon is.'

'A request, sir,' Njangu said. 'I'd like to tell my friend what you said. And you said something about needing volunteers with ACVs.'

'Your friend's on a Grierson?'

'He is. Third Platoon, A Company, Second Infantry. A gunner, sir.'

The lanky *alt* hesitated.

'His TC's a big bastard named Ben Dill,' Petr said.

'I know him . . . know of him anyway,' Hedley said. 'Bad attitude. Violent sort. About the size of a Zhukov. If he wasn't prejudiced against walking, he'd make a great I&R noncom. Good. Go get Dill's Pickles for us. We can always use another asshole.'

Striker Garvin Jaansma bounced into A Company's orderly room, stripped his fatigue cap off, and stood attention, dripping a bit of transmission oil on the freshly waxed floor. There was no one in the orderly room except the company clerk, a snotty little *finf* named Calmahoy. 'The CO wants to see you,' he said.

'That's what *Tweg* Ric told me,' Garvin said.

'She's in her office. Knock first.'

Garvin marched across the room, counting his sins, and rapped in a businesslike manner.

'Come in.'

It wasn't true that *Cent* Dian Haughton ironed military creases in her brassiere every night, but it should've been. She was all army, from her closely cropped hair to her perfect posture to her immaculate uniform. Nobody knew how good or bad an officer she was, for in the three months she'd been in charge of A Company she ran things through her efficient bully of a first *tweg*, Malagash. Garvin threw her his best salute, stood at rigid attention, suddenly aware of the microcalipers and circuit reader sticking out of his coverall pocket.

'At ease,' Haughton said. 'You know what the company policy is for taking personal coms during work hours?'

'Yes'm,' Garvin said. 'You don't.'

'And your friends aren't supposed to call, either.'

'No ma'am,' he agreed.

She handed him two pink message slips. 'Read them.'

Garvin wondered who might've – and then his eyebrows crawled toward the ceiling. The first was from a 'Jaseeth Mellusin,' the second from a Loy Kouro.

'Your business is your business,' Haughton said. 'But if I might, I' d like to ask a couple of questions.'

'Yes ma'am.'

'Is this Mellusin any relation to the mining family?'

'Yes ma'am.'

'Hmmph. And therefore this Loy Kouro's connected to the holo *Matin*?'

'He is.'

'Friends of yours?'

'One . . . I hope is,' Garvin said. 'I think the other's more of an enemy.'

'For a brand-new striker,' Haughton said, 'you certainly travel in interesting circles.'

'Do you think so, ma'am?' Garvin's voice was neutral, his expression bland. Haughton waited until she realized Jaansma wasn't going to elaborate. She grunted.

'Very well. You have my permission to return the calls now. Use the executive officer's office. The blue com goes directly off camp, so you'll have privacy.'

'Thank you, ma'am.'

Haughton looked him up and down. 'I'll be very interested in your progress, Striker. Dismissed.'

'This is Jasith,' the throaty whisper came.

'This is Garvin Jaansma. I'm the—'

'Soldier,' she interrupted. 'I hadn't had hardly anything to sniff or drink, so I remember everything.'

'I guess I owe you an apology,' Garvin started.

'No,' Jasith said. 'I called to tell you I was sorry. I'd had a fight with Daddy before I came, about how I was lazy and not willing to work and not worthy of being a Mellusin, and I was just in a perfectly foul mood, and trying to pretend I wasn't.

'So when you and Loy started fighting, I'm afraid it struck me wrong, and I just made an ass of myself. I'm sorry, Garvin.'

'No,' Garvin said. 'I'm sorry. I should've learned to control my big mouth and my temper by now.'

'And things were going . . . just so nicely,' Jasith whispered. 'I remember your kisses.'

'I remember some other things.'

'Like a big bed of flower petals?'

Garvin found himself breathing a little hard. 'Something like that.'

'If you let me . . . if you want . . . maybe there'll be a next time sometime.'

'I'd like that,' Garvin said.

'I know you've got those stupid war games in four days,' Jasith said. 'Daddy and everybody else are going to go watch their end, up on Mount Najim. After they get finished, will they give you a leave?'

'Probably.'

'You have my number,' she said. 'I'll keep my com with me everywhere. Please call me.'

'I promise.'

He heard a smack – a kiss? – and the line went dead.

'I *shall* be dipped,' Garvin said in some astonishment, and dialed the second number.

'*Matin* publisher's office,' a female voice cooed. 'How may I assist you?'

'This is Striker Garvin Jaansma, A Company, Second Infantry Regiment, Strike Force Swift Lance, returning Loy Kouro's com.'

'Please stand by.'

A moment later: 'This is Loy Kouro. I called to apologize for starting a fight with you at Bampur's party the other night.'

I'll be dipped and dunked, Garvin thought. 'That's all right,' he said amiably. 'It wasn't much of a fight.'

The voice became a trifle frosty. 'I hope I didn't injure you or anything.'

'Nope,' Garvin said. 'You missed clean, then decided to go swimming.'

'Perhaps the next time we meet,' Kouro said after a moment, 'you'll allow me to buy you a drink.'

''Fraid not,' Garvin said cheerily. 'I only drink with my equals.'

There was a hiss of anger, then the line went dead. Garvin turned the com off, went out. *Cent* Haughton was standing over Calmahoy's desk, pretending to read a sheaf of orders.

'Thank you, ma'am,' Garvin said. 'I appreciate the favor.'

Haughton looked at him closely. Jaansma had spoken as if she were his equal. She wondered for an instant if perhaps he was, then just who Jaansma really was. He went to the door, put his cap on, and left.

Haughton stared after him, then saw something: 'Calmahoy, look at that oil! This is an orderly room, not a hogwallow! Get a mop and clean that up!'

'So my fame travels,' Ben Dill said. 'An asshole, hmm?'

'That's what Alt Hedley said to tell you,' Njangu said, glancing surreptitiously around for something large and heavy to lay Dill out with when he exploded. The only thing suitable was the Grierson the *dec* was standing next to. Yoshitaro decided on flight. Instead, the huge man bellowed laughter.

'Asshole Ben, eh? 'Kay, that's what it is.' He beat on the Grierson's armor with a fist. 'Unass the sardine can, folks. We're gonna have a small discussion about volunteering before we go and do something stupid like volunteering.'

'A question,' Garvin asked Dill, as they carefully reassembled one of the Grierson's chainguns.

'Ask and ye shall receive,' Ben said.

'I&R is the ground-pounding scouts, right? And Mobile Scout Troop does the same thing, but with vehicles.'

'Veddy basic.'

'Howcum I&R plays bad guy, and MST sticks with the main force? Wouldn't it be more like what'd actually happen for anybody we'd fight, other than bandits, to have a real air capability?'

'Excellent question,' Dill said. 'First, the guy who

plays aggressor in any war game shouldn't be very good, because if he does something outrageous like beat the butt of his CO, guess what'll happen come promotion time? *Alt* Hedley of I&R doesn't give a shit about making rank by kissing ass, so he thinks it's a hoot to be the bad guy. *Cent* Liskeard, of Mobile, does . . . and you notice he outranks Hedley, even though both job slots call for a *cent*.

'You also notice nobody talks about real fighting, like going after the 'Raum in the hills, because nobody outside Hedley and some other blood-drinkers want to dirty their hands shooting at folks who might be women, children, and general backstabbers who look like everybody else.

'Smart folks . . . that is, those who're careerists on the brown highway, don't think playing aggressor is a treat either. That's why the two companies that're helping I&R were ordered, not volunteered. You don't think their canny COs went and stuck their paw in the garbage grinder of their own accord, now do you? See why you never want to be an ossifer an' gruntleman, young Garvin?'

EIGHTEEN

Twenty men and women were lined up in the clearing. Jord'n Brooks stood in front of them, and, to one side was Jo Poynton and Comstock Brien. 'I greet you, brothers and sisters,' he said, 'warriors all, and am proud of you for volunteering for this vital mission the Planning Group has honored me to lead. One day, when we 'Raum seize D-Cumbre and reach for the system and then the stars, people will look back and say, "Here was when it began," "Here were the heroes who began the freeing of our race, our people, our culture."'

His voice rose.

'This is the beginning of the end for our enemies, the Rentiers, and for all those in the Universe who doubt our truth.

'Take up the packs and weapons you see in front of you. There are instructions inside. Read them, memorize them, and then we shall begin rehearsing for action. Our Task will be a shining torch in the eyes of men and women everywhere, a torch for freedom and liberty.'

The twenty cheered. Brooks stood very straight, eyes half-closed, listening.

NINETEEN

Chance Island rumbled as Swift Lance lifted away from
its base, climbing out toward the mouth of the bay. Five
kilometers above the ocean, the Force moved into a mas-
sive swirling formation, hundreds of Zhukovs, Griersons,
Cookes, almost seven thousand men. There were errors —
a dozen near collisions, half a dozen real ones. But casualties were light and most of the shattered ACVs were
able to land under their own power or emergency antigrav. A handful of crewmen took to their personal
droppers. Three of these malfunctioned, and two other
troops who'd managed to avoid mandatory swimming
lessons drowned in the bay. Then the Force went back to
sea level and accelerated to a safety-conscious 200km/h
for the assault. Simulated AA missiles took out thirty-
two of the ACVs as the Force approached land, then the
equally simulated missiles of the Zhukovs and air-support Griersons suppressed the missiles, and Strike Force
Swift Lance closed on the Landing Zone, just as the monsoon rains rolled across Dharma Island.

The assault was considered very successful by *Caud*
Williams, who disregarded his maneuver losses, saying
they were meaningless, and only due to the low speed
dictated by circumstances. He also paid no mind to the
nine percent of his assault craft who'd either aborted at

Camp Mahan or at lift; as well as the nearly one thousand men and women of the Force with 'other duties' that kept them out of the games.

The Aggressors, unimaginatively named Blue Force, had been out for twenty-four hours already. The two companies of Third Regiment anticipated the worst, and had been ready to spend the day digging and blasting out fighting positions. But the trenches and bunkers of four years earlier were still in decent shape, and all that was necessary was a little sandbagging here and there and rousting out the wildlife that'd colonized the sites.

'Just like camping when I was a kid,' one soldier said.

'Mebbe,' one said, hefting her weapon. 'But at least back then I had rubber-band guns to fight back with. A real weapon! A woman's weapon! Not this poppity-poppity-poppity goddamned Mark 21!'

'Shaddup and load yer blanks,' her teammate said.

The Strike Force Shrike battery hovered along a dirt road, movement hopefully concealed by tall overhead trees. The battery commander kept checking his SatPos, which insisted on telling him there was a turn just beyond his present position that'd let him swing north, find an open meadow, and prepare his missiles for 'firing' in support of the Swift Lance attack. The *cent*'s SatBox had been promising this turn for about two kilometers.

The road was mucky and getting worse as the rain drenched the Griersons, and the trees were close on either side of the column. He knew he was close to the Blue lines, but without Zhukov support dared not pop up above the trees and get a 'real-world' position by eyeball.

He grunted relief as they rounded a bend and saw the promised fork. Better yet, there was a grounded Cooke with Military Police stripes, and a smartly uniformed *dec* standing next to it.

'Set it down,' he ordered, 'we need a fix,' and his driver obeyed. The *cent* slid his hatch open, and the *dec* saluted. 'I think I'm a little misplaced,' the *cent* confessed.

'That's why they've got me out here,' the *dec* said. 'The map's pi-skewey, and you'll want to take the fork on the left.'

'Good,' the *cent* said in relief. 'My Box was telling me entirely different.'

'That's why we're here,' the *dec* said. The *cent* closed his hatch, glad to be out of the rain, and gave orders. The battery lifted, went slowly down the narrowing track.

Dec Monique Lir grinned wolfishly, jumped into the Cooke. 'Hook it on out of here,' she ordered. She keyed her com. 'Vara Seven, this is Sibyl Beta. Fire Mission.'

'This is Vara. Go.'

'This is Beta. Battery of Shrikes, from Marten up one, left two, target moving north, rate of movement approximately four kph.'

'This is Vara. We have indicators enough to fire. Shall we launch?'

'This is Beta. Negative. In about . . . oh, fifteen minutes them li'l suckers'll run out of road and pop up right in front of you, and you can blast 'em over open sights. Reverting fire control to you. Have fun. This is Beta, clear.' She turned to her driver. 'Let's go find a hilltop and watch the fireworks.'

Fifteen minutes later, the track petered out into the trees, and the cursing *cent* ordered his vehicles up into open air. They'd reset their course after getting a decent bearing.

'Fire,' the *alt* in charge of the Blue missile detachment five kilometers away ordered, then turned to an umpire. 'I call four dead Shrike Griersons.'

'Agreed,' the woman said. 'You wiped 'em out clean.'
She opened her com. 'Maneuver control, I have Swift
Lance casualties to report.'

The Griersons came across the Landing Zone in open
vees, Zhukovs giving simulated fire in support. Rear
ramps dropped, and infantrymen doubled out, went into
assault formation, charged the Blue lines. On schedule,
the 'enemy' was forced out of his prepared positions,
falling back into the foothills toward Mount Najim.

'You know,' one *finf* advised a new striker, 'if you just
holler "bang," and don't fire your blanks, your piece'll be
easier to clean when the bullshit's over.'

The mess line clanked forward in the rain toward the line
of cooks.

'Whaddawe got?' a private asked.

'Good stuff,' a *finf* said enthusiastically. 'Real scram-
bled eggs; some kind of sausage, least I think that's what
it is; toasted seed-bread; fruit; tea.'

'Any of it hot?'

'Most,' the *finf* said. 'Well, some of it. Tepid, anyway,
which is better'n basic rats, isn't it?'

'Yum, yum, frigging yum. Just what I need,' the
striker said, 'to turn me into a Stupor Soldier, ready to
beat the antlers off that nasty ol' Blue Army.'

'You suckin' for promotion or something?' another
striker asked suspiciously.

'Not me. I'm just *wild* wit' enthusiasm.'

'Would you rather be back in barracks polishing shit?'

'Hmm,' the first striker said. 'Can't say as I ever polished that . . . about the only thing I haven't. But you're
right, it's *nice* to be out in the open air, breathing pure
water and smelling dirty feet and drive exhausts. I'm a-
ready to kill!'

'Who?'

'Dunno,' the striker said, 'and it don't matter much. You just point this here trained killin' machine in the right direction and stand back from the spatter!'

Anonymous with the hood of his anorak over his helmet, Erik Penwyth shifted his full mess kit into his left hand and dipped his mug into the kettle of bubbling tea.

The half-awake cook nearby didn't notice that Penwyth's mug was already nearly full of small purple crystals. He dumped them into the kettle, pretended to scoop up tea, wandered away, looking for an unoccupied tree limb or vehicle hood to use for a table. Out of sight, he looked at the glop in his mess kit, grimaced, dumped it, and trotted away toward Gamma Team's camouflaged position.

The effects of the potassium permanganate crystals would be interesting. In a few hours, depending on bladder capacity, everyone who'd had tea with his breakfast would be urinating a nice, passionate red, which would work *real* wonders for morale.

Caud Williams cleverly disengaged his right flank, pulled it back to a hidden LZ with waiting Griersons, then sent it and his reserve regiment in on the left, closing off any possibility for the Blue Force to retreat west, into the rolling hills behind Leggett's Heights. Now their only retreat was Mount Najim.

'Flipping clever,' Hedley said cynically. 'Now, if I were Strike Force Commander and running this flipping mess, and it was a real flipping war, I'd want to punt my enemy back into those nice open foothills, where he's wide-open for arty and air, and I could obliterate his flipping ass in detail. But what do I know about war? I'm only a flipping *alt*, and I didn't write the script, either.

But let's see if we can't use this hooraw's nest to have a little fun.'

Four I&R Teams rode Cookes south-southwest, in the dying light, between the Swift Lance main line and the oncoming Swift Lance left wing. One Cooke's drive blew, but the other three successfully arrived deep behind 'enemy' lines, setting down in scrub jungle about two hundred meters in from the road from the coast to the Strike Force lines.

"Kay,' Petr Kipchak ordered. 'I'm gonna take Gamma first, then Alpha, then Delta. Monique, you want to cover my flanks with Beta?'

'Why do you get to go first?' Lir asked. 'I outrank you.'

'Same reason I'm running the patrol. This was my idea.'

'Things are liable to get interesting,' Alpha Team Leader's *dec*, Nectan, muttered. 'You realize there isn't one of us who's operated with any other team? Nice on-the-job training.'

'So what?' Petr asked reasonably. 'We're just beating up crunchies. It isn't like they're 'Raum, knowing the turf and lugging a real gun or two, now is it?'

'Strong point.'

'However, you did bring up a valid issue. Brief your teams — if we step in the doggie-doo, pull back across this river we're gonna come to and hit 'em once, hard, move on out. We'll RV fifty meters back of this here vehicle park, giving them the Cookes, which should be a surprise; then pull back another three hundred meters, backtrailing and ambushing anybody who's still on our ass. Set up a defensive perimeter, and we'll move out for home at false dawn. But that's only if everything's blown. Let's go find somebody and ruin what's left of their day.' He looked around. 'Njangu . . . take point.'

Yoshitaro covered his surprise – he surely didn't feel ready. He started to protest, saw Petr's expression in the twilight. 'Moving out, boss.' He paced forward, remembering how he'd gone down city streets, every nerve, every tendril feeling for something strange, something hostile. *A game, sure*, he thought. *Next time it'll likely be 'Raum. Good practice, like they say.*

He moved up to the river, peered across it from under a bush, saw no enemy waiting. He motioned for flankers, waited until a weapons team came up. Njangu motioned, as he'd learned. Me first . . . then you two . . . then the rest will cross in file. Flankers go wide on either side of the main column. He realized that, for a moment, the Force's greenest soldier, he was in command of thirty people's lives – and relished it, just as he'd reveled in leading his clique into villainy.

The water was cold, about waist-deep. He went across the ten-meter-wide water, facing upstream, scuttled quickly up the far bank. Secure. Cross. The I&R patrol followed him. On the farside they re-formed, and went on to the road. Njangu crouched in brush beside it, weapon ready.

Petr and Monique came up, motioned for him to keep watch to the south. They went to the center of the fragmenting pavement, knelt, and held some sort of conference, frequently examining the roadbed. Njangu had no idea what they were looking at or for. Monique made the motion of flipping coin, Petr tapped his butt. She shook her head in mock dismay, motioned him to go south.

Kipchak came back. 'Patrol south, staying on this side of the road,' he whispered. 'I'll have two SSWs right behind you. If you see them before they see you, pull off to the side, grenade 'em, and we'll attack. If they see you first' – he shrugged – 'try to "die" neatly.'

They moved about two kilometers, and it was very dark when they heard the whine of vehicles and saw the flicker of headlights, very much against maneuver regulations.

"Kay,' Petr said in what Njangu thought was a shout, jolting him, then he realized Kipchak had spoken in a normal voice. 'Alpha, Beta, right side of the road, one SSW right here, the rest of you flank on back. Beta, Gamma, filter on back with 'em. Dorwith, set your SSW up here, back of Njangu. Monique, move your Squad Weapon back of 'em after they stop, and when I holler run a burst out.'

'Got it, boss,' Dorwith said.

"Kay, *Finf* Kipchak,' Monique said. 'I'll be running the blaster myself. RHIP.' She disappeared down the winding road.

'Njangu, take off your Aggressor armband.'

Njangu obeyed. Kipchak did the same, setting his blaster against a tree. He unfastened his combat vest, let it hang open, rolled one sleeve up, tossed his helmet on the ground.

'If they win, they can shoot us as spies,' Petr said. 'Now, you lie down here, just to the side of the road, and I'm going to look desperate. You fell over with some kind of creeping crud, and we desperately need help. Here they come.'

The six Griersons were configured for cargo, their rear deck a sealable single compartment from the TC's hatch back. Their only armament was a single heavy blaster in each turret, and the guns were pointed skyward, unmanned. They were traveling about ten feet above the ground, as maneuver doctrine prescribed this close to the lines, below the horizon of any TA radar.

The Vehicle Commander in the lead Grierson saw a disheveled *finf* waving frantically, shouting for help, and a man sprawled at the side of the road.

'Drop it, Sy,' he ordered, and the driver obeyed. The VC, a warrant-two, clambered out of his hatch onto the Grierson's roof before the vehicle grounded.

'What happened?' he called.

'Sir . . . we lost it, tryin' t' lift over them trees,' Kipchak panted. 'Think my *aspirant's* dead . . . he's not moving . . .'

The Vehicle Commander went quickly down the climbing indents to the ground and to the distraught soldier.

'Easy, man . . . gleet!' The gleet was caused by a somewhat non-issue stubby blaster pressed against his face.

'Shoot!' Kipchak shouted, and Lir let a burst out of her Squad Support Weapon. The I&R troops came out of concealment, weapons ready. 'You're now the prisoner of the Blue Force,' Petr shouted. 'Hiccup and you're slotted.'

'You can't do this! You're not in enemy uniform,' the warrant stuttered.

'Yep,' Kipchak agreed. 'Illegal as all hell. Immoral too, probably. Two men to each vehicle. Anybody moves, secure 'em properly.'

Men and woman swarmed aboard the Griersons. Njangu heard a shout from one vehicle, then a squawk. Nectan's grinning head came out of the VC hatch. 'Secured. One black eye.'

'This isn't part of the game,' the warrant objected.

'Nope,' Kipchak said. 'I'm ashamed of myself. What're you carrying?'

The warrant pressed his lips together.

'Look, friend,' Petr said mildly. 'All I have to do is look for myself. And you didn't bother blanking your bumper letters, so I know you're support for Fourth Regiment. Just tell me what's in the back of the putt-putts, or I'll behave like a real guerrilla and shoot your young ass. Which means throwing you in the river, then tying you to a tree somewhere up the hill and not telling anybody where you are for a day or two.'

The warrant stared at Petr, decided he was as big a madman as he'd heard I&R noncoms were, and would do exactly as promised. 'The first two Griersons have portashelters and sleeping bags, the next hot rations for dinner, and the last has supplies for the Regimental Officers' Mess.'

The Swift Lance POWs had been prodded off their vehicles, and corralled to one side of the road. Monique came up in time to hear the last of the warrant's report.

'Oh dear,' she said, not meaning every syllable. 'It's going to be wet, cold, and hungry tonight for some folks. Bet that'll make Fourth Regiment real nasty fighters by morning. I hear it's gonna monsoon like a bastard, too.'

'You can't do this,' the warrant tried again.

'But we just did,' Kipchak said. 'You got an umpire with you?'

'No.'

'Hmm. Presents a problem. We could actually strip everything out of the Griersons and burn them for authenticity, but I think Daddy Williams would spank. Lir, you know how to disable a Grierson, not too permanent?'

'Yeh.'

'Do it, then.' Kipchak turned back to the warrant. 'Raiders can't afford prisoners. I could let you go on parole, but you look like one of those sneaky types who'd deny anything happened. What we did to you enemy sorts was line you up against those trees over there, and commit a war crime. To prove it, we're going to take everybody's ID card. That ought to convince the umps we done you wrong, and you're officially dead. Plus we'll take your pants with us.

'As far as actual damage, gracious freedom-loving thugs that we are, we're going to turn you loose. It's about six kilometers up the road to something resembling Swift Lance people, I'd guess about the same distance back to your friends. Have a simply wonderful evening stroll.'

The Swift Lance attack continued. Holo teams hovered over the front lines, recording the bravery of Our Fighting Men and Women for viewers throughout the Cumbre System. It was a very dull week for news.

The Blue Force fell back and back to more prepared positions, left from the last time around, ringing the crest of Mount Najim. Overjoyed they wouldn't have to be doing much digging, they prepared for their last stand, which would be followed by the reception on the final 'battleground' by *Caud* Williams and his staff for the Rentiers of D-Cumbre.

The men and women on both sides hoped there'd be a few crumbs falling off the table for them.

'This won't make us well loved,' *Aspirant* Vauxhall said, after considering Hedley's suggestion.

'Probably not,' Hedley said. 'Big flipping deal.'

'But it surely will cause some hootin' and hollerin',' Senior *Tweg* Gonzales said thoughtfully.

'Which is what I&R's supposed to do, isn't it?'

'I guess.' Gonzales eyed his superior. 'Jon, let me guess why you came up with this idea. You figure that'll put us on the shit list, and the worst thing Williams could do to . . . or for . . . us is to make us get out there on the Highland walls and work for a living hunting real-life bandits.'

'Why, Brer Rabbit, you perspicacious son of a bitch,' Hedley commented.

*

'Lower,' *Caud* Williams ordered. 'I want a closer look at that knoll.'

'Yessir,' *Finf* Running Bear said, and took the Cooke down to about thirty meters above the ground. 'We're getting simulated fire, sir.'

'Ignore that,' Williams said impatiently. 'This has nothing to do with the war games.' He studied the terrain, rechecked his projected map. 'That'll do,' he decided. 'Easy access from the road. Our guests will be able to see the entire maneuver area, and there's more than enough room for the tents, in the event of rain tomorrow.'

His com buzzed. He keyed the mike. 'Lance Six Actual . . . very well, *Mil* Rao, I'm scrambling.' He listened, and his eyes widened. 'Oh brother.' Williams caught himself. 'Message received, understood. Will arrive back in your area in . . . one-five. Have my staff ready to discuss this matter. Out.' He replaced the com in its slot. 'Back to field HQ.'

'Yessir.'

'This'll put a fine crimp in things,' Williams said. Running Bear maintained an interested silence.

'This is classified,' Williams said. 'But PlanGov has just had a deep-space com.'

'From the Confederation?' Running Bear blurted hopefully.

'Negative,' Williams said. 'Don't interrupt, soldier. From Alena Redruth, the Protector of Larix and Kura. He'll arrive in-system within an E-week for a conference with Governor General Haemer.'

Running Bear waited the appropriate time, then asked, 'About what?'

'We don't know,' Williams said. 'But he wants the conference on C-Cumbre, not here. Governor General Haemer wants us to provide an appropriate escort.' He thought for a moment. 'I think we can still bring the games to a satisfactory conclusion . . . but some units'll have to be withdrawn to prepare for the ceremonies.'

'You're *what*?' Hedley snarled.

'Gone, sir,' Ben Dill said. 'I go bye-bye. All the Griersons you've got are out of the games and pulled back to Mahan.'

'Why?'

'No word, sir. Not even a rumor. But we're supposed to prepare for offplanet service.'

'Nobody tells me flipping *shit*,' Hedley said. 'So I don't have any transport but those lousy flimsy flipping Cookes, which is gonna throw a crimp in my goddamned plans. Or are the goddamned games canceled?'

Dill shook his head. 'Dunno, sir.'

'Probably not,' Hedley said. 'Continue the mission and all that crap . . . without any support.'

'I don't understand,' Vauxhall said. 'Why'd they lift our air, instead of taking it from the general reserve?'

'A simple reason. Dill, stick fingers in your flipping ears so you don't get a big head or think ill of your superiors.'

'Yessir,' the big man said, not moving.

'Aggressors Always Lose, so they're making it easier for us to take it in the shorts. Remember which end of the stick we're holding?'

'Oh,' the *aspirant* said. 'So what are we going to do?'

'What we always do,' Hedley said. 'Improvise and come up with Plan B.'

TWENTY

The Blue Force held a semicircular line about a kilometer below the plateaulike summit of Mount Najim. Half a kilometer downslope was the knoll *Caud* Williams had chosen for his reception, promptly dubbed the Pimple by everyone below the rank of *mil*. Williams positioned his headquarters, in a collection of hasti-domes, behind the Pimple, masked from enemy fire. No sensible officer would have considered sending a missile into the area. Promotions were hard enough to come by in the Force. Covered bleachers were set up atop the Pimple and to one side was a large gaily striped tent rented for the banquet. *Caud* Williams was ready for final victory.

Governor General Wilth Haemer arrived with a flurry of aides and a harried expression. *Caud* Williams saluted him, and Haemer drew him out of earshot. 'I'm amazed you aren't worried,' he said.

'I see nothing to worry about,' Williams said. 'The maneuvers are proceeding precisely as I'd anticipated.'

'I don't mean them,' Haemer said in exasperation. 'I mean' – he glanced about – 'Redruth's visit.'

'I've learned,' Williams said with more than a touch of pomposity, 'to worry about one thing at a time. I'm sure Protector Redruth merely wishes to discuss the current problem with the Confederation. Perhaps he has good news for us, or has a plan for us to work together on. His last visit was most amiable, wasn't it?'

'Yes, yes,' Haemer said. 'But still . . .'

'Everything will be fine.'

'I certainly hope you're right.'

The two moved apart, each wishing the other fool would slip into a garbage pit in the near future.

Twenty-one men and women in Confederation uniform were hidden about a kilometer west of the Pimple. Using a trick learned by the first settlers on D-Cumbre, they'd found a *kwelf* grove for concealment. The *kwelf* grows in a circle, sending out runners that root and then climb upward as first saplings, then trees. The trees grow closer and closer together, until it appears the mature *kwelf* is a solid hedge. But the interior is open, covered by overhead growth and is anywhere from ten to thirty meters in diameter and makes a perfect shelter. An entrance is generally made by cutting away, and then replacing, a single tree.

Jord'n Brooks checked his watch. 'They will begin their stupid endgame in thirty minutes. Let us go. May the One help us complete our Task.'

Wordlessly, the twenty picked up their weapons and moved toward the grove's entrance.

'I resent that, Daddy,' Jasith Mellusin said. 'I wanted to come see this because, well, because you said you wanted me to take a bigger part in the family business, and we do business with the soldiers, don't we?'

Godrevy Mellusin lifted an eyebrow. 'Jasith, don't take me for an utter fool, just because I'm your father. No, we don't do any business with the Confederation forces, unless you sell them something in that money-losing lingerie shop I let you talk me into. Nor do I believe you wanted to come out here in the rain just to keep me company to watch a bunch of muddy soldiers run up and down.

'Who is he, and I hope he's high enough in the ranks to keep me from grinding my teeth?'

Jasith rounded her eyes innocently. 'I'm *sure* I don't know what you're talking about.' She started giggling, and her father smiled wryly as one of his aides led them to their reserved place in the bleachers.

'What's going on?' Loy Kouro demanded irritably of the soldier.

'Sorry, sir, *Caud* Williams' orders,' Reb Gonzales said 'We're commandeering this vehicle for the duration of the maneuvers.'

'Whaaat? You can't do that! This is a *Matin* news lifter! You know what *Matin* is, don't you?'

'Yessir. A holo, sir. But I have my orders. Please step out of the vehicle.'

'But we're covering your little games, dammit! If you grab this lifter, there won't be any coverage from us!'

'Yessir,' Gonzales said. 'A terrible pity, sir. Now if you'd step out of the lifter, sir?'

'The hell I will,' Kouro said. 'Driver, take it up.'

The driver's hand touched the controls, and Gonzales pulled the door open and yanked the man out.

'You son of a—' The driver came up, fists ready, and Gonzales' spear hand went forward into his gut, came back, slammed into the side of his neck.

'I saw that!' Kouro said.

'Saw your driver slip and fall?' Gonzales said. 'Knocked himself out on a rock, he did. Half a dozen other people saw what happened, too, and will be happy to testify if you choose to press charges. Now, if you'll unass the lifter . . . sir . . . we can go about our business.'

Kouro got out, and two strikers had him by the elbows. 'Put him with the others,' Gonzales ordered. 'And drag this poor stumbling lad over to see if he needs medical attention.'

There were seven other civilian lifters, private and commercial, pulled off the main road. Their drivers and passengers were guarded by half a dozen I&R troops. *Alt* Hedley came out of the brush.

'This is going to make a bit of a stink,' Gonzales observed.

'Probably,' Hedley said. 'But if we'd let him go on by, he would've said something, and Swift Lance isn't totally brainless. Pity about that journoh, though. Do you remember how they stand on pay raises for *alts*?'

'Dunno, sir. I only read *The Economist*,' Gonzales said.

'And aren't you the high-class tart.' Hedley tapped fingernails against the side of the lifter, thinking. 'On the other hand, this could make things very sneaky ... Three, no four volunteers from, who's in the barrel this week? Gamma.' He raised his voice. 'Give me Kipchak, Dorwith with a Squad Support Weapon, Heckmyer and that new guy. Yoshitaro.'

The four came out of the brush. 'Get your respective asses in this here journalistic vehicle and stand by. We're gonna get real flipping dirty, stinky, illegal, and immoral.'

Simulated missiles launched as the first wave of Griersons swept in from the east, through drifting clouds of rain, and landed on the rising ground on one side of the knoll. It was spectacular, with preplanted demolition charges going off, smoke bombs arcing through the air, and the slam of practice charges from the Griersons and supporting Zhukovs.

If anyone noted the Griersons came in for rather gentle

landings to avoid damage, no one commented, nor did anyone ask why Williams ordered a high casualty-producing frontal assault on the Blue lines rather than a flanking attack.

The Swift Lance soldiers, shouting aggressively as ordered, mucked their way toward the Blue positions.

Then the second wave struck, coming in from the west, landing closer to the Blue lines. The spectators were enthralled, battle on all sides.

'Hey, idiots,' the *dec* shouted. 'Where the hell did you come from? The battle's over there, you—'

Jord'n Brooks shot him, and the woman beside him gunned down the noncom's two flankers. A fourth soldier gaped at the gore, frozen by the dying gasps of his teammates. Brooks shot him before he could recover.

'Hurry,' he ordered. 'We're behind the soldiers' assault lines.' The 'Raum pushed through the trees, paying no attention to the war cries to their right as the second wave attacked Mount Najim. Ahead was their target – the knoll with a brightly painted tent and bleachers beside it.

'Land the third element,' *Caud* Williams ordered, and his executive officer, *Mil* Rao, spoke into the com.

Five waves of Griersons – the Force's First Regiment – lifted from concealed LZs and drove toward Mount Najim as the rain broke, and the sun blazed through for a perfect moment. *Caud* Williams looked around his command center, saw the smooth efficiency of his staff, heard the roar of the ACVs and thought with enormous pride, *This is all mine. I raised this unit and built it from nothing.*

The First Regiment would overfly this knoll, and land just behind the Blue Lines, and the war . . . the battle game, he corrected himself, would be over, and a triumph.

Williams saw a small news lifter, with the logo *Matin* on it, dart across the battlefield's rear, in front of the onrushing Griersons. *If that idiot gets in the way of my people and there's a collision . . .* Then he relaxed, seeing it level out well below the Griersons' flight pattern. *Must be that young firebrand Kouro. His father told me he'd be covering this for his holo. Good footage he must be getting, thrilling for Cumbrians to watch, make any real Confederation citizen's heart pound. Must remember to get a copy of the disc.* Williams put the matter out of his mind, turned back to his conquest.

The lifter banked and drove directly for Williams' command center. From the jungle to the east, seven other lifters joined it.

Jasith Mellusin peered about, trying to see where her . . . well, not really, at least not yet, *her* Garvin might be. She wished she'd asked just what kind of a job he did, for she didn't know where to look.

Garvin Jaansma boredly put the touchup sprayer to a scratch on his gleaming Grierson. He wondered if he could ghost out and chance a call to Jasith's com number, decided it wasn't a good idea. Ben Dill had assigned him this job, not Senior *Tweg* Ric or somebody not worth obeying if you could get away with it. He went back to his work, wondering if this secret mission they' d been pulled out of the field for would be interesting, and if it'd keep him from being able to get a pass into Leggett.

An MP, elegant in dress uniform, held up his hand. 'Hold on, troops. This is the VIP area, and you can't—'
One of Brooks' men shot him in the head, and he

spasmed back and down. Brooks heard alarmed shouts, paid no mind. The bleachers full of the enemies of his people were just two hundred meters away. He was ready for his Task.

The news-lifter grounded outside the command center, and two of Wllliams security men came toward it as the hatch opened. Five bearded, dirty men wearing Blue armbands tumbled out. Dorwith fired a burst of blanks, and Njangu shouted, 'You're dead,' and the five crashed into the command center.

'Hedley!' *Caud* Williams sputtered. 'What in the name of—'

Hedley thumbed a blue smoke grenade, tossed it toward Williams. 'We're brave idiots on a suicide mission, sir,' he said. 'I'm afraid you're dead!'

'You can't—'

'I did, sir,' and the command center swirled into a chaos of rattling blanks, varicolored smoke grenades and shouting, screaming staff officers. Outside was the drive-whine as the other commandeered lifters landed, and the shouts of the company as they rolled out and began 'slaughtering' Strike Force Swift Lance's command elements.

Over all was *Caud* Williams' parade-ground roar: 'You're doomed, Hedley, you bastard! I'll have you court-martialed! Your career—'

Then Njangu heard the hard blast of *real* gunfire.

Three 'Raum knelt, sprayed the bleachers, and then the blaster explosions were drowned by the screams.

Gonzales was bellowing: 'Come on, you stupid bastards! Get rid of those frigging blanks! This is for real!'

*

Jasith Mellusin stood, trying to see what was going on, saw a man suddenly without his head fall two meters away in the bleachers, blood spraying. Her mouth opened to scream, then her father knocked her down and threw himself on top of her.

A man in civilian clothes, with a pistol in his hand, ducked around the side of a lifter, hastily shot at Brooks, missed. Before Brooks could react, the man shot the woman next to Brooks, then Brooks fired two rounds, and the man fell. Brooks' teeth were skinned back in a silent snarl as he ran closer to the bleachers.

A 'Raum beside him pulled the trigger on his blaster, gun set on automatic. Rounds yammered away into emptiness and the blaster was silent. He stood, stupidly staring at the empty weapon, finger moving on the trigger, then he was gone, and Brooks didn't see who killed him.

Njangu ran out of the Command Center, finger pushing the magazine release, blank magazine dropping away, left hand reaching into his combat vest, finding the heavy magazine with real rounds, pushing it home in his blaster's receiver, somehow remembering to tap the magazine base to make sure it was seated, then he was going forward, and heard, for the first time in his life, the slam of blaster explosions around him.

'Around here,' Hedley shouted, running toward a hasti-dome, and Njangu, Dorwith and a scattering of other I&R soldiers followed, running past an utterly motionless staff *haut*, mouth gaping open, shut, like a beached fish.

Njangu came into the open, into insanity. Confederation soldiers were systematically shooting into the VIP stands. What the hell was—

'Kill 'em,' Hedley shouted. 'They're phonies! Kill 'em all!'

Obediently Njangu knelt, pulled his blaster into his shoulder, put his sight's dot on the center of one shooter, touched the trigger. He never saw the flame, never felt the recoil-tap, but saw the man convulse, flinging his weapon high into the air, and slump. Yoshitaro moved his aim to a woman reloading her blaster, fired again.

Dorwith's SSW yammered, and blasts exploded across the ground, swept over the killers, then a bullet smashed his shoulder, and he rolled away, groaning. Njangu remembered his training, picked up the gun, and darted forward, hearing rounds slam in nearby. He crouched behind a wheeled transportall, used that for a rest, sprayed three attackers, saw them fall.

Someone was shouting, pulling at him, and the words came through: 'Stop, dammit, you're killing our men!' then a bullet took the fool, and Njangu found the shooter, killed him in turn.

A woman wearing a black dress stumbled toward Jord'n Brooks, bloody hands covering her face. She took them away, and there was nothing but gore and torn flesh. He shot her twice in the chest, looked for another target.

Two 'Raum beside him fell, and he twisted sideways, went down, gun turning, firing. His shot took *Dec* Alyce Quant in the side of her chest.

Njangu saw a man fumble a thick cylinder from his backpack, come to his knees, lean back for the throw. Njangu killed him. The explosives thudded next to his body, and another attacker rolled away, screaming. The charge exploded, red fire, black smoke, mud cascading, shrapnel hissing, and bodies pinwheeled away.

Brooks saw his grenadier die, saw the blast kill half a dozen or more 'Raum, saw there were only three of his team left. 'Away,' he shouted. 'Away,' and ran, zigzagging, for the distant jungle.

'That's it,' Njangu heard. 'That's it! They're all down. Cease firing!' He realized with some surprise he was the one shouting. The firing stopped for an instant, and he faintly heard screams, moans from the VIP bleachers, saw men and women wearing crosses on their sleeves running toward them. Ahead was a scatter of uniformed bodies, shredded and torn by gunfire and the bomb blast. He saw movement, and someone fired, and the body contorted, lay still.

There were still a dozen rounds in the belt of his SSW. Weapon ready, he walked toward the dead madmen, barrel sweeping back and forth. Petr Kipchak was beside him shaking his head, eyes glaring in rage and disbelief. 'What a *hell* of a way to run a war.'

TWENTY-ONE

The Force buried its dead under a gray, lowering sky. The seven who'd died in war-games accidents were laid to rest with the same ceremony as the five men and women of Intelligence and Reconnaissance Company and the four other Force soldiers who'd been killed stopping the 'Raum attack. If anyone in I&R objected, they said nothing.

Nineteen civilians had been killed by the 'Raum, twice that number wounded. Six innocent 'Raum were murdered by roving gangs, and the Eckmuhl was put under a dawn-to-dusk curfew 'for its own protection' by Governor General Haemer. The Rentiers suggested the 'Raum community have penalties levied against it, but Haemer refused to order this. The non-'Raum of Cumbre seethed – *something* must be done about this outrage.

'That was a damned-fool stunt,' *Caud* Williams told *Alt* Hedley. Hedley stayed at attention, and silent. He didn't think Williams wanted either agreement or disagreement. 'But you ... and your men ... must be commended for the swiftness you responded with when those traitorous backstabbers made their murderous assault,' he went on.

'Thank you, sir.'

'I have a question,' Williams said. 'It appeared that all your men carried live ammunition, which you should certainly know is prohibited by regulations.'

Once more Hedley said nothing.

'If I were a fool ... which I am not ... I might ask why you allowed this, and where your men procured these rounds, when all our munitions are rigidly rationed. Would you care to volunteer any information?' He waited a bare second. 'I thought not. Under normal circumstances, the heroism of your men would merit appropriate medals and promotion, just as your mischief requires punishment. It's my thinking that the two even each other out. What's your opinion?'

'Frankly, sir?'

'I doubt if you know any other way to answer.'

'Very well, sir. I don't care about myself. But I think it's a bit rotten for you to do that to my women and men, who were merely following my orders.'

Williams' ears reddened. He took a deep breath, held it, then exhaled. 'I asked your opinion ... and I received it. What I said, stands. Let us move on to other matters. There is a special mission required of me, and of certain Strike Force personnel in two days, on C-Cumbre, which is of all-encompassing importance. It should only take a day, little more. When I return, we shall finally dispose of these hill-bandits. Every effort must be expended, and I require the utmost diligence.

'I expect my Intelligence and Reconnaissance Company to be in the forefront. You'll be reinforced by the band and the Honor Guard — that is, the Headquarters Security Section — when they return from C-Cumbre — and you will be supported by a section of Heavy Assault Vehicles and the Mobile Scout Troop. If you need further transport, *Mil* Rao will either call for volunteers or detail additional elements.

'Yessir,' Hedley said, saluted, and left, wondering what his line-slime would think of xylophonetinklers and brasspolishers being added to their ranks.

TWENTY-TWO

C-Cumbre

Winds swirled across the planet's man-scarred surface, sent dust devils curling up into emptiness. Its dry, hot atmosphere was breathable but unpleasant, each breath tasting of invisible razor blades.

The human Planetary Headquarters was a series of cold temporary-looking buildings sealed under a low dome, as if it were precariously situated on an airless moon. Half a planet away was the Musth Center, two four-story buildings with inverted-C roofs.

Great jagged pits, inverted ziggurats, dotted the landscape, and machinery, some robot, some remote-controlled, a very little hands-on-operated, churned around the diggings.

The two fly-on-fly-off transports that'd brought the Strike Force's Griersons and two Zhukovs hovered a dozen meters above the ground, side ramps gaping, and a stream of combat vehicles floated out, each disgorging its antenna array as it did.

Garvin and Kang were out of their stations, hanging over Ben Dill's seat, looking through the curving windscreen at the desolation.

'I know all this digging pays the rent,' Kang said. 'But does it have to be so ugly?'

'Shaddup,' Dill ordered. 'Stanislaus's working his usual magic, and I'd as rather he not ram one of these cargo pigs while he's listening to your brillig repartee.'

The two stayed silent while Gorecki maneuvered the Grierson away from the starship to the line of ACVs parked outside Planetary Headquarters, where a guide waited. He motioned the ACV back, forth, to the side, until it was precisely aligned then brought his forearms across his chest in a chopping motion. Obediently, Gorecki grounded the vehicle. 'We're down, Ben,' he reported.

'Power stays on,' Dill ordered. 'But you can lock the controls .'

''Kay.' Gorecki came back from his position in the nose. 'What now?'

'Just exactly what we're trained to do,' Ben said. 'We wait.'

'You got any idea what we're waiting for?'

'Hell no,' Dill said. 'We're mushrooms. Kept in the dark and fed only on shit.'

Caud Williams had ordered the combat vehicles detailed for the Protector's visitor to be at Condition Yellow – missiles, rockets, shells out of their lockers and in the launchers/guns. Garvin remembered the *Malvern*, Protector Redruth's cold-eyed bullyboy Celidon, decided that if he were Williams, he'd have more artillery loaded and locked on Condition Red, and in the air, not sitting around waiting to be hit.

Half an E-day later the com ordered: 'All personnel disembark.'

'With or without sidearms?' Garvin asked.

'With,' Dill said. 'When in doubt, carry.'

Ten minutes after they'd formed up in front of the Grierson's nose, a starship on secondary lowered out of the yellow-brown murk toward them.

'Good gods, what's that?' Garvin asked.

'Uh – I think it's a *Remora*-class destroyer leader,' Kang said. 'It would've commanded a flotilla of smaller Confederation destroyers. I built a model of one when I was a kid. But the one I built didn't have all those extra blisters and gun stations.'

'That's what happens here on the fringes,' Dill said. 'The Confederation finally grants a goodie, figures that's enough for a generation or two, so whoever gets the goodie has to do field modification until his eyes bleed.'

'That makes sense,' Gorecki said. 'But what did they use to make the mods with? A sledgehammer? And what the hell are *those*?'

Those were four very sleek, very modern darts of patrol ships, flying close formation around the DL.

'Damfino,' Dill confessed. 'That big hog's something that looks like my grandfather commanded it, and it's flanked with some trick stuff that looks like it came straight out of Centrum last week.'

'Son of a bitch,' Garvin remembered. 'You know, we were told the *Malvern* had some real zoomie new spit-kits back in the hold when we were coming out. Wonder if ol' Redruth traded for 'em with the "pirates," or –'

'Shaddup,' Dill said. 'Don't go out of your way to get in trouble.'

The DL grounded, but the patrol craft kept orbiting. There was an emblem on the large ship's nose Garvin couldn't make out. The ship's name was the *Corfe*.

Their earpieces clicked, and they heard *Caud* Williams' voice: 'All Strike Force Swift Lance elements . . . stand by to render full honors to Alena Redruth, Protector of Larix and Kura.'

Governor General Haemer, flanked by *Caud* Williams, *Mil* Rao, and a bluster of staff officers plus a color guard and a few bandsmen, came out of the dome and went to the *Corfe*. A lock opened, a ramp slid down, and four men walked down. The Cumbre colors dipped and music played.

'Now please God, let 'em walk on by,' Gorecki said. 'I got no interest in playing pet for offworlders.'

But the officials seemed intent on trooping the line.

'Stand tall, fellers,' Dill said, and his crewmen obeyed, peripheral vision at Condition Red. Garvin especially wanted to see Alena Redruth, never having been this close to what was supposedly the last of an endangered breed, an absolute dictator. Redruth wasn't that impressive, smallish, balding, in his late thirties, more like a minor bureaucrat than a warlord. He wore a simple dark brown tunic and pants, with a single decoration around his neck. Flanking him were two obvious bodyguards.

Garvin's attention was jolted away by the man just behind Redruth. The man was tall, muscular, with the inadequately repaired remnants of a scar across his forehead. His expression was mixed cold amusement and mild dislike. He wore a dark green dress uniform with decorations, black knee boots and a black-leather Sam Browne belt with a dagger sheathed on one side and a pistol on the other. Garvin remembered him well, from the troop compartment of the *Malvern*, Celidon, the leader of the 'pirates.' *I'm invisible*, Garvin thought as the party came abreast of the Grierson. *Of no interest. Just another ranker*.

Naturally Celidon paused. 'If you don't mind,' he said to Williams, 'I'd like to ask a question or two of your men here.'

'Of course not,' Williams said, a trifle nervously.

Celidon went to Dill, looked at the single row of decorations on his chest. 'You're on your . . . second enlistment?'

'Yessir,' Ben said.

'Plan on making a career of the service?'

'Haven't decided yet, sir.'

Celidon nodded, then his eyes went, like a stooping hawk, to Garvin. 'You, Striker. What's your post?'

'Gunner, sir.'

'What's the maximum effective range of one of your Shrikes?'

'Classified, sir.'

'You can tell me, troop,' Celidon snapped. 'Larix and Kura are allies of yours, and I spent a good deal of time as a Confederation officer.'

Garvin didn't answer.

'Go ahead, Striker,' *Caud* Williams said.

'In theory, ninety kilometers once the target is thoroughly acquired,' Jaansma said by rote. 'In fact, probably fifty or sixty should be the maximum allowed for, and that in extremely favorable conditions.'

'Pretty close,' Celidon said. 'Try forty in combat. You fired one yet?'

'No, sir.'

'You think you could hit something under real-world conditions?'

'I know so, sir.'

Celidon smiled briefly. 'May your confidence be rewarded. What about your chainguns?'

'Four thousand meters effective range, best used under visual conditions, either natural or amplified.'

'How long does it take to reload?'

'About three minutes, sir.'

'I'd guess you could do it in less,' Celidon said. 'You're a big lad. My congratulations – you appear to know your tools. Let me ask you another question, if I might. Does it worry you that your Strike Force has no interstellar capability, that no elements of the Confederation Navy are stationed in the Cumbre System?'

'No, sir, it doesn't bother me. Things like that are *Caud* Williams' concern, not mine.'

'What about the Musth?'

'What *about* the Musth? Sir.'

'Do they worry you?'

'No, sir. We're at peace. Should they?'

Celidon nodded, as it satisfied. 'One final question: How long have you served with the Strike Force?'

'Eight months, sir. I came out on the *Malvern*.'

Celidon jolted slightly, tried to cover. 'Not familiar with that ship,' he said. 'Carry on,' and started away.

The dignitaries moved on. *Caud* Williams remained next to Jaansma. 'I told you once to rethink what you told me, didn't I?' he asked.

'Yessir,' Garvin said.

'I'm not a total oaf. I saw Celidon's reaction just now. And I'm capable of reevaluating things when necessary. I assume you haven't blathered your theories about the *Malvern* to everyone?'

'Nossir,' Garvin said truthfully. 'You ordered me not to.'

'Good man.' Williams looked after Redruth. 'Yes, some things might just be worth reconsidering. Tell your company commander I authorized you to add another slash, *Finf* Jaansma. You did well today.'

'Yessir,' Garvin said. 'Thank you, sir.'

Haemer escorted the out-system visitors to C-Cumbre's elaborate if seldom-used conference room, and aides offered refreshments. For a time, he tried light conversation, which Redruth seemed amiably willing to continue indefinitely.

Finally, the governor general couldn't restrain himself: 'Protector Redruth, what have you heard of late from the Confederation?'

Redruth smiled wryly. 'Nothing. I was about to ask the same question, but you just answered it for me. Absolutely nothing. No coms, no visitors, no naval ships, no convoys, and the handful of independent merchants who've visited my planets also come from the fringes, and are as much in the dark as we are.

'I chanced sending a corvette with two escorts toward Centrum almost two E-months ago. They've vanished . . . or at least we've had no word, and they've not responded to any of my coms.'

Haemer and Williams looked carefully at the Protector, trying to see if he was lying, but his bland face showed nothing but mild worry and concern.

'And that, of course, is the reason for my visit.'

Haemer stiffened. 'Oh?'

'I must plan my economy, my strategy, as if some sort of possibly long-lasting interregnum has occurred,' Redruth said. 'I don't know what's happened with the Confederation . . . certainly there were reports of civil unrest and even systems withdrawing from its umbrella before this strange silence.

'But I'm a man of action, not thought, so my plans are simple – I stand alone, and must guarantee peace and security to my people. I've begun a significant ship-building program, and will need additional ores, which I propose to procure . . . purchase . . . from the Cumbre system.'

Haemer relaxed slightly. 'Good,' he said. 'Obviously, being cut off from the Confederation has done our metals trade no good whatsoever. I'm delighted you've decided to increase your quota, and our mining corporations should have no trouble meeting any requirements.'

'I didn't think there would be a problem,' Redruth said. 'However, I'm concerned about the Musth.'

'In what way?'

'I know well their ambitions,' Redruth said. 'They aspire to control the universe, a step at a time, and I was afraid that, with their learning the Confederation no longer stands behind us they might become, shall we say, ambitious.'

'I've been worried about the same thing,' Haemer said. 'But as yet our relations continue cordial.'

'Perhaps,' Celidon said, 'we might offer increased security to the Cumbre system, since you have no naval capabilities and we do. Perhaps we might think of stationing half a dozen of our ships on D-Cumbre. I'm sure the system's resources would be sufficient to fund them, and the citizens would be grateful.'

Haemer's mouth was dry. He considered his response carefully.

'Thank you for the offer,' *Caud* Williams said smoothly before Haemer spoke. 'It's magnificent seeing fellow humans jump to our aid. But your presence might well trigger the response we all fear.' There wasn't a trace of sarcasm detectable in his speech.

'I don't follow,' Celidon snapped, but Redruth was nodding thoughtfully.

'Just this,' Williams continued. 'The Musth, as you point out, are a very ambitious species. They think their presence in the Cumbre system is justified, and would, I'm very sure, be delighted to increase it. In fact, I wouldn't be surprised if they would like total domination of at least this planet and its resources.

'If Larix and Kura suddenly show an increased military presence in the Cumbre system, that might serve to tip the balance, and give some of their more aggressive warlords reason to exacerbate the situation.'

'What of it?' Celidon said scornfully. 'Certainly you're not suggesting these aliens are superior to Man, are you? We've never stepped back before any challenge, and sure as hell can't start now. All beasts recognize fear, which gives them reason to attack.'

'The Musth are hardly beasts,' Williams said.

Celidon shrugged. 'They aren't human . . . I need no other description.'

Haemer stepped into the silence. 'My military commander makes an excellent point,' he said. 'Any incident, here on the frontiers of Man's expansion, might well spark war, and without the possibility of reinforcement from the Confederation, that might prove disastrous. I include Larix and Kura in my assessment.'

Celidon snorted disbelief. Redruth nodded. 'You have a point,' he said. 'So let us consider the details of our new trading agreement. That should be more than enough.

'For the time being, at least.'

TWENTY-THREE

'Well, Mary dipped in creosote,' Njangu Yoshitaro exclaimed. 'Just who do you know . . . or blow?'

'Rather attractive, ain't it?' Garvin said, smugly admiring the two stripes of a *finf* on his sleeve. 'Nice to see that Strike Force Lit Twit is finally recognizing its best.'

'Talk to me, little white brother,' Njangu growled. 'Or I'll smite the living hell outa thee.'

Nganju whistled when Garvin told him about Celidon, had him stop the story, found Petr, and had Garvin start all over.

'Oh boy,' Kipchak said. 'So Redruth's got big eyes for Cumbre, eh? It sure never shits, but it pours all right. Musth to the front of us, 'Raum to the left, Redruth's bullies to the right, and frigging nobody to cover our young rears. Oh dear, oh dear, oh my spectacles and gloves.'

'I got a question, Garvin,' Nganju said. 'Everybody's bustin' ass getting ready to go to the field to haunt the wild 'Raum, and you've got time to flaunt your newly striped young butt around. In a word, howcum?'

'Six hours off, reward from *Alt* Wu, my lovable and never sufficiently blessed platoon leader. *With* permission to honk into civilization for those six hours.'

'But you had to come all the way to I&R to rub it in on your ex-best friend, eh?'

Garvin's smile vanished. He looked pointedly at Petr, who inclined his head in understanding. 'Private business, eh? Thanks for coming by and telling me, Garvin. I always need something new to brood about.' Petr went back into the squad bay.

''Kay,' Yoshitaro said. 'What's whupping?'

'Wanted to ask you about options.'

'What sort?'

'The sort that we don't appear to have, Njangu. Look. I joined the army because . . . because things were getting a little interesting. I figured I'd give it an honest straight shot, get out after one term, and have those certain problems half a goddamned galaxy away.'

'And *I* joined because a judge was going to fry my brain otherwise. How come you've always been so close-mouthed about what happened?'

'That doesn't matter right now . . . and stick to the subject, dammit. Anyway. I never figured I'd end up out back of God's behind, and I sure as hell didn't plan on the goddamned Confederation doing a vanishing act on me,' Garvin said.

'Nor me,' Njangu confessed. 'I was sort of hoping to get a nice soft assignment somewhere close to Centrum where I could shuffle stage right at the proper moment and continue doing what I was doing before. Except this time without getting caught. Or, if I couldn't manage that, like you, finishing one term and having a clean record to counterbalance future villainies.

'It looks, now that you brought it up,' he went on, 'like both of us are a little light on controlling what comes next. If that's what you meant by options.'

'It was,' Garvin said. 'You got any brilliant ideas?'

'Mmmh,' Yoshitaro said. 'We stick around here,

somebody's liable to blow our silly fool heads down around our butts.'

'Right.'

'Things don't appear like they're going to get any more peaceful, either,' he said.

'Right again, I'm pretty sure,' Garvin agreed.

'So that leaves three options,' Njangu said. 'We could buy our way out.'

'You know anybody with money?' Garvin asked.

'Nope, so that's dead, unless you find a Real Friend with your new comrades up there in the Heights. Option two – desert.'

'To who?'

'Shit, I dunno. I'm thinking out loud. It'd be pretty hard to disappear into Leggett, even if I don't think the Force'd look for us too hard. But there doesn't appear, at least from the outside, to be any really good rogueries for somebody like me to disappear into. You could always do some fine gambling to pay the rent. Maybe I should be your bodyguard.'

'Gambling don't cut it,' Garvin said. 'Not on a long-range basis. Sooner or later some bastard figures out you're better than he is, and always hold the aces, and so he breaks your thumbs out of general dissatisfaction. Hard to deal seconds with busted finger bones.'

'Sounds like you know for sure,' Njangu said casually.

'Stop digging,' Garvin warned. 'Some day I'll tell you. Anyway, not only can gambling get dangerous, but everybody I know who chased the speckled cubes sooner or later started betting on something else that he didn't know squat about, and lost his shorts.'

'So deserting for a life of crime doesn't appear too good,' Njangu said. 'We could sleaze our way to another island, and actually *work* for a living.' He shuddered slightly. 'I know a village where we could go fishing.'

'That really thrums a string deep within,' Garvin said sarcastically.

'With the exception of a certain girl-child, it doesn't,' Njangu said. 'What about you? You've been swinging around with the rich. Anything there?'

'Not yet,' Garvin said. 'But I'm going into Leggett in a few minutes. Maybe something'll develop. That's a very thin maybe. But so far, nothing.' He thought. 'We could always see if the bandits need a training cadre.'

'Not bright,' Njangu said. 'Maybe we're a bunch of clonkheads at the moment, but sooner or later we'll get moves. When we do I'd rather be looking down the sights than be looked at.'

'True.' Garvin sighed. 'So what do we do? Just soldier on?'

'That's the best I can think of, right now,' Njangu said, a bit disconsolately. 'You know, since I've always thought of myself as a dude with an eye for the main chance, you've just managed to depress me.'

'I managed to depress myself,' Garvin said. 'Guess we'll just have to keep thinking.'

'Guess so,' Njangu said. 'There's got to be *something*. And thanks for dropping by, *Finf* Jaansma.'

'My pleasure, *Striker* Yoshitaro.'

Garvin was pacing back and forth outside Leggett Station, looking for Jasith's little red lifter. He paid little attention to the long black antigrav lim that slid up beside the curb, other than a mildly envious stare until the side door lifted, and Jasith leaned out.

'Garvin,' she called. 'Over here.' She didn't sound happy.

Garvin, with thoughts of lim backseats dancing in his head, hurried over. He started to bend over for a kiss, got a swift, tiny headshake no.

'Garvin, I'd like you to meet my father,' she said. The

tall, bluff man sitting beside her in the back leaned over, holding out a hand.

'Godrevy Mellusin,' he said. 'Jasith said you had a short pass into town, and neither of you had specific plans, so I thought it might be appropriate for me to buy you dinner.'

Garvin was very pleased with himself for not spreading his arms to the heavens, and bellowing, 'Why frigging me alla goddamned time, God! All I wanted was some frigging flower petals!' Instead, he shook Mellusin's hand with a firm, manly gesture.

'It's the least I could do for anyone who saved our lives two weeks ago,' Mellusin said. 'Besides, I wanted to meet my daughter's young man. I remembered when I was young, with strong appetites but nothing to satisfy them with, and thought I might help.'

Garvin couldn't tell if there was a twinkle of slightly malicious amusement in Mellusin's eye. 'Get in, lad,' he said. 'I've already made arrangements at the club.'

'Sorry,' Jasith whispered as he got in. 'I got mouse-trapped.'

Garvin, in his travels, had eaten at a couple of exclusive clubs, and shuddered at the thought of a third. Not only wasn't he going to have a romantic evening, but he was going to be fed a dinner slightly worse than the mess-hall meal he'd passed on back at Camp Mahan.

But he ate liver-and-nut pâté with consomme; a roast with a tart berry stuffing and mustard sauce; a red, astringent vegetable; a warm salad with hot bacon and a sweetish brandy dressing; and a chocolate soufflé with vanilla sauce for dessert. Before that, Mellusin had summoned a waiter, and asked if there was any of the Earth Taittinger left. The man grudged there were a few cases.

After the man had left, Mellusin shook his head. 'Most

sommeliers think they own the cellar or at any rate are paid on its size, not for their service. Sad.'

'Earth champagne?' Garvin said. 'I'm not sure a one-stripe promotion's worth it.'

'Anything's worth champagne, Garvin,' Godrevy said. 'At my age, just having survived another night's enough. Still, I suppose we're going to have to think about that, what with the present situation. The local fizzy grape's only fit for shoe polish.' He turned serious. 'What do you think about losing contact with the Confederation?'

'I don't know anything, sir,' Garvin said. 'But I don't like it.'

'Who does?' Jasith said. 'No new fashions, gossip, celebrities, music, holos . . . we might as well be living in a vacuum.'

'We are, my dear,' her father said.

'You know what I mean,' Jasith said.

'Sometimes I think my daughter wants me to believe she's an airbrain,' Mellusin said. 'It'd make me more vulnerable.'

Jasith laughed. 'Now you're onto me.'

The champagne came, was uncorked, tasted, pronounced acceptable, and poured around; then the dinner began arriving.

'Since you avoided my question, Garvin,' Mellusin said, 'let me ask another. What's your opinion of Protector Redruth's visit? Don't look startled. I know about most things that happen in this system a few seconds after they occur. The Mellusins are among the Rentiers, after all.'

'I'm not sure I should say anything, sir,' Garvin said. 'Most everything that happened recently is classified, I'm pretty sure.'

'Careful, aren't you? I notice you didn't even admit to Redruth's being here.'

'Yes sir.'

'Most people your age can't wait to make sure every-one knows they've got a secret, if they have one.'

'I learned better some time ago.'

Mellusin waited, but Garvin didn't explain. 'Well,' the man said, 'I'm not at all pleased. He shows up on C-Cumbre, meets with Haemer and his staff for half a planetary day, then returns to Larix/Kura. No banquets, no ceremonial visits to D-Cumbre, no coms with any of the people he met when he was here last.'

'Such as myself,' Mellusin added. 'I do not like *that* at all. Since he went to C-Cumbre, his visit must have had something to do with the system's minerals. Yet he made no contact with me, and I own one of the larger mining establishments . . . even after the sabotage a few months ago. That I find worrisome. Wouldn't you?'

'I suppose so, sir,' Garvin said. 'This roast is really excellent, isn't it?'

'Very well. I give up, *Finf* Clam,' Mellusin said. 'Your young man has a great deal of discretion.'

Jasith giggled, remembering Loy Kouro's swimming lesson.

'What's so funny?'

'Nothing, Father.'

'Very well . . . I'll now look for a completely neutral topic of conversation. As an offworlder, what do you think of D-Cumbre, Garvin?'

'Interesting.'

'What planet are you from?'

'Various, sir. My people traveled a great deal.'

'What line were they in?'

'Promotion, sir. Family entertainment.'

'Very interesting. And you chose not to follow them in the same field?'

'I did for a time, sir,' Garvin said. 'But circumstances changed, and I decided to enlist in the army.'

'Not a bad idea,' Mellusin said. 'I've often wondered what would've happened if I'd chosen the colors instead of what I did. And so you were sent here, to the edge of nothing.'

'So far,' Garvin said, 'I like Cumbre.' He gave Jasith a meaningful look, and was rewarded when she slipped her foot out of her shoe and rubbed it up and down his inner thigh, hidden by the table's long cloth.

'Good,' Mellusin approved. 'There's a place on the frontiers for an ambitious young woman or man.'

'As a matter of fact,' Garvin said, 'a friend of mine and I were talking about that very idea this evening. Assuming I take my discharge here on D-Cumbre after one term, what might my options be?'

Jasith slid her bare foot into Garvin's lap, began moving her toes.

'I noticed you know which fork to use . . . and I've already complimented you on your discretion,' Mellusin said. 'That would make you distinctly employable with one of the Rentier firms. For instance, Mellusin Mining could always use a good man in security.'

Garvin nodded. 'Actually, I think, by the time I finish with the Strike Force, my fascination with being shot at will be a thing of the past.'

Mellusin smiled. 'Ambition is well rewarded here,' he said. 'As I assume you've noted, D-Cumbre has its own class system.'

'So I've seen,' Garvin said, his voice flat.

'Some say it's the natural order of things,' Mellusin said.

'I've noted that as well.'

'Garvin was the one who had the, uh, encounter with Loy Kouro,' Jasith said, then looked at the two men questioningly, unsure whether she should've said anything.

'You're the one who toppled that young fool into the lily pond?'

'I was, sir. But there was provocation.'

'With Kouro there generally is, just as there generally is with his father. They're both idiots. I assume he was running his mouth about the natural inferiority of the 'Raum, and how anyone around him was an obvious Superior Being?'

'He was, sir. With a 'Raum standing beside him. I thought that was in fairly poor taste.'

'That,' Mellusin said, 'is the reason people get waylaid in dark alleys. I've warned him to keep his opinions to himself, or at least voice them in front of the right people or save them for the ed-pin section of *Matin*. But he won't. One hopes he learns discretion before someone teaches it to him, in a more painful manner than you did.

'As I was saying, there *is* a class system here on D-Cumbre, and has been since shortly after the first colonists arrived, opened the mines, and the 'Raum showed up a bit later and began working them for us. Most people, from top to bottom, like things the way they are – comfortably ordered. The human race becomes unsettled when it's unsure of its future, and it's the task of a natural leader to guide it carefully. Is something the matter, Garvin?'

Jaansma was sweating gently – Jasith's toes were moving in his crotch, and she was barely suppressing her glee. 'Nothing, sir. A bit warm in here.'

Mellusin nodded for a waiter, told the man to increase the overhead fan's speed. While his attention was turned away, Garvin pinched Jasith's big toe. She hid a yelp, pulled her foot down.

'Now,' Mellusin said. 'Where were we?'

'You were explaining why the Rentiers were the rightful masters of the Cumbre system,' Garvin said.

Mellusin looked sharply at Garvin, was met with an open, interested expression.

'Come on, Garvin,' Jasith said. 'They've called your shuttle.'

'Coming,' he said, stepping carefully out of the lim, aware he was just a little drunk. 'Thank you for dinner, and an . . . interesting conversation, sir.'

'Thank you,' Mellusin said. 'I enjoyed meeting you, and, like my daughter, am a bit impressed. Come back and see us again, Garvin Jaansma.'

'Thank you, sir. And I *shall* see you again.'

'Come *on*,' Jasith shouted, and Garvin trotted toward her. He eyed the schedule flashing on the board.

'I thought you said the shuttle was leaving. I've still got fifteen minutes.'

'And I wanted to kiss you, dummy. That ought to take at least fifteen minutes, unless you want to go back and gibber some more with my daddy.'

'Nope. Let's find a nice secluded corner. But you know what I really want to do?' He leaned close, whispered.

'Garvin Jaansma! Such language!'

'Just wanted to make sure there wasn't any confusion about what we might think about doing next time around.'

'Talk like that certainly prevents confusion,' Jasith said, trying to pretend shock. 'Here's what I'd like to do.' In turn, she whispered.

'Great gods,' Garvin said. 'I didn't know rich girls talked like that!'

'We do,' she said throatily. 'And you should see what we do with our mouths when we're *not* talking. That's even more shocking.'

TWENTY-FOUR

Alt Jav Hofzeiger felt a little like crying. No one . . . not his revered retired-Haut father back on Mauren VI, not his instructors at Centrum's Military Institute, not even his fellow junior officers, had told him combat would be like this.

Combat . . . for their blasters were fully loaded, the orbiting Zhukovs and Griersons high overhead carried live missiles and rounds, and his orders were to kill any armed man or woman who refused a single shout to surrender.

Combat . . . but he hadn't seen anyone to shoot at, let alone anyone worth shooting at. Just ignorant hill-dwellers, completely perplexed at his questions, who didn't even seem to know where on the map their lousy little villages were.

Three coms shouted questions and orders at him and each other, carried by three sweating troops who'd been riflemen or -women before this patrol.

One com: 'Assegai Delta Deuce, this is Assegai Delta . . . give your present map locations please . . .' Assegai Delta was Fourth Infantry Regiment's Commanding Officer, a bluff man he'd respected until this nightmare began, *Mil* Fran Whitley.

Hofzeiger was Assegai Delta Deuce – Fourth Infantry,

Delta Company, Second Platoon, commanding seventeen
other infantrymen .

Another com: 'Assegai Delta Deuce, this is Delta
Six . . . come on, Hofzeiger. I've got your Bravo element
on visual, and they're separated from your line of march.
Suggest you take up a defensive perimeter until they join
the main force, over.' Delta Six was Delta Company
Commander, *Cent* Theresa Rivers, and at least all she
sounded was harried. Hofzeiger thought she was a
damned good officer, if a little too eager. He realized his
men would say the same about him, at least the eager
part.

'Assegai Delta Deuce, this is Lance Six. Why are you
moving so slow? Imperative you complete ordered day's
sweep on sked . . . you are at least four kilometers behind
projected march . . . blip your present location, over.'
Lance Six was God – *Caud* Jochim Williams, orbiting
just overhead in his Cooke. Rivers was in a Grierson, and
the Regimental Commander in another Cooke.

Three levels of command were riding close herd on
this patrol, ordered to sweep the reaches from the coastal
lowlands of Dharma Island into the ominous, unpopulated, and fog-hung Highlands. II Section – Strike Force
Intelligence – said the 'Raum hid out on these slopes,
oppressing the rural farmers and requiring them to provide food, shelter, and fresh recruits at gunpoint. But
there'd been no bandits so far, nothing but the endless
yammer of Hofzeiger's officers since he'd off-loaded from
his Grierson before dawn, far downslope.

He wanted to grab all three mikes and scream shut
up, give him a moment to think, a moment to try to find
where he was on the completely inaccurate map which he
wasn't even sure was of Dharma Island, regardless of the
legend, a moment to get his platoon rested and re-
formed. Dammit, he wasn't a bad officer . . . maybe not

the best in the regiment but always with SUPERIOR ratings, and they weren't giving him a chance to prove
himself.

One com-carrier eyed Hofzeiger with sympathy — the
alt wasn't a bad guy, and these dickheads up in the sky
had no idea of what it was like to be down here in the
slime on a forty-five-degree slope of sticky, wet clay
trying to keep from sliding all the way back down to the
ocean, glimpsed longingly in the distance now and again,
rain-soaked, pack straps digging into shoulders, waist,
back, blaster weighing half a kilo more each step you
took, goddamned vines pulling, whipping, thornbushes
clawing, and strange noises in the brush just out of sight.

No idea at all.

'Level ground,' the man ahead of a com operator whispered, as per orders, although why quiet was important
with the drive roar of the aircraft overhead and the chatter on the coms was beyond anyone. 'Level ground,' the
operator obediently told Hofzeiger, who nodded dumbly,
then remembered his own orders, and passed word back
down the column, wiped sweat, and reached for the com
to Williams, figuring he was the most important.

'Lance Six, this is Assegai Delta Deuce, blipping . . .
map not accurate . . . terrain nearly impassable . . . cutting our way as we go . . . over.'

'Delta Deuce, this is Lance. I did not ask for excuses,
soldier! Follow my orders, or I'll have someone down
there who will!'

Hofzeiger wanted to swear, but just clicked his mike
twice — message received. Another whisper came down:
'Village ahead. Occupied. Six up.'

'Son of a bitch,' Hofzeiger muttered. 'Another one
that isn't on the map.'

He keyed the mike. 'Lance, this is Delta Deuce. Stand
by. We have a village to clear.' He repeated the message

into the other two coms. 'Six coming up,' he whispered
back, and pushed his way up the track they'd been slash-
ing through the undergrowth. His com operators started
after him, then Hofzeiger had a wonderful idea. ' You
three maintain position. I'm doing a personal recon.'

The first com man grinned – not bad. If Hofzeiger
wasn't there to be shouted at, he couldn't be shouted at,
now could he?

Hofzeiger's platoon sergeant, *Tweg* Adeon, was waiting
on the edge of a scrubby cornfield. Ahead was the village – a scatter of huts around a central square, a single
large public com sheltered by a round wooden canopy, a
half-domed prefab building with peeling paint that was
the STORE; and a long open-sided shed that would serve
as the village social center, pub, and meeting place.

'See any hostiles?' Hofzeiger asked.

Adeon shook his head. 'Two kids, one scrawny woman
who looked about thirty-six months pregnant, two *giptels*. No goblins. Goddamned village doesn't look like it'd
support more'n one bandit, and he'd have to take his loot
in corncobs.'

The *giptel* was a mostly domesticated native of D-
Cumbre, and served the hillside peasants as pet, watch
animal, and dinner, its white porklike flesh frequently
the only meat, other than game, these poor people would
see. Chickens had been imported with the original settlers, but became an instant favorite for the planet's small
two-legged snake-bodied predators known as *stobor*.

Hofzeiger saw a man peer out of a hut, duck back
inside. 'They know we're out here,' he said. 'Bring the
patrol up, skirmish line, and we'll sweep the village.
Adeon, you and I'll see if that peekaboo sort knows anything.'

'And,' Adeon muttered, 'if he's willing to tell it to us.'

Fifteen minutes later, the platoon had gone through

the village, found nothing except twenty-six scared peasants: children, women, and old men. That should have triggered an alarm from experienced soldiers, but Hofzeiger was thinking of other matters. All three coms were alive with questions from the overhead brass, trying to find out what was going on, if the patrol had found anything, what disposition was being made of this, that, and the other. Hofzeiger ignored their yammering, and asked the villager he'd prodded out at gunpoint his name.

'Eichere,' the man said reluctantly.

'And what's the name of this village?'

'It doesn't have one,' Eichere said. 'We just call it the village.'

'Cosmopolitan sort here,' one of the com operators said.

'Quiet,' Hofzeiger ordered. 'Are there any bandits in this area?'

'Bandits? I don't know what you mean.'

'Men with guns. Men who refuse to obey the government's laws,' Adeon said impatiently.

'The only men with guns I've seen are you,' Eichere said. 'I don't know if you obey the laws or not.'

'Kick the bastard a few dozen times,' a *finf* said. 'Bein' funny's not one of his available options.'

Hofzeiger glared at the noncom, went back to Eichere. Half a dozen villagers came up, cautiously, watching, listening.

'Are you sure there aren't any bandits?'

Eichere compressed his lips, looked away, nodded.

'He's lying,' a woman said. The woman was in her early thirties, looked a little less work-hammered than the others, and her rags were a bit cleaner and mended.

'Who're you?'

'Balcha is my name.'

'You've seen bandits?'

'Of course,' she said. 'We all have. But he . . . and the others . . . are too scared to say anything.'

'Why? We'll protect you from them.'

'At night?' Eichere said cynically. 'You'll come back from your city to make sure they don't burn my hut . . . with me inside it?'

'You're a coward, Eichere,' Balcha said scornfully. 'We must trust the government.'

Eichere snorted.

'Where do the bandits go?' Hofzeiger demanded.

'They use the trail that goes from there' – she pointed to the farside of the village – 'up toward the Highlands, or so I was told. They have a camp not far from here.'

'A camp?'

'Yes, sir,' she said.

'Could you take us there?'

Balcha hesitated.

'I will pay you,' Hofzeiger said eagerly.

'No,' she said. 'I will take no money. But if I take you to them, will you kill them all? Then we can be safe.'

'I will only kill those who resist me,' Hofzeiger said. 'The others will be arrested and taken to the city for trial, and punishment.'

'But they will never come back to our village?'

'No,' Hofzeiger said firmly.

'Then follow me. It is about . . . two, perhaps three hours from here.' She started toward the path.

'Wait, Balcha,' Hofzeiger said. 'I must report this to my leaders.'

Twenty minutes later, Balcha, who was walking just behind the point man, hesitated at a split in the trail. 'This way,' she said, not sounding sure of herself.

'Great,' a striker whispered. 'Another far-traveler. Gets lost half a klick from home.'

A few minutes later, she stopped beside a two-meter-tall mound of mud built by the industrious insects the Cumbrians called ants. She puzzled a moment, then turned to *Alt* Hofzeiger, who was just behind her with *Tweg* Adeon and the three com operators. 'I think I am leading us in the wrong direction. Let me go back to that turning and look at it again. Can I have one man to keep me safe?'

Hofzeiger growled under his breath, caught the eye of one striker who hadn't looked away fast enough. 'Habr. Go back with her.' He held out his hand, and a com operator slapped a mike into it. 'The boss is gonna love this,' he muttered. 'Delta Six, this is Assegai Delta Deuce . . .'

Balcha waited until she and Habr were just around a bend in the trail, stumbled, went to her knees. Habr knelt to help her, grunted, and stared in shock at the knife handle sticking out of his solar plexus, just below his ballistic combat vest. His face wizened in agony, then went blank, and he collapsed. The woman who'd called herself Balcha put two fingers in her mouth, whistled.

Up ahead, concealed in the brush about five meters from the trail, Comstock Brien heard the whistle, nodded to the man with the small plas box with a single button. The man unlocked the box, pressed the button.

The abandoned anthill had been hurriedly dug out from the rear when the Fourth's patrol was seen dismounting from its Grierson. Broken bottles, rusty nails, and other debris from the village dump were packed against the hill's inside wall, then two hundred kilos of mining explosive added. Some of the explosive came from the raid on C-Cumbre, months earlier. Two radio-controlled detonators were inserted in the explosives, and wet clay tamped to seal the hole.

The blast vaporized *Alt* Hofzeiger, his com operators, the rest of the command group, and six of the other twelve men and women. Half of the survivors were down, screaming, moaning in pain, and others were in stunned shock, staring at red-rain-drenched bodies.

Brien shouted, and thirty men and women burst out of their hiding places, and a ragged volley from sporting rifles and shotguns blasted. There were only two still making sounds, mewling like wounded kittens as they squirmed. Brien shot one with his pistol, and a woman shotgunned the other two 'Quickly,' he ordered. 'Take weapons, boots, everything.'

A woman rolled a young soldier over, saw her chest move, lifted her archaic rifle. 'No,' the soldier whispered. 'Please.' The rifle fired once.

One com unit had, freakishly, survived the blast.

'Delta Deuce, Delta Deuce, this is Delta Six. What the hell's going on down there? Delta Deuce, respond at once.'

'Take that, too,' Brien ordered. 'Our Task is easier when we can listen to them.'

Balcha trotted around the bend. 'Good,' Brien complimented her. She nodded thanks, knelt over a body, and unfastened its combat harness.

'Is there anyone in the village who tried to collaborate with the *giptels*?' he asked.

'No,' she said. 'They are well trained. We need punish no one.'

Four minutes later, there was nothing on the trail but twelve naked bodies.

Caud Williams stepped out of his Cooke, walked slowly from the clearing that'd been hastily carved out of the jungle to the ambush site. The last of the corpses were being slid into body bags. *Cent* Rivers, Delta's

Commanding Officer, sat on an uprooted tree, head in her hands. *Cent* Angara met him, saluted.

'Don't do that,' Williams said. 'We're in a combat zone!'

'Sorry, sir,' Angara said. 'I was thinking about . . . other things.'

Williams nodded, stared down the trail. 'Do you have any idea how many casualties these brave soldiers were able to inflict before they were overrun?'

'None, sir. No blood trails, no blood patches at all.'

'They must've cleaned up before they fled, the bastards,' Williams said. 'Very well, then, we'll have to make an educated estimate.'

'Sir?'

'How many bandits do you think they were able to take with them?'

'Sil there was no sign of *any* enemy casualties,' Angara said.

'It's impossible for me to believe women and men that I trained weren't able to fight back,' Williams said firmly. 'And do you have any idea what would happen to morale if we were to tell the men of the Force their fellows were helplessly butchered where they stood?' Angara said nothing. 'Very well,' Williams said. 'Eighteen of our people killed . . . probably they were able to take at least one with them. The unit diary will give the casualties as twenty-one probable kills, fifteen wounded.'

Angara still was silent.

'I assume you heard me, *Cent*?'

'Yessir,' Angara said. 'Twenty-one probable kills, fifteen wounded. Sir.'

Williams stared, and Angara looked away.

'What about the village?'

'I've sent two interrogation teams in. So far, nobody

knows anything. The woman who said she wanted to help came to the village just as they heard the sounds of our landing, and said they'd treat her as one of them, or be very, very sorry, and anything she said, they must agree with. Most of their young men have already joined the bandits. The villagers said they were forced to go. I'm not sure that's the truth. They've got no idea where the bandits came from, no idea where they went, how many there are, or anything else.'

'Very well,' Williams said. 'Carry on.'

He took a deep breath, went over and sat down beside Rivers. She lifted her head, and Williams saw the tear streaks. 'You make them into soldiers . . . and then you lose them,' he said gently. 'That's the way it's always been. The first time's always the hardest.'

'Jav . . . *Alt* Hofzeiger was one of my best.' she said. 'I'd recommended him for the next *Cent* Board. Now . . .' She blinked, swallowed very hard. 'They murdered my whole platoon, *Caud*. They shot *Finf* Zelen in the face . . . she would've lived, if we could've gotten her evacked in time. But . . .'

Her voice trailed off.

'Come on, Theresa,' Williams said. 'There's almost one hundred sixty people still alive. They're depending on you.'

'I know. I just hope there'll be some way to make them pay for this.'

'There will be,' Williams said firmly.

Rivers looked at a dark, drying stain. Her lips compressed. 'Yes, sir. Someone *will* pay. Soon.'

Two nights later, a Grierson grounded gently about half a kilometer from the village, just at last light. Twenty-five men and women, wearing dark coveralls, faces and hands darkened, got out. They carried pistols and fighting knives. All were volunteers. It was fairly dim — only the two smaller moons, Penwith and Bodwin, were out.

They gathered around *Cent* Rivers. She drew her knife, held it up. 'I want everybody on D-Cumbre to know the Force never forgets . . . and we always punish murderers. And everybody in that village is guilty. I'll take point.'

She sheathed her knife, and the twenty-five filed off, into the jungle, toward the village.

'Did you hear the skinny?' Garvin said.

'I heard,' a glum Njangu said.

'Which version?'

'Both,' Yoshitaro said. '*Matin* claims the 'Raum out-laws did it because one of the villagers must've given us some good intelligence. That's the official word.'

'And you know that's bullshit.'

'I know.'

'Damn, but that'll teach 'em,' Garvin enthused. 'Mess with the bull, and you get the horns. How many did they kill?'

'About forty,' Njangu said. 'Mostly women and kids.'

'I heard *Cent* Rivers led the raid in person.'

'I heard the same thing," Njangu said.

'So what're you so gloomy about? That'll put a chill in all those illegal settlements out there. Teach 'em they can't play on both sides.'

'Garvin,' Njangu said tiredly, 'come on, man. *Think*.'

'Think what? That's the way to run things. They kill one of us, we kill a dozen of them. That'll teach them not to be aidin' and abetting.'

'It'll teach them, all right,' Njangu said. 'Teach them to be guerrillas.'

Garvin stared at his friend. 'How do you figure?'

'Real simple,' Njangu said. 'First, think about things from the villagers' perspective. We come through for half an hour, then go back to this island. The 'Raum live next door. The villagers can add . . . half an E-hour for us, twenty-six and a half for them to get even.'

'Yeah,' Garvin nodded.

'So if you were a villager, and you wanted to stay a live villager, who would you be more polite to?'

'I guess the 'Raum,' Garvin said reluctantly.

'Now, we've started patrolling the hills. We're going to bring law, order, and justice, right? So the first thing we do, when a patrol gets shot up, is send out a death squad and obliterate the village. Fine court of law there, and a *really* good way to get people to love you, last time I heard.'

'Who said we were supposed to be loved? That's why they gave us guns.'

'Hide and watch, my friend,' Yoshitaro said. 'Every dirt-gobbler that was wondering about things, after that dumb bitch created a slaughterhouse, shouldn't have much trouble making up his mind. Which side would you pick if you were out there?' Njangu finished.

'Shit,' Garvin said. He slumped down on Njangu's bunk. 'I *wasn't* thinking.'

'It doesn't look like anybody is,' Njangu said. 'And I'll bet they don't start now. Williams can't court-martial Rivers, even if he wanted to. Which is going to set a real fine example for the next idiot who's standing there with a gun in his hand, pissed off because his bunkie got his head shot off.'

'I guess you're right.'

'I *know* I'm right,' Njangu said.

'How'd you get to be so damned smart?' Garvin asked.

'I'm not smart, I'm cunning,' Njangu explained. 'Cops can make all the mistakes in the world. Crooks only get to make one.'

'So I'd better leave the thinking to you from here on out?' Garvin said.

'Might be safer. And I'll make you another prediction. This batshit won't stop anything. There'll be more patrols hit, and pretty soon we won't go into the hills at all in anything other than company strength. And then they'll start sniping at us while we waddle through the jungle, grinding us down one by one.'

'You're sure a cheery bastard,' Jaansma said.

'I am that,' Njangu said. He put down the sight he'd been carefully cleaning, grabbed his cap from the end of his bunk. 'Come on. I'll let you buy me a beer and maybe that'll make me into a laughing idiot like the rest of this murderous goddamned Strike Force.'

An assault team was wiped out three days later, and, four days after that, HQ Honor Guard was almost sucked into an ambush making a sweep five kilometers beyond the Heights.

Less than half a dozen 'Raum were confirmed killed, although the claimed body count was ninety, and only seven had been captured. About six villages were cleared as suspected 'Raum strongholds, and another dozen razed after weapons or other banned materials were found.

Caud Williams announced a change in tactics – henceforth the Force would patrol in company-sized elements, remaining in the jungle for up to five days, being resupplied from the air while hiving smaller units off on close-range sweeps. 'Once these small patrols locate the bandits,' he said, 'it'll be a simple matter either to smash them from the air or hit them hard with the main force. Another advantage we have, and one I propose to exploit to the fullest, is our command of the air. These bandits will become like field mice, always looking over their shoulder for the hawk – and I guarantee it'll be there.

'This campaign should last no more than another month or two before we bring peace to the hills.'

'I've decided,' Garvin said gloomily, 'God ... or the gods ... hate me.'

'Why?' Jasith asked. 'And why is the pickup so spotty?'

''Cause I'm calling from the public line outside our orderly room,' Jaansma explained, 'and there's about a kazillion taps on the line to make sure I don't say anything classified. There's also a delay in the transmission, I think. Not that I would say anything I'm not supposed to. Hell, I don't *know* anything classified.'

'So why are you so hated by gods and such? You got a chance to call me, didn't you,' Jasith asked.

'That's about all I'm going to get to do,' Garvin said. 'Because ...'

The sound blurred for a moment, then cleared as he said, 'so you see why I said that?'

'No,' Jasith said. 'Your voice went away.'

'I guess I do know something secret,' Garvin said. ''Kay, lemme rethink how to put it.'

'Uh, was it something about us?'

'Yep.'

'Maybe something like it'll be a while before you see me again?' Again, the sound blurred, but Garvin had nodded while speaking. 'I already figured that out,' Jasith said. 'Daddy told me what – some real big people told him.'

'That figures,' Garvin said. 'Everybody out there, including probably the 'Raum, knows more about my future than I do.'

'Can I come see you?'

'I don't think so,' Garvin said. 'All of our civilian workers have been told to stay away, and they've doubled the . . .' Again his voice blurred. 'I'm sorry, Jasith,' he said, sounding as completely pitiable as only a celibate twenty-year-old can. 'I really hoped, well, that . . .' His voice trailed off. 'Maybe, someday . . . aw, hell.'

The two stared at each other for a moment. 'I gotta go,' he said finally. 'There's two or three other guys waiting to use this com.'

'Garvin,' Jasith said softly. 'Do you still want to . . . see me?'

'Of course. You know I do.'

'Then let me give you something to remember, when you're out there.'

She swiftly unfastened her blouse, opened it. She wore nothing under it, and her breasts stood up firmly. She ran a fingernail around one nipple, and it stood up firmly. 'I wish it was you doing that to me,' she whispered.

'Me too,' Garvin said, his voice a little hoarse.

'I'd show you more . . . give you something more . . . but a housekeeper's just around the corner. I'll miss you, Garvin. And I'll be there when you want me.' She ran a tongue slowly around her lips, then cut the connection.

Garvin sat, staring at the gray screen. Someone hammered on the booth's door. 'Come on in there! Other people got girlfriends, too.'

'Not like mine,' Garvin said. 'Not like mine.'

Two months later, there were about twenty confirmed 'Raum killed, fifty-six captured, eighteen surrendered. Thirty-eight Force men and women were dead, about half that many again wounded. Seventy-three civilians had been killed by one side or another. Forty-six 'illegal' settlements had been burned by Force patrols or civilian vigilance patrols. And no one in the Strike Force, beginning with *Finf* Garvin Jaansma, had been granted a pass.

*

'You see,' Comstock Brien said, 'this is the way to victory. Slow, proven, but little by little we whittle them down, without any expensive adventurism, such as you advocated.'

Jord'n Brooks smiled thinly. 'Let us hope, brother,' he said, 'that your way continues to be successful.'

'It shall,' Brien said smugly. 'And now is a good time to show how our power has increased.'

Five days later, an estimated two hundred or more 'Raum came from nowhere and seized a suburb of Leggett. They held the holo station long enough to make a planetwide 'cast proclaiming that justice and equality for the 'Raum must come to the Cumbre system, or the worlds would run with blood. They held a drumhead trial in the town's police station, and hanged the town's officials and seven of the local police force. The others had either fled or been killed in the assault.

Another thirty-nine civilians whom the 'Raum accused of being traitors to humanity were shot before the assault force vanished as silently as it had come, a full half an hour before police reinforcements arrived, and forty-five minutes before the first Force reaction element was deployed.

TWENTY-FIVE

They came out of the Griersons fast, blasters ready. Overhead, unseen in the mist, three Zhukovs howled close orbits around the buildings, gray in the gray dawn.

But there was nothing waiting except bodies.

Bodies and the Musth. There were thirty-three of the aliens, a platoon, wearing the combat harness that identified them as soldiers, and they moved in pairs, from human corpse to corpse, methodically making sure each was adequately dead.

Njangu and the rest of Gamma Team ran around the Musth headquarters, and set up a hasty perimeter. Not two meters from Yoshitaro was a very dead man, who wore the simple coveralls of a farmer, but wore a Confederation battle vest and carried an issue blaster. There was a fist-sized hole in his chest. Njangu glanced at the body, away, then quickly back, for something in the hole had moved. White-gray worms wriggled, then returned to their burrowing. Njangu swallowed hard.

'That's one of their weapons,' Kipchak said calmly. He was crouched, blaster ready, to the team's rear. 'It's a projectile weapon that blows a frigging great hole in you with a capsule, the capsule breaks, and those worms eat you to death before you've got time to scream more than once or twice. Supposedly the worms then die.'

'Not that it'd matter by then,' Penwyth said.

'Silence over there,' Gonzales snapped.

'Your men need not mire themssselves,' a Musth told *Alt* Hedley. 'Thessse creaturesss have gone beyond, and will not be troublesssome, and there are no more of them, or we would have found them on our detectorsss.'

'So it appears,' Hedley said. He glanced back at *Caud* Williams and his staff, coming out of a C&C Grierson. 'But I have my orders.'

'Then continue wasssting your time,' the Musth said. 'It isss no concern of mine.'

Hedley nodded, made the rounds of the I&R company. The 'Raum must've come out of *that* ravine, he guessed, seeing the sprawl of bodies from there almost to the main buildings. The first to die had been hit with conventional blasters, and left not completely unpleasant remains. But the closer the raiders got to the Musth, the more nastily they'd died. Here was a clot of bodies shredded by something, there was—

'You are interesssted in what happened?' It was the Musth.

'I am.'

'I have the name of Wlencing,' the Musth said. 'I have the lead of the sssoldiers who dessstroyed thessse bunglersss, I believe the word is.'

'Why bunglers?' Hedley asked. 'Jon Hedley is my name, by the way.'

'To make an attack, and be utterly wiped out without causssing any casssualties in return doesss not sssuggesssst the most ssskilled of warriorsss to me. Or am I making a misssevaluation?'

'No,' Hedley said. 'Not considering the results, you're not.'

'Are thessse the same sssort I have ssseen on your holosss? Banditsss, I think you term them?'

'Yes. Renegades from the 'Raum.'

'I know the 'Raum,' Wlencing said. 'Wormsss who burrow at the ordersss of your authority-onesss. From thisss, I would think they ssshould know their ssstation, and not presssume to be fighters.'

'They didn't do very well,' Hedley agreed.

That makesss me wonder about certain . . . thingsss,' Wlencing said. 'About how good your warriorsss really are.'

'I am not familiar with your weapons,' Hedley said. 'Blasters killed those men and women over there. But what about this group?'

'A very sssecret weapon,' Wlencing said. He opened a pouch took out a box with rounded corners. 'I touch thisss stud, then throw the deviccce. When it ssstrikes, sssmall creaturesss explode out, sssmall creatutcsss with . . . bitesss? Isss that the word?'

'Stings?'

'Yesss. Ssstingsss. Quick, but not pleasssant.'

'You said it was secret,' Hedley said. 'Why are you telling me?'

'Why not? I do not think there isss anything that ssspecial about the deviccce. Ssstarshipsss' performance, ssstrategies, misssiles, yesss, sssecret. But a sssimple killing tool? That isss ridiculousss. Besssides, sssince I command our warriorsss, no one will contesssst what I decccide to do. Or not to do.'

'I see,' Hedley said.

'Are you not plagued by thossse-far-from-the-fight, who think it their right to make rulesss for all?'

'Lord knows we are that,' Hedley said. He looked at another body. 'How did she die?'

'By a hand weapon like this,' Wlencing said, taking something from a pouch. It had a short, stubby barrel, and the 'grip' was a double strap. Wlencing touched it to his upper paw, and the grip curled around it, as his double thumbs clasped it. 'A very, very fassst acccid, sssprayed by ultrahigh-presssure air. As fassst asss one of your blasssters, if ssshorter-ranged.' He put the weapon away, looked back at the command group. A Musth had joined *Caud* Williams. 'That isss Aesc,' he said. 'Our sssystem-leader. He isss telling your leader what happened, and warning him.'

'Warning him?' Hedley said.

'No Musth died here today at the handsss of these sssavages,' Wlencing said. 'That isss good. That isss the way it mussst continue. If one Musth . . . jussst one . . . isss killed by these rebelsss, thessse banditsss, all humansss, innoccent, guilty, everyone in the Cumbre sssystem will either die or become our digging worms, and these worldsss will become part of the Musth Empire.'

TWENTY-SIX

Word of the Highland Massacre swept through the 'Raum mining colonies on C-Cumbre, the 'Raum settlements across D-Cumbre, and especially in the Eckmuhl, the 'Raum ghetto in Leggett. The 'Raum exploded in blind rage and hatred. There were no Musth in Leggett, but there were the hated police and the Rentiers who exploited the sect. Police lifters were overturned and burnt, and the officers in them beaten or worse. Riot squads were driven back, and police stations became fortresses under siege. Stores were looted, including two of Angie Rada's family's Markets. Gangs of 'Raum ravaged the streets, and anyone not armed and traveling in company was in danger.

The Force was brought down from the hills to bring order. The soldiers swept the streets, set up roadblocks. Unfamiliar with civil disorder, the soldiers behaved as if the 'Raum, all 'Raum, were their enemies, sweeping the rioters back into Eckmuhl, arresting any 'Raum who couldn't give an instant explanation for who he – or she – was, and what he – or she – was doing, or even for just having a 'Raum-sounding name. Sometimes the 'Raum fought back, and sometimes they ended up in hospital. Others, not so 'lucky,' ended in the morgue.

The streets were quiet again. The holos, especially

Matin, cheered the Force as saviors of Cumbre. The soldiers gloried in the praise they received so seldom, or at least some did. *Alt* Hedley, *Finf* Kipchak, *Finf* Jaansma, Striker Yoshitaro, *Cent* Angara and others kept their own counsel.

'Now,' Jord'n Brooks told Jo Poynton quietly, as the Group assembled for another meeting, this time in a burnt-out village, 'you see my idea of moving against the oppressors in the city might have merit.'

'Our people were defeated,' she said.

Brooks shrugged. 'They were rioting, not fighting a war. And they weren't beaten in their souls, their hearts, their minds. Can there be any of our people who don't realize their enemy, and that only one can survive?'

'I can't argue that,' Poynton said carefully. 'But Brien's view of the Task has been more successful than yours, at least as far as external results, and success will rule this Group's thinking.'

'True,' Brooks grudged. 'But how long will his success continue? The Force is still fighting us with only one hand, and that one bare. Sooner or later, unless they are total fools, they will learn to fight our way. And then what?'

Jo Poynton nodded once, turned away from Brooks as Comstock Brien began speaking.

TWENTY-SEVEN

'You're free,' Jasith squealed.

'Or anyway reasonable,' Garvin said. 'Since we're such hee-roes, I wangled a pass.' Jasith didn't notice the sarcasm. 'Any possibilities of getting together?'

Jasith's voice went husky. 'You tell me where.'

Garvin thought of the Shelburne's bar, remembered Marya, discarded the notion. 'I'm from out of town, remember?' he said. 'You pick the spot.'

'Are you still at the base?'

'Yeh. Next shuttle to Leggett's in . . . ten minutes.'

'You just wait there,' Jasith ordered. 'Concentrate on looking cute. I'll get you.'

Garvin peered through the gaggle of shuttles, cabs, and private lifters, spotted a familiar, long black lim nosing toward him. 'Aw shit,' he moaned. 'Now I'm gonna have to listen to more batshit about how the frigging Force is saving frigging civilization. God *damn* it, Jasith! Are we failing to communicate?'

The lifter grounded, and the pilot's door lifted and Jasith stuck her head out. 'Surprised?'

'Oh Lordy lord, am I ever,' Garvin said fervently.

'Then get in,' she ordered. 'Up front, with me.'

Garvin checked the backseat. No father. Jasith had her

hair tied back and wore a red halter top and baggy black crepe pants. She was barefoot. Wordlessly, the two leaned together, and kissed. After some time, a horn blasted, and they broke away.

'Take me,' Garvin said. 'I'm yours.'

Jasith touched controls, and the lim took off and floated along the ramp toward the ocean. 'Daddy's got two bodyguards keeping me safe,' she said.

'Where'd you hide them? In the baggage compartment?'

'I managed to convince him that I was perfectly safe, if I came out here to see you. He said we couldn't get in any trouble with soldiers all around us.'

'There aren't any soldiers all around us,' Garvin said.

'You noticed.'

'So where are we going?'

'Nowhere.' Jasith touched sensors, and the lim turned until its nose was pointing toward blackness. 'On this heading,' she said, 'we'll reach' – she hit another sensor and the SatPos screen lit – 'Lanbay Island. About dawn, at this speed.'

'What's there?'

'Nothing. Rocks. Trees. Waves. But I wasn't thinking about going there.'

'What were you thinking?'

'First, about putting this lifter on auto . . . like this,' Jasith said. 'Then about putting an anticollision alarm on. Then about toggling this sensor here' – the dark canopy of the lim cleared, and they were looking up at storm clouds racing overhead – 'and getting in the back, like this.' The seat swiveled, and Jasith moved past Garvin. 'Join me?'

Garvin found seat controls to the side, pressed one. The seat back collapsed.

'Not that button, silly,' Jasith said. 'The one in front of it. But put the seat back up first.'

Garvin obeyed. 'Now what?'

'I had the head cook flash-defrost one of our picnic baskets,' she said. 'I put it in the storage compartment in the back of this seat. It's got all kinds of good things in it – roe, pâté, chilled filet of beef with sour cream dressing, endive salad, and a fruit ice, plus a couple of bottles of that Earth Taittinger champagne you sucked up so fast when Daddy and I took you to dinner. So we could eat. Or . . .'

'Or what?'

'Or you *could* always press that button over there, under the window.'

Garvin obeyed, and the lim's rear seat gently collapsed, and pillows inflated on either side. Jasith swung her legs up, until she was lying on the seat.

'I wondered why Daddy ordered this feature on the lim which came all the way from Centrum,' she said. 'He said there'd been a mistake. I don't believe him. Do you think he might be unfaithful to my stepmother every now and again?'

Garvin didn't answer. He was staring, hypnotized, at Jasith. She sat up, unfastened her hair, let it fall free, then her fingers touched the button of the halter top between her breasts.

'Let me do that,' Garvin said.

'All right.' Jasith lay back. Garvin's fingers were suddenly thumbs, but the top came away. He bent his head, nibbled at her nipples. She sighed, stroked his close-cropped hair. He put both hands in the waistband of her pants, slid them off. She wore nothing under them.

'Undress for me,' she whispered.

He obeyed, Jasith's eyes on him. 'You're very pretty,' she murmured.

'So are you.'

'Now,' she said, lifting one leg and resting it on the

doorsill, and putting her hands together, over her head, 'come here. Hold my wrists to keep me from moving. Now, my Garvin. Oh, please, now!'

Half an eternity later, the lim bumped softly against something. Jasith murmured, sat up, peered out. 'Oh dear,' she said.

'What's the matter?' Garvin said.

'We appear to be lost. Oceans don't have shacks.'

The lim had gently bumped into a low shed, turned, and was drifting away from it. Garvin saw a sign: FIRING RANGE SEVEN. TARGET STORAGE SHED.

'We sure as hell are lost,' he said. 'Lost and in trouble. We're back on Chance Island, out on one of the target ranges, on the east end. We will get our heinies slapped if they catch us.'

'How'd we get here?' Jasith wondered.

Garvin looked over the now-lowered front seat, noted flashing lights on the control panel. 'I think we must've kicked Something,' he said. 'Or everything, starting with the collision sensor. And I think we better rectify the matter. I see headlights coming toward us.'

Jasith slid past him, into the driver's seat, and her fingers rippled over sensors. The lim lifted to two meters, accelerated, and sped over the range, then down a rocky beach and back out to sea.

'Do you think they'll shoot at us?'

'I don't know,' Garvin said. 'Whyn't you drop it down some, and I'll say a prayer.'

She obeyed, and small waves crested barely a meter below the lim's bottom. 'Now what?'

'Now we wait until we make sure we're out of range and beyond challenge.' Garvin said. 'Are we going back toward Lanbay Island?'

'More or less,' Jasith said.

'I don't see any missile flashes,' Garvin reported, looking back. 'So I guess we showed 'em clean skirts . . . well, not that. Bottoms, maybe. Whyn't you drop the speed down?'

'And then?'

'And then come back here where you belong.'

'All right,' Jasith said. 'And then?'

'Is there some way to open this roof?'

'Surely.' The canopy opened, and a light, warm, tropical rain misted down.

'Now what?' Jasith said.

'You just stay on your knees like that,' Garvin said, getting carefully to his feet, 'and let me surprise you.'

A moment later Jasith squealed. 'Oh God, God, God,' she moaned. 'Oh yes. All the way in me now. Oh, Garvin. Garvin . . .'

At dawn, the men and women of the Force were stumbling out of their barracks for reveille as a black luxury lifter floated down the enormous parade field. It grounded, a door lifted, and a disheveled Garvin Jaansma got out, went to the driver's side.

'Wasn't Daddy right?' Jasith said softly. 'Wasn't I perfectly safe?'

He kissed her.

'Give me a call, soldier, when you're of a mind to.' The lim window slid closed, and the craft lifted, spun on its own length and accelerated away, toward Leggett across the bay.

Garvin Jaansma took a deep breath, started across the parade ground as the whistles and catcalls built from the Force.

TWENTY-EIGHT

'Again . . . you know *nothing* about the murder of Mister Scryfa and his family?' the interrogator asked, slipping, letting a bit of incredulity into her voice.

'Nothing,' the 'Raum said calmly.

'But you were their housemaster,' Technician Warbeck insisted.

'I was.'

'You were in the house when the murderers came in.'

'Evidently I was.'

'But you heard nothing? Nothing woke you?'

'I am a very sound sleeper,' the man insisted.

'Warder!'

The door opened, and the guard entered.

'He's cleared for release,' Warbeck said. 'But you're to stay in close touch with us, in case we need to question you again.'

The man stood, a trace of a smile on his lips, and walked out. The warder lingered. 'Why didn't you nail him? The bastard was there . . . we know that . . . we even found a blood trail from the Scryfas' bedroom to his quarters.'

'Look at this trace,' the woman said, and lifted the hood away from the machine she sat behind. 'Zero flickers on the readouts, zero wiggles, zero anything, which means the frigging scan insists he's innocent, innocent, innocent, and that's all a judge will listen to.'

'That's not possible,' the guard said.

'Sure it is,' Warbeck said tiredly. 'If somebody doesn't believe lying to us is really lying . . . they'll fly every time.'

'That's what it's come down to?' the warder asked. 'Somebody can slaughter a Rentier . . . and his whole family . . . and hike?'

'That's what it's come down to.'

A Cooke hovered up the jungle trail, hovering at intervals, and a small white spike spat into the ground from a cylinder bolted to its hill. Within an hour, three women and two men went the length of the trail. The leader carried a small homemade case. Every now and again, the case buzzed, and the five looked carefully through the undergrowth, dug in the ground until they found one of the spikes. Every time they did, a woman covered it with a dark metallic cone. They did this to all of the people-sniffers except one. That one they put a very filthy pair of pants next to, and one man urinated in a circle around it. Then they ran, back toward their camp.

Three hours after that, three Zhukovs dived toward the spike. Three salvos of the semiguided Fury rockets shot toward the ground. and the jungle rocked under explosions. A single Grierson sailed through the whirling smoke, and an I&R team dropped off its ramp. 'Kursk Leader, this is Sibyl Beta,' the team reported. 'Negative contact.'

The *alt* commanding the Zhukov flight forgot his communications discipline. 'Whaat? We had positive indicators!'

'This is Sibyl Beta,' the com told him. 'I say again . . .

negative contact. No casualties found, no traces found. Your trickshit machinery's wonky. Out.'

Two Cookes swirled about the village. 'No sign of life,' one reported.

'Keep checking,' the battalion commander, overhead in his Grierson, ordered. 'We have positive intelligence about this village.'

One Cooke dived low, the second close behind.

'Maybe there'll be something up that draw?' the commander of the first Cooke suggested on the between-ship channel.

'On your tail,' the other responded.

The first entered the ravine, hovered around a bend and thick, hand-woven nets rose up before, behind. The gunner on the first ship pulled the triggers on his autocannon, and shells slammed uselessly through the holes in the net. Another net came up, trapping the second Cooke. The commander of the ACV shouted a warning, just as six 'Raum, each with a captured Squad Support Weapon, rose from spider holes and bullets yammered into the scout vehicles.

'Relax,' Comstock Brien said quietly. 'Does it not always come this route?'

'It does,' the young man said. 'But it'd just be my luck—'

'Don't talk of luck,' Brien ordered. 'The greater your decision, the harder you work, the better your luck shall always be.'

The young man sniffed in skepticism. The third man leaning against a crude frame said nothing. A few minutes later, the first man stiffened. 'I hear it.'

Moments later, the drive-whine was audible to Brien's older ears, and, a hundred meters below, a Zhukov nosed into view, following the overgrown road as it curved below the cliffs. The young man and his partner tore away the concealing foliage, pushed the wooden frame with a Shrike lashed to it to the edge of the bluff. The missile had misfired during an air-support operation two weeks ago, been recovered by the 'Raum, fuel only half-expended. Its firing mechanism was replaced with a simple contact detonator, and the missile carried far down island.

The second man moved away from the launcher and watched the Zhukov close on a peculiarly shaped bush the three men atop the hill had designated as a firing marker, while the third ran back a few meters and picked up a small switch that was wired to the missile's rear.

'Wait ... wait ... wait ... wait ... NOW!' the second man ordered, and the third closed the switch. The Shrike hissed, then heat waves flared from its exhaust. The rack bucked, and the missile launched, almost straight down toward the Zhukov. It struck the attack ship just behind the main turret. The Shrike's primary charge exploded, and a jet of incandescent gas seared through the armor. The main charge, a gaseous explosive, sprayed into the Zhukov's crew space and detonated. The Zhukov exploded, pinwheeling into the jungle, thrashing like a dying beast.

The three men allowed themselves a moment of exultation, then trotted away.

'How the hell did those bastards manage to kill a Zhukov!' *Caud* Williams raved.

'As I said, sir, from above,' *Mil* Rao said. 'Armor's a few centimeters thinner there. And nobody expects to be hit from topside unless they're in space.'

'What was that goddamned vehicle commander doing that low, anyway?'

'Doing as he'd been ordered, sir. Closely patrolling the old highway toward the Highlands, looking for enemy sign.'

'Very well,' Williams said. 'Very well. We'll have to . . .' His voice trailed off.

Rao waited. 'Yes, sir?' he said after a time.

'Give me a moment,' Williams said. 'I'm trying to figure what we'll do next.'

There were five Cookes, flying west, fast, about a hundred meters above the jungle. The bluffs leading to the Highlands were to their left. Three times one or another of the combat lifters dipped into a clearing, hovered for an instant, then climbed back to the formation. The fourth time was almost like the others, except that the diving Cooke hovered long enough for eleven men to drop off the sides, and double into the thick brush around the clearing, crouching in a perimeter.

The eleven were Gamma Team, First Troop, I&R Company plus *Alt* Jon Hedley. They wore dark green-and-black camouflage matching the jungle, their faces and hands were blackened, and they carried heavy packs. They waited, weapons ready, for five minutes. The jungle was silent, except for the drip of rain. A wind stirred. A howler called from a distance. Then a gunshot blasted from somewhere, dull, dead, muffled by the undergrowth. A moment later, another shot came, from some distance, then a third and a fourth, each blast fainter than the last.

'Shit!' Petr said, standing. 'They made us.'

The team stayed in a crouch, except for Hedley, who slid to the team leader. 'Now what happens?'

'We evac,' Petr said, 'or else there'll be thirty or more of 'em coming in on us. A man could get hurt sticking around an insertion zone these days.'

'Every time?'

'Just about,' Petr said. 'They seem to be able to tell whether it's a phony insert or for real. Looks like the bastards have every clearing either bugged . . . although we can't find any telltales . . . or under visual. This is my fourth patrol this week that's been blown.' He motioned to the team's com man, took the microphone: 'Sibyl One Control, this is Sibyl One Gamma. Outski. Eyeballed. Clear.'

'This is Sibyl Control,' the voice came. 'Nice short visit. Stand by. Pickup inbound.'

'See what I mean, boss?' Petr said.

'I do,' Hedley said. 'I know you're good, and I know the other insert teams are good. The flipping problem seems to be flipping simple. The flipping villains are flipping winning.'

TWENTY-NINE

Caud Williams was glooming over a glass of sherry – his last case from Centrum, which made his mood worse – in his quarters when someone tapped. 'Enter.'

Jon Hedley opened the door. 'A word, sir?'

'Come in, Alt.'

Hedley obeyed.

'A drink?' Williams asked. 'There's almost anything you could want behind the false bookshelves.'

'Nossir,' Hedley said. 'I'd like to ask a favor.'

'Petr, Monique,' Hedley said genially. 'Grab a cup and drag up a chair. I'm looking for flipping volunteers.'

'Boss,' Kipchak said, 'I'll be honest. You've got me for anything that's better than this dumbshit stumbling around like we've been doing.'

'I'm in, too,' Lir said.

'I'm not just looking for single volunteers,' Hedley said. 'I want two flipping teams, one as the main operators, one as support.'

'You've got Gamma,' Kipchak said.

'And Beta,' Monique said.

'You're not going to check?'

'Don't need to,' Lir said. 'I speak for everybody. If I don't . . . they can go back to groundponding with the line-slime.' Kipchak nodded agreement.

I had a little chat with God,' Hedley said. '*Caud* Williams listened, said it was worth a try. He sounded pretty beat-up by the course of flipping events.'

'No offense to ossifers and like that,' Kipehak said, 'but he damned well ought to. This Operation Clean Sweep's a goddamned joke.'

'With any luck, things'll get serious now,' Hedley said. 'Here's the drill. We're going to put one patrol out on a hot scent . . . I've figured out a way to get on the ground without being snooped, I hope . . . and they're going to stay flipping out there until we bag the lot of 'em.'

'How long?'

'If necessary,' Hedley said, 'until everybody's dead, retired or their enlistment's up.'

'What about rcsupply?'

'You'll lug ultraconcentrates, and won't get anything more until you're starving,' Hedley said. 'Then we'll do it with some kind of masked airdrops.'

'What about commo?' Lir said. 'Nice to be runnin' through the jungle, all sneaky-like, with half a dozen goddamned Command and Control dicks ten meters upstairs.'

'That's part of the deal Williams bought,' Hedley said. 'I run things from insert until it gets serious and you call for the big dogs. Nobody hangs over you.'

'Let's go back to this bagging lot,' Petr said. 'How's that going to work?'

'The insert team stays after the villains,' Hedley explained, 'and follows 'em to where they're going. If it's a raid, the patrol either wipes 'em out or gets them to surrender. If things get too big, I've got authorization to call in all kinds of flipping support.'

'How much is all kinds of flipping?'

'The whole flipping Force, if that's what it takes,' Hedley said.

Lir whistled soundlessly. 'What did you do? Catch Williams in bed with a dead woman or a live kid?'

'Oh ye of little faith. He merely listened to my wisdom, then began salaaming.'

'Yeh,' Lir said. 'Right.'

'Go get your teams ready,' Hedley said. 'I've got some coms to make . . . there'll be a little augmentation made before you tromp the turf.'

'Asshole Ben is looking for volunteers again,' Dill said. 'With I&R one more time . . . except this time it's for real. Trying something new, new being classified.'

'Why not?' Kang said. Dill looked at the other two, got nods.

'I'm not sure how it's different, but we're going to be part of the immediate. And Garvin . . . we're backing up your chingo Yoshitaro with Gamma Team.'

'This might be really real, then,' Garvin said.

'I surely hope so,' Kang said, a little wistfully. 'I'd really like to kill somebody who's not a computersim before I get too old to gloat.'

Caud Williams watched the fifty soldiers file into the hangar and find seats on the floor. He waited until security specialists closed the doors. 'Good afternoon,' he said. 'I'll make this short. This operation is being directed by *Alt* Jon Hedley of Intelligence and Reconnaissance, and it's all his show. All I have to say is the Force has always thought of itself as a team. You half hundred are going to prove we are. That's it.'

Hedley saluted, he returned the salute, then, surprisingly, sat cross-legged on the concrete as if he were no more than a striker.

'A team,' Hedley began. 'That's as good an image as any other. From now on, I want all of you to lose any idea about who's better, scouts, armor, commo or whatever. We all have the same job: Kill or capture 'Raum dissidents.

'That's what we're going out to do. Not take territory, not make friends with villagers, not look good in holos. We're also not going to kill anybody who isn't flipping trying to kill us. Nobody's going to call in a target they "think" might be goblins, nor are we going to launch because we "think" a village might have 'Raum. There's been enough of that nonsense.

'We want the goblins and only the goblins, either dead or in our hands, singing like little dicky birds about their friends. Once we've nailed them, good and hard, two things'll happen: First is the little guys in the jungle will start wondering if they're on the right side; and the bigger guys will think about going back to the mines or whatever they were doing before they started messing with the wrong people. And there'll be no rest for us until we're done.'

It was a bit like basic training, Njangu thought, but not much. Their instructor was Petr, and the entire team was trainees. 'The first order of business is Contact Reaction,' Petr said. 'We'll go through it until it's pure muscle response, and your brain is still playing diddly-do-wah and it's all over.'

Reaction — when hit, everyone jumped to the side, first man left, second man right, and so forth. Turn in the direction of the fire, first man sprayed a burst of ten rounds, runs back, second man did the same, and so on until the patrol was back far enough to break contact and retreat or find a better fighting position. Again and again they went through it, marching up and down through the comparatively safe jungles of Chance Island, always with live ammunition. There wasn't any punishment for error, just Petr's sad eyes and a slow shake of the head; but somehow, probably because things would get very real in the next few days, that was a worse penalty than anything Lir could've devised.

Monique was doing the same with her team, over and over again. Slow-walking, step by step, utter silence, toe coming down first, then heel, then rest, then another step forward. Knowing where everyone carried everything – spare ammo in the lower pouches of the vest, any personal medication in upper-left shirt pocket, snacks in upper-right pocket, med-pouch on right hip, and so on and so forth. Any team member could find anything she . . . or the possible casualty . . . needed on anyone else by day or night, whether the other was conscious or bleeding.

'Well,' Petr announced one day, 'we're not ready, but I don't think there's anything more to be gained by farting around out here. I think it's time to go play in the forest.'

'Got a min?'

'Sure,' Njangu said. He eyed Erik Penwyth carefully, wondering what was coming – his tentativeness suggested Penwyth was about to confess to some great sin, and Yoshitaro wasn't in the mood to play confessor.

'Uh . . . did you hear about Angie?'

'Nope. Been too busy trying to figure out what I'm gonna carry to the field.'

'She's gone.'

'*What?*'

'Yeh. Bought herself out two days ago.'

'Where'd she get the credits?' Njangu wondered. 'She would've had, what, two years, maybe three left on her hitch? Going rate for a bare-bones crunchy is a thousand credits per year, plus I'd guess I&R adds more to that.

Say another five hundred? That's a pot of money for a striker.'

'Her family's got money,' Erik said.

'I thought she wasn't on speaking terms with them.'

'You saw some of their stores got burned out?'

'Saw it on the holos. I was going to ask,' Njangu said. 'But we're not exactly on speaking terms these days.'

Erik didn't go back to his bunk. Njangu put on a bland, waiting expression. 'Uh . . . there's something else. She and I . . . well, we had a thing a couple of weeks ago. The last time they gave us a pass.'

'So? She told me to pack my ass with salt and piddle up a rope two months or more ago,' Njangu said. 'And even so, we weren't in love. I'm not crying up my sleeve over her . . . at least, not as far as I know.'

'We weren't talking love, either,' Erik said. 'But something weird happened . . . maybe you can tell me what it means.'

'I don't think, knowing what I don't know about Angie, I can tell you squat.'

'We ended up at my folks' place,' Erik said. 'And, well, sort of vanished for the weekend. I've got my own apartments with my own entrance and so forth. I asked her if she wanted to meet my parents, maybe go out to a party or something. Since she's kind of wild, I thought she'd get along 'kay with some of my rowdier friends. She said she wanted to go out . . . then changed her mind. She sounded a little angry when she said that. So all we did was, well, be together.'

'Angie was like that with me, too,' Njangu said.

'It was, well, I guess I'd call it a little exotic,' Erik said.

But don't think I'm bragging or anything. just trying to explain. Then, the night we had to come back, she told me to whack off, and if I said anything to anybody about what happened, about the things we did, she'd dry-gulch me.'

'That's just about exactly what happened to me,' Njangu said.

'What did I do wrong?' Erik said. 'I mean, we weren't in love, or anything. But she was 'kay, and I thought we were getting along. And then . . . whambo.'

Njangu shook his head. 'Sorry, my friend. I haven't a clue.'

'Weird,' Erik said. 'Just plain weird.'

Four days later, yet another sweep went out, two companies from Second Regiment. Plus ten extra men, who, except for outsize packs for their Squad Support Weapons, looked no different from the others. There were other, less obvious differences – they'd bathed in chemical potions the Force's IV Section – Logistics – said would mask their scent from sniffers, either animal or mechanical; and their uniforms were coated to mask heat radiation.

The two companies laboriously moved through the flatlands below the bluffs, then swept a village reported to be 'Raum-controlled. They checked identity cards, asked for cooperation with the government, promised great rewards for any 'Raum who turned himself or anyone else in, and left with negative contact, negative results. At dusk, Griersons lifted them back to Chance Island.

No one had noticed the ten men and women – Gamma Team, I&R Company – who'd dropped away into thick brush a kilometer outside the village. The recon team formed a defensive perimeter, took whisper coms from their packs, fitted them, and Kipchak made a commo check.

An hour after the companies crashed away into silence,

three women, loudly and ostentatiously calling for an escaped *giptel*, came past. Kipchak glanced at Njangu, grinned tightly. No one spoke – the team's coms were set on a frequency between the normal military channels, but there wasn't any point in being sloppy. The 'Raum's three scouts had missed them.

Half of the team ate, while the rest kept watch. Their rations were high-concentrate protein bars, four thousand calories per meal, and each soldier carried two dozen paks. They could travel long and far on these, with their only worry being the notorious side effect of the bars clamping their bowels shut for perpetuity. 'At least,' Kipchak had said, 'that keeps us from exposing our flanks.'

It rained at dusk. They were glad of it – the drizzle, the dwindle of the rainy season, would hide any noise they made when moving. An hour later, Kipchak signaled. They crept to the trail and went back to the village. There were lights on in the buildings, and the common building was occupied.

Petr held one hand out, an the team went into cover. He shed his pack, pointed toward Heckmyer, and the two slithered forward. Kipchak took night glasses from a pouch on his combat vest and swept the village and the crowd outside the common building. *Ho, ho, ho*, he thought. *Where did all those hale hearty yongkers come from? They sure weren't around when the troopies were. And they're all carrying guns. Tsk. Perhaps these kiddies don't mean to bring happiness and health on honest soldiery.*

There was a meeting going on, but Kipchak was too far away to make out any words. He thought of getting a shotgun pickup from one of the team, but decided not. Revolutionary cant was revolutionary cant. He keyed his whisper mike. 'Go back for the others,' he told Heckmyer. The man slid away, came back with the team.

Again, Petr touched his com. "Raum in the village,' he said, waited for the team to survey the situation. 'I count seventeen.'

'We could nail 'em good right now,' Penwyth suggested.

'Negative,' Petr decided. 'There'd be civ casualties. We'll sweep wide of the village,' he said, 'and lurk beyond the pathway on the south. I think they'll take that route back to wherever they live sometime tonight or tomorrow. We'll take a chance on losing them on the way. But I'd rather get a whole bunch of goblins than wipe 'em up one at a time.'

'What about the reaction team?' *Finf* Newent asked.

'I don't see any chance to put them on the ground without alarms blanging. Poor Monique.'

Just before false dawn, Striker Deb Irthing heard sounds from the village. She nudged Stef Bassas, her watchmate, and he crawled back, tapped heels of the sleeping Gamma Team, lying in starfish formation. Petr Kipchak crawled up beside her, listened, and keyed his com to the main frequency assigned to I&R. 'Gamma. Moving.' He flipped the com back to the team frequency.

Five minutes later, dark figures came up the trail. Petr counted sixteen. He didn't move, and the last 'Raum came past. *Not good enough or tricky enough*, he thought, *you'll never trap Mrs. Kipchak's favorite boy like that*, counted half a hundred, then said, 'Go,' stepped out of concealment, and Gamma went after the 'Raum.

They moved very slowly, thinking of silence, breathing slowly, knowing the 'Raum were moving faster, confident on their own ground, certain they weren't being tracked. Once an hour Petr touched a tiny transponder on his combat harness. and a red blip flashed back at Camp Mahan, in the I&R Company's Plotting

Room. It was about half-full of officers, mostly from II Section, plus *Mil* Rao, the Force's executive officer. They spoke but little, and the occasional scrape of a coffee cup or suppressed cough was very loud.

The day was clear and hot, without clouds, the muddy trail starting to dry out. Kipchak changed point men every hour, but refused to let anyone else walk slack — just behind point. He regularly knelt and checked the tracks left by the seventeen. If the footprints were water-filled, he kept moving, but twice, when mud was seeping into the tack he stopped the team, letting the 'Raum get farther ahead.

Even with all the caution, he almost led the patrol into them, just at midday. The 'Raum had moved off the trail for a meal, and it was only by luck that Bassas, taking point, saw the dull gleam of a weapon ahead. He froze, motioned once, and very slowly, very carefully, Gamma backed up twenty-five meters. They waited, heard movement after a time, and went on.

It was late in the day when they heard the whine of a lifter. Gamma slipped off the trail, didn't look up, even though their faces were camouflaged. The lifter passed overhead. Petr Kipchak felt blood pound at his temples. *Bastards, bastards, bastards, and they promised no goddamned overheads, probably frigging Williams not able to keep his god-damned hands out of the pie . . .* The lifter came back, and Kipchak chanced looking up, saw the aircraft, saw a flash of the logo on the lifter's side; *Matin*. He swore again, in a new and different key. *So there's a leak somewhere, somebody must've let the journohs know there was something going on in this sector, and they're out looking.*

Njangu, too, had seen the markings. *I'll have to tell Garvin*, he thought. *Next time, stand on that pigfuttering Kouro's neck and make sure he's drownded dead, not just soggy.*

The lifter made another pass over the featureless jungle, then its whine receded. The patrol went on.

An hour before dusk, Gamma smelled smoke, heard the yap of *giptels*, and knew there was another village ahead. It was a bit larger than the first, and had three paths leading in and out. Sounds of laughter, cheering, came, and Gamma smelled something barbecuing. Something very tasty. They avoided looking down at the hi-pro rations as they chewed mechanically.

'Two men,' Kipchak said into the whisper mike. 'Take the team's canteens and go back a quarter klick to the stream. Njangu,' he went on, 'I think they'll take the upper trail tomorrow. But bug the lower one, just in case. Take Irthing for backup.'

Njangu took two tiny devices that looked like nails with enlarged heads from a pack pocket, slid out of his pack straps, and moved toward the village, blaster ready, as dark closed in. He wished he had a pistol, but those weren't issue, but private purchase. Only Petr Kipchak carried one. Once a *giptel* heard or smelled him, and yapped, but no one paid any mind, too busy with celebrating whatever. He found the trail, turned the sensors on, buried them on either side of the track.

He was only about three meters from the back of one hut, and heard the sound of a man panting, a woman moaning. The woman squealed, and the man grunted several times. *I am in the wrong end of this business*, he thought, then thought nothing as the man came out of the hut, a dim, naked form. Njangu slowly raised his SSW, wondering why his gut turned at the thought of killing someone who was naked.

The man peered into the gloom, and Njangu's finger tightened on the trigger, then the man laughed hugely and began urinating. Njangu felt spray on his face, and acid burned at the back of his throat. The man finished, scratched, went back into the hut, and more laughter came. Yoshitaro swallowed hard, and started back toward the patrol. Irthing was squatting next to a tree, shoulders shaking. *So this is how to become a legend in the Force,* Njangu thought.

Petr led them up a slope to a flat ground above the village gathered the patrol around. He closed the whisper mike, spoke in a low tone. 'This is safer,' he said. 'We can see the trail they'll take . . . I think . . . from here, and nobody's going to get stumbled over. Or pissed on,' he said with a bit of a laugh. 'There's a big pool about twenty meters on, Njangu. You can go sluice off, and we'll try to remember not to shoot you when you come back.'

There were three on watch, Kipchak, Jil Mahim, and Njangu. The party in the village had died down, and there were only two or three lights burning. They were high enough on the bluffs to look out over the bay, and could see the faint lights from Leggett to their right, in the west, and Chance Island, home, warmth, dry clothes, and real food glimmering like a jewel in the bay's center.

Petr had said it was all right to talk, as long as it was quiet, but neither Mahim or Njangu had anything to say, night, jungle, and the 'Raum close about them.

It was very clear, and the stars shone with a hard beauty. Njangu wondered, if he knew where to look, if he could see the star Waughtal's Planet orbited around. He hoped not.

He jumped a bit as Petr began talking in a very low voice, almost as if he were thinking aloud. 'When I was a boy,' he said. 'I remember a holo. Old sucker, and the colors were starting to bleed a little. Anyway, it was about a planet called Rome, and how they carved themselves an empire. Their soldiers were called legionaries, and the empire kept them on the frontiers. keeping it safe.

'Maybe that's where I decided I wanted to become a soldier. Keeping people safe's not a bad thing to do with your life. Anyway, there were barbarians, and they kept hammering at the empire, and little by little it shrank, and bits were lost, and eventually Rome disappeared.

'I kept thinking about that, and what it would have been like to have been one of those legionaries, out on the far end of nowhere, looking at the stars and knowing they were enemy, and knowing there was nothing behind you, you were cut off, that there was no support, nobody to shout for when the barbarians came. I wondered what it was like to be part of a last legion like that.

'Never thought I'd find out for real.'

He fell silent, and there was no sound but a tiny, whispering wind.

'Intelligence says Gamma Team's still on them,' Dill said. 'The 'Raum have holed up in another village for the night, and Gamma's sitting on a hill, waiting. So far the 'Raum don't seem to be anything but fat, happy, and dumb.'

'What's their team leader going to do?' Gorecki wanted to know.

'According to *Cent* Angara . . . and none of this are we supposed to know, being dumb-ass flyfolks in the rear rank,' Dill said, 'he's going to track 'em until they lead him to a bigger target. Or, if they realize they're being tracked, scrag 'em.'

'Hope he finds a big, wet, creamy target,' Kang said. 'Something like a headquarters, right out in the open. Yum!'

'Restrain yourself, Ho,' Garvin said. 'All things come to she who waits.'

'I'm not talking about coming, dammit. I'm talking about killing!'

'You should've been the gunner, the way you talk.'

'Nope,' Kang said. 'Any fool can pull a trigger. It takes brains to handle electronics.'

'I'm gonna shatter your whole world,' Jaansma said. 'I'll bet if we find them, they won't have anything more sophisticated than what they've stolen from us for you to worry about.'

'Then I'll ask for a turn on the guns.'

'Fair enough.' Garvin turned to Ben. 'You know, O big-time and enlightened Vehicle Commander, I've been thinking.'

'Tsk,' Ben said. 'Brains aren't authorized until you make *dec*. But try your feeblest.'

'I'm wondering about these 'Raum,' Garvin said. 'Mostly they live in the cities, with the biggest concentration over in Leggett, right?'

'Except for the mines on C-Cumbre, pretty much,' Dill said. 'But there's got to be a kiloton of 'em scattered around in the bush in little bitty villages.'

'Scattered around doesn't make for anything very impressive.'

'I don't see where you're going.'

'Sooner or later, we're going to start nailing them,' Garvin went on. 'We can't keep being clusterbrains forever, can we?'

'With *Caud* Williams anything's a possibility.'

'When we start hurting them,' Garvin went on, 'it'll be hard for them to get support from the villagers, fishermen, whatever, right?'

''Course,' Kang said. 'Especially if we do something smart, like start controlling the groceries and keeping track of city-bought supplies so we can see what villages are quartermasting the shitheads.'

'Not bad,' Garvin said admiringly. 'Promote that woman. Now, once we start hurting them, we'll be hunting them pillar to post, right?'

'Right,' Dill agreed. 'Relentless pukes that we are.'

'Hold that line,' Garvin said, 'and consider something else. They slot somebody out there in the wilderness, it doesn't make much of a dent in the holos. What would happen if they started killing people here in Leggett? Wouldn't *Matin* go apeshit about the third body that got splattered on the front steps of their building?'

'Sure,' Dill said. 'Look how wiggly everybody got when that Rentier . . . Scryfa, I think it was, and his family got butchered last month. The 'Raum start doing that on a regular basis, and maybe leaving a bomb here and there to keep life interesting, D-Cumbre'll start skreekin' and hollerin'. Stands to reason.'

'So shouldn't they be moving into the cities and pushing things to make PlanGov knuckle under and talk about whatever changes the 'Raum think they're fighting for?'

Dill looked carefully at Garvin. 'You know, troop, I'm sorta glad you're on our side. 'Cause what you just said makes way too much sense.'

Njangu woke before dawn, his head throbbing, his gut wrenched in a knot. He tried to vomit, couldn't. Jil Mahim, the team medic, crawled over.

'What's the problem?' she whispered.

'Got the creeping cruds,' he managed. 'Probably from bein' pissed on.'

'That can do it to you,' she said, went back to her pouch. 'Here. Painkillers and anticrud.'

Njangu unscrewed his canteen, swallowed the tablets

with a gulp of water. Seconds later, everything came up. 'Oh *frab*,' he moaned.

Kipchak crawled up beside the medic, found out the problem. 'Can you march?'

'Hell yes,' Njangu managed. 'That's better'n the alternatives.'

Petr nodded. The only option was for Njangu to be left behind. After the 'Raum and the patrol cleared the area, the Force would evac him. Assuming there was something left to evac. 'Saddle up, then.'

Njangu feebly got into his pack, picked up his blaster. Penwyth and Mahim helped him up. 'It ain't gonna get any easier,' he managed. They moved to the trail, and were waiting for the 'Raum when they moved past.

The day was hot, dry, and a blur. Njangu felt like he was on fire, pain in every joint. He wanted to crawl off to the side of the trail, lie down, and hope for sleep. Or death. But he didn't. He kept plodding. The universe narrowed to one hand carrying his blaster, the crushing weight of his pack, and one foot in front of the next, over and over. Every time he brushed against a branch, or scraped a rock, it felt like a burning brand.

Once, he found tears running down his face, hastily scrubbed them, and a portion of his camouflage, away with a filthy sleeve. Nobody's ever seen Njangu Yoshitaro cry, and they wouldn't now. No one since . . . since he couldn't remember when. He hated himself, and everyone else. Kipchak for moving at such a killing pace, the bastard on point who always took the steep way, the rocky way, the son of a bitch behind him who wouldn't do the decent thing and carry his pack for him. Bastards the lot.

He dully swallowed the broth Mahim fed him around midday, lost it minutes later. The medic held an airblast to his arm, and he was vaguely aware of hissing.

Somebody was lifting him, and he got his feet under him. He stumbled, the pack almost bringing him down, but he found his balance. 'Hep ho,' he managed, and they moved on again.

The day was an agony of months and years, and when the tears came back again he didn't bother to wipe them away. He didn't see anything on either side, didn't care if the goddamned 'Raum ambushed him. At least they wouldn't be moving, at least the 'Raum'd let him rest, and being shot couldn't hurt more than he already did.

Eventually they stopped, and somebody led him to a tree, slid his pack off, and told him to sit down. Somebody else fed him some more broth, and this time it stayed down. Mahim gave him another injection, and he was instantly unconscious.

He awoke in a gray dawn, feeling marvelous. He didn't believe it, and cautiously felt his arms, his legs. He wasn't dead, at least not unless dead included still being in a jungle. He could smell his body, and it still smelled sick. But he was alive. He remembered crying the day before, and, strangely enough. wasn't ashamed.

Faintly the thought came – *you just pushed through something, my friend. Like you did on the cliffs. Taught you, didn't it?* He put the thought aside as being hopelessly romantic and got ready for the day's march.

They followed the 'Raum for two more days. Now the villages were fewer and smaller as they moved closer to the Highlands. The 'Raum made their camp in *kwelf* groves. Gamma didn't have that luxury and slept in the open. But at least the rains had stopped – the dry season had arrived.

Njangu was on point. He was utterly alive, every nerve singing, and the brush of a breeze on his skin was like a blow. The air was sharp, clean, and every tree, every flower had a different, distinct scent. His breathing came slowly, regularly, from below his diaphragm, as he'd learned from his *sensei*, long ago on Waughtal's Planet. He could feel the enemy ahead, maybe two, maybe three hundred meters, feel the careless, confident way they moved.

He jumped when Petr tapped his shoulder, thumbed him back into the column, almost got angry, then obeyed. It was someone else's turn – no one could maintain perfect alertness for long. *Finf* Newent slid past, flashed a tight, meaningless grin, teeth pulled back in a near snarl. Njangu followed him at slack, a respectable distance from Newent.

The jungle blew up in front of him, and Newent stumbled back, arms splaying, his SSW spinning, and fell against him. Yoshitaro heard the thud of gunfire, and Newent convulsed, grunted, went limp. 'Hit them,' someone was shouting, and Njangu realized it was Kipchak. He pushed Newent's corpse away, fired four bolts at waist-level, fought the urge to go flat, found a grenade on his belt, thumbed, and hurled it, then crouched and sprayed more rounds. Other blasters were stuttering, and the volume of fire from the 'Raum slowed, and he tossed another grenade, rolled, and the three behind him sharded into splinters. He forced himself up to his knees, lifted the heavy SSW, sprayed fire across blank green jungle.

For an instant there was silence, and Kipchak shouted, 'Back,' and he obeyed, stumbling away from the ambush and a bolt clipped a branch over his head, and he almost tripped and fell. There was a cluster of rocks, and the patrol was behind them. 'Come on,' Kipchak shouted. 'Fall back . . . you're the last,' and the patrol was moving again, at a shuffling trot.

Njangu realized he was last in column, closest to the enemy, and fought panic. Kipchak was there, firing past him. 'Back to the trail fork,' he ordered, 'we'll mousetrap 'em there,' and Njangu obeyed, hearing the air rasp in and out of his lungs. Gamma spread out at the fork, and Njangu spotted a thick cluster of brush to one side.

'Jil,' he ordered. 'You and Stef keep running back. Make a lot of noise. Stop about fifty meters down the trail and drop off to the side. Slot anything that comes down. We'll shout you back up when we need you. The rest of you, over there and get ready to smash 'em when they come.' He wondered dimly what made him give the orders, but Gamma was obeying, and Petr came back. He saw what Njangu had ordered, nodded. Seconds later they saw motion up trail, and five 'Raum half ran toward them.

'No . . . no . . . no . . .' Petr was whispering . . . 'NOW!' and five Squad Support Weapons blasted fire. Screams, and staggering bodies, and Njangu let another burst go into their midst.

'Up, up,' Kipchak ordered, and shouted for Mahim and Bassas. 'Now we've got them going . . . don't let up.' They went back the way they'd come, past four bodies and one sobbing boy. Kipchak's pistol fired, and he was silent. *Five down*, Yoshitaro thought. *Twelve to go.* Njangu saw Newent's blank, staring eyes in a mask of blood, looked away. Mahim stopped long enough to tuck a sensor on the body, turn it on for later pickup.

All that day the patrol followed the 'Raum. The com started chattering, and Petr keyed the mike: 'This is Gamma. All frigging units stay off this freq or I'll close the com down. Clear.' There was a squawk of outrage from someone, but then the com was quiet.

'We're tracking 'em,' Petr explained as he ordered a halt. 'And we're too close. Look. They're leaving a blood trail. Let 'em get a few minutes ahead,' he said. 'Then we'll go on.'

'What happens next?' Penwyth asked. 'We need a piece of the bastards for slotting Newent.'

'They'll try to trap us,' Kipchak said. 'And if they can't bust us, they'll try to lose us, which we aren't gonna let them do. Don't worry. We'll get ours.'

The 'Raum backtrailed three times, but all three times their hasty ambush was spotted before it was sprung. Then, as Kipchak had predicted, the 'Raum went more slowly, into thick brush, up rapidly drying creek beds, over stony ground. But each time Gamma was able to stay with them.

They rounded a bend and saw two sprawled bodies, moving slightly. 'They're worried,' Petr said, 'They're dumping their casualties.'

Mahim started forward. 'No!' Petr shouted. He sprayed a burst into each body. One was knocked aside by the impact, and Njangu saw the primed explosive charge set under her, and then the charge blew, shredding the woman's corpse. 'Nice try, but no *daggah*,' Petr said, and the pursuit went on.

By dark, they were high up on the bluffs, and mist from the Highlands rolled down over them. Njangu thought he was breathing fire, his lungs searing, and the rest were gasping as loudly. 'Com,' Petr ordered, and Irthing, who was carrying the set, handed him a mike. 'This is Sibyl Gamma. Scrambling.' He touched buttons on the com. The scrambler not only ate power, but reduced broadcast range on the coms. 'Do you have me marked?'

'Sibyl Gamma, this is Sibyl Control,' the com whispered. Kipchak recognized Hedley's voice. He made a quick status report. 'I think they're holing up for the night. Anyway, they should unless they're brain-dead. Can you get me a sniffer in the air?'

'Affirm.'

'Don't hit them,' Kipchak ordered. 'I say again, don't hit them. Let me know if they move before first light. We've got them going, and I think they're heading for something solid.'

'This is Control,' Hedley said. 'Understood, will comply. But watch it. They could be planning a surprise.'

'This is Gamma. Understood. That's one reason I want the sniffer up, to give me a little early warning if they put the hounds out.'

'Understood.'

'Just give me a chance to nail them down, and you'll have your big target. 'This is Gamma. Clear.'

Everyone, even revolutionaries, fall into the trap of routine. So it was with the 'Raum. In spite of their policy of never meeting in the same house or village twice, or on the same night, the huge cave at the rim of the Highlands had become a permanent headquarters. The tiny entrance was still well guarded, but now there were paths leading to it. The Movement's records, computers, coms were centered there, and so it was necessary to garrison the outside of the cave. Other 'Raum units, after action, retreated there to report and get new instructions. Since it was perfectly safe, they also lingered for a day or two, finding a chance to relax, to raise their voices above a whisper, to laugh without looking over their shoulders.

The cave's inner chamber held the twenty men and women of the Planning Group, plus another fifteen of the 'Raum's most respected fighting leaders. Comstock Brien stood by at an easel, with a Confederation-issue map on it.

'This is an excellent opportunity to hit the Rentiers and their dogs hard,' he said. 'That patrol is obviously a stalking horse. It's trailed our unit for several days, without forcing contact. The Force wants a battle, and I think it should have it.'

Jo Poynton stood. 'Brother, what makes you think that we can outfight the Confederation soldiers?'

'We have consistently done so this far,' he said. 'And their response time with reinforcements has been miserably slow. I've put myself in their commander's mind. He wants to draw some of us into the open. He's thinking perhaps we'll send out a hundred, maybe a hundred fifty men, so he'll be prepared to respond with two or three hundred. Excellent odds, from his perspective. But what are the chances of the Force's unreliable air-delivery vehicles being able to put a full three hundred men into the mountains? I would say very, very slim. Plus whatever vehicles they successfully launch can be hit by the anti-aircraft missiles we've acquired. That should make them cautious.

'My plan is simple: I have three hundred troops mustered outside this cave. Our team is less than three hours distant. By dawn, we could reach them and first obliterate that patrol with, say a hundred men, giving the patrol time enough to report the enemy strength. The Force will then bring in reinforcements. Just when their men are landing, we'll hit them with the rest of our fighters.

'I'll com immediately for another two hundred fighters from the regional units in the area, which will give us overwhelming force. By the time the Force realizes its surprise assault was expected, the men on the ground and, hopefully, a great number of their combat vehicles will be destroyed. They will, of course, panic and counterattack with every man, every vehicle remaining at Camp Mahan.

'But we will be gone, gone with more weapons, perhaps

even some of their vehicles if the chance presents itself. I've already set a rendezvous for any seized aerial vehicles to be secreted in the middle of the Highlands, where the *giptels* will never look for them.

There were shouts of approval. Jord'n Brooks stood. 'No,' he said loudly, and there was sudden silence. 'This is the worst, most dangerous sort of adventurism. For you . . . not we, but you . . . are pinning the hopes of the future, the struggle of years, on a single engagement. If we win, that is marvelous. But if we lose, brother? What if we lose?'

Brien glowered. 'We shall not lose, *brother*. I know that. But let it not sound like this is just my decision, or that I am somehow trying to become some sort of Supremo. Tell me, brothers, sisters. What should we do?'

Brooks listened to the shouts of 'Fight,' 'Hit them,' 'Yes!' 'Attack!' His face was still, unmoving. 'Very well, Brother Brien,' he said. 'We shall attack. But I hope the doom that comes will not be for all of us.'

'Oh my aunt Fanny who sitteth on Buddha's right frigging hand,' *Cent* Angara said. 'Get your sorry ass off that cot, Hedley, and come look at Nirvana.'

Hedley was instantly beside the big screen that relayed data from the Electronic Warning Grierson orbiting a kilometer above the 'Raum team. 'Why kiss my money-making ass,' Hedley said. 'Look at all those little red dots streaming along. We done sprung 'em out of the woodwork.'

'Sure as hell,' Angara agreed. 'Officer of the Watch!'

'Sir?'

'Get the Old Man up, and the troops moving. Full alert, ready to launch in three-zero minutes. *Caud* Williams'll give the attack order.'

Hedley was at another com. 'Roll the pickup team,' he

said. 'Get my people off the ground.' He changed channels. 'Golan Flight, I need one of your Zhooks for a quick-and-dirty. Hell yes, now. If I wanted them in ten minutes, I would've called you in ten minutes. Direct authorization from Lance Actual.'

'Roll out,' Dill snapped. 'Gamma's ready to come out. And they're warmish.' The hangar lights went full on, and Dill's crew jumped off the cots set up beside their aircraft. Gorecki had his boots on, unfastened, and flopped his way toward the Grierson's cockpit. The hangar door lifted, and Camp Mahan was a flare of activity as the Grierson's drive whined on.

'Sibyl Gamma, Sibyl Gamma,' Hedley broadcast. 'This is Sibyl Control. Get 'em up and ready. You're coming out. The birds are in the open.'

'This is Gamma,' Kipchak, who never seemed to sleep, snapped. 'What about the boys I've been chasing?'

'We'll do it sanitary from the air,' Hedley advised.

'They're mine, goddamit!'

'Not anymore, Petr. Now they belong to the meat-grinder.'

Ten minutes later, a Zhukov dived in on the 'Raum team half a kilometer from the Gamma Team, weapons systems slaved to the EW Grierson's sensors, and a ripple-salvo of Furies spat. The Furies exploded, and the small camp was a hell of flame. The Zhukov banked across the holocaust, came back, 35mm chaingun ravening, the vehicle commander's cupola-mounted 25mm spitting fire. All ten of the 'Raum patrol died before they came awake.

The Grierson settled into the tiny clearing, smashing through branches and small trees. The back ramp dropped, and yellow light, honest, man-made light flared through the night.

'Mount up,' Kipchak ordered, and the exhausted survivors of Gamma stumbled into the Grierson. Kang and Dill passed out boiling hot coffee and heatpaks containing a fresh roll stuffed with wine-baked *giptel*, mustard, pickle, and a fried egg on top. Garvin helped Njangu to a bench, and he slumped down, unaware he was still wearing his pack. The ramp closed, and there was blessed sllence, and the Grierson lifted out of the jungle.

'You did it,' Garvin enthused. 'You got them into the open.'

'No shiteedah for sure?' Njangu said.

'No shiteedah for sure. The whole Force is gonna roll on 'em. You'll probably get a medal after we obliterate them.'

'Probably,' Njangu said, through a double mouthful. 'And if I'm real good, maybe a bath or even a fast hosing-off?'

Garvin sniffed. 'Lord. Since you mention it, you folks do smell a little ripe around the edges.'

Deb Irthing snickered. 'Like somebody pissed on us, maybe?'

'Not quite *that* bad. But close.'

'Real close,' Njangu said, and took another bite.

'Very good indeed,' *Caud* Williams told his regimental commanders and staff, staring at the screen. 'We'll put First Regiment in against these troops in the open on the left . . . Second on the right closing in a pincers, then Third assaulting straight into that base of theirs, whatever and wherever it is. Fourth will remain in reserve.'

Hedley turned from the photo montage he was studying, took off the interpreter's tri-dee glasses. 'Sir?'

'What is it, *Alt*?'

'I think I've got their base spotted,' he said. 'I think it might be this area here. Tracks lead to this cliff face, and vanish. I think our goblins use a cave for their hideout.'

'What of it?'

'Caves can be hard to clean out.'

'*Alt*,' Williams said firmly, 'your people did a good job of finding the enemy. I'll take care of finishing them.'

Hedley inclined his head, didn't respond.

It took almost all of the Force's Griersons to load the combat elements of First and Second Regiments, and the troop compartments were still crowded. The air was a staccato chatter of commands as the Griersons, in three elements, slashed low to the west of Leggett, toward the 'Raum columns. Their drive-hum shrilled over the jungle, and hunting beasts heard and scurried for cover.

Lead elements of the 'Raum head the Griersons and ordered antiaircraft crews to the alert. These men and women, still not familiar with their confiscated weapons, fumbled with the controls as the sound grew louder and the first wave could be seen, dots against the morning sky.

One Grierson was Ben Dill's – they'd barely had time to offload Gamma when they were ordered to the parade ground to pick up a load of First Regiment soldiers. 'Somebody's looking for us,' *Finf* Kang announced calmly from her 'turret.' 'Scanning . . . scanning . . . he's got a lock.'

'Gorecki . . . maneuver on her command,' Dill ordered.

'You tell me, Ho,' Stanislaus said.

'Tracking . . . tracking . . . he's launched! Go low!'

The Grierson dived hard, and Garvin tried to ignore his stomach as he waited behind his weapon sights.

'Gunner,' Kang said, very calm, 'TA my beam . . . I've got the launch site . . .'

Garvin switched acquisition systems to Kang's antimissile tracker. 'Locked on,' he said.

'What about the frigging missile?' Gorecki snapped.

'It's still coming on . . . still tracking . . . Garvin, throw something at the launch site,' Kang ordered. 'Driver . . . hard left to nine o' clock . . . missile at three o'clock . . . incoming . . . climb hard!' The Grierson moaned as Gorecki slammed full power. 'Ah-hah, little bastard, went and screwed its mind,' Kang said. 'It's searching . . . blanking it . . . blanking it . . . gotcha! Missile toppled, skipper . . . Garvin, are you ever gonna shoot at anything? And by the way, you owe me a beer for saying they weren't gonna have anything trickshit for me to worry about.'

'Target acquired,' Garvin said, as his head banged against the sight and water filled his eyes. 'Tracking . . . locked . . .'

'Launch when ready, Mister Gridley,' Ben Dill said.

'Launch one, launch two, launch three . . . lost target . . . bring me left, more left, dammit,' Garvin snapped, and Stanislaus obeyed.

'Target acquired . . . launch four . . . HOLY SHIT!' Jaansma shouted as the jungle in his sight turned flame, black, then brown and cloudy and he saw equipment and men fountaining. 'Target destroyed.'

'Mister Jaansma,' Dill said. 'Watch your commo discipline.'

'Sorry, Ben. Searching . . .'

'Three minutes from LZ,' Gorecki said. 'Get the crunchies ready.'

'Searching,' Kang echoed Garvin. 'Searching . . .'

The first assault wave came out the back of their Griersons into a sheet of fire. They went down, and a few stayed there. SSWs and blasters returned the 'Raum fire, at first spattering, then a solid roar. Noncoms bellowed orders . . . move, move, you sorry shitheads, get off this LZ and on them . . . stay here and die, you idiots . . . come on, move, move . . .

Soldiers were up, zigging, maneuver elements going forward, fire support blasting at seen targets or just the area, and the Force overran the 'Raum's forward positions, blasters, rocket launchers stuttering destruction.

'Where are the rest of our fighters?' Brien asked.

'Twenty minutes, perhaps more, away,' the woman carrying his com reported.

'Too far. Tell them to drop everything but their weapons and ammo and come at the run, or we're lost.'

The woman nodded, touched her mike's sensor.

The Second Regiment hit an unprotected flank, and the 'Raum fell back, re-formed. A few of their fighters broke, ran, and were cut down. The others firmed their resolve, and continued fighting. There would be no mercy shown on either side on this battleground.

'Oh you dumb sons of bitches,' the woman aiming the portable rocket launcher gloated. 'Didn't anybody ever tell you about bunching up?' She pressed the stud and the rocket hissed out of its tube and exploded in the middle of the 'Raum. A moment later, a 'Raum sniper saw her weapon, caught her in his range finder and fired. The round caught the rocketeer in the calf, and she howled, dropped her weapon, and rolled on the ground in agony. Her sometime lover, a rifleman, hesitated, then followed orders and picked up her heavier weapon and its ammo vest. He moved on, hoping the woman would get her med-pouch open, or there'd be a medic, before she bled to death. He shut off that part of his mind and looked for a target.

Dill's Grierson had just cleared land, going back for another load of troops, when it bucked, slewed sideways in midair, rolled twice drunkenly. Garvin heard the drive cut out, then start again, then cut out once more.

'Hang on, people,' Stan said. 'Trying to restart it.'

'Stand by for ditching,' Ben ordered. 'Ho, Garvin, out of your turrets.' The two obeyed, strapping themselves down on a troop bench. 'Seventy-four meters above water,' Dill reported. 'I'll try to pancake the turd in.'

The drive caught, hiccuped, then caught again, but whining shrilly, like a high-speed motor with sand in its bearings.

'We're going again on sixty percent,' Gorecki reported. 'But for how long is crystal ball territory.'

'Remembering that a Grierson, sans power, has the glide pattern of a brick,' Dill said, 'stay at ditching stations. I'll try to lumber this prick to something a little solider than what's underneath us.'

Garvin listened to the drive whine, break, whine, break, and found his lips moving. *No*, he thought. *You are not praying. You do not believe in anything more than Garvin Jaansma. So stop with the stupid prayer already.*

The Grierson, smoke pouring from its vents, limped over the beach and slammed across the parade ground at seventy-five knots, wallowing, sliding, slewing from side to side.

Eventually the crashing and slamming stopped. Garvin opened his eyes, looked up at Kang, realized the situation was unusual, because she'd been across from him when he closed his eyes and the bouncing had started. Dill clambered from the VC compartment into the troop box, yanked the manual hatch release, and the rear ramp fell away. 'Come on,' he shouted 'Griersons don't burn, but this one just might. Outside, outside, outside!'

Garvin punted Kang out in front of him, jumped clear, ran to the front of the Grierson, and pulled Gorecki bodily out of his compartment through the emergency hatch. Not looking back, the four ran, bent over, then went flat. Eventually they realized there wasn't any explosion, any fire, and lifted their heads to the accompaniment of onrushing sirens.

'Aren't they going to be all pissed off,' Garvin said, 'when there isn't anybody bleeding for 'em?'

'Yes there is,' Dill said. 'See? I scratched my pinkie. Medal time, medal time, medal time!'

Four Cookes darted across the smoking jungle, autocannons roaring, and a 'Raum counterattack hesitated, broke. They spun, blasted the area again, and caught two AA missile crews in the open.

'Cambrai Leader, got a whole bunch more of them,' an electronics Grierson reported. 'Humping like they're late for something. Passing the target along to you.'

'Thank you, Big Eye. Guess they're afraid they'll be late for the ball.' The Zhukov commander switched channels. 'All Chambrai elements . . . we have a big target. Men in the open . . . looks like reinforcements. We'll use main arty, finish them with the chainguns. Let's go collect us some heads.'

The four Zhukovs dived on the 'Raum, and collision alarms screamed. Their pilots pulled control wheels back into their laps, and the Zhukovs shuddered, nearly stalling, as five alien ships flashed out of the cloud-cover over the Highlands. They were scythe-shaped, the curve of the C forward, about twenty-five meters from horn to horn. On the top and bottom of the ships were pods, each containing one prone Musth. The Musth called them *aksai*, after a snakelike creature of their home-worlds, known for viciousness and lethality.

The standard watch frequency came to life: 'It isss perceived you have isssolated our mutual enemiesss. Perhapsss we ssshould offer asssistance.'

Without waiting for a response, the Musth ships rolled into the attack. At the horns of each *aksai* air ionized, and a line seared into flame. The ships sprayed fire across the 'Raum formation, then again.

The Zhukov pilots recovered, came back. But there was few targets for their 150mm autocannon except roaring fire, as everything, trees, brush, men, and women, even, it seemed, the ground itself, burned.

'It isss good to sssee the wormsss burn, isss it not?'

'Shit,' a rifleman said. 'I don't see anything left to kill.'

'Nope,' his teammate said. 'Guess we—'

'There's one,' the other interrupted. A 'Raum got out of a shell crater and stumbled toward them. He was holding something against his chest, and shouting incoherently. Both infantrymen fired, and the body spun sideways, lay still. 'Wonder if he was carrying anything worth souveniring?' the first asked.

'Let's go check—'

The explosives the 'Raum carried blew up, and the two soldiers flattened. Dirt rained, and the two stared at each other. 'That guy,' the first soldier said thoughtfully, 'took things way too serious.'

Comstock Brien picked himself up, wiped blood from his eyes. There were no more than fifteen or twenty of his fighters still moving, and all were wounded. His com carrier was unconscious, blood spurting from a severed artery. He picked up her mike. 'Base, this is Brien.'

There was a crackle, then: 'This is base. What is going on? I tried to contact you twice, without result.'

'This is Brien. Don't know. Some kind of shell hit us.' Brien wiped his face again. 'We are surrounded. Are there any reinforcements? Are there any more reinforcements?'

Jord'n Brooks looked around the cave at the thirty men and women, touched the com's sensor. 'There are no more reinforcements. Can you break away?'

Silence, then: 'No. We are trapped.'

Again a pause. 'Brooks . . . this is Brien. You were right.'

Brooks looked at Poynton, grimaced. 'I wish I wasn't.'

'This was one ending, but a beginning, too,' Brien's voice said. 'Now, it is your Task to see it to its end. Don't mourn for us, Jord'n Brooks. See that we did not die in vain.' The com went silent.

'You heard him,' Brooks said. 'I want you . . . you . . . you . . .' He pointed around the cave at ten people. 'Your Task is with the guards outside, holding back the enemy, for they will be attacking in minutes. Fight to the last, and keep them from following us. The rest of you . . . take what records, what files you can carry. Be ready to move in five—' A bomb blast outside rocked the cave. 'No, three minutes. Take what is essential. For we are now the heart of the 'Raum, heart of The Movement, heart of the Revolution, and we must not fail.'

The Force swept across the battlefield, found only a handful of wounded to take prisoner, and some of those suicided or made soldiers kill them. One might have been Comstock Brien, for one soldier said a wounded man with a livid scar played dead, then shot three soldiers before being killed himself. But when II Section realized who the tenacious warrior might have been and went back, no trace of his body was ever found.

Force casualties were comparatively light – fewer than seventy-five killed, twice that wounded, for almost five hundred 'Raum killed.

'Now we take their base,' Williams ordered. The Third Regiment, augmented by I&R Company, started forward, a little cockily, sure the battle was over, and fire sheeted. Four officers were down in the first blasts, and half again as many noncoms. They fell back, regrouped, attacked once more, and again the 'Raum drove them back.

'All right,' *Caud* Williams said. 'If they want it the hard way . . . *Mil* Rao, we'll use Zhukovs to reduce their base from the air.'

'Sir, if we could take some prisoners, it would be—'

'*Alt* Hedley, you can do your scavenging among the dead after the smoke clears,' Williams said furiously. 'I will not lose another of my men uselessly. And I'd advise you to hold your tongue, for the goodwill you've gained by finding these 'Raum is being rapidly dissipated.'

Hedley started to say something, turned and stamped out of Williams' command vehicle.

'Hey, Monique,' a Beta Team *finf* called. 'The boss wasn't whistlin' through his bum. There *is* a cave.'

'Team forward,' *Dec* Lir ordered. 'Two volunteers, with me. The rest, blow the shit out of anything that moves.' Blaster ready, she entered the dimness of the cave. Smoke billowed, and she coughed, came back out. 'Anybody got a light?' Someone tossed her one, and Lir pulled on her gas mask, went back inside. Her light played around the rocks. There were half a dozen corpses, all killed by blast, none appearing hurt except for slight trickles of blood from their ears and mouth.

'Come on in,' she shouted. 'We got them all. Goddammit, that horseshit Kipchak had all the fun.' She moved the light more slowly around the chamber, across the stacks of paper, fiches, and shattered computers. 'But I think we got a ton and a half of good shit ourselves,' she said to herself. 'II Section's gonna come all over themselves.'

The five Musth ships landed beside *Caud* Williams' C&C Grierson. A center pod on one opened, and Wlencing got out. Two armed Musth flanked him, as he stalked across the waste to Williams. The *caud* saluted, and Wlencing lifted a clawed arm in acknowledgment.

'Finally,' he said, without preamble, 'you have defeated thessse not-worthiesss. Perhapsss, when the time comesss, and we make war on each other, you will not be a helplesss babe.'

Caud Williams could not find a response.

'With thisss,' Wlencing continued, 'you will be able to sssmasssh the remainsss of thessse?'

'I hope so,' Williams said. 'I think we will.'

'Good,' Wlencing approved. 'It isss not fit for the grown to be disssstracted by cubsssss.'

That night, the surviving 'Raum found shelter in a village. The nervous farmers reluctantly fed them.

'Don't worry,' Jord'n Brooks said. 'We are not remaining here, but will leave within the hour.'

Within two days, they would reach, and disappear into, Eckmuhl, the 'Raum district of Leggett, and the war would continue, but on another front.

*

Njangu Yoshitaro, Petr Kipchak, Erik Penwyth, and the others of Gamma Tearn slept through that gore-drenched day, and if they dreamed of blood or slaughter, none of them remembered their dreams when they awoke, late the next day.

THIRTY

'Should I tell you what I'm wearing underneath this jumpsuit?' Jasith whispered.

'Not unless you want me to explode all over your windshield,' Garvin said, a bit hoarsely.

'My *windshield* doesn't want that,' she said. 'So concentrate on the scenery. For a minute, anyway. See . . . there's my house down there.'

Garvin forced his eyes . . . and his attention . . . out the canopy. He looked down at a tall buttress nearly in the center of the Heights that had evidently been hollowed out – large glass windows and balconies dotted its face. 'Which one is yours?'

'All of them, silly. All those rooms are connected, plus there's others that're completely under . . . not ground, but rock. But none of those are mine mine. My place is over there.' She cut power, and pushed the lifter into a gentle descent. They closed on a huge abandoned mining site, now overgrown with flowers and plants iridescing the colors of paradise. In its center, next to a fountained pool, was a fairly small house, all dark wood.

'That used to be a quarry,' she explained. 'One of the first things my great-how-many-times grandfather owned. It produced a multicolored veined rock, like granite, and it was a great favorite when the early

Rentiers started building their mansions. I guess the Mellusins have always been miners, even back on Corwin VIII, which is where we came from.

'The quarry made grand-whatever even richer, and then he started buying great chunks of C-Cumbre and other things. But he built his house near where he started. Then the vein played out, and the quarry just sat there, until my mother married my father. She was a Kemper, and their money's from holding companies, so she always thought she was better than my father. At least, that's what I heard, even though Daddy never snides her. She died about ten years ago.'

'I'm sorry,' Garvin said.

'Don't be,' Jasith said. 'I never thought she liked me very much, and I guess I must've been a brat and returned the favor. Anyway, she's gone, and so it doesn't matter. She took a look at that quarry, after she and Daddy got back from their honeymoon, and said she wanted to turn it into a garden. She and about three hundred 'Raum she had Daddy hire full-time. She built a little house on the shore of the lake, that's supposed to be a copy of something called a teahouse from ancient Earth, and spent time there. When she wasn't buying things, anyway. She was gone a lot when I was growing up. She went to Larix a lot. I don't know if she had a lover there, or if the stores on Larix have better toys. I guess it wasn't much of a marriage.

'When she died, I asked if I could have the house, and Daddy gave it to me for my sixteenth birthday. And the garden, too. I still have about seventy-five gardeners working for me on the grounds. What's the matter, Garvin?'

'Nothing, nothing,' Garvin said. 'That was just the sound of my mind boggling. So you live down there, all by yourself? And Daddy doesn't happen to have a spy-beam on your front door or anything? Or has the servants bribed?'

'I don't know about any spy-beams,' Jasith said. 'That only happens in romances, anyway.'

'I wouldn't put large credits on that,' Garvin said.

'Of course he bribed my servants. But I've got my own trust fund, so I bribed them bigger.'

'The very rich *aren't* like you and me,' Garvin murmured. 'Just sneakier. Can I make a suggestion?'

'Of course.'

'Land this baby, or else we're liable to find ourselves bumping into range shacks again. I feel a certain set of urges coming on.'

'Anything you want, Garvin. Absolutely anything.'

'Oh dear,' Jasith said. 'I'm afraid my head gardener's going to be hot at me tomorrow. And I'll bet my back is all moss-stained and nasty like your knees.'

'You're the one who wanted to show me the garden instead of the bedroom,' Garvin said.

'But I didn't think you were *that* impatient.'

'Now you know. Still am, in fact.' Garvin moved his hips and Jasith gasped. 'You're ready already?'

'I never stopped being ready,' he said into her ear. 'Now lift your legs . . . slowly. Hook your ankles around my back.'

'Like . . . like this? . . . oh . . . oh . . . Garvin, not so hard . . . please . . . slowly now . . . now, yes now . . . oh gods, gods, gods . . .'

The restaurant, deep in the heart of the Eckmuhl, had only two things recommending it: It had an entrance on each of four streets; and those streets, unlike most in the Eckmuhl, had excellent line-of-sight perspectives for lookouts. There were two at each exit, armed with mil-issue blasters. A police patrol – three lifters, as was customary in the Eckmuhl – saw the gun guards and sensibly kept on going.

There were seventeen men and women in the restaurant, all armed. Jord'n Brooks and Jo Poynton sat at a table in front of them. 'We shall make this brief, brothers and sisters,' he began. 'This location can only be considered secure for minutes. You seventeen are the most highly regarded warriors and agents who survived the disastrous and poorly advised jungle campaign. I want to form the new Planning Group, for you to be The Movement's *sohs* if you will. A few of you were members of the previous Group, and I request you continue to serve.'

A 'Raum stood.

'Yes, Brother Ybarre?'

'This is very irregular, brother. According to custom, the Planning Group should be selected by the fighters, after due consideration, prayer, and discussion.'

'In normal times, true,' Brooks agreed. 'But these are not normal times. I cannot emphasize that too highly. We took heavy casualties in the forest and when we relocated to the cities. What are your estimates, Sister Poynton?'

'About forty percent,' the woman said. 'That's an estimate, but I think pretty close to the truth.'

There was a low murmur of dismay. Brooks nodded. 'Exactly. I do not wish that figure to be spread about, for fear of further destroying morale. We were beaten badly by the Rentiers' dogs. Let us never forget that, and let us never make the mistake of thinking the Task is completed until we see real victory.

'Our fight will be, must be, in the heart of the enemy. We will strike them hard, and take any target that we find. But these targets must be risk-free. If we are to be hit as hard again as we have been, I fear the Task may lie uncompleted this generation, and will have to wait for another generation of warriors to rebuild The Movement.

'I will not allow this to happen. We must practice patience and cunning, and we also must move swiftly. Time is of the essence. Let me tell you our new grand strategy: I propose the Grand Rising shall occur soon. Very soon. Within the next six months, in fact.' There were exclamations of shock, surprise. 'Yes, brothers and sisters. The day is at hand when we shall grasp power. We shall not fail this time. Before the year is out, Cumbre will belong to us.'

'You're 'Raum, right?' Njangu asked.

'What makes you think that?' the girl asked.

'My suspicious mind,' he said. 'Well?'

'What if I am?'

'Then I'd ask why you're so interested in a stinking soldier like me?'

'Why shouldn't I be?'

'Oh, I don't know . . . could have something to do with loud bangs and people getting hurt and nonessential things like that,' Yoshitaro said. 'Or have you been in a timewarp for the last year or so?'

'I don't pay any attention to politics,' the girl pouted.

''Kay,' Njangu said. 'Now, my next question . . . since you're on the, shall we say, youthful-looking side, might I ask if you're over the age of consent?'

'Is all you soldiers do is talk?'

'Not at all,' Njangu said, leaning closer and whispering in the girl's ear. Her eyes got wide.

'You talk dirty! And what's a bunny rabbit?'

'Never mind. Do you want to dance some more?'

'Uh-uh,' the girl said. 'Let's go for a walk. My name's Limnea.'

'And I'm Njangu the Adequately Equipped.' Njangu stood, dropped coins on the table, and put his service cap on. 'Where are we strolling to?'

'Down on the beach, maybe?'

'Sounds as good a place as any to get mugged,' he said.

The blaring music chopped suddenly when the insulated door closed behind them. The night was brilliant – all three moons were up. A breeze came off the bay, and Njangu shivered. The girl, who was wearing a pair of green silk-looking pants that flared hugely at the leg, supported by suspenders that served to hide the nipples of her firm, fairly large breasts, appeared to feel no cold. She had close-cropped red hair, and her eyelids, lips, nails and earlobes were tinted blue. Njangu eyed her, looked at the softly romantic shoreline, at the colorful beached fishing boat they were walking toward, and wished he had a pistol.

'So what do you do with the Force?' Limnea asked.

'Not much,' Njangu said. 'Push papers back and forth. Make sure people get paid on time.'

'Oh.' Limnea sounded disappointed. 'I thought you were one of those like I've seen on the holos. You know, carrying a gun and things like that.'

'Not me,' Njangu said. 'Loud noises terrify me.'

They reached the boat, and Njangu leaned back against it, Limnea beside him. 'You can take it as a compliment if you want,' he said, 'or not, but you remind me of some of the girls I used to clique with.'

'What's that mean?'

'Not a lot,' he said. 'And maybe I'm wrong. I'd sure like to be.' He put his hands on Limnea's hips, moved her in front of him, pulled her back against him.

'Isn't it pretty?' she said.

'Mmm-hmm,' he said, hands moving around and around on her belly.

'That feels good,' she said softly. He moved his hands up, cupped her breasts, tweaked her nipples with his fingers. She sighed, turned, put her arms around him. Her tongue darted into his mouth.

Limnea's open eyes flickered, and Njangu threw her into the man coming at him with a knife. She squealed, fell to the sand. The man slashed at Njangu, and Yoshitaro bent backward. The man recovered. tried a thrust, and Yoshitaro grabbed his wrist with his left hand, yanked him down, and snapped a knee up into the man's rib cage. Bones snapped loudly, and the man gagged and fell. Njangu kicked him in the face, and scooped up his knife as the second man came in. Yoshitaro slashed, and the man yelped, pulled his bleeding guard arm back.

The two fenced for an instant, then Njangu reversed his grip on the blade, jumped to the side and smashed a fist into the man's neck, snapped his hand back, swinging the blade out and ripping the man's face open. The man stumbled sideways, blade whipping back and forth, keeping Njangu off.

Njangu waved his knife flashily, the man's eyes flickered to it, and Njangu stamp-kicked the man's instep. The man grunted, lunged at Njangu, who sidestepped, and slashed the man's wrist open. Blood sprayed, and the man gasped, clutched his fountaining wound. Njangu kicked him very hard in the solar plexus. His attacker gagged, folded, went flat.

'I hate being right sometimes,' he said. Limnea was running hard down the beach. He went after her, caught up with her in a dozen meters, knocked her sprawling. She rolled over, looked up at him. He still held the knife.

'How did you know?'

'That you weren't just interested in my fair white young body? Easy,' Njangu said. 'The only time a soldier walks in a bar and the prettiest girl spots him and has to jump his bones is in the holos. Mostly we end up paying for it, or with a skunk, or pounding our puds after the money's been spent buying some who-gives-a-shit honey champagne cocktails. Plus you were a little obvious.'

'Don't kill me,' she said. 'Please.'

'Why not? You would've let your two goons kill me,' Yoshitaro said reasonably. 'Now answer my question. You're 'Raum?'

Limnea nodded jerkily.

'Were you and your friends interested in robbery? Or just a dead Forceman?'

Limnea didn't answer.

'I'll guess the last, you debonair revolutionary you. So now the question becomes, what should I do now? Scream shrilly in the key of C for a cop?' Limnea's eyes were wide in fear. 'I've heard rumors the noble Policy and Analysis policemen have some interesting interrogation techniques with 'Raum suspects,' he said. 'Particularly female ones.'

'Please,' Limnea whispered.

'Please my left testicle,' Njangu said. 'You wouldn't have shown me any mercy, now would you?'

'They might not have killed you,' she said.

'Yeh. And I'm the Queen of Sheba.' He looked around. 'Get up.'

She obeyed, eyes fixed on him, and on the knife.

'See those rocks over there? Go on over.'

She obeyed.

'Very well,' he said. 'Negotiations can begin. It's either the cops, or . . .? Remembering that a good revolutionary always knows how to think on her knees.'

Very slowly, she slid the suspenders from her shoulders, let them fall to the side. She undid a fastening, and her pants pooled about her feet. She wore only matching briefs, pulled them down and was naked.

'An excellent start. Now, come here.'

She came toward him. Her breath was coming faster, and her lips were slightly parted.

'When we were interrupted so rudely, you were doing something with your tongue,' he said.

Limnea kissed him, and her hands fumbled with his belt, his trousers snaps. She pulled her lips from his. 'We have a saying,' she said. 'The one who completes his Task is rewarded.'

'Or, to the victor belong the spoils,' Njangu said. He looked at the knife in his hand, sent it spinning, a silver circle splashing into the water. He began unfastening his shirt.

'No,' she said. 'When you do it to me, I want to feel your medals, want them to dig into me. But first, I must be on my knees, as you ordered me.'

The 'Raum hit post offices in half a dozen cities across D-Cumbre, including two in Leggett. The raiders knew just what they wanted, exploding safes for the credits inside, and all official correspondence for its intelligence values. There were only two 'Raum casualties, both minor, and they were gone with the other raiders by the time police units arrived.

PlanGov responded by suspending habeas corpus – suspects could be held, without trial, for as long as two months. Special internment centers were set up on outer islands and were quickly filled.

Governor General Haemer announced a new identity card would be issued to all 'Raum. After a certain date, anyone without a card or with the old identification was subject to immediate arrest. This would force the men and women of The Movement into the open. Or so was the theory.

The Rentiers' Council voted to levy a two-million-credit

fine on the entire 'Raum community, for sheltering criminals and dissidents and failing to support the properly constituted government, but Governor Haemer vetoed the measure.

The men and women of the Heights muttered angrily – the Confederation, or what was left of it, clearly was soft, spineless. Firm measures needed to be taken at once.

Policemen patrolled in at least pairs, frequently more, and wore combat vests, ballistic armor, and many carried mil-issue blasters.

There were three of them at the door of the shabby tenth-floor apartment. The odor of cooking, too many bodies, sweat, and grease hung heavy around them. Two paid no mind – they were 'Raum of the cities and had grown up in the stink. The third, who'd come in from a farm as The Movement ordered, fought nausea.

The woman who opened the door had a baby on her hip, and two little girls clamored behind her. They saw the guns, shrank back.

'Sister, we come from The Movement,' the man said. 'There's nothing to fear. We are here to collect your identity card, and the cards of your household.'

'But . . . what will we do without them?'

'Nothing will happen,' the man said. 'Every 'Raum has been ordered to do this.'

'Oh,' the woman said. 'So if no one has a card . . .'

'Exactly,' the man said. 'We all stand . . . or die . . . together. You understand our struggle better than most.'

'I'll get ours,' the woman said. 'Be sure and knock hard next door. The old woman there is very deaf.'

'There is great concern on our homeworldsss,' System-Leader Aesc told Governor Haemer, 'about your ability to maintain peace in thisss sssystem since contact with your Confederation has been lossst.'

'You know about that?' Haemer said, undiplomatically. The holo image of Aesc and Wlencing shifted slightly, firmed as the transmission beam relocked.

'Of courssse,' Aesc said. 'You ssshould be aware that there are variousss factionsss, I believe isss the word, in our Empire, and their desssired policiesss are not necessssarily the onesss currently in effect.'

'The Ssssytem-Leader meansss,' War Leader Wlencing interrupted, 'there are thossse in the homeworldsss who would like to intervene here in the Cumbre system, and gift you with what might be called a caretaker government. At leassst until your Confederation returnsss, at which time proper gratitude can be expresssed.'

Haemer could not detect any human emotion such as maliciousness or irony. He noticed Aesc look swiftly at his war leader, then away. 'I am sorry,' he said, 'but I am getting mixed signals. Don't you Musth share a common viewpoint?'

Wlencing started to say something, but Aesc interrupted. 'Our waysss are not that unlike yoursss,' he said. 'We rule by concensssus of all.'

'But sometimesss,' Wlencing put in, 'the common agreement changesss when a new reality presssents itssself.'

'Is that happening now?'

Wlencing and Aesc exchanged looks, didn't answer.

'Great God, what a mess,' Loy Kouro exclaimed.

'Isn't it just,' Police Major Gothian agreed. 'We figure there's at least a million ID cards all melted together. Probably more. I guess every goddamned 'Raum on D-Cumbre had a gun put to his head, and the P&A Team on C-Cumbre says the miners there did the same thing.'

Kouro walked around the pile of melted plas in front of the police station. 'No one saw them dump it off ?'

'No one's admitted to it yet,' Gothian said. 'We're still interrogating the night shift and the neighbors.'

'Why'd they do something absurd like this?'

Gothian started to snap something, stopped. No matter how thick, a publisher's son was treated gently. 'If none of the 'Raum have identity cards,' Gothian explained, 'then our identity checks are useless.'

'Oh,' Kouro said. 'Diabolical. Truly diabolical. What will be your countermeasures?'

Gothian hesitated, unwilling to admit that no one had devised one yet. 'My Policy and Analysis team is studying the matter right now, and a decision will be imminent,' he said.

'Good. Very good. We've got to nip these bandits in the bud,' Kouro said ineptly. 'You may rest assured that nothing of this matter will be reported in *Matin*.'

'That's exactly why I asked you to drop by,' Gothian said. 'That, and to see if I might buy you a meal.'

'Never averse to that,' Kouro said. 'But I think it would be more appropriate for me to stand treat. You, after all, are in the front lines of the struggle, and should be honored as best I can.'

Gothian blinked, unwilling to believe anyone actually talked like that, then smiled acceptance.

'Hey, Yoshitaro! Don't you ever pick up your friggin' mail?' the I&R Company clerk asked.

Njangu braked in considerable amazement. 'Nope,' he said. 'Nobody ever writes me. I'm awwl aaa-lone in the world.'

'Write, flight, spite. Somebody sent you a package.'

'Oh yeh? From where?'

'Now do I have time to read the return addresses of

every piece of mail?' the clerk asked. 'Of course not . . .
just the ones that smell pretty or have dirty suggestions
on the disc cover. C'mon, troop. Get your goodies.'

''Kay,' Njangu said. 'You know anybody at II Section
who's got an X-ray machine?'

'Well dip me in chocolate and call me turd,' Kipchak
said, examining the pistol closely. It was a mankiller, a
variable aperture blaster of cold gray alloy, as deadly as it
looked. 'Who's your unknown admirer?'

'Damfino,' Njangu said. 'There was nothing in the
package, other than a piece of paper with a com number.'

Kipchak looked at the pistol even more closely.

'I think I got some advice for you,' he said.

'Already taken,' Njangu said. 'After II Section X-
rayed the box and didn't find anything boomish in it, I
had the armorer take the piece apart looking for fiendish
thingies inside. Nothing. He said it was a perfectly standard Marley. About four hundred credits on the open
market. Then we took it out to the range, bolted it up in
a vise, and ran a string to the trigger. Shoots like a sum-
beech,' he said. 'Dead nuts on.'

Kipchak turned the weapon over and over. 'You try
the com number?'

'Not yet. But I'm sure thinking about it. Maybe this
is a new way to get in my shorts.'

The door to Njangu's room banged open, and Garvin
bounced in. 'Hey, look what somebody sent me!' He held
up a pistol identical to Njangu's.

Over the next week, about fifty Force soldiers got pack-
ages. of various shapes and configurations. All contained
identical pistols, and the same com number. Some recip-
ients were in I&R Company, including Petr Kipchak.

*

''Kay,' Hedley said, 'so that's it with these flipping pop-guns? You're the big-time Intelligence analyst.'

'To reassure you that your view of me as a potential messiah is accurate,' *Cent* Angara said, 'I do, in fact, have an explanation. They're bait.'

'What sort of flipping bait?'

'The people who got them,' Angara said, 'are either recent enlistees or people who've had a bit of trouble adjusting to military life. Some have been in the motivational platoon, two or three in the brig for various offenses. Quite a few of your I&R people, by the way. All good field soldiers, though.'

'What happens,' Hedley asked, 'when they dial that flipping com number?'

'I don't know,' Angara said. 'There's somebody e-monitoring, and they're fairly good, because I haven't been able to get a response other than a synthed voice that says 'Go ahead, I'm listening.' Evidently I'm not saying the right things, nor is anybody I've conned into punching up the number. I had Planetary Police's Policy and Analysis techs check the line quietly, and the goddamned thing's got about six bounces, so nobody knows where the base station really is, and if we dig any harder, it'll most likely self-destruct. But I can tell you what happens when somebody does say whatever the monitoring wants to hear. Eight of the people who got pistols have deserted.'

'Deserted? Not just gone on a spree?' Hedley asked.

'Vanished clean. The MPs tracked two of them to the 'rail station. A ticket clerk said he saw a good-looking soldier open a locker and take out a package. She went into the women's 'fresher, and came out in civvies.'

'Oh flipping really?'

'Yeh,' Angara said. 'He remembered which bank the locker was in, so we grabbed a couple of P&A types, and quite illegally opened all of the lockers. One had a rolled-up uniform in it that had been issued to Striker Mol Trengue, who is currently carried on the books as absent over leave. I looked at her holo on the roster. Real pretty. Sniper-rated, too.'

'Pretty good sign,' Hedley said, 'that somebody doesn't plan on coming back when they leave the monkey suit behind. So somebody's collecting flipping deserters?'

'Looks like.'

'Who?'

'Dunno.'

'Why?'

'Dunno that either.'

The four old women had worked together, cleaning offices in Leggett's business district, for years. They'd gone to each other's weddings, birth ceremonies, manhood rituals, Task-divinings, taken care of each other's children and grandchildren. They lived within a block of each other in the Eckmuhl, and walked the three kilometers to and from work together each day. Their chatter stopped for a moment as a police lifter cruised past – like the other 'Raum in their district, they'd obediently surrendered their cards when The Movement ordered. The lifter passed, and they talked on, of this and that.

A battered lighter, cargo space covered by a canvas tarp, lifted out of a narrow street and came after the women. One noticed the lighter, creeping slowly after them, was about to say something when the canvas fell away. Two men, one woman stood there, wearing dark clothing and hoods, and holding military Squad Support Weapons with drum magazines.

The woman started to scream, but it was too late as the blasters shattered the early-morning quiet. Bodies were smashed against the office wall next to them, blood spattering in a grotesque spray. The lighter lifted nearly straight up, against traffic regulations, banked over a rooftop, and disappeared, leaving a scattering of leaflets in its wake. They were all the same:

'RAUM!
The People of Cumbre
Have Taken Enough
You Have Nurtured The Serpents
At Your Breast Long Enough
Now Is The Time of Change
Reject Their Tyranny
Help Us Destroy Them
Or
We Will Destroy You
The Commitee for Peace

Eleven more 'Raum, none with any known involvement with The Movement, were slaughtered that day, and the same leaflets scattered over their bodies.

The people of Leggett, known for dark humor, dubbed the killers of the Committee 'beards.' If questioned why beards, the answer was because none of the assassins appeared to have them. It was the best . . . and only joke as the dry season ground on, and the killings continued. Some 'Raum quit their jobs and huddled in the Eckmuhl or other 'Raum ghettos across the planet. Others had their jobs terminated, for no citizen of D-Cumbre wanted to chance being in a crossfire if someone came for 'their' 'Raum. Police seemed unable to arrest any of the beards, or find any leads to the mysterious organization and its leaders.

Now D-Cumbre's cities flashed with violence. Not only Leggett, but Aire, Seya, Taman City, Launceston, Kerrier saw robberies, assassinations, intimidation of officials. *Caud* Williams broke the always-unlucky Fourth Regiment into independent companies, each to a city, generally barracked in the main police compounds. But there were never enough soldiers – the Force, badly undermanned, now was spread thin. Williams privately thought too thin.

The five men came through the door with a rush, guns leveled. Jasith's store manager boss squeaked and fainted. 'No one moves,' the leader said.

Jasith held up her hands, and the other three clerks followed her lead. She took a slow step sideways, and two guns were aimed at her.

'Don't even think about that alarm,' the first man warned. 'The one that's about two steps to your left.' Jasith froze. 'We know where all six of the alarms are,' he continued. 'Touch one, and you'll die. All we want is the cashbox . . . and which of you is Jasith Mellusin?'

Jasith licked suddenly dry lips. 'I . . . I am,' she said reluctantly.

'You're coming with us for a while,' the man said. 'You'll be assisting The Movement. Your father'll pay—' Very suddenly his head exploded, and he pinwheeled, falling, his finger clenched on the trigger, and bolts shattered mannequins, dressing-room mirrors. Jasith's bodyguard, standing in the doorway to the break room, swung his pistol toward another 'Raum, was gunned down. The bodyguard's teammate pushed over his partner's body, was killed before he could level his pistol.

Jasith went flat. She heard shouts, more shots. She noticed an earring she'd thought lost a week earlier on the floor about a centimeter from her nose. 'Break off!' she heard someone shout. 'Away from here!'

A police lifter cruising the boulevard heard the shots,

and its two cops jumped out, one keying the automatic
DISTRESS code. The four 'Raum ran out of the lingerie
shop, and the cops saw them. One fired, missing, and
was shot down. The other officer knelt, and fired back.
The 'Raum dashed down the street, shooting wildly at
anything or anyone that moved. A boy about ten, a
'Raum window cleaner, ran out of a doorway and was
killed.

Another police lifter spun around the corner, and three
policemen, armed with blasters, came out. The 'Raum
went down an alley, onto another street. Halfway down
the street was an old stone building, a bankrupt gymnasium.

'We have estimated four suspects,' the police com said
tonelessly. 'They're inside the old Silver Exertorium. One
officer down. Request heavy support.'

'On the way. Force also notified.'

The Grierson was armored, black with a POLICE EMER-
GENCY TEAM on the side. A gunner sat in the open hatch,
behind a 25mm autocannon, sweeping back and forth,
looking for a target. The Grierson's back ramp dropped,
and two platoons of Special Tactics police ran out, bulky
in body armor, combat vest, military helmet and blasters.
Officers shouting orders, they took position around the
gymnasium.

'We getting any fire?' a police noncom asked.

'Nothin' so far.'

'Good. We got 'em pinned,' the other said. 'Second
Squad – we'll go for the main entrance.'

The ten policemen came into the open, as a window of
the gymnasium smashed and an SSW's barrel poked out;
blaster fire boomed. Cops ducked for shelter, or screamed
and went down. A slim tube with a bulbous, finned

object on it slid out a doorway, and the 'Raum holding it aimed carefully, touched the firing stud. The rocket slammed into the pavement just in front of the Grierson, bounced, and exploded under the driver's compartment. The ACV bounced clear of the ground, pilot fighting for control, then rolled, crushing the gunner. Its drive still hissed, and then the Grierson bulged, flame flickering from its open ports and hatches. Another SSW opened fire, bolts crashing into the bottom of the Grierson, ricocheting wildly.

'It's a trap,' somebody shouted. 'The bastards had backup! Get the frigging army in!'

Alarms shrilled across Camp Mahan's parade ground, and a reaction element streamed toward waiting ACVs. Dill and his crew stood helplessly beside their still-unrepaired Grierson. 'Goddammit, goddammit, goddammit,' Ben swore monotonously. 'Somebody's having fun, and it ain't us.'

First *Tweg* Malagash came around a corner. 'I need one volunteer . . . you, Jaansma. Ammo detail on that Cooke over there. The poor little copsies are running out of bullets.'

Garvin felt orphaned, naked. He didn't know anybody in the Cooke's crew or the other man on the detail. He didn't belong with them, didn't know if they were any good. He wanted Dill, Gorecki, Kang, not these strangers if he was going close to danger. *At least*, he thought, *we're just taking the bullets in. We won't have to use them.* But he was very damned grateful for the pistol at his waist.

His headset crackled. 'Would you look at that?' the pilot said, and Garvin saw smoke billowing high from the city's center. *Hope Jasith's got a good view of the excitement, and she's not scared*, he thought. *Sure wish I could be there to do the strong right bower stuff.*

"Kay, gang,' the pilot went on. 'That's where the action appears to be. I've got contact with the LZ Officer. We'll go in high, get a view of what's going on, then go in fast. Get the shit off the bird so we can get out quick. I'll try to give you guys a chance to tourist a little on the way out.'

They crossed over land, and Garvin looked down at the high, ancient walls of the Eckmuhl below, then a flash and a thin stream of smoke rushed at them. 'Dive,' he shouted. 'Somebody's shooting!' The pilot gaped, turned to look at Garvin, and the missile slammed into the Cooke's nose, exploded. The vehicle tumbled, and two soldiers were pitched out, falling, screaming, a hundred meters to the narrow streets of the Eckmuhl.

'Hang on,' the pilot shouted. 'We're goin' in hot. It's gonna be a bastard!'

It was.

THIRTY-ONE

'Sit down, Yoshitaro,' *Alt* Hedley said, less an invitation than an order. The I&R Company commander sat behind a table, with *Cent* Angara, an *Alt* Njangu didn't recognize, and a grim-faced Ben Dill. Njangu obeyed, hoping he'd been called to Company Headquarters because there was some word about Garvin, missing for two days now.

'We have some information on your friend, *Finf* Garvin Jaansma,' *Cent* Angara said.

He's dead, Njangu thought. *Why else would everybody be formal and glooming?*

'*Finf* Jaansma may be alive,' Angara went on. 'We secured the wreckage of the Cooke at dawn today.'

Njangu inhaled in relief, then caught himself. *Good news . . . but hard faces? Careful.*

'We have a few questions about your friend,' Angara went on.

'Such as,' the unknown officer snapped, 'whether or not he ever evinced any sympathies with the 'Raum? I'm *Alt* Wu, Jaansma's platoon leader.'

'No, sir,' Njangu said, and the scene fell sharply into place – it felt like a police court. He certainly knew how to handle that.

'You know that he was one of the soldiers who was sent a pistol recently by an unknown person or persons?'

'Yes, sir.' *So was 1, and so what? And stop trying to sound like a cop, Wu. It don't become you.*

'There were five others aboard that Cooke,' the *alt* went on. 'We found three bodies in the wreckage. Two were obviously killed in the initial impact. The third, the pilot, appears to have been killed by internal injuries that left him outwardly unscathed. However, there were blaster holes in his back . . . blaster holes from a pistol, a pistol in the same caliber as the weapons that've been mystery presents to various members of the Force.'

Njangu's face showed no sign of his surprise, and he said nothing.

'Once again,' the *alt* said, 'Jaansma showed no sign at all of wanting to join the 'Raum?'

'None.' Yoshitaro counted two fast beats before adding 'sir.'

'Calm down, Striker,' Hedley said. 'No one's accusing Jaansma of anything.'

Not much they're not, Njangu thought.

'There was no sign of his body,' Wu said, 'nor any blood trails, and two others in the detail are also missing. One had just been reduced to the ranks, and was loudly complaining about life being unfair. Could all three of these have seized the moment, so to speak, and deserted?'

Njangu waited, stolid.

'I'm sorry you don't seem to be able to help this somewhat informal inquiry,' Angara said. 'If you think of anything that might help, please see *Alt* Hedley at once.'

Right. When giptel *dance.*

'Is that all, sir?'

'It is,' Hedley said. Wu looked at Njangu angrily, but said nothing. 'You're dismissed.'

'May I be excused as well, sir?' Dill asked.

'Very well.'

Both enlisted men saluted, walked out of the room.

Njangu was walking fast, back toward his quarters. Dill hurried to catch up with him. 'Yoshitaro, wait one.' Njangu stopped. 'That was a little raw in there,' Dill said. 'I just wanted to say, I don't believe Garvin's a traitor.'

'How could he be a traitor?' Njangu snapped. 'He's no more part of this world than you are . . . or I am.'

'Sorry. Wrong word. I meant to say I don't think he'd dump us. But do you have any idea about why that pilot would've gotten shot?'

'If I did, *Finf* Dill, I sure as hell wouldn't tell you,' Njangu said.

Dill flushed, stepped back, fists balling. Njangu was suddenly in a slight crouch, fingers together, slightly curled. The two stared at each other, then Dill opened his hands. 'Sorry,' he said. 'I was thinking about a certain platoon leader I know. Like maybe you were, too.' He walked away, quickly.

Njangu waited until he was out of sight, started toward the two coms that connected with civilian lines, then caught himself, and went toward Force Headquarters, and the bank of lines outside the commissary that he hoped weren't monitored. *But if they are, what of it?*

The Cooke had slammed in hard, but flat, spun in two lazy circles skidding up the narrow street and came to rest halfway through a low masonry wall.

Garvin Jaansma sat up, spat blood, and the world unspun around him. He was lying against the body of the gunner, who'd cushioned him from the crash, and died in the process. The fourth ammo-pusher had fielded a case of blaster drums with his skull. The pilot . . . the pilot was slumped over his controls, and the boneless way he lay told Garvin all he needed to know.

Garvin heard shouting, and bleared out at the street, through the litter of spilled cargo and debris, and saw fifty or more 'Raum running toward him. Some had clubs, others knives, and still others were hurling rocks as they came. Garvin's pistol was out and he was about to fire when his mind caught up with him. Very deliberately he fired four shots into the dead pilot's back.

'Take that, you bastard,' he shouted, then turned. The fastest of the mob, a woman in her thirties, wailing vengeance and waving a pair of long scissors, was almost to the Cooke.

'Here, sister,' Garvin shouted. 'Forever The Movement.' He tossed her the gun. The woman's eyes went wide, but she dropped the scissors and caught the gun in both hands, then reversed and aimed. Clumsily, but straight at Garvin's chest.

I'm rescued,' Jaansma shouted, wishing he could have come up with a better line

The woman looked stupefied, but the pistol lowered. Three men were beside her. 'He shouted that he was one of us,' she managed. 'And gave me this.'

'No,' Jaansma corrected. 'I'm not a brother, not yet. But if I'm allowed to, I'd be honored to help in the Task of freedom. That's why I deserted the Force.'

Njangu touched sensors, waited. The com buzzed twice clicked three times – the contact was being bounced from repeater to repeater, then a synthed voice said, 'Go ahead. I'm listening.'

'Uh . . . somebody sent me a pistol a couple of weeks . . . no, about a month ago, with this com number attached.

'Go ahead. I'm listening.'

'I just wanted to thank whoever's at the other end of this for the present. I'm Njangu Yosh—'

'Wait.'

There were more clicks, then a human voice came on. 'What took you so long to get off the pot?'

'I know you,' he said.

'Damned well should,' Angie said.

'What're you looking for?'

'People who don't like the way things're going. And are willing to do something about it, starting with a whole lot of dead 'Raum.'

'Suppose I'm interested?' Njangu asked.

Silence for a moment. 'You remember a village?'

'I do.'

'Go there. Somebody'll meet you. No tricks, no tails.'

'Suppose I'm not quite sure yet? What about cover? What about keeping me out of the slam if I do go with you? Killing 'Raum's all real good, but what about the far end?'

Another silence. 'You jerking me off?'

'Negative,' Njangu said.

'Better not,' Angie said. 'We don't have time to preach for converts. When . . . if . . . you're ready . . . call this number again. But don't take too long. Time's running out for wafflers.' The line went dead.

The police began escorting those 'Raum still brave, or needy, enough to go to their jobs outside the Eckmuhl, using prisoner-transport lifters as shuttles. There were nineteen 'Raum already aboard the lifter, and a twentieth hurrying toward it, the others chaffing him for wanting to stay behind and have a party with the beards when the bomb exploded that'd been planted in a small lifter parked just ahead of the pickup point.

Two Planetary policemen died with the nineteen. The only survivor was the latecomer, and he swore, as he lay on the pavement, feeling what he knew was not rain patter about him, that he would never be on schedule for anything in whatever life span the One had granted.

'There have been very few men or women of the Force who wished to join us,' the slender, not unpretty woman observed. 'And most of those were 'Raum who had erred, lost sight of their Duty for a time, joined with the Rentiers' dogs, then realized their horrible error. Two of those had completely lost their way, and thought they would be double agents.' The woman paused. 'They did not die easily. But they died, without accomplishing anything at all.'

'That was well,' Garvin said, trying to sound a bit approving, a bit enthusiastic, and scared. Only the last came easily.

'Garvin Jaansma . . . promoted *finf* for merit . . . off-worlder, which may be a plus . . . gunner on an Aerial Combat Vehicle . . . Third Platoon, A Company, Second Regiment . . . yes, don't be surprised, we have people inside Camp Mahan. Were you in trouble, Jaansma?'

'No, ma'am.'

'Why do you wish to join us?'

Garvin took a somewhat theatrical breath. 'I joined the Confederation to become a fighter, a warrior. I didn't join to become a policeman, especially not one who smashes the little people and keeps the fat-asses in power.'

'But isn't that the nature of any soldier?'

'Maybe so,' Garvin said. 'Maybe I didn't think things out enough.'

'Perhaps not,' the woman said. She gnawed at her lower lip, thinking 'What were you before you enlisted?'

'I was a salesman,' Garvin lied. 'Not a very good one. 'If we . . . The Movement . . . were not pressed for time,

I would have you taken to some rear area and given instruction. It would be impossible for you, if you're really a spy against The Movement, to maintain your role over that long a time. But time is something we have little of, and you're a trained soldier, which very few of us are. What military skills, disciplines we have, we've had to learn by error and by others' deaths. You could be of infinite value.

'However, we are hardly fools, so we must devise a certain test, something that will irretrievably bind you to us, even if you had thoughts of double betrayal.'

'I'll welcome any test you want to put me through,' Garvin said fervently, his stomach turning.

'The Old Man is biting credits in half,' *Cent* Angara said. 'And shitting quarter-C pieces. Deserters are bad enough, but now we've got one who's found a new career as a gunman for the 'Raum.'

'So it seems,' Hedley agreed. 'Flipping wonderful, ain't it. Run the tape again. With the sound off. I've heard enough shittin' and shoutin' for one day.'

Angara touched a sensor, and the stage in front of them came alive. They were the only two in the II Section screening room.

It was a Leggett street. A heavy stone building almost filled the block, and the camera was across the street from it. The building had a discreet sign: MELLUSIN MINING. Three armored lighters were grounded next to it, with four armed guards pacing back and forth.

'Poor goddamned Mellusin,' Hedley murmured. 'First they try to snatch his daughter, then they do grab his flipping gold.'

'Wonder which one hurt the most?' Angara said.

'The daughter,' Hedley said. 'He's real big on her, and she's an only child. These credits the 'Raum're after are just a bit off the top. But he's got another reason to feel bad . . . I just got something from the interrogation of Jaansma's Grierson crew . . . one said the kid was having a thing with Mellusin's daughter.'

The scene flashed off, and Angara stared at the younger officer in surprise. 'That's too goddamned coincidental to be coincidental.'

'That's what I was wondering,' Hedley said calmly. 'Sure is flipping interesting. Run the tape, my friend. Maybe we're missing something.'

Angara touched the sensor, and the security recording spun on: Six men came out of Mellusin Mining, each rolling a half-meter-square safe. Side doors slid open on the middle lifter. Thus far, it was a standard payroll shipment for Mellusin's mines on C-Cumbre, hard credits instead of an electronic transfer because the 'Raum miners, not without justification, insisted on 'real' payment from the bosses they hardly trusted. In mid-transfer, the process went sour, as two cargo lifters careened out of an alley, and rammed the front and rear lifters. 'Raum leapt out of the backs of the lifters, and started shooting. Guards fought back, ran, were shot down. Two other cargo lighters came up the street, and rear doors banged open and ramps slid down. 'Raum began loading the safes aboard the lighters. All the 'Raum wore hooded masks. All except one.

'Push on our boy,' Hedley requested, and Angara obeyed. Garvin Jaansma, holding a blaster, filled the screen. 'Very good. Go back on him, until he first comes off the flipping lifter.'

The three-dee hologram reversed itself, and Garvin became one of the 'Raum who jumped off a lighter, gun ready. He aimed, pulled the trigger, aimed again . . .

'Go back on that one again,' Hedley said. 'Now freeze it right at the moment when he shoots. Good. Not much of a recoil from that blaster, now was there?'

'There isn't much anyway.'

'Widen the angle,' Hedley said. 'Tell me who he shot.'

Angara ran the record back, forth, back and forth again. 'Nobody,' he said. 'A shitty shot?'

'Qualified marksman,' Hedley said. 'Or maybe they didn't trust him enough to give him any flipping ammo?'

'Not proven. But we'll accept this was a test,' Angara grudged. 'They surely must've known there's cameras all over the Street outside Mellusin Mining, and with him the only one bare nekkid for all to see . . . guess they were making sure he was committed to the flipping cause. Even if they didn't give him any bolts, Jon, just partici-pating full-heartedly in this will be enough for him to be dancing Danny Deever when we catch him.'

'Maybe,' Hedley said. 'Run it forward. Okay, he pre-tends to shoot . . . look at that woman just behind him. The one with the cut-down sporting weapon. Notice it isn't pointed anywhere but at young *Finf* Jaansma? They *didn't* trust him.

'Keep it running. Now he's done what he was ordered to, so now he just stands there, waiting, until they shout for him to load up with the flipping gold. Like a good little rebel he jumps in the lighter and off everybody goes with Mellusin's money End of episode, beginning of legend. Now we'll have Jaansma the Flipping Rebel to contend with. Right?'

'Right,' Angara agreed. 'But it'll be the end of a legend when we hang his young ass.'

'*Not* right,' Hedley said. 'Run it back one more time, to when he lowers the blaster. Push in on his face. Look at that.'

'He's scared,' Angara said. 'Got a twitch. I'd twitch, too, if I were selling out everything and everybody I knew on the permanent record.'

'A flipping irregular twitch,' Hedley said. 'I think there's something sneaky going on.' He asked an increasingly irritated Angara to run the scene two more times, then got a pad and pen. 'How'd you do in Basic Commo?'

'Acceptable,' Angara said. 'But that was so long ago we were communicating with smoke puffs.'

'Always suspected that. One more time. Slowly.' Hedley scribbled as the scene unwound. 'Now I need to use the flipping com.' He touched sensors, asked for some information. disconnected with thanks.

'Well, well,' he said. 'Things are a leetle more complex than they seem. I just checked *Finf* Jaansma's record again. Did real well in everything, which we know. Including Communications training, both programmed and conscious. That's interesting as all hell, considering I noticed our rebel's twitch is very flipping military. That eyelid of his is twitching in basic code: O, N, I, N, S, I, D, E, G, E, T, C, O, M, M, O.'

Angara ran the letters through his mind. 'Pile it in, Hedley. Nobody's that sneaky.'

'Yeah? How come he has time for another O, N, I, N before they hustle him off?'

'Oh shitola on a green leaf,' Angara grunted. 'This does muddy things up a bit, doesn't it?'

'Yeh,' Hedley agreed. 'Do we decide to believe him? And if we do, how do we make contact with him? Come on, Messiah, gimme some flipping suggestions.'

'Don't know," Angara said. 'I'm still stuck on the first question.'

'Njangu.' *Alt* Hedley said cautiously, 'I have a proposition.'

Njangu it is now. Be very careful, little brown brother.

'Yes, sir,' Yoshitaro said, looking brightly interested.

'All this is highly classified,' *Cent* Angara said. 'Please sit down.'

Please? Hoboy, this is going to be cute.

'We misjudged your friend Garvin Jaansma,' Hedley said. 'We're now operating on the basis that he's innocent, and a very quick thinker.'

Angara explained about the holdup, which Njangu'd already be heard about through the rumor mill, and Garvin's coded blinking. Njangu almost nodded – his friend *was* thinking fast. *Probably all those goddamned 'Raum wanting to tear him a new asshole kicked his brain into high gear. He sure wouldn't have come up with something that stinky all on his own. And he better be careful, in whatever warren they've got his young ass, or he's going to start thinking he's thinking, get cocky and get thin-sliced. Stinky shit's my department.*

'Very interesting,' Yoshitaro said when Angara'd finished. 'And I'm not surprised at all. But why're you telling me all this?'

'We want you to go in and get him out.'

'Uh . . . *Cent*,' Njangu said, with a twisted grin, 'I'm not Stupor Soldier. No steel teeth on me, and no pocket nukes up my ass. Perhaps the word that's gone before me's been a little excessive.'

Angara glanced at Hedley. 'Your Recon boys are as big wise-asses as their leader.'

'Hope so,' Hedley said. 'Otherwise, all that training would've gone to waste.'

'We'd put you in with some mini-coms the Planetary Police's P&A Section has, and a good cover.'

'Such as?'

'Such as you're going to desert.'

Now why would I do something like that?' Njangu said. 'Jaansma might be a friend, but we ain't banging assholes, to put it bluntly. It'd have to be better than that.'

'What about,' Angara tried, 'that we think you had something to do with his desertion?'

'Not enough.'

'Even if we're going to court-martial you?'

Njangu started to say something, then caught himself.

'Go ahead,' Hedley said.

'I better not, sir. I've got enough enemies.'

Angara lifted an eyebrow. 'I don't bruise easy. Keep talking.'

'Very well . . . *sir.* That's the flash shit they do in holos. Thrown out of the regiment in disgrace, epaulettes, whatever the hell those are, torn off in disgrace, medals thrown in the dirt, drums thumping away. Real dramatic . . . sir . . . but *giptel*-piddle as far as I'm concerned.'

Hedley grinned at a flushing Angara. 'Why?'

'Because the real world . . . at least when it comes to crookery, isn't all that dramatic,' Njangu said.

'You have some expertise in the area?' Angara asked.

Njangu just looked at him.

'Sorry. Go on.'

'Look at it from the 'Raum point of view. I show up with cops chasing me, hollering and screaming, and it looks flash, like I said. So the first thing they're going to do is check me out every way they can.'

'We don't think they have a scan.'

'I don't give a shit about scans,' Njangu said. 'I can beat them, most times.'

Hedley blinked. 'How? Sorry . . . some other time you'll have to show me that little trick. But go ahead. Sorry I interrupted you.'

'What I'm worried about is the records. Charge sheets, court-martial scheduling, all that sort of thing, right down to who was going to stand in for officers who were gonna be on that court-martial. Other things, like what

hard evidence did you get to think I was a 'Raum convert
to get this court-martial rolling? '

'You're being paranoid.'

'Am I? Even paranoiacs got enemies, sir.'

'As long as we keep everything inside the Force, and at
the highest level, we should have no trouble,' Angara
argued stubbornly.

'Inside the Force, sir? Last time I was at Headquarters,
I saw a dozen 'Raum clerks. Don't try to make me believe
Caud Williams and *Mil* Rao do their own filing.'

'Just because one of our clerks happens to come from
a 'Raum background—' Angara started.

'Means they're the enemy. Not to mention I don't
believe somebody in II Section, some Force person, won't
tell this tippy-top secret to a buddy of his with the cops'
P&A Section. And of course I don't believe the 'Raum
just might happen to have an agent or two inside the
coppery. Pretty soon, everybody'll know good old
Njangu's out there playing games, including the 'Raum.
I've *got* to take a one-way, chicken-shit point of view, sir.
It's my ass you're talking about dumping in there. Let's
say that I've had some experience in things going wrong,
and if they can go wrong, they will. And I'll be the dead
meat.'

''Kay,' Hedley said. 'Drop the idea. We'll find some
other way to get Jaansma into contact with II Section.
But we'd like you to help us plan whatever we're going
to do, since you know him better than anybody else.'

'Not a chance,' Njangu said. 'I'm the one that's going
in. But we're going to do it my way or no way.'

Njangu stamped back into the barracks with a black look
on his face, and obvious rage in his heart.

'What's the matter?' Kipchak asked.

'Dirty sons of bitches,' Njangu snapped. 'They won't

get off this shit about Garvin being a traitor, and maybe I know something and maybe this and maybe that.'

'Hey, Njangu,' Gerd said. 'They don't know any better.'

'No,' Yoshitaro said. 'No, they don't. Tell you what they'll do . . . they'll put Garvin's face on a poster and some Planetary oinker'll gun him down, and then they'll find out different and all it'll be is "oh, so sorry, we made a little mistake." Which won't do the late Garvin Jaansma a goddamned bit of all right. Idiots practicing to be morons, every goddamned one of them.'

'Maybe it'd do some good if I talked to Hedley,' Penwyth said. 'I spent time with Garvin myself.'

'You can try. But I'm through talking to butthooks with their fingers in their ears.'

'You better get some sleep and stop raving,' Kipchak said mildly. 'They've got you on guard, third watch, tonight.'

'It never frigging rains but it pours, doesn't it? All right. Lemme start spit-shining on the off chance I make supernumerary,' Njangu growled. 'I *really* didn't need this shit.'

Very quietly, PlanGov announced normal traffic to and from the far-distant island/city of Kerrier and three other islands had been interrupted because of 'civic unrest,' to be resumed as soon as possible.

Caud Williams had ordered Garvin Jaansma and Njangu Yoshitaro to keep a low profile. Probably no order has ever been so lavishly disobeyed: First Garvin deserted, then Njangu Yoshitaro, at least in the eyes of the Force, vastly outdid him. According to the charge sheet, Striker Yoshitaro, when detailed to guard duty, was observed to be loudly and obnoxiously drunk when his watch was called. The commander of the guard attempted to quiet him, and he knocked him unconscious, broke the *Tweg* of the guard's left arm when he tried to quiet him, drew a pistol on other members of his guard, and told them to get inside the guardhouse or die, then locked them all in cells and hurled the key into the bay.

He proceeded to the Camp Mahan main commissary, which was just closing, broke in the back door, terrorized several civilian clerks at gunpoint, and stole the evening's receipts. Yoshitaro ran out the front entrance of the commissary, shot out the overhead lights, commandeered a passing Military Police patrol lifter, struck one of the policemen when he attempted to reason with the berserk striker, and stole the lifter. Civilian authorities were not able to respond in time, and the Military Police lifter was abandoned outside one of the gates into the Eckmuhl.

Njangu Yoshitaro and Garvin Jaansma were placed on the Planetary Police's Most Wanted list, and orders were given to the police and army that both were considered armed and extraordinarily dangerous, and authorization was given to shoot on sight, without warning.

'This,' Garvin explained, 'is Jo Poynton. She's the equivalent of the head of II Section for The Movement. She gave me a chance when I first decided to join the 'Raum.' He sounded impressed, and Njangu looked respectful.

'You others can leave,' Poynton said, and Njangu's guards vanished. She took a pistol from her desk, and laid it in front of her. 'You two are interesting,' she said. 'Your deeds make you sound like terrible desperadoes.'

Njangu shrugged. 'People got in my way.'

'Perhaps,' she said. 'Although I'll admit it's very hard for me to believe the Force would allow anyone to create as much chaos as you did to create the rationale for a false deserter. And we do appreciate the contribution to The

Movement's treasury. It came to a bit over ninety-seven thousand credits, for your information.'

Njangu smiled wryly.

'Since you arrived in the Eckmuhl four days ago,' Poynton went on, 'I did some thorough checking within The Movement about you. You already know, Jaansma, how careful we are in documenting all members of the Force, requiring all brothers and sisters to report on any contact with soldiers, but perhaps that's new to you, Yoshitaro.'

Njangu tried to ignore the constriction in his throat, remembering his 'contact' with the woman named Limnea.

'The first appearance you, Yoshitaro, have in our records is when you, without any rationale, chose to help a 'Raum boy who was being bullied by some drunks Why?'

'I'd had a bad day, and needed to relieve my tension.'

Poynton blinked. 'That's an unusual answer. At any rate, because of this uncommon event, I had you and your group followed. You, Yoshitaro, managed to elude my not-inexperienced operative. I then decided to have you, Jaansma, picked up for interrogation later that night. I sent two men after you, both skilled warriors, and one you crippled, the other was a long time recuperating and still can't be considered fully capable of combat.'

'I m sorry,' Garvin said, trying to sound ashamed. 'I thought they were trying to rob me.'

'Then,' Poynton went on, 'first one, then the other of you desert, and make your way to the Eckmuhl and want to join The Movement. Don't either of you find those events a bit suspicious?'

'Maybe,' Njangu said. 'But I think life's a bit suspicious.'

Surprisingly, a smile came, and Poynton's compressed lips were attractive for an instant. 'I discussed my problem with the one who now leads The Movement's Planning Group, and what should be done. On one hand, I don't want to lose the potential of your valuable services. You've already given us excellent information on your unit's codes and procedures, although the Force has already changed its signal operating procedure, so what you told us is important less in practice than in theory. Both of you will be very useful in the days to come, both training new fighters and as warriors yourself, so the first option that was suggested I found unpleasant.'

'I assume,' Njangu said, 'your leader suggested shooting us.'

'Correct.'

'That *does* seem a little wasteful,' Garvin said.

Again Poynton smiled. 'Sometimes I forget how grim we've all gotten,' she said. 'I hope both of you can keep your humor alive.'

'Easy, as long as *we're* alive,' Njangu said.

'Which brings me to the second option,' Poynton said. 'Both of you are aware of the Rentiers' own terrorists, the ones they call beards?'

Both men nodded.

'We have excellent intelligence that they are not only funded by the Rentiers and other medievalists, but that most of their operatives, at least the most effective murderers, were recruited from the ranks of the Force. Some of us think they are actually still members of the Strike Force, operating under deep cover so they can butcher with a free hand. What's your opinion?'

'I'd think not,' Njangu said. 'I came from Intelligence and Reconnaissance, and we work closely with II Section – Force Intelligence. I think I would have heard some whisper if we were running death squads.'

'Perhaps . . . or perhaps not,' Poynton said. 'I must allow my opponents credit for some intellect, and being able to keep a few secrets. Not to mention the possibility that you are both double agents, in which case you're lying.

'Not that it matters, for the head of our Planning Group and I have devised a mission for you two, a further test. I will control your team, and you will have access to any resources the 'Raum can provide which you need.

'Your assignment is to track down and eliminate those death squads, those they call beards. If you fail, that might suggest you are still with the Force, but the problem will have been solved for us by the beards. If you succeed . . . you have done everyone on D-Cumbre a great favor.'

THIRTY-TWO

'I frigging despise eavesdroppers,' Njangu snarled. 'Even when they're on my frigging side.'

'So I see,' Garvin said calmly. He sat on one of the small apartment's beds, feet on a table. Their room was a mess working on a shambles – wire ripped from the ceiling and walls draped across plaster-strewn tables; three spike-mikes that'd been boot-tested and found wanting, a shattered grid-mike that'd masqueraded as a bad scenic view of the bay invisible behind the high walls of the Eckmuhl, and an archaic standard microphone that appeared to have been planted by one of D-Cumbre's original settlers.

'Did you get all of them?' he asked.

'Every bleedin' one,' Njangu said, shaking his head, holding up one finger and pointing to one of the ceiling lights. He scrawled on a notepad: *I boogered that one so it's only got about a meter's range. Let them think they're still hearing something, so they don't get worried. Keep the important shit in writing.*

''Kay,' Garvin said. 'By the way, where'd you learn your techno skills?'

'Can't a girl have a few secrets?'

'Why not. So what're we gonna do about nailing your bearded honey?'

Njangu slumped down on another bunk. 'That's a poser, ain't it?'

'Actually, the first question is, *can* we do anything about ol' Angie?'

'We better.' Njangu said. Or The Movement's gonna have us 'dobe-walled.'

'Appears like,' Garvin agreed. 'So what're the options?'

'The first and easiest would be to nark her off to the coppers,' Njangu said. 'Which'd piss off our new lords and masters, 'cause it's a little hard to believe she and her crew'd get Handled Harshly, since me and some other people have this sneaky and obvious hunch the Rentiers are bankrolling them. Plus I ain't big on snitching.'

'So you want to do her yourself ?' Garvin asked.

'Not really,' Njangu said honestly. 'I'm not that hard-assed. But we've got to ensure she . . . and the rest of the beards . . . are inactivated. Permanently. Unless we want the same treatment.'

'This keeps sounding like killing,' Garvin said, grim-acing.

'It do, doon't it?'

'But first things first,' Garvin said. 'I know we're incredibly gifted, intelligent, analytical and well hung, but how are we gonna *find* young Angie? I understand there's been some other folks looking.'

'I think I can get ahold of Rada,' Njangu said. 'She did gimme her com number, and suggested a meeting place. I think we ought to establish contact, see what shakes, then play it by ear.'

'So commence to button-pushing, my friend.'

'Not here,' Njangu said. 'Let's go grab our quote escorts end quote and find a neutral com. No. Better idea. Let's go tell Poynton what we're going to try.'

*

Njangu waited until the monorail car was almost empty, then picked up his battered case and got off, trying to think like he looked – a young, not very successful sales-man having a bad day out here in the tules, hoping the little fishing village of Issus would change his luck. He left the station, walked through the park, eyeing the businesses around the square for possible customers. His eyes swept left, right.

There's one . . . even wearing his old service boots . . . good camou, Angie . . . another one pretending to scan the holo board . . . now one of ours, shit, gotta break that woman's thumbs and get her to stop playing spy, peepin' around like she ought to be wearing a veil with a codebook in one hand . . . god-damned amateurs . . . pity the frigging Movement's down on hiring crooks . . . He bent, adjusted a bootstrap, glanced casually behind him. *Another one back there . . .* Angie's gift-pistol in the small of his back felt very comforting.

A man came toward him, a familiar face, brushed against him, and was past, and Njangu realized his sidearm had been quite neatly lifted. Before he could figure what to do next, Angie Rada came out of a net repair shop's alcove and was beside him, holding his right elbow in her left. She was dressed like a day tourist from the capital, but kept her other hand in her wind-breaker pocket. 'Smile like you're having fun,' she whispered. 'We're two old friends who just happened to run into each other.'

'Aren't we?'

'Why'd you take off ?' Angie asked.

'Things got a little henhouse back at good old Camp Mayhem, and I decided to seek grander horizons.'

'What took you so long to call me again?'

'I thought I'd check the other options first,' Njangu said. 'I've got a pretty good idea a man could get killed working for you . . . with damned few credits in the process.'

Angie's grip tightened, and she swung the hand in her pocket until it pointed toward Njangu. 'What others? The 'Raum?'

'Jesu Joy of Man's Desire, Angie! Just 'cause you've turned into some kind of bigtime death squad leader doesn't mean you have to pack in what little goddamned humor you had!'

'Careful, Yoshitaro,' Angie warned. 'What I'm doing isn't a joking matter.'

'Yeh, well I always learned that it's a good idea to keep a smile on your lips and a song in your heart when you're smashing the State.'

'We're hardly doing that,' Rada said. 'Rather, we're backing it up, doing the work it's reluctant to do, so it can become as strong as it's supposed to be.' She looked critically at Njangu 'You know, I'll never understand you.'

'Nothing to understand,' Njangu said easily. 'I'm just a charming feller with an eye for the main chance. I checked around with the local mobbies, but they're lying pretty low and not hiring outside talent at the moment.'

You better realize something, mister. Once you're in this thing of mine . . . of ours, there's no getting out until it's over.'

'And that'll be?'

'When these frigging 'Raum have been taught their place and put in it.'

'Which is?'

'The bastards that have been killing women and children and policemen . . . dead or in prison. Dead by court, dead by our hands, it doesn't matter.'

'What about the others? Not every 'Raum is rebelling.'

'Shit they're not,' Rada said fiercely. 'They're backing these murderers in everything they do, and that's just as bad as if they were pulling the trigger or setting the bomb themselves. So they'll have to pay. We ought to just stamp 'em all out, but I know my Cumbrians. They think they're too good to go offplanet and work the mines, or dig the ditches, so we'll always need the 'Raum, I'm afraid. But we can keep them off Dharma Island, off the other major islands, and out of the cities.

'Maybe we'll isolate them on some of the Windward Islands or something, and build ports to transport the miners back and forth to C-Cumbre, and have temporary camps for those we need to have doing scut work in the cities. I don't know. That's for the pols to work out, after we give the government back to them.'

'We?' Njangu asked.

'You don't think I'm alone in this? Killers, for your information, are high-maintenance tools. My family, after their stores got burned, have realized which side they're on, and that helps. But there's others . . . real big names, names that'd surprise you, who're contributing. Credits, vehicles, target tips . . . you name it, we've got it.

'So are you in?'

'As if I've got a choice.'

'Good,' Angie said. 'Now, we'll arrange to get back to Leggett, making sure you didn't bring any friends along, and then we'll start training you.'

'More training?' Njangu wailed, but felt vast relief. It looked as if he'd done it, stepped through the door the minute it fell open. *Ho-ho, Njangu Yoshitaro, master infiltrator and double agent.* And then everything fell apart around his shoulder blades.

A cheery voice called 'Aay! N'anju! Angie!'

Njangu jolted . . . *shit, blown*, saw a smiling, long-haired beauty. Deira, of long months ago. He sagged in relief, lifted a hand in greeting. Then he saw Angie's face, cold in rage, and her hand came out of her jacket pocket holding a heavy pistol, and she crouched, bringing her off hand up in support, the gun aiming, in utter madness, at Deira. Njangu reacted without thinking, snapkicking, the gun spinning away, into the park. Angie scrabbled after it, snarling incoherently, and a gun blasted behind Njangu, blowing a hole in a parked lifter.

Njangu rolled, hand going for his bootheel, not as nonsensical as it looked. One heel had been modified by 'Raum craftsman, and held two old-fashioned shot-shells, each in an alloy barrel, with spring firing pins. He had the weapon, brought it up, saw a heavyset man he thought he remembered from the Force aiming at him, not five meters away, and snapped the first pin. The gun blasted, nearly breaking his wrist, and the pellets spattered the man. He screeched, dropped the gun, grabbed his face, and staggered backward.

Angie recovered her pistol, was aiming, and Njangu let the other barrel go. Both of them missed. Njangu ducked away, into some brush, heard Angie screaming, 'Kill him! Kill him!' and for the first time in his life, the cops came to the rescue.

There were three of them, big men wearing riot gear, and they saw Angie, pistol in hand, and reached for their guns. She shot one, he grabbed his arm, and she ran toward the monorail station.

Njangu went after her, cutting through the park, not sure what he'd do if he beat Angie to the station, hoping to hell his backups had seen what'd happened and were coming, but seeing, hearing no one, the crazy thought repeating, *all right. bitch, all right, you went and made it personal and now it's gonna be payback time.* Behind him, the cops shot again, then a third time, and he wondered at what. Someone shouted 'Halt,' and he threw a rude gesture over his shoulder, kept going.

He stopped behind a tree thick enough to stop a

blaster bolt. He looked back, and saw Deira on her hands and knees, scuttling behind a grounded lifter, felt an instant of relief, then dashed on.

A grenade boomed ahead of him, then he was out of the park, seeing smoke curl outside the 'rail station/town hall, two sprawled bodies and shattered glass jeweling the ground. Angie was going up the steps, two men with her. One paused, aimed carefully, and shattered the top of the com tower on the hall's roof.

A 'rail car was inside the station, turbine whining. Another grenade blasted, and shots echoed from inside. Njangu, a crazy whirl in his guts, ran up the steps of the hall, used a shattered window frame for a step, pulled himself to the roof of the hall. He shinnied up the lattice of the blasted tower, just as the 'rail eased out of the station, two meters below him, three meters awsy.

Not letting himself think, he jumped, and thudded down on the car's roof. He slid, almost going off as the car picked up speed, found a pressure hold, squirmed to a rotating beacon, clutched it as the wind roared about him.

Now what, you silly bastard, now what, hoping they didn't hear the thud as you landed and this goddamned thing doesn't go fast enough to knock you off, and didn't you forget something important like maybe a bang-stick? His fingers fumbled at his other heel, pulled it off, and whipped the antenna free to flail in the wind. He touched the POWER sensor, the SEND button.

'G . . . this is N.' Static crackled, and Njangu winced, knowing this half-assed lashup the half-assed 'Raum techs had built, swearing it'd never be found, swearing it was set away from any Force frequency, was screwed and pretty quick blaster bolts would start punching holes in metal and then Njangu Yoshitaro.

'G. Go.' Garvin's voice was quite calm, and Njangu forced himself to sound the same.

'In a world of shit,' he said, and briefly explained what'd happened.

'What do you need?'

'Wings, asshole — but maybe somebody knows the 'rail routes, and can be waiting at the station with a hundred gazilhon Zhukovs.'

'Negative on the *Zooks*,' Garvin said. 'But there'll be people there. The Big Man's here, and he's giving orders. Hang on. We'll pull your ass out.'

'You better.'

But the 'rail never reached the main Leggett station. As the silver rails curved over the Heights, then down toward Leggett, it came close to the ground, not ten meters above a thickly brushed hillside. Blaster fire came from inside, then screams, and more shots. The turbine screamed up the cycle, then there was sudden silence.

Yoshitaro chanced looking, saw an emergency exit screech open, locks protesting. A man jumped, gun in hand, arms wide, coat flapping, landed, then Angie followed, then the third man leapt free. Angie glanced up at the car, and Njangu hastily ducked out of sight. The trio pushed through the undergrowth toward a nearby street.

Njangu Yoshitaro, unarmed, listed three dozen sorts of fools he was, jumped into the middle of a thornbush, rolled, and went after the three beards.

'G . . . this is N.'

'Go.'

'Obviously the party didn't make the station.'

'No shiteedah. What happened?'

'They jumped off outside Leggett, infiltrated into the city.'

'Eeesh. So we're starting all over again?'

'Big negative, my friend. I stayed with 'em. Present

location Yoke Itchie Seven Unyoke Q as in Queen, Yoke Medal Doolie Gik Gik Pod Sif Medal Pod Unyoke. Bring some big guys with sticks. These people aren't friendly at all.'

'On the way.'

The warehouse sat in the grimy port industrial area to the east of Leggett's main shopping district, with no signs of ownership. Njangu scouted the entrances — one on each of the streets the building fronted on, a fourth on the wharf to the rear. He found a vantage point in an alleyway and waited. Three times lifts with RADA MARKETS came and went. *Subtle.* Njangu shook his head. *More proof P&A are really incorruptible coppers.* Twice he talked Garvin closer, wondering what sort of big guys with sticks he'd been able to arrange.

A short man with a broom wandered up the street, paused at the alley, and grinned toothlessly. 'Go back one block,' he said. 'We're waiting for you in that burned-out building.' The street-sweeper ambled on. Njangu checked for watchers, obeyed.

The building had been a cargo-lifter park and maintenance works, and flame-twisted machinery still sat here and there on the grease- and smoke-blackened floor. Njangu blinked as he smoothed inside. There were at least fifty 'Raum gathered, none big with sticks, dressed in every guise from workman to *soh*, two-thirds men, some very young. But all were armed with a disarray of weaponry, holding their weapons fiercely. There were paired guards at the two entrances.

Garvin crouched atop an overturned, burned-out lifter. He saw Njangu and stood. He held a pistol in one hand. 'Brothers and sisters to be,' he started. 'I would have your ears. My brother, Njangu, has tracked these enemies of the people, these ones they call the beards, to their den. We know there are three of them in there, probably more. We do not know what the building contains. We do not know what weapons our enemies have inside. We do not have time to make further investigation.

'I hope I have brought you to the center of this conspiracy who have slaughtered your women, your children, your men. I would like to take one prisoner, to interrogate later, to determine how many more of these beards we shall have to find and eliminate, but if we cannot, we cannot.

'We must strike hard and fast, for the police will arrive shortly after the fighting starts. When you see no more targets, leave at once. If there are wounded, dead, try to take them with you, and don't leave them to the cruelties of the police. If you must, abandon your arms and attempt to melt into the people, for you, as a fighter, are more important than any gun, any bomb. I shall begin the attack, after I have been told each group is ready. Expect anything when you enter.

'This is the heart of the enemy. Show no mercy, and remember the blood on their hands, and repay them for their evil. Work well, for the Task is at hand.'

There was a murmur, and the men began filing out. Garvin jumped down, walked to Njangu. 'Ready?'

'Yeh,' Njangu said. 'I say again my last: What about the fancy talking?'

'In the circus,' Garvin said blandly, and went toward the exit.

The warehouse served not only Rada Markets, but, through them, another dozen smaller emporiums. To the nineteen deserters Angie Rada had recruited, it was, with the exception of sexual opportunities, fairly close to nirvana. They'd sectioned off the rear of the building, closest to the bay, for living quarters, set up bunks and stoves from the stored camping equipment. They made periodic forays into the warehouse for food liquor, holos, and such, taking a case at a time so there'd be little obvious sign of their presence.

Sixteen beards were listening to Angie Rada, who stood in front of a large-scale tri-dee pictomap of Leggett. A seventeenth guarded the main entrance the lifters used, and two others were in the city on surveillance duties.

Her voice was low, cold: 'Obviously it was a trap, or else no one would have been backing up the traitor Yoshitaro. It was lucky I sensed something going awry, or none of us might have made it out of that armpit alive.'

One of the men who'd been with Angie thought of asking why she'd shot at that girl, who didn't seem to be doing anything but waving, but thought better, remembering three other deserters who'd challenged her, and been dumped out the back door into the water, wearing sleeping bags wrapped in chains and neat holes in their foreheads.

'I don't know who he's working for, the Force, the police, the 'Raum, but we'll find him, eventually,' she promised. 'But in the meantime, we need to strike back, strike hard. Here is our next target. It's the main place of worship for the 'Raum, just at the entrance to the Eckmuhl. Elt, Wiglaf, you've been surveilling it, right?'

'Right,' one man said. 'It's a go target. Nice, soft, easy in, easy out.'

'We'll use a bomb this time,' Angie said, 'and station shooters around the sides. After it blows, we'll run two magazines through our weapons, then break contact.'

The first beard to die was the sentry. He turned, surprised, as the small door next to the lifter entrance opened and a spring knife went into his throat. Two 'Raum eased his body to the floor, and Garvin, Njangu and the rest of the first attack group slipped inside.

The huge room was bright, lights hanging in rows along the curved ceiling. It was filled with aisle after aisle of goods, some stacked, some on shelves. Steps led to an upper level with darkened offices. Njangu went up the steps, scanned the long aisles below, heard voices from the rear, pointed the way to the 'Raum, came back down.

The 'Raum on the other two street entrances got inside without raising an alarm, but the last group, closest to the beards, grated their door open.

Angie's hand blurred for her gun, and she shot the first two 'Raum, and another beard pitched a grenade into the doorway. The blast sent the group stumbling back.

Garvin, down an aisle at the warehouses' other end, saw a man with a blast rifle, shot him, knelt, and sent bolts spitting down the aisle. A beard shot back, and Garvin, as he rolled to the side, was blinded by a warm, sticky fluid. He wiped his hand across his eyes, saw red, had a panicked moment, realized the bolt had shattered a carboy of some sort of sweet drink on the shelf above him, rolled into the next aisle, and sent half a magazine roaring down toward the deserters.

The warehouse was a chaos of shouting, screaming, shots, and explosions. The two groups from the side deployed across the open loading area. Five beards, knowing they'd see no mercy from the 'Raum, were behind a stack of loading pallets methodically dropping their attackers.

'Surprise,' Njangu said, stepping out from an aisle behind them, a seized rifle at his shoulder. They spun, but too late as his blaster chattered, and four men and a woman curled, screaming.

Njangu couldn't hear anything, momentarily deafened by the ferocity of the firefight, and then a 'Raum was shaking him, his lips forming words – 'All down! All of them are down!'

An instant later he was proved false, as Angie blew the 'Raum's head off and charged toward the wharf exit, shooting as she went. She changed magazines, jumped over the doorsill onto the wharf. Her partner paused to fire back into the warehouse as flames flickered and smoke billowed from a pile of boxes.

Garvin took careful aim, and blew half his chest away, then started shouting, 'Break contact! Break contact! They're gone!' and slowly the 'Raum came down from battle madness, standing in haze amidst scattered bodies.

He thought, not surprised, *So much for prisoners*, shouldered a wounded, moaning 'Raum, saw one of the beards writhing in pain, shot him in the head, then ran, stumbling, toward the eastern exit, the farthest from where the police response should come. 'Raum streamed after him, their leaders shouting commands to pick up the wounded, the dead. Some obeyed, some just fled, Njangu was at the rear, the body of a 'Raum woman over his shoulder, then they were out of the warehouse. The fire inside was spreading, leaping from aisle to aisle, and smoke poured from the ceiling vents. Njangu heard the scream of sirens across the city, told his mind to disregard that, and began zigging through back alleys toward the Eckmuhl.

Angie Rada skidded around a corner, breath searing, saw the police lifter blocking the narrow street and the half dozen riot cops crouched behind it, guns aimed. 'Drop the weapon,' the lifter's PA set boomed.

Angie ducked into a shop entrance, snapped a shot at the lifter and the PA set screeched into silence. She shot at a cop, saw him grab his leg and convulse. 'Come on, you bastards, come on,' she shouted, and there was fierce joy in her voice.

The Eckmuhl exulted that night, and no one, not the Force. not the police, was stupid enough to send patrols inside the walls. Njangu and Garvin sat in that night's safe house with Jo Poynton. 'Shall we go out and reap our benefits?' Garvin asked. 'Not forgetting our "escorts"?'

'Wait a moment,' Poynton said. 'There's someone Njangu should meet.' A moment later the door opened, and a medium-sized man came in. He was unremarkable except for his thick chest and muscled arms, and then Njangu met his eyes, eyes that held and burned.

'This is the Big Man,' Garvin said, unnecessarily.

Njangu extended his palm, but Jord'n Brooks nodded instead of using the standard Confederation greeting. 'At the moment, I use the name Tver,' Brooks said. 'Although that changes. And I do not like being called the Big Man. There is no one in The Movement bigger than another.'

Njangu stared skeptically, couldn't decide if Brooks believed what he was saying.

'It would appear,' Brooks said, 'you two are a positive asset to our cause.'

Garvin inclined his head in thanks.

'My emphasis is on "appear,"' Brooks said. 'You helped us . . . but you also helped the cause of the Rentiers.'

'How do you figure?' Njangu said interestedly.

'Ccrtainly the Force is delighted to have these lunatics named beards out of the way. Their own killers work more subtly. And the real controllers of this system, those with real intelligence, can't be pleased with what happened, knowing every atrocity the beards committed drove more and more of our brothers and sisters into activism.'

'Your mind works in strange ways,' Garvin said, a little hostility in his voice.

'That's why I've remained alive, and why The Movement continues to grow,' Brooks said calmly, stating facts, no more. 'But I don't want you to be angry at what I said. Perhaps, even probably, it's not true, and you're sincere converts. As time passes, and you perform other missions for us, my words will perhaps be proven false, hateful.

'Perhaps.' He nodded, went back out.

Poynton shrugged. 'He is what he is. And we all serve him willingly.'

'Maybe so,' Garvin muttered. 'But I'm not sure I have to like him. I think I'm gonna go out and find some masses to lavish gratitude on me. Coming?'

'Maybe in a bit,' Njangu said. 'I want to shave, wash up first. I'll meet you, where? Around midnight, somewhere around that big church?'

''Kay,' Garvin said. 'If I'm not there, I've found a better party.'

'The same goes for me.' Garvin gave Njangu a thumbs-up, went out.

Your friend isn't afraid to speak his mind,' Poynton said.

No,' Njangu agreed. 'That's why he's got me around, to keep him out of trouble.'

'Perhaps I could show you a bit of our gratitude,' Poynton said. 'I happen to have a bottle of a very good wine, even if it is just from D-Cumbre, in my quarters I've been saving for some sort of victory. I don't like to drink alone.'

'You have a deal, Fearless Leader and Intelligence Honcho of the Universe,' Njangu said. 'But give me half an hour. I still smell scared to me.'

*

Njangu shut the old-fashioned shower off, considered its ending dribble through the ancient, rusted head. Not much of a 'fresher, compared to the omnidirectional water cannons in the Force's barracks, nor the lavish 'freshers in some of the expensive hotels he'd blown the profits from a successful villainy in. But it was better than being pissed on by a bandit, and just a bit better than the 'fresher in the crowded apartment he'd grown up in.

Outside the building, he heard the continuing roar of the celebration. He pulled the curtain aside a bit, and a hand extended a towel.

'I'm not looking,' Jo Poynton said.

Njangu took the towel and dried himself, thoughtfully re-evaluating the 'Raum intelligence chief. Just because he was terrified she'd expose him . . . although not quite this literally . . . didn't mean he couldn't, wouldn't, at least if she were interested? She certainly wasn't hard on anybody's eyes, and was an equally long way from being stupid. *Very strange*, he thought. knotting the towel around him and putting a smile on.

'You're sure you're not peeking?'

'Maybe . . . just a little.'

He stepped out of the shower. Poynton was sitting cross-legged on the wooden laundry hamper that opened on a drop from aeons ago, when this building had prosperous tenants, before it'd been divided and divided again into a warren. She wore a loose, blue-velvet jumpsuit whose top wrapped around and tied at her waist. She was barefoot, and smelled of exotic fruits. Looking as she did, rather than the dedicated warrior, Njangu realized that she was probably no more than two, perhaps three years older than he was. He felt his body stir. It'd been a long time since Deira and . . . he closed his mind off, admired Poynton.

Beside her was her always-present pistol, an open bottle of wine, and two mismatched glasses. She poured a golden wine into each, handed Njangu one. 'To victory.'

'To victory,' Njangu replied, honestly.

She picked up the bottle, went out of the 'fresher into the apartment's main room. There were still scars from Njangu's redecoration on the wall.

'You didn't have to destroy my apparatus quite so thoroughly,' she said.

'Sorry. But I don't like being spied on.'

Poynton grimaced. 'If we don't know everything, then we are vulnerable.'

Njangu didn't answer, went to the window, looked out. The streets were full of 'Raum, shouting, singing, and the intermittent, seldom-repaired street lighting was augmented with flaring torches. He heard music from two directions, wildly differing tunes.

'This,' Poynton said, coming up behind him, 'is what it was like, before, during our holidays.'

'And will be again.'

'I hope so,' she said, drinking. 'But many of us have died.'

'People get over pain,' Njangu said. 'That's one of the things that lets us keep living.'

Poynton considered him thoughtfully. 'That's a fairly profound observation from someone as young as you.'

Njangu lifted his glass to her, drank.

'So,' she said, coming toward him, 'shall I turn my back while you get dressed, and we can go out and see what manner of amusements are to be found?'

'If we did,' Njangu said, 'it would be with my "escorts" behind me. And your bodyguards.'

'Yes,' Poynton said.

'In here, there aren't any extraneous people.'

'No.'

'I'm not particularly hungry, are you?'

'No,' she said. 'Not . . . not for food.'

'And we have our wine.'

'Yes.'

Njangu reached out a finger, ran its nail from her throat down the vee of her neckline. Poynton caught her breath. 'That feels very good,' she said, her voice low. 'Perhaps better than it should.'

'Doesn't The Movement have rules about fraternizing with low-rankers like me?'

'Why should we?' Poynton said. 'We 'Raum are sensible about things. At least about some things.'

She stretched, hands lifting over her head. She was only a few centimeters shorter than he was. Njangu came very close, and she lifted her lips, eyes closing.

He kissed her, and her tongue came to meet his, and her arms dropped around him. Their mouths worked together, becoming more frantic, and his hand found the tie of the jumpsuit, pulled, and it fell away. Her nipples rose against his chest.

The kiss ended, and she whispered, 'It was a very long time, out in the jungle, where your own smell disgusted you, and you wouldn't want anyone to smell your stink.' She untied the knot on his towel, tossed it away, let the jumpsuit slide down her long legs, and pool on the floor. Njangu picked her up, and she was very light, and carried her to the waiting bed.

Garvin sat, comfortably alone, back to the stone wall of the great church, watching the crowd eddy around him. He was slightly drunk, and quite content. *I guess Njangu found something better to pass the time with. Wonder if Poynton . . . naw. Never the chance. She's too wound up in revolution to ever think about getting naked with anybody. Pity,*

*because when I think about it, she's not that bad-looking. Get
her to smile more often, and——*

'Mister?'

Garvin saw a very young redhead in front of him. Her
hair was cut short, and her lips, nails, earlobes and eyelids
had been tinted blue. She wore a deep red, loose-fitting
pair of pants. matching blouse, with cloud patterns that
made her look even younger than she was.

'Heh-lo,' he said, reflexively putting on an ostentatiously lascivious grin.

'You're one of the people who came over to us from the
Force, right? That man over there said you led the raid
against those bastards today.' She pointed, and Garvin
saw one of his escorts.

I shall do something about that bigmouth, he thought.

The girl caught his expression. 'That's all right, mister.
I'm with The Movement, too. I do decoy work, outside.
I've brought down seven myself,' she said proudly.

Garvin covered his reaction. 'So what can I do for
you?'

'I saw you, and another man from the Force yesterday,
going into one of our houses.'

'Ah?'

'He was a tall man, dark-skinned. Short hair. Good-
looking.'

'Maybe I know somebody like that,' Garvin said cautiously.

'He told me his name was Njangu once?'

'That could be my friend.'

'Do you know where he is? I spent a little time with
him . . . before he decided to join us. It was . . . sort of
nice. I wanted to know if he wanted to . . . get together
again.'

'No idea where he's at,' Garvin said honestly. 'No idea
at all.'

'Oh,' the girl said disappointedly, then brightened. 'Are you with anybody? My name's Limnea.'

Garvin shook his head.

'Lonely?'

'Not really.'

'Oh,' the girl said. ''Kay, as you Force people say.' She turned away. 'I guess I'm the only one who doesn't like being alone.'

Garvin thought of Jasith, far distant in the Heights, looked again at the girl. It was late, and he was alone, senses alert, his mind still not believing he hadn't been killed in that brief nightmare of blood in the warehouse.

'No,' he said slowly. 'No, you're not the only one.' The girl turned, and he saw hope in her eyes. 'So what does a stranger in the Eckmuhl do to celebrate?'

'I'll show you,' Limnea breathed. She licked her lips. 'I'll show you.'

Njangu made sure Poynton was sleeping soundly, crawled over her and out of the bed. He dressed hastily, slipped out of the door, and let it close behind him. The door to his escorts' rooms was shut. He listened, heard someone snoring within. *Sure. Why worry when your boss is making sure the subject's quite firmly in place.* He went down the long, worn stairs to the street.

It was only a few hours before dawn, and the celebration was mostly over, although he could still hear a few drunks singing loudly. *For straight-laced culters,* he thought, *these 'Raum sure have an open mind about unwinding.*

Two blocks away was one of the few unbroken public coms. He went for it, circling back twice. There was no tail. He fed coins in the slot, grinning at the sudden thought of a spy dooming himself by not having correct change, listened to the dull ringing.

An alert voice came: 'Sibyl Monitor.'

'Wake Hedley up,' he ordered.

The voice protested.

'Dammit, wake him up! This is Sibyl Black.'

The voice went away. Njangu waited, back to the com. If anyone came . . . he wished he'd taken Poynton's pistol . . . and then Hedley was there. 'Listening. Recording.'

Njangu spoke briefly, a report he'd rehearsed waiting for Poynton to fall into deep sleep. There was silence when he finished.

'That was pretty bold work,' Hedley finally said.

'Seemed like the best plan.'

'No way you could have dropped the dime to us? You haven't checked in since you went over the wall, and we were starting to worry.'

'Goddammit, boss, you want to come in here and play boo with these bastards?'

'Sorry,' Hedley said. 'Shouldn't second-guess. Is this a continuing commo point?'

'Negative. Still looking for some kind of secure way to report regularly, and this ain't it.'

'What's going to happen next?'

'More shootings, more bombings,' Njangu said. 'They're building up.'

'That doesn't take anybody on the inside to tell,' Hedley said. 'Is there anything we can do for you?'

'Yeh,' Njangu said. 'Get that AC of Garvin's . . . Dill. And his crew, and the best Grierson the Force has got. With a couple of Zooks. When this thing breaks, we're gonna want to come home at lightspeed, and we may be a little hot around the edges.'

"Kay,' Hedley said. 'Keep us posted.'

'What option do I have?'

*

'You know what I want you to do now?' Limnea said. She sprawled across the bed, naked. A candle burned on either side of the bed.

'What?' Garvin said, trying not to sound exhausted. *Goddamn that Njangu anyway. Just because he kept himself from getting killed by this decoy by screwing her until she was too shot to signal doesn't mean I'm up to playing Superstud. Lord, how I'd like to be doing something sensible, like sleeping.*

'Open up that drawer,' Limnea said. Garvin found long scarves. 'Take four of them,' Limnea ordered. 'Tie my hands, my ankles to the bedsteads.'

Garvin did as told, considered her pert buttocks, rearing at him, decided he might not be *that* tired.

'Now I can't move,' she said. 'Now you can do anything you want to with me, can't you? You could whip me if you wanted to. Or . . . or hurt me.'

'I, uh, guess so. But I don't like—'

'I *like* strong men,' she whispered. 'I *like* not being able to stop a man from doing whatever he wants. Lean close, and I'll tell you what I want you to do to me.'

Garvin did, and she whispered. He blinked, a bit shocked. 'You're sure?'

'Oh yes, oh yes,' she breathed. 'Please? Now, oh please do it to me now!'

As far as Njangu could tell, Poynton hadn't moved since he left, curled on her side. He slid out of his clothes, and started to climb over her.

She stirred. 'Where were you?' she said, voice sleep-sodden.

'I had to use the facilities.'

'Mmmh.' She rolled onto her back, and slid the blanket away.

'As long as we're both awake,' she said, lifting her legs

around his waist and pulling him down toward her warmth. 'Tomorrow the war begins again.'

The last two beards were shot down by police, trying to rob a delivery truck, two days later.

THIRTY-THREE

Poynton was right – the war did go on. Nastily, messily, fought in alleys and at night or on sun-drenched streets, beaches and around calm lagoons.

'Victory is just within our grasp,' *Caud* Williams said to the assembled journalists. 'There will be no more than a few short months of turmoil, lessening as time passes, and if all of us pull together, from Rentier to 'Raum, Cumbre will have the peace it deserves.' The media reps cheered him, the cheering led by Loy Kouro of *Matin*.

Three more islands were privately conceded to be under the control of the 'Raum, and a security hold placed on all media regarding the loss.

Njangu and Garvin were detailed for special assignments by Jord'n Brooks, training recruits in weapons-handling and tactics. They were always accompanied by their escorts, and never left the Eckmuhl.

Twice, Jo Poynton asked Njangu if he wished to spend the night with her. Otherwise, there seemed to be no change in their relationship. When they were alone, Njangu asked as many questions as he dared – and Poynton seemed happy to repeat the legends of Brooks, his invulnerability, and his rapid rise to head The Movement.

Neither Yoshitaro nor Jaansma were able to break free to make contact with the Force.

A meteorite shot over Dharma Island, lighting the night sky brighter than all three moons at full and disappeared toward the unpopulated, heavily jungled island of Mullion to the west. Many Cumbrians took it as a sign of change, although no one could agree on what the change would be. The 'Raum quickly decided it was a sign from the One who created them, and their day was close at hand.

'Sir!' Now-*Finf* Hank Faull snapped a salute.

'Pull up a pew,' Hedley said. 'I got a request this morning, for anybody in the company who's got any experience with the 'Raum. It'll mean transfer to II Section, a one-grade promo to *dec*, and maybe a chance to strike for *tweg*. Warmer, better-fed, and a damned sight safer'n running patrols with us. In case you didn't notice, we aren't exactly getting I-A flipping skinny these days, not from prisoners nor from just listening about.'

'No thanks, sir.'

'You didn't even have to think about it?' Hedley asked.

'Nossir.'

'None of my business, but why not?'

'I'm not a windy-ear,' Faull said, a bit of anger in his voice.

'Which means you won't spy on the people you used to be with?'

'Nossir. Not a chance, sir.'

'Spying blows goats, eh? But it's 'kay to shoot?'

Faull didn't answer.

'Won't argue,' Hedley said. 'Hell, if I were you, I might do the same flipping thing. No hard feelings?'

'No hard feelings, sir.'

'Then get the hell out and do something useful.'

'I won't lie to you, sir,' *Cent* Angara said. 'We were just damned lucky.' *Caud* Williams and *Mil* Rao scowled at the holo, an overhead shot of a crashed spaceship half-buried in jungle. 'We just happened to have an EW ship airborne, slaved to a Zhukov flight, waiting for possible ground targets when that 'meteor' entered atmosphere. One of the techs on the Grierson scanned the meteor, found it was a starship, checked with Cumbre Control and found nothing was inbound. The Grierson Commander challenged it, and the ship commenced evasive action.

'He alerted the Zhukovs, and their flight commander . . . Golan Flight, one *Haut* Chaka . . . decided to treat the ship as hostile, and ordered a Shadow launch. They got a strike, and Golan Flight tracked the intruder until it crashed. Again, luck was on our side, and the ship didn't burn, although all three of its crewmen were killed.'

'Who were they?' *Mil* Rao asked.

'No idea, officially, sir. Their uniforms, gear were sterile. But I went in on the site after dawn, and checked their supply cabinets. The foods, drinks, were Larix and Kura in origin – I'm familiar with their ways.'

Rao glanced at *Caud* Williams. His face was flushed with anger, although he forced calm into his voice. 'And the hold was full of these?' He indicated the open case. It was plas, padded on the inside, and held five very simply designed projectile rifles.

'About two thousand of them, sir. And ammunition. No manufacturer's stamp or serial number on any of them,' Angara said.

'Primitive,' Rao offered, picking one up and squinting through its fixed vee-sight.

'Good enough to kill Forcemen,' Williams snapped. 'Where was the ship going to land?'

'We're not sure, sir. I ordered the Grierson to scan all frequencies, and put up two more ships as backup. I picked up a faint signal about ten kilometers from Leggett on the coast, but it cut off when I ordered the EW ship to home on it.'

'Son of a spraddle-legged bitch,' Williams swore. Rao looked at him in considerable surprise – the Force commander almost never used profanity. 'We've not only got these 'Raum to worry about, but somebody who's supposed to be on our side is obviously trying to backstab us.'

'Certainly not a total surprise, sir,' Rao said. 'Not after the way Protector Redruth was so interested in "helping" us a few months ago.'

'If the 'Raum win,' Angara added, 'they'll have to do business with somebody, and they hate the Musth too much to deal with them . . . plus they'll probably drive the Musth off C-Cumbre, then need somebody to protect them. Redruth. And in the long run Redruth's no doubt thinking that he can smash the 'Raum at leisure – he's got spaceships and a lot more troops than we do – and end up with the whole system.'

'But how'd he make contact with the 'Raum? Do you have any intel on Redruth having any kind of a liaison man with them?'

'Nossir.'

'What about those men you have on the inside? Have they heard anything?'

'Sir,' Angara protested, 'this isn't a secure location.'

'For the love of Hildegard . . . my own base not secure . . . very well,' Williams grumbled. 'Sorry for the slipup.' He shook his head. 'Extraplanetary economics, trade routes, mineralogy . . . they never told me I'd need any of this back on Centrum, when I was an *aspirant*.'

'Nor me, sir,' Rao said. Angara kept silent.

'Did you destroy the rest of these weapons?'

'Nossir,' Angara said. 'Had the usable ones put in one of our dumps. Just in case.'

'Probably a wise move,' Williams said. 'You can never be too well armed or fit. Come on, *Mil*. We're going to make PlanGov Haemer most unhappy . . . and see about modifying a starship or two and putting them out on the fringes of the system As if we didn't already have enough enemies.'

Njangu encountered Jord'n Brooks that afternoon. The man gave him a hard look and stamped past, into Poynton's office. *If I were insecure, which of course I'm not,* Njangu thought, *I'd think that maybe the Big Man is suspicious of me. But there's no reason for that. None at all. Something all his very own must've gone wrong.* Nevertheless, he covered the bug in his and Garvin's apartment and spent two or three hours diligently working.

'Chief.' Monique Lir said heavily, 'I'm just plain sorry. But none of those 'cruits were fit to lick the sweat off the balls of an I&R man, so I dropped 'em.'

Hedley grimaced. 'It isn't enough we're getting our flipping butts beat by the flipping 'Raum, but now we can't find any new crunchies qualified to help us in our hour of flipping despair. I'll be flipping glad when this is over, Monique, assuming we win, so can start getting some real talent into the company.'

'Like who?' Lir asked. 'You think we'll link up with the Confederation again?'

'I'm not holding my breath on that one,' Hedley said. 'I mean when we can start recruiting 'Raum.'

Lir goggled. Hedley chuckled. 'Sure. Where do you think your best soldiers come from after a war? From the side whose butt you just beat, if you' ve got any sense.'

'Which means,' Lir said, after considering things, 'if things don't go like they should, I'll be applying for the First 'Raum Throat-slitters.'

'Uh-huh. And, most likely, I'll be standing in line right behind you,' Hedley said.

Poynton went to Brooks that night, very late, in the basement that was that night's headquarters. The room was spare – Brooks refused even to allow his commo man to share the same building with him, for fear the gear could be tracked. All that was in the room was a cot, a table with a map and a pistol on it, and Brooks' small day pack that held what few personal items he thought he needed.

'May I have a moment?' Brooks nodded. 'There was a message from my main agent on C-Cumbre,' she said. 'In a private code. There is a cargo lighter that will leave the Mellusin Works the E-day after tomorrow. The crew has been thoroughly converted to our ways, so it will carry explosives and other devices for The Movement.'

'I'm aware of the shipment,' Brooks said.

That lighter is fitted with a small passenger compartment for Mellusin's executives,' Poynton went on. 'I was informed that your wife and children can be placed aboard without any hazard. Once the ship's landed here, I can spirit them into the Eckmuhl without discovery.'

Hope flashed across Brooks' face, then he hastily shook his head.

'There's little risk,' Poynton said. 'The explosives are all binary, and perfectly—'

'*No,* ' he said more sharply.

'Yes, sir,' Poynton said.

'Wait,' Brooks said. 'Don't misunderstand me. I'm not saying no because I'm overly concerned for my children's safety . . . nor for that of my estranged wife. When I left C-Cumbre, I swore I would live only for The Movement.

If I allow myself to have my children here . . . or to allow The Movement to waste the slightest of its energies bringing them to me, no matter how much I wish to see them, then I am diminished, and the strength within me is diminished.

'And if I allow myself this weakness, when someone else wishes to devote some of The Movement's time to his or her private affairs . . . well, then I would have little space to criticize them.

'Is that not correct.' It was not a question.

Poynton stared into his blazing eyes, then nodded, and left the room. She was a little frightened by his fanaticism . . . but a pan of her mind thought: *But that is why we serve, and he leads . . .*

'When the hell are we gonna get Garvin out?' Kang asked. Ben Dill shook his head. 'Dunno. They haven't told me anything .'

'You think he's still alive?' Gorecki asked.

'*They* think so,' he said. 'Or else they would've put us back on scut patrol instead of sitting here with this ickle-pretty Grierson.'

'You know who I feel sorry for?' Kang said. 'That girl he's got. Mellow or Mellis or whatever her name is. She's got to be living on her fingernails.'

'She's rich,' Gorecki said. 'The hell with her.' But he didn't sound as if he meant it.

Ben Dill stared out the hatch of the Grierson at the deserted landing field, then, after a time, returned to polishing the ACV's peephole to an even clearer luster.

'Brothers Jaansma and Yoshitaro,' Brooks said, 'I've determined on the special task I promised. You should be aware our Time is racing close, and that we will be ready to bring our persecutors to final battle shortly.'

Garvin blinked, but Njangu managed a 'Yes, sir. We're ready.'

'Good,' Brooks said. 'You will continue training our warriors as you have been, but they won't be recruits any longer, but some of our more experienced fighters. You will determine which are suitable for sub-leader roles under your dual command, and you will work with them very carefully, for they'll be your unit on the Day, when your Task will be presented to you.'

'And what'll that be?' Garvin hazarded.

'It would be foolish to tell any warrior exactly his Task,' Brooks said, 'for fear of compromising that Task, and others if he were captured. However, I'll tell you this . . . it is something you two are uniquely qualified for, and will give you the greatest moment of glory you could imagine.' He nodded the two of them out.

Njangu waited until they were in open air, and around a corner. 'Did you figure out what he's going to do with us?'

'No,' Garvin said. 'But something tells me it's shitty.'

'I'll bet large credits that he's going to use our club-swingers and us, against the Force,' Njangu said. 'In his eyes, that'd be a real treat.'

'I'll be dipped . . . but I'll bet you're right.' Garvin was silent for a moment. 'You know, Njangu, I'm starting to think I'm going to like killing that *giptel*-screwer. What a shitty thing to ask of anybody. Doesn't he have any loyalties to anything?'

'Probably not. Except his goddamned Movement. And the only way you'll slot him is if you get there before I do,' Njangu said.

'There's a soldier here to see you, Miss Jasith,' the servant said.

Jasith felt her heart beat twice, then stop for an instant. 'An officer?' She remembered seeing a holo once where a soldier was killed, and how an officer brought word to the soldier's wife.

'I don't think so,' the servant said. 'Officers got things up here, on their shoulders, and he's got slashes on his sleeve.'

Jasith started toward the door. One of her omnipresent bodyguards slipped from his alcove, loosening his pistol.

Standing in the huge mansion's foyer was the biggest man she'd ever seen. Big, but he had a kindly look on his face, so she felt no fear. 'Uh, Miss Mellusin,' the man said. 'My name's Dill. Ben Dill.'

'I've heard of you . . . you were . . . are, Garvin's leader in that tank thing. The man who tells him what to do.'

Dill nodded.

'What can I do for you . . . have you heard anything?'

Dill looked at the bodyguard, who stared back. 'Tell him to go away,' Dill said. 'Or I can't say anything.'

'Dak?'

'I've got my orders, ma'am.'

Jasith waited, and he reluctantly left the room.

'I can only stay a second,' Dill said. 'And I can't let you ask me any questions. I just wanted to tell you that Garvin's still alive.'

'How do you know?'

Dill shook his head. 'Can't say. And I'm busting security even telling you what I did, so you can't tell anyone at all, not even your father, for fear of what could happen to him. But we thought . . . I mean, I thought . . . you ought to know. . . 'Scuse me. I've got to be going.'

'Wait. I'll drive you to wherever—'

But the big man was out the door, and it closed silently behind him. By the time Jasith had it open, he was gone, and no one, not the roving grounds patrol nor the two stationary security posts at the end of the long drive had seen him come or go.

*

'This is your alert,' Jo Poynton told Njangu and Garvin 'You will be required to perform a certain Task within the next three days. Rest and ready yourselves, for there will be no more important Time in your life.'

There was a glow on her face, as if she'd just been promised Nirvana.

'We're ready now,' Garvin said, trying to sound heroic.

'I know you are,' Poynton said. 'I know you are.'

'So the shit's coming down,' Garvin said, 'and we're stuck here, with no way to blow skibbereen on the operation.'

'Probably,' Njangu said, 'but not absolutely. I've been doing some looking about this old house.'

'And?'

'Two floors down, sixth door, there used to some kind of office. Or maybe a gambler's den. I found four com lines when I checked the building out after we moved in, so I knew your average peasant-type 'Raum hadn't lived there. And guess what? One line is still live.'

'Shitfire and save matches,' Garvin said. 'If it's still hooked up, what're the chances it's not bugged?'

'Damned near nonexistent,' Njangu said. 'That's why I thought you should be the one to make the try.'

'And get killed?'

'Better than me, isn't it? Besides, you're the hero type, remember?'

'Bite,' Garvin said.

''Kay,' Njangu said. 'I'll be fair. You want to flip a coin?'

'Nope,' Garvin said. 'I'll go. Dummy that I am. When it quiets down and everybody's pretending to sleep.'

There was a man in their building who seldom slept and, when he went out, kept his face turned away, to hide his shattered features. His name was Lompa, and he was one of the two agents Poynton had ordered to take Garvin Jaansma alive, long ago as he walked back from Bampur's party, where he'd first met Jasith. He still had periodic headaches from being kicked in the head, and had to be careful what he ate.

He'd heard about the Forceman who'd deserted to the 'Raum, and instinctively knew his leaders were wrong. Those *giptels* never changed their ways, their habits, and when he saw the traitor was the tall, blond man who'd beaten him so badly, he became very sure. He was on light duties because of his injuries, so it was easy to hang about, and unobtrusively follow the tall one wherever he went.

Now, late at night, he saw Garvin Jaansma creep out, and felt triumph surge. The two traitors would finally be exposed, and he would not only be revenged, but be rewarded for diligence and cunning. He went down the hall after Jaansma.

THIRTY-FOUR

Lompa watched Garvin, slinking along like the dog he was. The blond *giptel* went downstairs, and Lompa waited for a count of three, followed. He paused at the landing, then peered uound the lintel post, keeping low. His quarry'd gone down another flight. Lompa crept toward the next set of stairs, and Garvin came out of an open doorway. Lompa started to scream, but Garvin had him by the throat, squeezing, squeezing. The world darkened, went to a pinpoint as Garvin pressed harder, and Lompa's feet flailed, crashing against the wall.

The man went limp, and Garvin dropped him just as a door came open. One of Poynton's security men came out, rifle ready. The rifle came up, and there weren't any options. Garvin crouched, and the pistol was out of his waistband and firing.

The blast reverberated through the building, and lights went on, and shouts began. Garvin started back toward his rooms, but heard rapid footsteps coming down the stairs. He fired three times quickly – the near-universal symbol for distress, hoping Njangu would catch the message, and ran down toward the exit. A woman was on guard, and she swung her blaster toward him. Garvin shot her, scooped up the rifle, and took an instant to tear her ammunition belt off. A bolt smashed into the wall above him, and he automatically shot back, started for the rear of the building, when a hatch opened in the wall and Njangu Yoshitaro slid out.

'Guess you screwed things up, huh?' was Njangu's greeting. 'See if I ever let you have all the fun again.'

'Come on,' Garvin said. 'The whole goddamned Eckmuhl will be after us in a second.'

'Sounds like they already are,' Njangu said, and they were out into the night streets. Garvin took a moment to muscle a large can of trash across the door, then they were running down the narrow alleys, darting here, there.

'Where'd you come from?' Garvin managed.

'Did . . . a few basic mods on the laundry chute yesterday,' Njangu managed. 'With a rope or two I happened to run across. Good back door, eh?'

Garvin shot at somebody who was showing a bit too much curiosity, skidded into a narrow alley that curved around a building with only a single dim streetlight. The alley came to a dead end, except for a single doorway into a ramshackle building. 'Back,' he said, and a bolt screamed off the cobbles beside him.

Njangu booted in the door, heard screams. 'Out! Out!' he shouted, and 'Raum streamed down the stairs. Njangu shouldered past into the building, Garvin after him, as a dozen armed 'Raum rounded the corner into the alley.

They were in one of the typical tiny Eckmuhl groceries, with almost-bare shelves. Njangu scooped up two liter bottles of cooking oil, went up the stairs, shouting 'Out' like a maniacal traffis director as he went. More screams, more shouts, and more 'Raum men, women, and children boiled downstairs. They pushed through the frenzy, saw an armed man, shot him, and the frenzy got louder. Njangu peered in an open door, saw bolts of cloth and half-finished garments. He put a round into a cloth-bonding machine, and its solvent sprayed. He hurled the cooking oil bottles against the wall, and they shattered, then shot into the mess, and nothing happened. 'Goddamn modern weapons,' he snarled, saw an emergency lantern and its igniter, went across the room, lit it, and dropped it into the pooled oil. There was a satisfactory *foomf*, and Yoshitaro lost most of his eyebrows and short-cropped hair.

The screams were louder, and the 'Raum panicked, trying to get out before the building was engulfed. Shouts came below as someone tried to order chaos.

'That takes care of the back door. Now where?' Garvin asked.

'We got any options?' Njangu panted. 'Up. To the roof. We'll cross to the next building from there. These goddamned warrens all connect to each other.'

But this one didn't. The seven-story building's neighbors were all just a bit too far for jumping. Garvin set the rifle down, scuffled through the trash on the rooftop, found a long plank. 'Pray for me,' he said, and lugged the plank to the building's ramparts. It looked just about long enough, and he let it fall across to the next building's roof to become a bridge. His eye was about a meter off, and the plank pinwheeled on down to smash into the street, and blaster fire came back up.

'They would've shot you off it, anyway,' Njangu sympathized.

'So what are we gonna do now?' Garvin asked.

'Hope like hell the smoke attracts attention,' Njangu said. 'And that the fire department still makes house calls. Dawn's what, an hour or so away?'

Smoke boiled up through the stairwell, and Garvin surveyed the billow. 'Guess they won't come up that way.'

'Guess they don't have to.'

Garvin heard a whine, saw the lights of a lifter coming
over the rooftops, jumped to his feet, and waved wildly.
'It's the police,' he said. 'We're saved!'

The police lifter sped overhead, banked, and came
back. Garvin stupidly stood in the middle of the roof,
pistol in hand, waving, and then Njangu tackled him,
knocking him away as the autocannon opened fire, and
25mm slugs chewed up the tar paper and debris around
them. 'Next time . . . try waving without the goddamned gun!' Njangu managed. 'Lie still and look dead,
for Allah's sakes, and maybe they'll figure they got us.'

The lifter made another pass, very low, low enough so
Garvin felt the wind of their passage. 'See what happens,'
Njangu said, 'when you go and depend on a cop?'

'*Cent* Angara,' the voice said. 'Wake up.'

The II Section officer rolled off his bunk, bleared at
the displays around the Command Center. The Officer of
the Watch stood next to him. 'Sir, the scan reports a fire
in the middle of the Eckmuhl, and the police frequency
says they silenced two snipers on the rooftop of the building.'

It didn't appear to have anything to do with them . . .
but still. 'Turn out the alert unit,' he ordered. 'Put an
electronics bird over the Eckmuhl. If nothing else, we
can relay for the civilians. Wake up *Mil* Rao, but let the
old man sleep.' He hesitated. 'If they've got snipers out,
maybe the whole thing's a blind to suck in the fire
people. Get the alert unit in the air, and have one, no two
Zhukovs seconded to them.'

'Sir.'

'And is there any of that coffee left?'

Poynton burst into Jord'n Brooks' headquarters – a commandeered snack bar. There were a dozen com sets

around the room with their waiting operators, all tuned to various Force and PlanGov frequencies. Brooks paced back and forth, listening, eyes half-closed, sorting through the chatter. His eyes came fully open as he reached a decision. He went to one silent com, a high-frequency interplanetary 'caster, picked up the mike. Brooks touched the mike's button. 'Leviathan, this is Tver,' he said.

'Leviathan,' a voice came back. 'Listening.'

'This is Tver. Situation altered. Begin Leviathan at once. I repeat, at once.'

'Leviathan. Operation under way.'

'The traitors failed,' Brooks said. 'This is now the Day, and the great Task begins.'

'Sir,' Poynton started. 'I'm sorry they managed to deceive me, and I promise—'

'Sister,' Brooks said, without a hint of anger, 'we're all fools to someone. The point is to ensure it never happens again.'

'It won't,' Poynton said. 'Do you still trust me for my Task?'

'Trust has nothing to do with it,' Brooks said. 'There is no time to choose and train another, even if I wished. Forget about what happened, as I told you, and make your work reap twice the rewards as compensation.'

His smile appeared quite sincere. Poynton hurried away, remembering, however, the time Brooks had smiled just as honestly, and then shot a double agent in cold blood.

Ben Dill was already awake, unable to sleep, when the sirens blared across Camp Mahan's parade ground.

"Zat for us?" Kang asked sleepily.

'No. Don't think so.'

She sat up, reached for her deliberately old-fashioned

spectacles, and turned on the antique two-dee vid that had been their only entertainment while waiting to extract Garvin and Njangu. They watched the various 'casts, saw nothing but the usual early-morning drivel, then the stations started cutting away to sleepy-looking journohs.

'*Something's* going on,' she said, pointing out the obvious.

'And it's in the Eckmuhl,' Gorecki said, the noise having wakened him.

'Awright, awright,' Dill said. 'Let's warm it up. Maybe it is for us.'

'You're gonna have to have a word with that idiot Garvin,' Gorecki said. 'First he goes and lets himself get volunteered, then starts doing something or other with the 'Raum. Your boy better straighten out, Dill, for I'm getting tired of being his goddamned fast ship every time he wants to stick his heinie in harm's vise.'

Njangu and Garvin lay motionless on top of the roof as smoke rose, ever thicker, ever more choking. The air above was alive with the whine of lifters, from police to fire to media, and the sky was beginning to gray.

'You got any bright ideas?'

'If we move,' Njangu said, 'they'll start shooting at us again.'

'And if we don't,' Garvin said, 'pretty soon we won't be able to.'

'As long as it looks like we're for it,' Njangu said, 'mind if I ask just what the hell you did before you joined the Force? Hoping for an honest answer.'

'I told you the truth,' Garvin said. 'I ran a circus.'

'Yeh. Right.'

'I shit thee nix,' Jaansma said. 'Come from a long line of circus families. Managers, ringmasters, once every now and then a high-wire act, but those were mostly the black jeeps of the family.

'Generally a Jaansma kid'd work for one of the family shins, doing everything from being a joey . . . that's a clown . . . to a slanging-buffer in an arcade, then go out on the road, somewhere out on the fringes to get seasoned, finally end up with one of the big shows on Centrum or somewhere. But my folks were killed in a fire, and I ended up with an uncle who wasn't that connected. He did the best he could, and I worked the circuit some, but when I got to be seventeen I jumped at the first circus that offered a graft for a Jaansma, any Jaansma. That was Altair, on a world called Willy's Fortune, believe it or not.

'The show was a gam, crooked from the go. Snakier than any of the hustles you've told me about. Rigged wheels, girls, boys, anything for a credit. About the only thing we had that was worth a shit were the animal acts. I was the ringmaster, but since I was just a kid, I didn't have the pull I should've, and the owners didn't listen when I said things were going sour, and even the diddly flatties . . . normal citizens . . . we were gaffing were starting to catch on. So I started hanging out with the acts and trying to figure out what I was going to do next, and where I was going to get the graft to pull out.

'The whole thing went to shit about the fourth month I was with them. Somebody started a rube on the midway . . . a fight in the middle of the circus . . . and it got nasty, going from fists to clubs to knives to guns. I heard an animal scream, and saw some asshole trying to set fire to the tent we had the grai — that's Earth horses — in. I went a little apeshit.'

'You shot him?' Njangu said, fascinated in spite of the madness around them.

'Not quite,' Garvin said. 'I opened the big cats' cages.'

'You *what?*'

'And the bears,' Garvin said. 'Sic'ed them on the flat-ties. Then I took off. Ended up on the neighbor world of Klesura, about busted, seeing the stories of how many deaths I'd caused get bigger and bigger, and all of a sudden there was this recruiting office.'

'Remind me,' Njangu said thoughtfully, 'never to get you seriously pissed at me.'

C-Cumbre

The 'Raum at the controls of the cargo lighter had been the best, most reliable pilot at his mine, and there'd been considerable wonderment at his disappearance with his craft. He. and a few other 'Raum, hid in an abandoned survey station in the middle of nowhere, resupplied and equipped by sympathizing crews of the ships that shuttled back and forth between D-Cumbre and C-Cumbre.

The strange device in the back of the lighter had come from a park monument dedicated to the memory of the early settlers of the Cumbre system. It had been mounted in an archaic lifter, and fired explosives in long rows, clearing lanes through the jungle. The apparatus had been stolen from the park, carefully cleaned and refurbished by 'Raum technicians who guessed at what they were doing without manuals, without anything other than old holos, then, after testing, smuggled to C-Cumbre.

The pilot took the lighter out of its 'hangar,' a haphazard-looking pile of scrap plas, and, barely two meters above the ground, drove toward the horizon.

'This is *Matin*,' Loy Kouro bayed into the mike, 'giving the News You Need, When You Need It, Loy Kouro transmitting. Our *Matin* lifter is above the suspicious fire raging in the Eckmuhl. Our firefighters have been unable to enter the district and combat the fire due to sniper fire from 'Raum banditry

'But your *Matin* crew is over the scene, as you can see. We're trying, with our high-powered stabilized light-amplified cams, to show you two of the snipers who made the mistake of shooting at a police lifter, and were shot down for their pains.

'Here . . . come in a little closer on that . . . here we are . . . now you can see them, and . . . Great God, from what I'm seeing on my pickup one of them at least appears to be one of the degenerates who've deserted our fighting Force to join with the scum who call themselves The Movement.

'Yes, look at that one's blond hair . . . no 'Raum ever looked like that! *Matin* sends its compliments to our best, our police, and if you'll stand by, we'll give you more coverage of the fire that's raging out of control in—'

'Son of a bitch,' Gorecki swore, staring at the screen. 'Ben. Look. That's Garvin on that goddamned roof.'

'No,' Dill said. 'Yes. The bastards got him . . . no, look. His lips are moving. He's still alive . . . and so's Yoshitaro, next to him.' He took a deep breath. ''Kay, troops. There go my stripes. Saddle up. We're on our way.'

'No ideas?' Garvin said.

'Shut up. I'm thinking.'

A blaster round spanged off metal a meter or so away.

'Now they've got shooters on the rooftops around us,' Garvin said. 'This isn't playing out as any fun at all.'

'At least the smoke makes it hard for them to get any accuracy,' Njangu said.

'Don't be such a pessimist.'

Garvin edged one hand down to his pistol. 'I don't have any intention of *frying*,' he said.

'Nope,' Njangu agreed. 'Give me another minute, and if I can't come up with something, we'll take on those snipers.'

'Good a way to go as any,' Garvin agreed.

Dill's Grierson floated out of the hangar, Ben in the open hatch, wondering what lie he'd use for takeoff clearance, as a column of troops double-timed out of the I&R barracks toward waiting Cookes. At their head was *Alt* Hedley. He spotted Dill. waved him down. 'You saw the news flash?'

'Yessir.'

'And were gonna cowboy off to the flipping rescue?'

'Something like that.'

'Dumbshit. Hang back. I've got clearance from *Mil* Rao – the old man's in another flipping conference with Haemer – to go beat things up a little bit. We're going to suppress whatever snipers they really have on the rooftops, and there'll be a flight of Zooks inbound if we need heavy hitters. Rao's got the rest of the flipping Force saddling up now. You go on and get those two flipping idiots out. Or bring back their bodies.'

'I'm gone,' Dill said, and touched his throat mike. 'Take it on up at speed, m'boy, and balljack toward the smoke. Kang, anything that you see shooting, level the suckers. It's time to quit fiddle-farting around.'

C-Cumbre

The cargo lighter came out of the low valley it'd been following, and the Musth Mining Center was in front of it. There were two of the *aksai* attack ships grounded on the landing field, and half a dozen cargo ships that looked like bloated seedpods, but nothing in the yellow, dirty air. The scattering of missile sites around the headquarters was unmanned.

'Be ready,' the pilot commanded. Two of the 'Raum were already at the controls of the explosive planter in the back, and didn't bother responding. The last, sitting beside the pilot, muscled a 20mm cannon on an improvised mount into position.

'Strike at the animals' combat ships first,' the pilot ordered, and the gunner opened fire, and dust spurted across the field and over the *aksai*. One gouted flames, the other crumpled to the side.

'Good,' the driver approved, then was too busy to say more as he closed on the buildings. A 'Raum in the back closed a large breaker switch, and the launcher chugged rhythmically, each blast hurling impact-fused charges of Telex to either side. The explosives spattered across the rooftops, shock waves rocked the lifter, and smoke and black flame gouted. The lifter cleared the buildings, and came back in another pass, X-ing across its first line of destruction.

On its third pass, two Musth had reached a launch station. A missile blasted out of its tube, smashed into the lighter, and it snap-rolled upside down, dived into one building, and exploded. Moments later, black flame shot high into the greasy atmosphere as something within the Musth buildings detonated. Of the approximately eighty-four Musth at the mining station, fewer than half a dozen survived.

'This is Tver. Begin Plan Tumbril,' Jord'n Brooks ordered, and on the outskirts of Leggett a rented storage shed's door came open, and a long, luxury lifter stolen six months earlier was pushed out.

*

Dill's Grierson soon outdistanced the swarm of Cookes soaring closer to the pillar of smoke in mid-Leggett and, in turn, was passed by three hurtling Zhukovs, each outlined by the rising sun.

'Unknown Grierson,' a voice came in Dill's helmet. 'This is Cambrai. Going our way?'

'This is Sibyl Black Recovery. That's a big affirm.'

'Good to have you along. We'll try to keep things nit and tiddy for our little brothers behind us.'

'Get some,' Dill said, and got a double-clicked mike in response.

'Straight in,' *Haut* Chaka ordered, 'and try not to obliterate too many civvies.' The Zhukovs roared across the lower city toward the Eckmuhl's walls. 'Not too fast,' Chaka advised. 'Gunner! Don't bother me with chitchat. Targets of opportunity.'

One gunner saw the sparkle of gunfire from a rooftop to the left of the burning building, swung the Zhukov's main turret and the 35mm chaingun sprayed the roof clean. The second gunner targeted a group of 'Raum in the streets below, and sent a single Shrike almost straight down, into their midst.

'Fiddleemee,' Garvin howled as the heavy gunships swep overhead. 'You can stop thinking now, little brother.'

Njangu rolled to where a blaster lay. A 'Raum two buildings away saw his movement, and blazed a burst across the rooftop. missing Yoshitaro by inches. Njangu fired back and didn't miss. 'Now, if the smoke doesn't get us,' he said, coughing.

Garvin leaned over the edge of the building and let half a magazine roll down the barrel of his blaster, spraying the street below. 'I do hope all good little boys and girls are sleeping in this morning,' he murmured, looked for a specific target. He found three 'Raum leaning out of a window two blocks down. aiming some sort of crew-served weapon, and blew the room in around them. The air came alive with the shrill whine of Cookes, swarming into the Eckmuhl like invading mosquitoes.

'All right,' Lir told her driver. 'I want you to put it—' The Cooke's engine hiccuped, died. 'Aw, goddammit!' she swore 'If you're gonna crash, find something worth hitting.'

'I can flare it, boss,' the driver said, yanking at the controls. 'How about that little round building?'

'Just get it down,' Monique ordered. 'Flying makes me nervous.' The Cooke pancaked onto the roof of the building. and Beta Team spilled off. 'First take care of anybody above us,' Lir shouted. 'Then we'll get the midgets down below.'

A spurt of flame sent the rooftop door spinning upward. 'Getting close,' Garvin said over the roar of the fire.

'Too close,' Njangu managed. Garvin noticed Yoshitaro's slightly toasted features for the first time.

'Aren't you a little young to be so bald?'

'Runs in the family,' Njangu managed. 'Get—'

A round spanged off the roof and seared through Garvin's upper shoulder. Njangu spun, saw the gunman on a rooftop, and shot him down.

Garvin sat down suddenly. 'Getting shot hurts,' he said thoughtfully.

'No kid. You gonna die on me?'

'Dunno,' Garvin managed. 'But I sure could use a painkiller and a soothing kiss.'

'Fresh out of both. Maybe—'

A long, mottled monster nosed out of the smoke onto the rooftop, its hatch opened and Ben Dill's head appeared. Kang appeared beside him. 'Come on,' Kang shouted. 'I' m missing pod targets!'

Njangu and Garvin stumbled across and up the ramp. A 'Raum shot at them, and the bolt spanged off the armor plate beside Yoshitaro. He managed the universal twin-fingered salute before the ramp slammed up and the Grierson nosed down and away at full drive.

'Look at all those flipping people,' Hedley said. 'And they've got flipping guns and everything. Alpha Troop . . . ground it in that open square, and advance by teams.'

The Cookes slid in for landings, and the men of I&R Company came out fighting. The 'Raum broke, began retreating deeper into the tangled web of the Eckmuhl.

Hedley picked up his mike. 'Lance Six, this is Sibyl Six.'

Rao's voice came. 'Sibyl Six, this is Lance Six. Go ahead.'

'I've got lots and lots of baddies, Lance, and they want to butt heads. We could use all the people you want to throw in.'

'This is Lance Six . . . First Regiment on the way. Use your people to guide them to targets.'

'Flipping-A,' Hedley said. 'Happy to help. Sibyl Six out.'

The Eckmuhl was no longer a sanctuary.

Ton Milot had his blaster slung over his shoulder, and three portable rocket launchers under one arm, and a case of ammunition beside him. He crouched behind a statue of something or other that'd been blasted into unrecognizability. *Take a minute to think about things. You don't want to go and do something stupid and get shot,* he thought. *The rest of the guys are over there . . . and the 'Raum are over there. So I'd best get my young ass moving, like yesterday, but cutting around this frigging statue, out of the line of fire.* He grabbed the re-supply, burst out into the open, thudding along, seeing bolts smash into the pavement, not letting his mind realize it, *come on now, twenty-five meters to go, you can fly over that, just like training, those bullets won't really hit you, you're doing fine, just fine*—

Something smashed his leg, and he crashed headlong, tasting grit, blood, smelling smoke, and pain grabbed him, like a red-hot clamp pulling at his thigh, and he saw blood, and other bullets were beating the ground around him. He felt a thud, saw blood stain his uniform sleeve black. He couldn't move, and guessed this was about all, that he'd die in this goddamned dirty-ass sun-baking square, never see the boats or Lupul again, and—

—And somebody had him by the back of his combat vest and was dragging him, and pain seared, but he bit his lip hard, *No, dammit, I won't scream.* And the sun was gone, and he was in the shade, being rolled over, and hands were tearing his pants open. Fuzzy shapes above him became figures, and he saw one of the Troop medics, and next to him was Hank Faull.

'Where the hell did you come from?' Milot croaked. 'You're in Vic Team, aren't you?'

'Saw you go down,' Faull said. 'Thought you might need a hand.'

'Hank, my friend, my father, my mother, my brother,' Milot said. 'You can have anything I've got. You can drink on me from now until the sun goes black. If you ever want to cheat on your wife, I'll provide the giggler and the alibi.'

Faull grinned, started to say something, then looked startled. He slumped forward across Ton Milot, as if all the bones in his body had melted. Another soldier was there, pulling Faull away, and Ton Milot saw the fist-sized hole in Hank Faull's back.

'No,' Ton Milot managed. 'That can't be. That can't be.' Then the universe went black.

The medic shouted, 'Get a lift in, dammit! I've got one down, one critical. Come on, people!'

'They're in that building over there, Petr,' Penwyth said. 'We'll need a goddamned airstrike to get 'em out. That goddamned door's solid steel or something, and they've got the windows sandbagged. Not to mention we're more'n a bit outnumbered.'

'Maybe,' Kipchak said. 'Maybe not. Gimme that SSW.'

The two were crouched in a shop door, catty-corner from the big building that held half a hundred 'Raum. The rest of Alpha Team held positions up and down the street. Penwyth licked his lips, ducked into the next store, and came back with the squad weapon, trying to ignore the two dead I&R men beside it and the bolts exploding around him.

'Find something to sandbag me,' Kipchak ordered, and Erik puzzled, found a flatiron and four sacks of washers, piled them for Kipchak to rest the forehand of the Squad Support Weapon on.

'See that little bitty window?' Kipchak asked.

'Hell yes. They shot at me out of that.'

'Spot me.'

'Huh?' Erik said.

'I said spot me, dammit! Like on the range.'

'Oh. 'Kay.'

Kipchak fired a single shot.

'Uh . . . high. Left.'

Kipchak tsked, moved his sights a little, fired again.

'High. Center.'

Another round went out

'I didn't see it. I think a hit. Yeh. You put it in the window all fight!'

'Nail this bastard down.' The weights went around the bipod legs of the Squad Support Weapon. 'Now lemme show you something,' Petr said. 'They're all nice and bulletproof outside, right?'

'Right.'

Peh braced the butt of the SSW, let twenty bolts slam through the tiny window, paused, then another twenty, then another pause and the rest of the belt. 'More ammo,' he ordered, but the door to the bank, if that was what it was, came open and bleeding 'Raum, waving white rags, handkerchiefs, even pieces of paper, came stumbling out. 'Bulletproof outside means bulletproof inside,' Kipchak said in satisfaction. 'Bouncing bolts bedazzle and baffle bandits.'

No one except a couple of radar techs noticed the luxury lifter as it climbed high into the sky, Leggett no more than a dot below.

Griersons dropped into the Eckmuhl, and troops trotted off. I&R men were waiting to escort them.

'Just follow me,' a grimy soldier told a group of officers. 'I'll put your men where they're supposed to be.'

The *haut* in charge looked suspiciously at the man, who wore no insignia. 'Follow you? Might I ask your rank?'

'*Cent* Radcliffe's my name,' Striker Penwyth said. 'And I've got personal authorization from *Mil* Rao.'

'Oh. Then I guess everything's all right. Come on, troops,' the *haut* said.

Njangu came to his feet, surprised, as Garvin walked out of the hospital entrance. He wore oversize fatigues, and one shoulder was lumpier than the other.

'What ho,' he said. 'I thought you'd be flat on your ass in a ward, trying to play giggle and pinch with the nurses and feebly taking visitors.'

'That's what they wanted to do to me,' Garvin said. 'I didn't like the idea.'

'Why not? Some nice days off after the shit we've been through. Float back, relax, and get some ghost time.'

'Uh-uh. I'm going back over, as soon as I can scrounge a combat vest and a blaster.'

'You're what?'

'I promised I was going to kill Tver . . . his real name's Brooks, by the way . . . if I got a chance. So I'm making the chance.'

'*Aw shit*, Garvin. I barely had time to take a shower and you want to go jump back in the shitter. You getting medal-happy or something?'

'Nobody said you had to go.'

'Not much they didn't.' Njangu growled. 'All right. Let's scout up some bangsticks. You got any ideas how we're gonna find our boy?'

'Yeah. But I'm not telling you 'til we're on the ground. You might jump the line and kill him first.'

'Is the fuse set, my brother?'

'It is.'

The pilot of the luxury lifter bowed his head, and his lips moved silently. 'Then we go, and may the One bless our Task.' He pushed the control wheel forward, and the lifter nosed over. It dived down and down, starting to shudder, and the lifter's computer pushed out dive brakes and the shuddering went away.

The driver tried not to look at his friend next to him, tried not to look out at the blue of the bay and the white stone, now smoke-covered, of the Eckmuhl, whose every alley he knew and loved. All that existed, all that should exist, was the swelling mass of the fortress below.

*

The sentries at the gates of the Planetary Government's headquarters had a bare moment to react to the sonic boom, look up and see the blurred black lifter as it dived almost straight down into the main PlanGov building, centering on the mosaiced stained-glass dome over the main conference room, where most of D-Cumbre's governing element were concluding a day-long meeting.

In the explosion died Planetary Governor Wilth Haemer, and most of his staff; about half of the Rentiers on the Council, including Bampur and Loy Kouro's father, publisher of *Matin*; Godrevy Mellusin, Jasith's father; Police Major Gothian, head of Planetary Police's Policy and Analysis Division; and *Caud* Jochim Williams, along with his aides and heads of II Section (Intelligence), III Section (Operations) and V Section (Civil Coordination).

Jord'n Brooks watched the holo of central Leggett, the cauldron of destruction where Planetary Government had been for a brief moment, then slung his blaster, started out of the snack bar.

'There have been enough words,' he said, 'Now is the Time. Our time to kill them all.'

He smiled.

THIRTY-FIVE

The 'Raum boiled out of the Eckmuhl. Some were disciplined assault forces on their assigned Tasks. Others were looking for revenge or loot.

About two hundred trained warriors attacked the ruins of the PlanGov fortress, with orders to leave no officials alive, and destroy all PlanGov records, from police files to mining deeds to land documents. The firefighters and medics swarming around the capitol didn't see the formation trotting up the winding avenue, but one man did.

Finf Running Bear, *Caud* Williams' driver/orderly, was crumpled inside his Cooke. The explosion had sent the vehicle tumbling across the avenue, flattening Running Bear on the floorboards, as he tried to keep from being thrown out and crushed. The Cooke came to rest halfway up a grassy bank, windscreen shattered. Stunned and bruised, Running Bear half sat, opened an eye, saw armed men and women running toward him, perhaps two hundred meters away. He vaguely identified them as 'Raum, and wondered why they were attacking him. He looked for *Caud* Williams for orders, saw no one.

He unclipped the autocannon from its travel lock, swung it up into position. He opened a box of ammunition, fed the belt of dully gleaming shells into the breech, ratcheted the operating handle twice, as he'd been trained so long ago, chambering the first 20mm round. Running Bear turned the range-finding sight on, hit the RANGE sensor as the oncoming 'Raum closed, and touched the trigger between the twin handles. The gun chattered, and he swung it across the formation. The hand-long shells, intended to penetrate light armor, sliced through the crowd. Bodies spun, shattered, and blood sprayed.

Running Bear heard blaster bolts explode around him, paid no mind. He swept the 'Raum again, and again. Something – an almost-spent bolt – cut his side, and he saw blood, but he had no time for that. 'Raum were falling back, some running, others, braver or more disciplined, found firing positions behind debris or in the open. Running Bear corrected his aim, and in two- or three-round bursts, killed them as well.

The gun stopped firing, and Running Bear realized the two-hundred-round ammunition box was empty. Moving carefully, slowly, he took another box from the rear of the Cooke, opened it, and fed another belt into the cannon. Something was running in his eyes, and he wiped his sleeve across them, saw blood, but felt no pain. He saw a group of 'Raum on their feet, about to charge, cut them down, swung his aim to the other side of the road, blasted three 'Raum who thought an overturned lifter would be adequate cover.

The dullness was fading, as if he were waking, and he felt the slash across his scalp, the wound in his side, another one he hadn't noticed on his upper arm, but they didn't matter. He shouted, a long, ululating cry no one on D-Cumbre would have known, but might have been familiar to warriors a millennium earlier, on battle-grounds around Fort Phil Kearney, on the banks of the Rosebud River, at a place called Little Bighorn.

Again the gun clanked empty, and again he reloaded. He was aware there were other soldiers behind him, and he heard their guns firing. He looked for more 'Raum to kill, saw none. There were a few of them, running hard, far down the avenue, then they, too, were gone, their attack shattered before it began. The street was carpeted with broken bodies, and the wounded groaned, screamed.

Finf Running Bear got out of the Cooke. Someone came up, but Running Bear looked at him, and he stood away. He did not need, would not allow, anyone to help him. Proudly, slowly, he walked up the avenue, to where a Grierson with a bright red cross waited.

Loy Kouro stared blankly out of the screen at *Mil* Rao. 'My father . . .' he said brokenly.

'Was killed with Governor Haemer,' *Mil* Rao said patiently. '*As* was *Caud* Williams and most of the other officials of the Planetary Government. I have assumed command of the Strike Force, in the name of the Confederation, and have temporarily taken charge of Cumbre's government. I want my proclamation broadcast by *Matin* . . . you are now its publisher . . . and the other holos immediately.'

'Yes,' Kouro said. 'That is good. My father would approve. Yes. I can do that.'

Mil Rao broke contact, turned to *Cent* Angara. 'Damfino if he understood. He's shocky.'

'A lot of people are,' Angara agreed. 'Now, sir. What are your orders?'

Rao drew a deep breath, walked away from the knot of Command and Control Griersons backed up to each other just outside the Eckmuhl's main gates, ramps lowered.

'All right. I'm thinking out loud. Tell me when I miss

something. First, is it legal for me to continue martial law without dealing with whoever survives from PlanGov?'

'I think so,' Angara said. 'But there's surely no one who'll argue. Not now.'

'That's done, then. I'm bringing you up as Force XO. Put whatsisface, Hedley, in charge of II Section. Operations . . . I'll control that myself, appoint someone else when the smoke clears. Civil Coordination . . . we'll find somebody to give excuses and press conferences later, when we're through killing them.' He spotted Hedley coming toward the command group with two soldiers. '*Alt* Hedley! Over here!' The three hurried over, and Rao told the *alt* of his promotion. 'You'll be a *cent*, maybe a *haut*, I'll figure out what your rank should be later.'

'Yessir.'

'Who're these two?'

'Our agents inside the Eckmuhl. We just extracted them. *Finf* Jaansma, Striker Yoshitaro.'

'Oh. Right. Well-done. You're both kicked up to *dec*, effective immediately.' Rao put them out of his mind. 'Now, let me collect myself. First thing, we'll withdraw First Regiment from the Eckmuhl. The 'Raum have broken out into Leggett in two places already. We'll have to pull back to Camp Mahan, regroup and—'

'Sir! We can't do that!'

Rao stopped cold, stared at Garvin. 'I beg your pardon, *Dec*.'

'I said, sir, begging your pardon, sir, we can't do that,' Jaansma went on. Hedley, behind Rao, was motioning for him to shut the flipping hell up if he knew what was healthy, and Njangu was trying to look like he was somewhere else. 'Sir, we spent time around that 'Raum named Brooks. He's the leader . . . or anyway as much of a leader as they have . . . of The Movement.'

'I don't have time for this, soldier.'

'I'm sorry, sir, but this is important. Sir, Striker, I mean *Dec*, Yoshitaro knows a great deal about the man. Don't you, Njangu? He knows what he'll do next.'

'I'm listening,' Rao said, in a dangerously cold voice. 'I hope I'm not listening to the two shortest-lived *decs* in the history of the Force.'

Njangu gave a hard look at Garvin, but they were for it now. 'Yes, sir. His intelligence chief, a woman named Poynton, told me a lot. The way he handles a problem is to hit it hard. He leads from the front. But if something happens, if it doesn't go right, he'll break contact immediately. He thinks The Movement is more important than anything, and it must be preserved. If he loses today, there's got to be fighters for tomorrow or next year. Poynton told me he was the one who ordered the 'Raum out of the jungles into the cities, where it was easier to fight and hide.'

'So what should I do?' Rao's voice was a little less cold. Hedley was suddenly very glad that Williams was gone, for he couldn't picture the late *caud* doing anything in this situation beyond ordering up a firing squad.

'Hit them where they're breaking out of the Eckmuhl, sir,' Garvin said. 'Hard enough so that you cannot just stop them. but wipe them out. Hit them hard enough, and you'll have Brooks, and maybe that'll break them for good. If the attack breaks, hit the stragglers, and that'll maybe finish this.'

Rao nodded. 'Thank you, *Dec*. Now, if you and your mate'll excuse us . . .'

Garvin saluted, and he and Njangu hastily backed away.

'Nice going,' Njangu muttered. 'Bigmouth.'

'You wanted a chance to kill the bastard,' Garvin said. 'If we pull out, he'll go back into the frigging woodwork, and we'll have to start all over again going up and down those goddamned hills.'

'Maybe you're right. So now what?'

'So now we go get Dill,' Garvin said firmly, 'then look up Petr, and go hunting.'

'Oh joy,' Njangu said. 'Nothing like a nice, private little war in the middle of all this nutsiness.'

Mil Rao looked at the two rankers as they hurried away. 'He made some sense. But we're spread very thin.'

'Not necessarily,' Angara said. 'Second Regiment's in reserve. Dump them with First into the Eckmuhl. Get all those independent companies back, and that'll give you Fourth Regiment as reserve.'

'What about the other cities? The 'Raum are hitting all over D-Cumbre . . . and the mining companies' police on C-Cumbre are about to break.'

'If we lose Leggett,' Angara said, 'nothing else matters.'

'You're right,' Rao said. 'And I've got to stop thinking like . . . like the way things were done before. You didn't mention Third Regiment.'

'Third'll be the bastard,' Angara said. 'Grab all the MPs from the whole goddamned Force, and put them in the streets with PAs going, saying anybody . . . and this means anybody . . . who's on the streets and armed is a dead pigeon. Then dump in Third Regiment and make it so. Hammer the 'Raum back into the Eckmuhl, and kill any vigilantes the Rentiers put in, as well as any private looters.'

'We'll have some innocent dead out of that.'

'When it's all over, we'll make reparations and apologies, which is easy when nobody's shooting. Just like we're going to have to make sure somebody changes the way this goddamned planet's run, unless we want Son of The Movement coming back in five or ten years.'

Rao thought for a moment. 'You know,' he said, 'when

you read about great battles and things, there always seems to be a single point that everything devolves from. Is this one of them? If it is, damned if I don't feel uncomfortable, having figured out a long time ago I don't fit into a star marshal's boots.'

'I don't know, sir,' Angara said honestly. 'But what do we have to lose? We're cut off from the Confederation, the Musth are probably going to want our ass for breakfast after what happened to their mining center, and sooner or later Redruth's going to show up again. I'd just as soon not have to worry about our backs when everybody else comes a-knocking.'

Raum nodded grimly. 'Like you said, what do we have to lose?'

The 'Raum attack in Leggett was three-pronged. The first, against the ruins of PlanGov, had been broken by Running Bear. The second, deliberately planned to be as much a riot as an assault, was against the city center, intended to do as much damage as possible, demoralize the citizens of Leggett, and mask the other two assaults.

The third was against the traditional enemies of the 'Raum, striking southwest toward the Rentiers' district, the Heights.

Dec Nectan, Alpha Team Leader, ducked back as a rocket exploded against the huge tree he was sheltering behind. It creaked, groaned, but held steady. He leaned out, snapped a shot back that he secretly knew missed, and looked down the line of soldiers. Some were his, others were infantry from line units that'd somehow joined up with his troop of I&R. *Aspirant* Vauxhall wriggled toward him, covered up as a bolt blew dust, then was safe.

'We're surely pinned,' Nectan said.

'What's your plan?'

'Wait 'em out,' Nectan said.

'That's NG,' Vauxhall said. 'For all we know, they're holding us with a blocking force, and the rest of the bastards have cut around our flanks.'

'Okay, boss,' Nectan said. 'Your turn in the barrel.'

'Let's try to shock them out,' Vauxhall said. 'I'll grab one of the Cookes and make a strafing run. You get the troops up. and hit 'em hard as soon as I'm clear.'

'I dunno,' Nectan said. 'You'll be wide-open if they've got AA.'

'Aw, shit,' Vauxhall said. 'You ever know a 'Raum who could shoot?'

Nectan thought of answering – damned right he did, and he'd buried the men and women who didn't believe it, but said nothing.

'Give me five minutes,' Vauxhall said. He squirmed away. Nectan shook his head and darted from tree to tree, giving orders.

Five minutes ticked past. Nectan heard the whine of a turbine over the clash of fighting. 'Get ready!' he shouted, and a battered Cooke banked around a corner, flying below the rooftops. He didn't recognize the pilot, but saw Vauxhall strapped behind the cannon. The cannon blasted holes in the storefronts, sent dust cascading.

'Come on! Up and into 'em,' Nectan shouted. He didn't see the flash, but heard the blast as a rocket smashed into the cockpit of the Cooke, and the lifter exploded. 'Let's go! Go!' he shouted, and the line of infantrymen was moving forward, ragged, but moving, from a walk into a trot and their blasters were firing steadily.

'The goddamned 'Raum are cutting us to ribbons in that frigging ghetto,' *Cent* Rivers said. 'We need reinforcements.'

'We don't have any to give you,' Rao said evenly. 'The independent companies are trickling back slow . . . the 'Raum are keeping them busier in the tules than we'd allowed for. What you have is what you've got.'

Rivers nodded jerkily and trotted toward her Grierson.

'The issue,' Rao said very softly to Angara, 'remains in doubt.'

Lir chattered a long burst from her SSW into the luxury department store, saw flames lick up, embrace the knot of looters lnslde. 'This is like stomping mice.'

'Careful, Monique,' Senior *Tweg* Gonzales warned. 'Thinking like that gets you killed '

'I'm not getting sloppy.'

'Better not,' he said. 'How do you think I've made it through as many wars as I have?'

Lir was about to answer when she saw, out of the corner of her eye, something flying toward them. 'Grenade!' She went flat. The grenade hit, bounced, landed next to Gonzales and three other I&R men.

Through the din, Lir heard the tiny whine of its fuse, then Gonzales said, in a mildly angry voice, 'Oh shit,' and rolled on top of the grenade. It went off with a muffled thud, and his body bounced with the shock.

'Goddammit to hell,' Lir said, and the soldier next to her swore she had tears in her eyes for a minute.

'Come on, you assholes,' she shouted. 'Kill me some goblins for Gonzales!' Her voice was very sure, very certain.

There were 'Raum who died well. One was the young woman Limnea. Her group was hit by a roving patrol from Second Regiment, her Task leader killed almost immediately. The 'Raum hesitated, almost broke, but

Limnea shouted them into cover, made them shoot back.

The Forcemen attacked, and she ordered the group to retreat to a central intersection. They occupied the waist-high concrete traffic warden's post, and let the soldiers attack them. The Force came in three times, was driven back three times. Each time, though, the volume of fire from the 'Raum was less and less.

A Forceman clambered to the third story of an over-looking building and sent a handheld rocket smashing into the warden's circle. The dirty smoke cleared, and there was silence.

Three Forcemen zigged forward, chanced peering over the edge. One threw up, seeing the butcher's bill inside. The other two, more hardened, checked to make sure all the 'Raum were dead.

'Look at this one,' one soldier said. 'Prettier'n hell, if she wasn't missing most of her guts. Wonder what made her get into this nonsense?'

Limnea's eyes opened.

'Shit, she's alive!'

The soldie'r bent over her, and Limnea spat a stream of blood in his face, twisted, and was dead.

'What are your suggestions, *Cent* Radcliffe?' the Officer asked.

'Why, no suggestions 'tall,' Penwyth drawled, trying to sound like one of the elite leaders he'd seen in holos. 'There's simply nothin' else to do but attack.'

'Attack. Yes, that's it. Of course. Brilliant,' the *haut* said, turning to give his staff orders.

The seafront central avenue was a brawling mass of 'Raum and poor people from other quarters. The MP lifters had gone overhead twice, warning them to clear the streets, and had been hooted at. One Cooke had been shot down by a team of 'Raum, and the military police-men aboard torn apart.

One woman smashed a storefront, pulled a liter of wine out, snapped the top, and drank heartily, then spat. 'Sour, dammit! Goddamned rich don't drink right,' and reached for another, more promising bottle, then stopped, hearing a strange high whine. She saw heavy lifters, flattened cylinders, bristling with turrets and mis-sile launchers swoop in from the sea, and glide slowly in pairs up the avenue, about ten meters above the ground. Zhukovs, led by Griersons.

The woman screamed, ran up an alley, escaped. Others weren't as lucky. The first salvos were irritant gas, then live rounds sprayed carefully high. But there were still people in the streets, some shooting back.

'Open fire,' the *cent* in charge of the flight ordered, and cannon roared and echoed in the heart of the city.

'Your Task has been changed,' Brooks told the grimy 'Raum cell leader. 'Instead of attacking the University, I have a far better goal for you. The Force has set its field headquarters up just beyond our walls. That is the last vestige of government the Rentiers have. Wipe that out, and the enemy will fall apart, because they've never learned to think for themselves.'

Poynton said nothing. The cell leader nodded jerkily. 'Good,' he said. 'But we have taken casualties.'

'I can see that,' Brooks said. 'I shall accompany you on the attack, and any 'Raum we encounter will join us. Come. We must hurry, for victory is just within our grasp. We must not falter.'

As the column re-formed, Brooks waved his com oper-ators away and dropped back beside Poynton. 'If we fail, and I do not believe we shall, your orders are to break

contact, gather any senior operatives you find, and
reassemble in the forest to continue the struggle.'

Poynton covered her reaction. 'If those are your orders,
sir . . . but if we are failing, I'd rather stand with my sisters and brothers.'

'No!' Brooks snapped. 'The Movement must live.'

'Very well,' Poynton said rebelliously. 'But where in
the jungle do we meet?'

'In the one place they would never look for us,' Brooks
said. 'The cave we used before. Then we'll relocate to an
even safer place I was told about, on Mullion Island, and
rebuild there.'

'Still nothing?' Garvin asked.

'Lots of fighting,' Ben Dill said. 'Nothing that looks
that impressive.'

Njangu looked back over his shoulder into the troop
compartment, at Petr Kipchak, the rest of Gamma Team,
and other I&R troops who'd wanted in on the blood.
'Not good, m'boy,' Kipchak said. 'Maybe you better set
us down near some goblins and let us get some action,
even if it's not what you want.'

'Trying one,' Kang said into the intercom. 'This
Brooks you want . . . is he a proper commander, or
does he use runners and carrier birds like barbarians
did?'

'Of course not,' Garvin said.

'Well, I just happen to be monitoring some 'casts,
coming on three and four frequencies, not on any Force
lengths. They're not coded, but they're real cryptic. I put
a locator on them. They're coming from just inside the
Eckmuhl's walls down there, moving toward one of the
exits. Damn near blanketed by the 'casts from Force HQ,
which is right over there.'

Njangu hesitated, looked at Petr. He had a bit of a

smile. and nodded once. 'Garvin,' Yoshitaro said, 'I think
maybe we've found our fight.'

'Or anyway one worth worrying about,' Petr added.

'Put us right in the middle of that, Ben.'

'Sure,' Dill said. 'I'm easy. Take her down, Stanislaus.'

The Grierson dived toward the Eckmuhl.

There were about fifty men and women in Brooks' group,
most of them experienced fighters, moving quickly along
the inner curve of the Eckmuhl's caverned wall. They'd
seen no sign of Force soldiers, although the sounds of
fighting were all around.

Poynton allowed herself a bit of hope – the gate was
no more than three hundred meters distant, very close, if
Brooks was right, to the Force's command post. Maybe
there *was* a chance, if they killed enough of the officers,
maybe the Rentiers *would* panic, and surrender. Certainly
they wouldn't have the guts to fight for themselves, and
with their mercenaries dead—

Her thoughts broke as someone screamed, and she saw
the fat pencil of a Grierson. She went to her knee, unslung
her blaster, and the ACV's guns opened up, and a missile
exploded nearby, sending her spinning into a wall, cannon
bursts exploding nearby. The Grierson slammed down,
and its rear ramp dropped, and soldiers spewed out.

The 'Raum found cover, started shooting, and fire
ravened back from the Grierson's guns and the SSWs of
the I&R soldiers. A grenade launcher thunked, and the
grenade landed next to one of Brooks' commo men. He
panicked, kicked it away, and the grenade exploded, and
killed all three com men.

Brooks was kneeling, shooting at the Forcemen, saw
his brothers and sisters dying, fired again, saw a soldier
drop, realized they were almost overwhelmed and ran,
crouching, through a doorway into the wall's tunnels.

Garvin went after him.

'You idiot,' Petr shouted, and followed.

A burst of fire came from nowhere, sending Petr spinning, agsinst the wall. He slid slowly down it, looking at the smear beside him, realized it was his own blood. A tiny knife came into his hand from nowhere, then his fingers opened, it dropped onto the cobbles, and he died.

Njangu leapt over his corpse, shot sideways at whoever had killed Kipchak, was in the doorway and in sudden silence. Explosions came dimly from outside, but they weren't part of his world.

There was a winding corridor, and steps led upward. He saw legs, almost shot, recognized them as uniformed. Garvin.

Brooks wouldn't have gone up, Njangu decided – Garvin was full of hooey – and startcd along the corridor. A shot seared past, and Brooks came from nowhere, blaster raised to club him down. Yoshitaro twisted sideways, took the blow on his right shoulder, yelped, and his fingers opened, dropping his pistol.

Brooks was hard on him, trying to push him back so he could get room to level his blaster, and Njangu snapped a knee up. Brooks screamed, staggered back, and Njangu kicked the gun out of his hands. Before he could recover, Brooks was on him, strong miner's muscles knocking him back, and a fist thudded into his gut. Njangu fought for air. Brooks' fingers were trying for a stranglehold, but Njangu had his chin buried in his chest. Brooks' hands clawed up his face for his eyes.

Njangu's free hand moved smoothly along his belt, found the snap of the sheath he'd worn on that faraway parade field. The blade was in his hand, and he drove it into Brooks' side. Brooks screamed, pulled away, the knife still hanging from him, stumbled to his feet, and Garvin shot him three times, very fast, in the chest.

Brooks pirouetted as if he were on a turntable, hands reaching toward the unseen sky, and he crumpled.

'Not that I needed any help,' Njangu said, through a throat that felt like it'd been sanded, as he used the wall to push himself up, 'but thanks.'

'No help?' Garvin said indignantly. 'He would've taken that knife out and shoved it right up your ass if it weren't for me.'

'Shee-yit,' Njangu managed, and stumbled toward the door.

He came out into sunlight and the scattered dead of Brooks' attack team, but it didn't matter. Njangu looked down at Kipchak's face, tried to find some last expression – hate, peace, anger – but there was nothing.

'Hey,' somebody shouted. 'I got a live one.'

The soldier lifted her blaster.

'No!' Njangu shouted. 'We need a prisoner.'

The soldier reluctantly lowered her weapon, and Niangu picked up a blaster from a corpse, limped over, looked at Poynton.

She stared up. 'Kill me now,' she said.

'Are you wounded?'

She shook her head. 'The blast.'

'Get up, then,' he said.

She obeyed, wincing as she moved.

'In front of me,' Njangu ordered. 'Back to the Grierson.'

'Are you afraid to shoot me in front of your brothers and sisters?' she taunted.

'Lady, right now I'm too tired to be afraid of anything. Now move!'

He escorted her back of the ACV, then motioned her into an alley. Face pale, eyes fixed on his, she obeyed. 'Go ahead,' she said. 'I'm ready.'

'Jo,' Njangu said. 'Get the hell out of here.'

'Shot while attempting to escape? I'd rather die where I stand.'

'I said, get your pretty ass the hell out of here, dammit! And don't you ever, ever, ever get involved in this kind of shit again.'

Jo Poynton stared, then backed away. When she was about ten meters from him, she spun and ran hard, disappearing around a corner.

Njangu turned, saw Garvin standing there, pistol dangling from his hand. 'Now why'd you want to do something like that?'

Njangu shrugged. 'Seemed like a good idea at the time.'

THIRTY-SIX

Two weeks after Brooks' death, *Caud* Prakash Rao was commed by Aesc of the Musth. Behind him was Wlencing. 'We are departing your sssystem.'

'I'm listening.'

'We are returning to our own worldsss,' the Musth said. 'You were warned once before asss to what might transsspire if any Musssth died. Now I musssst have conssultations with my leadersss. I do not plan to advissse them to continue this foolisssh coursssse of peacccce.'

Wlencing stepped forward. 'When next we meet,' he said, 'it ssshall most likely be with unsssheathed talonsss. It ssshall not be with engineersss and minersss we return with, but warriorsss. Then ssshall come interesssting timesss.'

THIRTY-SEVEN

Alt Garvin Jaansma, resplendent in dark blue dress uniform, a row of new medals on his breast, paid off the lifter.

'You want me to wait?'

'No,' Garvin said, and went up the steps of the mansion. The columns on either side of the entrance had wide black ribbon tied to them, and there was a black wreath on the door. Jaansma grimaced, touched the bell. He heard the hum, saw a spyeye turn. Nothing happened for a long time, and he was about to ring again, when the door opened, a big, well-dressed man, with a bit of a shoulder rig showing, stood there.

'Yes, sir?'

'I'm Garvin Jaansma. I'm a friend of Jasith's. Is she at home?'

'She is,' the bodyguard said, unfolding a bit of paper. 'And she told me what to say, exactly.' He read from the paper: '"Please go away, Garvin, and don't try to see me anymore. I'm going to be busy, taking over my father's company. If I see you, I'll just be reminded of what happened, and how you, and the others in the Force, couldn't keep my father from getting killed."'

Garvin blinked. 'That doesn't make any sense.'

'A Mellusin doesn't have to make sense,' the bodyguard said gently.

'I guess there's no way . . . nothing I could say that'd let me actually see her? Maybe if I could talk to her, she wouldn't . . .' Garvin's voice trailed off

The bodyguard shook his head. 'Sorry, *Alt*. But that's the way things are.'

Garvin started back down the steps. He heard the door close behind him.

He looked down the long, winding street toward Leggett.

'Guess dreams don't usually work out,' he said quietly, and walked away.

THIRTY-EIGHT

'So it's over?' Garvin tipped the bottle up, found it was empty, tossed it over the railing of the Bachelor Officers' Quarters. He scrabbled in the ice chest for another one, puzzled a bit drunkenly at its cap. He drew his combat knife out, reversed the blade, and snapped it against the neck of the bottle. The bottle's neck broke off cleanly. He drank, passed the bottle to Njangu.

Yoshitaro drank twice. 'I think you were one ahead of me,' he explained. 'Yeh. I guess it's over. Assuming *Caud* Rao makes sure there are straight elections, and the Rentiers get told to shut up and just make money. Good luck on that one, and on the goddamned 'Raum who're left suddenly becoming society's darlings. Sure, this is gonna be the best of all possible worlds.'

Garvin thought of Jasith, swallowed hard, and took the bottle back. 'This isn't the way it is in the holos when you win a war,' he complained after drinking.

'Nope,' Njangu said. 'Things got a little expensive. Williams, Vauxhall, Gonzales . . .'

'Hank Faull.'

'Petr.'

'Yeh. And Petr.' Njangu tried to keep bitterness out of his voice. 'But everybody's got medals, and you and I are officers, even if you somehow wangled it so I'm just a stupid *aspirant*.'

'Careful, young soldier,' Garvin said, trying to be cheerful. 'Promotions come to he or she who serves well. You know they commissioned Penwyth, too. It was either that or courtmartial him for impersonating an officer.'

'And we've got the I&R Company all for our very own.

'Which isn't going to be run business-as-usual,' Garvin said. 'I had a long sit-down with Jon and Angara today, and we're gonna reorganize. Liskeard's gonna go over to a Regiment, and Angara's gonna fold Mobile Scout into I&R, so we'll have Griersons with maybe a couple of Zhukovs for instant backup. No more frigging Cookes. Ben Dill's going to be commissioned and take over that end of things. Monique takes over as First *Tweg*, no matter how much she pisses and moans. I tried to get her to take that commission they waved in front of her, and I thought she was gonna smack me.

'The way things'll be is you and me work as a team, you being the supposed brains, me sounding like I know what the hell I'm talking about with the crunchies, Dill gets us into the fighting, and all's as it should be.'

'So the good are rewarded,' Njangu said.

'Supposedly.'

'How come I don't feel any better?'

'You aren't drinking enough.' Garvin handed him the bottle. 'Life's gonna get interesting, when those goddamned Musth come back. Or when Redruth gets the hots for our young asses.'

'I'll worry about that shit when it happens,' Njangu said.

They drank in silence for a time.

'You remember,' Njangu said, 'way the hell back when

we were hauling ass from the *Malvern*, and Petr was showing off all the stuff he'd memorized?'

'Yeh?'

'He had a poem. Can't remember much of it, but there were lines that went something like "those I fight, I do not hate, those I guard I do not love."'

'Petr's epitaph?'

'Or ours,' Njangu said.

'What a shitty way to make a living,' he said, after a space. Garvin grunted agreement, retrieved the bottle.

'Pity it's the only game in town.'

APPENDIX

The Cumbre system has a medium main sequence sun, about 1.5 million kilometers in diameter.

There are thirteen planets in the system, named, rather unimaginatively, after the letters of the alphabet. A- and B-Cumbre are too close to the sun to be habitable, with limited atmospheres, and have only solar and astronomical observation stations.

Mineral-rich C-Cumbre is the reason for both Man and Musth colonizing the system. Its riches include manganese, tungsten, vanadium, niobium, titanium, godarium, natural gamma iron, and some precious metals.

Mines, worked by both races, stud the arid landscape. It's uncomfortable for both races, more for the Musth than Man. It has a single moon, Balar.

E-Cumbre is chill, just habitable for Man, comfortable for Musth, who know it as Silitric, and consider it the center of the system.

F-, H- and I-Cumbre are ice giants.

G-Cumbre is a half-destroyed world from an out-of-system asteroid, and moonlets litter its orbit

J- and K-Cumbre are small planetoids and have small observation stations.

L- and M-Cumbre are little larger than J- and K-, and are almost certainly trapped asteroids, with extremely irregular orbits.

D-Cumbre is – mostly – Man's world. It has three

small moons: Fowey, Bodwin, and Penwith. Only the largest and nearest, Fowey, affects D-Cumbre's tides

D-Cumbre is about thirteen thousand kilometers in diameter at the equator, and its axial tilt is fourteen degrees, producing a more even climate than Earth's. Unlike Earth, there are no continental masses, but many, many islands, mostly in the temperate and tropical belt, although two significant landmasses are at the poles. Some of the islands are large and of volcanic origin. Their peaks have been worn into plateaus with an entirely different climate than the lowlands – still wet, but chill and mist-hung, with the vegetation fernlike, from tiny to enormous. The Musth make their headquarters on the largest of these, the Highlands on Dharma Island.

Man settled at sea-level, mostly in the tropics, with his capital, Leggett, on the northwestern portion of Dharma and three smaller islets. There are two dozen smaller cities, some not more than villages, on other islands in the temperate or tropical zones.

The climate is balmy, and there are few weather hazards, although open seas away from the island masses produce enormous globe-circling waves, and the stormy season can be uncomfortable.

The environment must be considered benign, although there are still-unclassified predators in the jungles and several species of fish, from large sea serpents to marine carnivores to coelenterates that must be considered hazardous to life.

Chris Bunch is the author of the Sten Series, the Dragonmaster Series, the Seer King Series and many other acclaimed SF and fantasy novels. A notable journalist and bestselling writer for many years, he died in 2005.

Find out more about Chris Bunch and other Orbit authors by registering for the free monthly newsletter at www.orbitbooks.net